Rebmann

Rebmann

A Novel

Marjorie Oludhe Macgoye

Washington, DC

Library of Congress Control Number: 2014937222
ISBN 978-0-9915047-3-2 paperback (alk. paper)

 An imprint of New Academia Publishing

 info@newacademia.com - www.newacademia.com
P.O. Box 27420, Washington, DC 20038-7420

In memory of my father,
Richard Thomas King
"Who would true valour see
Let him come hither;
One here will constant be,
Come wind, come weather. "

Contents

Preface   ix

Chapter I   1

Chapter II   29

Chapter III   55

Chapter IV   87

Chapter V   97

Chapter VI   113

Chapter VII   135

Chapter VIII   155

Chapter IX   177

Chapter X   209

Chapter XI   233

Chapter XII   247

Chapter XIII   267

Preface

This is a novel based on real events in real lives; therefore it tries to tell a kind of truth about the situation which the history books—even the church histories—do not tell.

Every person referred to on the East African coast or in Zanzibar has an actual, documented existence; there are so many records that there is no need to invent people, though one may have to spell out incidents which led to the generalizations the missionaries made.

I have also had to give names to the women and children, who are mostly anonymous, or attach some recorded incidents to known names.

Some of the characters in Europe or on shipboard have had to be imagined or adopted. The Rev. J. C. Tyler and Mr. J. S. Tyler both left the writings ascribed to them, but their relationship to one another or to Mrs. Rebmann is pure conjecture. Rebmann and Robert Moffat were in London at the same time and they knew one another. A grand-daughter of Canon Binns has told me that he was inspired by hearing Rebmann speak, though the missionary histories write Rebmann off as useless by the time he retired.

The spelling of place names at the time was erratic. Although Milton refers to Mombaza in *Paradise Lost* (XI. 399) Mombas or Mombaz was common up to about 1870, and here I reserve the usage to Rebmann, together with his consistent *Jaga* and *Kiriama* for the modern *Chagga* and *Giriama*. I have not attempted to improve on Rebmann's own understanding of personal names and forms of address, or of relationships and customs; Muigno does not have to be the same as Mwangi, this is not meant to be a work of hindsight. For instance the usage of *Maasai* and *Kwavi* for *Kwafi*, which

he must have adopted from African neighbors, is entirely different from modern interpretations. The insertion or omission of the
Bantu prefixes Wa- for the people and Ki- for language is tuned to
colloquial Kenya English today, and the usage in early letters is not
very different.

Most bible quotations are from the Authorized Version, which
Rebmann must have used, but since he must often have translated
in his head from the German I have used RSV where it fits better.

I am not a historian, though I have sought help from historians.
The main focus of this book is on what the missionaries, rightly or
wrongly, perceived in the mid-nineteenth century. Like most of us,
they contradicted themselves at times but (in case any reader con-
demns my interpretation as "too modern") the records are there to
show what they had to say about acculturation, conservation and
the universal application of the gospel.

A full bibliography would be out place here. I am indebted to
a host of travelers and officials for their published work. Most of
these are named in the three indispensable books covering recent
coastal history: Coupland, Reginald. *East Africa and its Invaders*.
London: Clarendon Press, 1938; Coupland, Reginald. *The Exploita-
tion of East Africa*. London: Faber & Faber, 1939; Nicholls, C. S. *The
Swahili Coast*. London: Allen & Unwin, 1971. A recent study by Dr.
Steven Paas is a valuable addition: *Johannes Rebmann. A Servant of
God in Africa before the Rise of Western Colonialism*. Nürnberg: VTR
Publications, 2011.

I have to thank in particular Dr. Walter Ringwald of Stuttgart,
Rosemary Keene of the Church Missionary Society Archives and
the Special Missionary Collection of the University of Birmingham,
as well as the McMillan Memorial Library, Nairobi, the University
of Nairobi Library and the Kenya National Archives.

I am endlessly grateful to Professor Emilia Ilieva and my son
Francis Oludhe for seeing this book through the press. Any error in
the interpretation of these materials is, of course, my own. And like
any other Christian writer, sinful and yet justified, I praise the Lord.

"In 1873 Sir Bartle Frere found a solitary and blind Rebmann at Rabai with about half a dozen converts."

J. M. Gray in *History of East Africa*. Vol. I, ed. Roland Oliver
and Gervase Mathew (Oxford: Clarendon Press, 1963), 242.

"To continue labouring in patience, says our venerated prel-
ate Oettinger, is in itself victory."

J. L. Krapf, *Travels, Researches and Missionary Labours* (London:
Trübner and Co., 1860), 507.

I

"I shall never see it again!"

The early morning air was pleasantly cool, with a light breeze which could be heard plopping against the broad palm leaves. Coral sand still gritted under the soles of their shoes against the moist planking of the boat. Isaac had stowed the luggage neatly under a tarpaulin.

It was little enough, and the old man did not show any concern over the possessions of a lifetime. The punt man was ready to steer along the creek towards the open sea, but no oar had yet begun to slap the water with the regular beat that implied motion and sprinkled drops of water over your head and shoulders. There was a scent of sweat, coconut oil, a lingering suspicion of palm wine from the seamen. The skipper fingered his koranic amulet and rosary unrebuked.

A cry from the shore wished them Godspeed in several tongues and intimated it was time they should be on their way. The older man raised a hand in vague greeting, the boatswain issued an order and the shallow, exploratory poling began. The proverb advises, 'Never row when you can punt.'

"I shall never see it again," repeated the old man, not quite resigned.

"You have not seen it for a long time now," Isaac replied. "You will always keep it in your mind's eye, my father."

"That I shall," said Rebmann heavily, "but there is seeing and not seeing. You remember the scriptures, Isaac. The host of the Lord is encamped about, more mighty than that of the enemy. There is much that we need to see. Thousand upon thousand of the Wanika clothed in white before the throne of grace and singing His praises in the Rabai tongue. Can you see them as well as I do with these blind eyes?"

"I believe there will be a harvest among my people..."

"You believe, you believe. You do right to believe. And you do well to claim no more than you have yet believed. Whatever else I have failed in, I have taught you this much respect for truth, Isaac. And that is something to be proud of if you remember the complaisance of your countrymen—'I will do it tomorrow,' 'I have nearly finished,' 'I quite agree'... But you do not see it, Jones does not see it, Price does not see it. What you see is a gang of useful people making tables and chairs and pressing their accounts for maize flour and copra. And this is needed too. To be close to Mombas, where you can get your trousers mended after they have been ripped on the march and receive letters forwarded from Zanzibar and be able to send within four or five months for a compass from Europe—we have these advantages which many of our fellow-missionaries lack. Other people have every right increasingly to want these advantages. You have read Dr. Krapf's book. You remember how these sentiments are reflected there from my mouth. Even in the old days, before your father came to read with us, King Kimweri asked for paper in preference to other gifts, for his Swahili scribes to use in writing letters for him. That was a sign of a new day coming, a sign we had not been taught about in Basel or Islington. It worked strangely on my heart... until others at Buyeni begged Krapf for paper to write charms on, and never understood how they dismayed us. But nevertheless the gospel is the gospel—it is not to be shouldered in exchange for freedom from slavers' whips, for trade apprenticeship, for neat houses or schools for the children. It is to be welcomed for its own sake and the rest can follow."

They must now, Rebmann sensed, be past Abdallah's plantation, where he and Krapf had sheltered, tossing with fever, the night before they had negotiated for the Rabai site. They would be among the mangroves, good, solid, saleable red mangroves, with green shoots pressing their way out among the dense, ripened timber, and little oysters clinging to the exposed roots. Eddies of pale sand must be rising from the bottom as the poles struck. It was necessary to keep talking, to subdue regrets to the continuing task.

"But you told the people your prosperity in Europe was a product of Christendom. You told them so, my father says, though of late I do not recollect your saying it. But I have been taught to tell them so, I who have not yet seen the marvels of land overseas or even the fancy oil-lamps of Zanzibar. So much the more do the Bombay Africans say so—Jones and Semler, George David and the others—for they do not remember much of their childhood here in Africa before they were rescued from slave ships, but they are always talking about their education at Nasik, in trade as well as in school, and the big buildings and fine clothes and the industries of British India. Jones, especially, angers the people by telling them there is nothing good in their way of life."

"It is true about the prosperity, Isaac, but there is no human society which does not have something good in it. We are all made in the Lord's image, after all, however far we may have fallen from it. When I was young I felt very strongly that prosperity is a blessing, and I still believe that to be true, though typically an Old Testament truth, not one of the most important. Even when you are old and broken, it is hard to think that the Lord has allowed a lie to pass your lips when you were seeking to guard them so zealously with prayer and self-searching as young missionaries do, but much has happened here since then to increase prosperity, with the clove sales and the sesame, and much to ponder upon has happened in Germany too. You may have a chance to see some of that for yourself. Perhaps that is the good that will come out of their throwing me off—that because of the infirmity of my eyes they allow me your company, and so you will gain experience that otherwise they would not have found the money for... Missionaries, like other men, put a great value on money."

He fell silent, and the young man, thinking him weary, was also quiet. True, the journey to London was an unlooked-for privilege, for Mr. Williams, had his own health been less precarious, might have escorted Mr. Rebmann and helped him present his report to the Home Committee. Up till now missionaries, apart from Rebmann himself, had not lasted long on the east coast. Mr. Price, of course, could not be spared, so providential was his arrival, with all his experience in Nasik, to open up the freed slave settlement which would take precedence over the sleepy old mission station at Rabai. But the younger missionaries did not seem to respect an elder as they ought, and an official might find it hard to travel with Mr. Rebmann after his confrontation with Sir Bartle Frere. In any case, Mr. Price said, he would find it difficult to keep up with their movements. They would want to jump off the boat at Genoa and on to a train, another boat, another train, to make the most of their precious leave. Indeed, in the five years since the Suez Canal had opened up, the journey from Zanzibar to London was almost as commonplace according to Price as that from Rabai to Zanzibar—not that this was commonplace to many people in Isaac's view, and even then you were not supposed to compare the mercantile city of Zanzibar with the great port of Bombay. Isaac had never seen either, and had no very clear idea of the mechanism of jumping on a train.

He knew English very well, and so had been able to deal with Mr. Rebmann's correspondence since his sight failed. Some of his agemates envied him, but they had not themselves sought to study the books of the white man or the Mohammedan either, though a few had enlarged their houses and gardens after the example of the mission. Old man Rebmann was always talking about Christian families, though his wife was dead. Outsiders mostly assumed that missionaries kept wives and children back in the home place, but Mr. Rebmann had never been back.

The boat was close into the shore and the stroke of the outer and inner oars was not quite even. It would take them about four hours to reach Mombasa harbor, and there Mr. Price would meet them. Next day they would board the big ship for Zanzibar, and there enter the international steamer. This would be a new experience. They shall mount up wings as eagles' was the text that had been given them.

"You see, Isaac," Rebmann was saying, "You must get these things clear before you reach the fleshpots of Europe. Fleshpots are not sinful in themselves. It is only if they take your mind off the work in hand that they become dangerous. The son does not have to live like the father. I certainly don't live like mine—it is 30 years since I tasted a proper German sausage or sat indoors before a blazing fire. You do not live altogether like yours, and this journey will change you more. Dressed up like a dandy, I don't doubt, as we used to say when we were young, sitting on a wooden chair at a table instead of on the uncomfortable round stool of a household head. You are writing business letters instead of holding your breath to see if the crops will grow (and not be stolen) without magic charms as I am sure your father used to do when he was first under instruction; and you argue with your old missionary godfather, instead of sitting in silence in the house and only letting your criticisms out when you are safely away in the bush trapping hares for the pot."

He broke off as the boatswain entered into ribald dialogue with a friend on the shore, but resumed with an old man's tenacity.

"I grew up in a quiet, rural place. It was more comfortable than Rabai, I should have said then, but we worried more over a cold winter or a low harvest than over wars and great inventions. I did my training at Basel, which looked like a big city to me: visitors from America and England used to come to see the mountains, the lake and the behavior of people who did not speak English, and felt themselves very adventurous.

Then I went to London and got used to speaking English instead of German: I was thought good at reading English, but to live in it was at first very hard. I got along, but I found that we Germans were expected to be more than humanly clever. Weitbrecht, when he was in training, had studied English, Arabic, Amharic and Tigre simultaneously, and because he was not too confident in his English (no wonder!) he was allowed to answer the Bishop of London's examination in Latin. I wonder if they have a proverb in Ethiopia like ours, *akili nyingi huondoa maarifa*, much expertise takes away wisdom!

In England we were treated as gentlemen rather than workers, and we found that a lot of people were proud of living comfortably with modern amenities such as gas lighting and the water closet. I wonder whether my good wife explained these to you? Myself, I wanted to present the gospel only in Nika terms. Poor Jones...

So, some of us got a feeling of being on top of the world and doing someone a favor by going out to wilder regions. It was in London that I saw Africans for the first time. Some of them worked in or around the ships in the docks, and would be going back to their countries. Others worked as house servants or porters. These had been declared free (or their fathers had) when slavery was abolished in Britain and they had just stayed around. They spoke only

English and lived and ate like everyone else in their own station in life.

One West African was in training with me: his name was George Nicol, and his English was a great deal more fluent than mine. Sam Crowther had left the year before—the same who is now a bishop in Yoruba land, a good man and clever too. The tutor, Dr. Scholefield of Cambridge, took away his answer papers to show how much better his presentation was than 'some of our Trinity fellows.' We never heard the last of it.

It was good for me to have been humbled already before I set foot in Africa, and know that what you people needed was not any superior faculties of mine but to share my privilege of praying and learning the gospel at my mother's knee. And indeed I wish it could be so for all—it *will* be so for you people of the land, but although Price thinks it easy to teach the slave souls, there remains that void in them where they were snatched from their own community. See how different Matthew Wellington is from the others because he still has his own name—Chengwimbe—and his own language— Yao. Polly is different too: I am happy that you have been able to share so much with her and perhaps help her to shake off that terrible emptiness. However close you wish to get to those others there is that alarming self-reliance that is afraid to trust anything less than the Lord—and we are all vulnerable to one another, my son: we need to admit it."

"Yes, my father, Polly is different, and I am glad you brought her to me from over the sea. My brothers laugh at me for conceding so much to a woman, but I wonder how I would have found a Christian wife among our girls, so set in the old ways. And I know she will manage everything while I am away. That will irritate my brothers too, but I am content, even though in my Nika fashion I am sometimes tempted to give contrary orders just to show her I am head of the household."

"It relieves me, my son, to hear so. For I remember when I went to Egypt to marry Mrs. Tyler, as she then was, an English schoolma'am, as you well know, and me a simpler farmer's son from Wurtemberg who people thought needed a wife—and I did, I did, and have given thanks for her every day since—I was near to turning tail and running back to Rabai. It is an awesome thing to pick a life-partner for another person, Isaac—and neat white tablecloths we must have, and tea with milk in it, and curtains, and little pots to hold the hair she combed out—oh, how good she was to put up with all my rough and readiness.

It was a great joy to her to see you and Polly married, and George and Priscilla David too, a few months before she died. Those were our first Christian weddings, and women all over the world love a wedding. They were the first I had conducted too, and made me think hard, though as you know, I have since come to the conclusion that marriages are not made in church: the church can only confirm what is made by human necessity."

"Yes, indeed," murmured Isaac, who had taken dictation on the subject until his wrist ached. "You were telling me about your training in London. All these years you have hardly mentioned it to me."

"Ah, yes. I tried not to hark back, you see, or to have you people look outwards over my shoulder. London, Bombay, Rabai, Kornthal, Cairo, they are all equally training-places for Heaven. But the West Africans, I was saying, were better than I at understanding the strange talk of the Irish courts where we went to do our practical work. Perhaps it is as well I did not learn to understand it all: English can be a dirty language when people set their minds to spoiling it.

So we were sent off to the mission-field, Isaac, with hymns and prayers round us, as though we were making a sacrifice by just going. In fact many were, because they did not live long in the countries of their calling, and this is a hard thing to accept or try to explain..." The boat began to rock, pleasantly enough, and the oars slapped more vigorously. They were out of the creek, then. The air was still, the sun almost overhead. No point in hoisting the sail. The hot salt stung.

"Your father will remember that Dr. Krapf had some hard words to say about young missionaries. 'The missionaries of this generation are effeminate and drifting; they are not fit to go out and conquer the world.' I felt them hard myself, especially when I was brought low with fever. I was only ten years younger than he was himself. But you grow in insight, not always consciously, as you grow in the flesh, and, indeed, as you get hollowed out with sickness and disappointment and the daily abrasions of living in a place where you feel yourself alien. For it takes some of us obstinate ones a long time to see that the notion of being alien is not something that others impute to us but something we impute to ourselves, and it takes digging and toughening rather than varnishing and polishing to make us fit into the niche the Lord has made ready for us. It is not nice, kind Johannes giving up comfort and society to represent the Lord in a reverential position in Rabai. It is the good Lord inviting arrogant, half-baked Johannes to accept the hospitality of Rabai and see how the words of scripture can take life within it. Do you understand?"

"Yes, I think I understand, though you are stretching the words to their limit…"

"Indeed I am, and tomorrow we must use English together, Isaac, in case the British officers think we are jabbering treason in Kinika. And in the days ahead I must say goodbye to you and learn once more to think in German. But it must be so, because now it is *your* turn to be the guest and try to penetrate every thought of his host in order to make the gospel message clear."

"Yet we have been taught so much about the superiority of Europe."

"Well, you have never traveled in a carriage with wheels. The only bridge you have seen is the little one at Ribe, apart from a few tree-trunks cut across a stream. You have not been down into the tunnels of a mine. You have not seen a factory with whole big rooms filled by machines producing goods. Indeed we have not even taken you to see the rope walk at Zanzibar or the boat yards of Mambrui. You will come across many gadgets that are better, in terms of usefulness or pleasure, than you have dreamed of before. Better, but not different in *kind*. I remember how eager you were to walk the 16 miles to Ribe to see the Wakefield piano that they managed to ship out without very much damage, but you recognize it so as instrument akin to the *marimba*. You have admired my big walking boots ever since you were a little boy, but you have never seen a Teita person going barefoot.

I shall also come upon many things that we could not have imagined in Germany 30 years ago. I believe there are little rooms now in which you can be lifted high up into buildings by a pulley and save the stairs, and wheels attached to foot pedals which will propel you along the road without the aid of a horse or donkey. But that does not make my young nephews better fellows than their fathers were.

In matters of relationships and morality, yes, you will find Europe has some advantages in having had a society instructed in Christian values through many centuries. People do not openly put a deformed baby to death as they do here, and those who leave all the labor to their wives, or beat them, try to conceal the fact. They do not like to be caught out in a lie, and those who exercise malice do not do so by crude magic but by sleight of tongue. There is a custom of affectionate behavior within families which is a directly Christian heritage, and in some places it extends to the master-servant relationship. There is some public provision for the relief of distress.

But this is not really what I mean. The missionary, at home or abroad, must obviously draw on all his experience in presenting the gospel and making his judgments live, especially his own experience of sin and repentance. What has he left behind that can be compared with the comforts of the gospel he carries with him? What are his few lonely fevers in comparison with the black night of sin and suffering his Savior endured? ..."

This seemed to Isaac uncomfortably like a sermon starting. Since his sight deteriorated, Mr. Rebmann had not gone in much for sermons, and had confined himself more and more to language work. But it was not the usual tenor of a sermon.

"They are wrong, they are wrong," the old man was muttering and Isaac was angry to see the sailors gesturing towards him as though invoking their Mohammedan angels towards one stricken with madness. "Or rather I am wrong to let their words prevail. And yet does it not seem arrogant to suppose myself always right, to stand out continually against them. They are better educated than I am, blessed with physical strength and use of all their faculties. They think it a matter of preaching and teaching, building houses and going on journeys. I have done all these things—who else? But if you think it is Rebmann's faculties that the Lord needs to use, so that when Rebmann is old and weary and blind he is no longer witnessing, then you do not see—I with my blind eyes see more than you do. It is not a matter of saying to Abe Gunga your father, as I used to say: 'Look, I can make a better house than yours and plant a better garden, learn of me,' though it may be good for him to learn. But it is—and your father, being a little bit my elder, was used to teach me this—a matter of being enabled to say to your father: 'Abe Gunga, is it well with the child'—that was you, Isaac—'who has been spared to you after so many disappointments?' 'Brother, I know your wife finds it hard that you are enquiring after what she sees as false gods, but women too are strong in the service of our God.' That one failed him, but your mother came back, Isaac, and helped keep you and others on course once she was strengthened in prayer. 'Brother, your village head has slighted you because of your loyalty to me, but God does not let his servants down.' 'Brother, we have received a gift of plantain and thought you might like to have a share of it.' 'Brother, I hear a leopard made off with your dog: have you got another one, for no Nika homestead can be complete without its dog.'

This is the daily habit of life, to be sustained whether one is feverish or not, whether one has had letters from home or not, whether the teaching is being well received or not. And this cannot be if half one's heart is in another place one still calls 'home.' On safari I—and you, who are embarking on the biggest safari of your life—may have to pause and calculate: is it proper to pay a visit here, to give a present there, to eat before marching or burden oneself with more provisions to carry. But at home in Kisulutini these things must become matters of course and expectation: only then is the vessel in place for the gift of God to fill.

This little I saw perhaps more clearly than brother Krapf, though he was more learned than I and also suffered more, having lost his wife and infant daughters before I joined him. He had great visions, in which I heartily concurred, and was well advised to plan our travels as he did, to point where other helpers may follow. But he was restless, here and there, here and there, and felt a need to husband his strength for the time to come. I never did till now. But to face Germany after all that has happened, I do not know how I shall find strength enough for that."

"We are coming to the harbor now," Isaac interrupted him. "There will be much to make you tired and upset. Let us prepare ourselves."

"Very well, my son, very well. It is a matter of burning one's boats, as they say in English—you follow me? It is not a pleasant idiom to think about when we are in the course of a journey. The baggage is in your hand, and when we board Mr. Williams may need assistance from you too, so you are the headman of the expedition this time."

Rebmann sniffed at the sea air and the increasing odor of the fish market as they approached the shore and the small noisy petrels wheeled around. It was March, the last days of the northerly monsoon season, and the harbor would be full, as he had seen it countless times. But his mind was not on the familiar bustle around him or even on the appropriate scripture,

> my heart panteth, my strength faileth
> for the light of mine eyes it also is gone from me

Over and over again he was mulling over the scene two years before when he *had* finally burned his boats by—what? Telling the truth to a human embodiment of the devil who would not be shamed? Or allowing pique and sarcasm to overcome his better judgment and dislodge him from the only place he ever felt at home? There was plenty of pique and sarcasm in the prophets—

> And it came to pass that at noon Elijah mocked them, say-
>   ing, 'Cry aloud,
> for he is a god; either he is talking or he is missing or he is
>   on a journey, or
> perhaps he is asleep…'

But one did not catch Sir Bartle Frere sleeping—oh no; that courteous, modulated voice from somewhere above one's head, that iron hand which had pushed out to the limits (or beyond) his powers as Governor of Bombay, that devastating logic which had refused government servants the right to spread the gospel in India, all bore relentlessly upon the stroke of fortune that had given him a new commission as the power of Bombay was curtailed. He had leave from the India Office and four ships of Her Majesty's fleet with which to impress upon the Sultan of Zanzibar his privilege of becoming an equal signatory with Britain to the end of the East African slave trade.

"Why, Mr. Rebmann," cried Sir Bartle Frere, seizing his hand with the violence of those who think the blind unaware of their proximity, "you are still here? I just heard it in Mombasa and hastened to pay my respects. In fact I feel like Stanley approaching Livingstone—overwhelmed. My name is Frere. I have lately come from Zanzibar."

"Welcome, Sir Bartle," replied the old pastor. "We heard of course that you were at Zanzibar. We have followed your career since you administered us from the Bombay Presidency. Now that the system of dependency has changed, we have to wait on the decision of the Viceroy. I have not the habit of being overwhelmed, as you see, even by the army you have brought with you. You have no doubt met Isaac Nyondo here, who is my hand as well as my eyes. And our evangelist, William Jones, one of those so excellently trained at Nasik and returned to help their fellow-countrymen."

The seven English gentlemen among the retinue were introduced, together with Kazi Shahabadia, a minister of the Rao of Cutch, whose father had long ago renounced slavery in his own dominions, so that they were now honorably associated with the anti-slavery lobby. Clement Hill and George Grey were from the Foreign Office, Colonel Pelly was the Resident in the Persian Gulf, the Reverend Dr. Badger was in attendance as interpreter, Captain Playfair had once acted as British Consul in Zanzibar and Major Euan Smith accompanied the Commission as Frere's personal secretary. Young Bartle Frere, just through Eton, had come along for the ride. The five European servants and 50 soldiers remained outside.

"Isaac, you can no doubt arrange some refreshment."

"I believe my wife and Mrs. David have this already in hand."

"Ah, do not trouble yourself," Sir Bartle Frere replied airily. "We do not come to descend on you like locusts. Our men have brought their own provisions and I am sure your mission people will show them where they can commence preparations. The boatmen, I believe, are helping the soldiers with the purchase of livestock. It is quite a little picnic for us amid this tedious business of arranging a new treaty with the Sultan to stop the slave trade. I am sure you know of our commission. I believe some of my colleagues would like to look around the station. It is a novelty for them."

Novelty indeed! But what kind of novelty would a slave camp then be?

"Of course: but you are not new to Africa and the East, sir, and you cannot fail to be aware that we expect to welcome our guests according to custom. After some small refreshment we can release you."

"Release? Ah, yes, very good. It is all a matter of releasing, after all. You know what that fellow Barghash said to me, 'We are a poor and narrow-minded people and require time to see your way.' Humbug! He has no alternative to complying with our demands."

"That may be so, but every missionary knows that compliance is not the same thing as change of mind. ... You are staying in Mombas?"

"Yes, we shall leave here well before dark. ... Your name is legend, Pastor Rebmann. I am ashamed that we have let it sink from view. Be assured that I shall not rest until some comforts fit for your station and infirmity have been arranged. I had no idea..."

His eyes roamed expressively from the rough-hewn walls I had labored over long ago to the flat roof supported by a criss-cross of rafters, the rickety wooden chairs and the shutters folded back from the uncovered window spaces. Although I could not seem him I was quite aware that they did so.

"I am quite comfortably provided, thank you," I replied, trying to still the note of reproof and avoid the ridiculous manner in which the English addressed their titled fellows, "and by no means lost. Any more, of course, than was Dr. Livingstone, whose skill with the instruments of travel we all revere. But, unlike him, I have not for these past many years journeyed beyond ease of communication. In fact the Home Committee is quite badgered—you will excuse the pun, Dr. Badger, old friend, you and I live by changing words—badgered, I mean, by the number of letters we inflict on them, Isaac and I. They are still sending us recruits. But alas the constitution of these days seems not to match that of the time when you and I were young." (Let him ponder that, for this heartiness. If I look older than him, that earns me respect in Africa, but I am not near 60 yet.)

"Your society here is limited, Mr. Rebmann. Do your converts support you?"

"Most gladly so. Isaac is the second generation of the first fruits: his father is my second disciple and his mother also attends. Of the freed slave people from Nasik, George David assists us here in the region, William Jones returned to Bombay for a while to seek further recruits, and Semler will escort them to Mombas. Three of our converts live nearby and take communion with us, so that we may strengthen one another: others live at a greater distance, and so spread the word. Some are hearers, not yet prepared for baptism. Patience, as my dear brother Krapf never tired of saying, in Africa (and elsewhere, I don't doubt) patience is of the essence. Men of my age have grown used to me as a neighbor: they drop in to hear a story from the Good Book and tell me one in return."

"And you have been here—20 years, is it? That is patience indeed. Think what enormous strides have been made in Zanzibar in that time."

"Twenty seven years. Think what strides have been made also in Europe. 1848, they say was the year of revolutions. And now Wurtemberg acknowledges the King of Prussia, if that is the sort of stride you have in mind. But here we have not stood still."

"The material progress is not—ah—very evident. You feel the Rabai people are better off than their neighbors?"

"Indeed, no. That is not what I meant at all. Hereabouts to promote inequality is to provoke witchcraft. And a good thing proclaims its goodness by spreading."

"You refer to...?"

"Well, for one thing the killing of infants with some slight abnormality appears to have become less over the years. Of course it is hard to be sure. To believe he is trusted is the mark of the novice. But whereas the people told us, when we first came, that they had stopped exposing twins, there are far more twins to be seen under 20 than there are above. And one does not hear—my wife used to tell me—such fearful enquiries into the order of teeth or precocious movement. I do not say none are done away with but the compulsion can be avoided. Children survive with a finger missing or a foot twisted, though no doubt serious deformities are still a cause of death. Perhaps it is as well, for there is little chance of living a physically inactive life here."

"But I heard that your first convert was a cripple."

"Yes, indeed. I understand his misfortune occurred when he was near to growing up, or else in those times he could not have survived."

"Are there other changes?"

"Oh yes. Do you not see the space we have here on open ground. Our first site was on a steep ridge, and many people lived in a fortress, within the kaya rampart. Now almost all the coastal communities have spilt over into the open countryside. Partly it is a growth of numbers, you may say, whether or not our simple health care has helped in that. But partly it is due to greater security—people mix more and do not feel the same tight bonds that led to fighting, group with group.

When I was new at the coast you did not meet a man by the roadside without his weapons, either bow and arrows or a spear. Now he is more likely to be carrying a hoe or a water-pipe or a gourd of palm wine.

I do not say everything is safe in the interior, even now. I warned New, *when he set off on his first trip to the snow mountain, things are more turbulent than when I made my journeys a quarter of a century ago—but on a broader landscape. I have often censured the Wanika for living only a day at a time. Gradually one comes to see that this carelessness is not the cause of slave-hunting, even at one remove, but its result. They fear too much attachment to something it is beyond their power to preserve.*

But, for better or worse, there is now more mobility, and so people learn more from one another—trade from the Digo, clothing from the Swahili, readiness to travel and take employment from the Kamba among us. And, if that, why not industry and order from the white man, more systematic gardening, German-style, and English concern for freeing slaves? They do not want to concede land to them or to forfeit labor they feel they have paid for, but few have tried to make a profit by turning runaways in. Their horizon has been enlarged. Only a few have whole-heartedly come to Christ, but many at least know His name and how our practices differ from the Mohammedan."

"Ah yes. An intelligent chief remarked to me that more missionaries would provide protection against the Maasai and the slave-traders. I made particular note of that for my report.—Does not the school provoke enquiry as to the faith?"

"We do not have a school at present."

"The people do most urgently desire a school, sir," broke in David. "On every journey we meet with their requests and would like to fulfill them."

"Ah, yes, George, on every journey. But let us remind ourselves— the Sparshotts had a school, and when they became sickly and moved to Mombas you took it over. The school moved to a breezy place—what is it called?—and then one of the families went away. A second family was raided—the father and his slave wife were killed, and two of the three sons captured. The third one moved to stay with relations, and for want of pupils the school collapsed. It has been so again and again, since I started the school at Bunni while Krapf was still here. You, Isaac, attended classes with my late wife, and how many others persisted? Classes come and go, but the reading of the gospel, somehow, continues."

"But people say…"

"Yes, George, people say. One at Jilore asks,

'How do you come to dress in these fine clothes and change words from one language to another?'

You tell him, 'I went to school,' and he says,

'I wish my son could go to school and become like you.' But at such a school as we might have here his son will not learn to earn money or speak like a Banian. One in Digo says to you,

'If we had a school, we could teach our young people to make chairs and boxes and fine sandals such as we see in Mombas.'

But if you tell him,

'Then bring good timber from the forest, and a hide for the sandals, and a goat to pay for the knife and the saw,' he will say to you,

'No, in other places people are paid to sing their ABC. We do not want a school enough to pay for it.'

They do not get paid at Ribe, but the freed slaves and the traders tell them this is so in distant places, so I suppose it must be true. Do not think, Sir Bartle, that we are cut off from news in this sleepy, slow-moving place. Compared with Gerlingen, where I grew up, East Africa is a hotbed of rumors.

And even if you do bring one man from each clan, William, to learn a trade, and a couple of young Kamba settlers who are good at craft work, how will you find a central place to suit them all and teachers which each one will respect? It is not yet time. When they hear the drum, they come to sing. They begin to understand what they sing. Those who can read, read aloud, and those who listen come when they are eager to read, or eager for baptism and therefore must try to read. Then a new class opens. It is as with their own initiations. You do not say, 'This will be the day: find candidates to be prepared,' but 'The candidates present themselves: therefore we will fix the day.'"

"One must start somewhere," exclaimed Sir Bartle Frere, looking suspiciously at the tea and fritters which had been brought in, while Mrs. David recited a long grace in English.

"Excellent, excellent," interjected Mr. Hill of the Foreign Office, "the cup that cheers but not inebriates."

"We find it so: palm wine from the village is refreshing too, in moderation."

Kazi Shahabudin condescended to a short conversation with Mrs. David in Hindi and complimented her on her knowledge of the language. Major Euan Smith compiled a report in his head, sensing that, as with oriental monarchs, it would not do to take notes. Dr. Badger glumly counted the odd cups and hoped for a chance of speaking with his old friend Rebmann later. In Arabic, may be. Inshallah. *It was too late to save him now.*

"One must start somewhere: this is exactly what I have been saying, sir," broke in George David, but was quelled with a look.

"Your catechumens, then, are required to read?"

"We like them to read, yes. Isaac's father, Abe Gunga, was the first, after Mringe died. I started him off and then left him with Erhardt when I went away to Egypt to bring my wife. That was in 1851, and by the time we came back he was doing well, very well. For the time, it was remarkable. It was not the same as for those who lived among the Mohammedans, as people increasingly do, and had the notion of book learning."

"Your wife?"

"Yes, I had a wife, sir. In fact we stayed with Dr. Badger, here, on our wedding journey back to East Africa. She was an English lady, and was 15 years here with me before the Lord took her, and a great blessing to us all. Our baby boy died early and we had no other: perhaps we should be thankful, or she might not have been spared so long."

"So. That is fortitude indeed. Did you not need to send her to Europe for her health in all those years?"

"Indeed, no. She came to serve as I did, and had lived a long time in Egypt before, used to the heat and other discomforts. And of course, compared with many missionaries we have lived a metropolitan life, so near to the civilization of Zanzibar. Nowadays there is even a hospital there: of course you know it. We used to go over often, when I had my sight, that is."

"And did Mrs. Rebmann take the women in hand? Sewing classes, that sort of thing?"

"Oh, she did much—so much. Not exactly making tiny garments—if you have looked around you on the way you will have seen that is hardly necessary. Until the Bombay ladies came there was no stitching of dresses. The women used to have their pretty pleated skirts they were so proud of, like a double petticoat, quite adequate for decency. You will still see them among our Kiriama neighbors—their movement from south to north is one of the big changes over the years we have been here. But that is less a matter of needle and thread than the art of winding it round and tugging and prinking—my dear wife explained all that to me, though she was hardly in a position to be worldly about her own dress.

And one would not particularly advocate dress-making as more of the women adopt the kanga *and* leso *from our Mohammedan neighbors.*

Those two pieces of cloth are adequate, cheap and easy to launder. Nor did they need any advice from her on what the training school calls inti-

mate matters. A lady of Siu had already done all that in a Kiswahili poem called Mwana Kupona. *These women here do not exactly hear Kiswahili, but I guess this sort of information gets about, as it does in Germany or Switzerland or England, even." Sir Bartle Frere coughed uncomfortably. Isaac looked at the floor. George David rustled some notes, finding a place ostentatiously.*

"I should be most interested to see a copy, Rebmann," put in Dr. Badger. "And any other manuscript you might have come across."

"I have collected what I could..."

"Bartle, my son," said Sir Bartle, "If you have finished your tea I expect you would like to take the opportunity to look round the place. Playfair, take a walk with him. And get some specimens of that wild cotton we saw in such abundance."

"Thank you, sir."

(Thank you for nothing. As though you finished Eton without getting hold of 'this sort of information.' As though you needed a naval officer to steer you past a bare-breasted woman carrying your gear uphill while the goddamn soldiery sat around waiting to be fed. As though this old German geyser was not capable of running rings round your exalted official papa.)

"Ah, yes, well, I thought you were discussing our impact on real life in Nika country... My wife was able to apply some unguent or plasters for women where their husbands had beaten them, and teach a little hygiene and just—well, you see, old-fashioned, evangelical love. 'She called her friends and they searched for the lost piece of silver,' that sort of thing. Naturally they didn't find her a very successful woman, not having a baby, getting married at what seemed to them a horribly advanced age to an old man of another tribe, living in a place like this. They were sorry for her, and a lot of virtues can grow out of sympathy..."

"But reading...?"

"Of course they would not learn to read before their husbands, would they? Imagine how they would have suffered. It was the young boys she helped with reading. But she taught the women songs and bible stories—I had to help her with the translation—and maybe a certain kind of—modesty, should I call it?

Terms vary so much from country to country. I had much to learn myself from being married to an Englishwoman"

"Indeed?"

"Oh well, I am ignorant. Perhaps a German woman would have sur-

prised me just as much. She seemed to be content with so little if you understand me. The women were heart-broken when she died."

"Quite so, quite so. ... We shall make the trip to Ribe from Mombasa another day. I hear that Mr. and Mrs. Wakefield have achieved marvels."

"Indeed, yes. They are very close to the people. They even have one convert from Islam, the first to my knowledge in East Africa, Mwidani by name, who has been in service with them. They have practically adopted a little Galla boy. Mr. New, you will be aware, is away on leave, and his book is being published in London."

"I understand they have even built a bridge."

"I hear so. Of course, I have not been in a position to travel recently. But Wakefield used often to be here, and their place in Mombas is near ours. A very likeable young fellow, not too proud to ask for advice when he needs it. Their little girl seems to flourish and I understand another baby is expected soon."

"Hmmm. We shall not be a burden to them, of course. We want to see the progress of the schools."

"Schools? Oh yes. Well, they will be glad to receive you. ... You say the soldiers will be cooking meat?"

"Indeed. They expect good rations. Do you not think your people will be able to supply?"

"These days everything has its price. Perhaps goats will do."

"That is hardly my province. Are there no cattle? I thought we saw a few?"

"Yes, of recent years there are some cattle, but the Nika do not ordinarily eat them. They require them for trading purposes."

"Ah, ingenious fellows like the Kamba, are they good with their hands and suitable for caravan work? What do they get for their cattle?"

"They are not very interested in caravans, and there are enough Wakamba settled near here to supply their peculiar skills. The Wanika trade their cattle for plantation labor. That is what they have learned from Zanzibar."

"Free labor?"

"The law of the Sultan's dominion does not insist on free labor, Sir Bartle. There used to be seasonal slavery during times of famine and warfare, to be compounded on agreement when things returned to normal. Now there is a new economic order. To compete with it people will take advantage of the times."

"*The spirit of the times is the spirit of abolition, Mr. Rebmann. You have been too long cut off from the movement of the age.*"

"*Not cut off, Sir Bartle, just attached to the receiving end. If we were all Christians, we should all pay just wages or go without service, which is what it would mean for many. I was glad when I heard, twenty five years ago, that the last feudal laws had been abolished in Wurtemberg: when I last saw that country some people still owed customary labor to their ancient masters, though not to the extent of serfdom. I was glad when Lincoln freed the slaves in America—only seven years ago, was it not? Alas that he was killed before he could oversee the implementing of that freedom. But I am not so far gone, Sir Bartle, as not to know that American ships delivered cotton cloth—*marikani *as we call it here—to Zanzibar all through the Civil War, though we knew it was bought at a loss from Manchester. The system did not allow those merchants from Salem and Boston and Providence, Rhode Island, even to admit to themselves that they might lose the advantage of cheap production. Do you suppose our Wanika are better informed than they are, sir?*"

"*Their education has lain largely in your hands, Mr. Rebmann.*"

"*Hardly as much as in England it lies in the hands of the British and National School Boards, Sir Bartle. (We studied the system, to great advantage, in Islington.) It is estimable indeed that pupil teachers should instruct poor children in reading and counting, but it is still their parents, if my grasp of English idiom does not forsake me, who teach them how many beans make five.*"

"*You are weary, sir, through long labor. You have lost hope of improvement.*"

"*Far from it, sir. Without hope, one does not labor so long. But my hope is, shall we say, less workaday than yours.*"

The servants came whispering. The picnic was spread in all its magnificence, villagers standing by to stare and comment. Rebmann refused to join his guests, making the ambivalent excuse of his blind clumsiness. Badger managed to waylay him, accompanied by Mr. Grey.

"*Pray excuse us for a while, Sir Bartle, and go ahead with your lunch. I have not met with Mr. Rebmann since—1862, was it, when Brigadier Coghlan and I slipped away from the Governor's reception to call on you here, Rebmann? And his language work is of great interest.*"

"*Indeed, indeed, Badger. Do impress upon him the urgency of publication. It would be sad indeed if new laborers to the harvest did not profit from his long application to the task.*"

"You came the same year, Colonel Pelly, to inspect our two stations, when you were in the consulate at Zanzibar."

"I remember it well, Mrs. Rebmann's gracious hospitality and the refreshing air up here compared with Zanzibar. I must say the Persian Gulf is hot, but it is less enervating than the island. I am distressed about your eyes, Rebmann, but that is the more reason for you to entrust the manuscript to Dr. Badger, so let me not detain you."

"You see how it is, Rebmann," said Badger, taking his arm. "They will take what they want from you. The Wanika already have much to remember you by. Do not fear."

"It is not a matter of fear," insisted Rebmann. "It is a matter of enlightened common sense. But let us not waste time—Isaac, Isaac."

"I am here, sir."

"Now those manuscripts, Isaac, that I made to take with me to the Cape. We should have gone, Badger, if my wife had lived. Afterwards I had not the heart. Some you made spare copies for me—no, not the English poem, nobody values that, the coastal manuscripts, I mean. Make haste and bring the spare copies. And bring the single copies in another folder, so that you may note those which Dr. Badger would like to have, and prepare them later. If I had had more notice, my dear fellow, it would have been done. Isaac's hand is so like my own, you would hardly tell the difference."

"You are more than kind."

"I should have liked your help with the Arabic, too, Badger, but the time is now past for me. An Arab friend in Zanzibar assisted me greatly: the Kadhi at Mombas, Sheikh Ali Ben, also made great efforts, but Sheikh Muhuiddin is a true scholar: both of them showed me how the gospel appears to the Mohammedan."

"And the English poem?" asked Grey.

"A toy I trifled with when my mind was disturbed: I don't think there is any urgent need for preserving that."

"You under-rate yourself. Your facility in the language astonishes us, Mr. Rebmann. Is it not very difficult? Or is it that you have special gifts?"

"I would not say special, Mr. Grey. To some are given tongues and the interpretation of tongues. And by a tongue I assume the apostle to imply something that intends meaning, not just a sounding brass or a tinkling cymbal.

If you fall into water you usually find you can swim. Too bad if you are one of the few who can't. If you are thrown into a place where no-

one understands you, you are likely to find a way of understanding those others. For months together my alternatives were Kinika or Kiswahili if my fellow-missionaries were away. It is a matter of asking the lord for strength and patience. But of course acquaintance with a few other languages broadens your understanding and sharpens your ear.

Even now, I do not claim to have a perfect comprehension of Kiswahili or Nika conversation. It is easy for people to exclude the outsider, if they wish, by adopting a tone of banter, of intimidation or of ribaldry in which words change their meanings."

"Are the languages as flexible as Arabic in this way?" asked Badger.

"Every language has its subtlety, its logic and its variations, which are not at all related to the deceptive simplicity of a people's mechanical culture. Even our missionary Intelligencer explained this, which must have come hard to people who feel that English is the supreme achievement of linguistic science. Our coastal languages are beautiful in their regularity and their precision. The art of oratory is greatly respected, and poets and story-tellers play upon the language like an instrument. (You have heard the special tones of our instruments—the zomari, the bungu—which is like the black notes of the piano?) This is a study by itself."

"And they write in Arabic script?"

"With the addition of three Persian characters to cover the sounds more accurately."

"Just a minute, Rebmann, let me get my notebook. Grey, why don't you go and have lunch? Tell them I'm collecting the manuscripts to take back with me—that will keep them happy."

"I am ready enough for some sustenance. Pastor, you will excuse me."

"He has had an audience with the Pope, Rebmann. He is even empowered to pay the Sultan's subsidy to Muscat for him. Canning laid it upon Zanzibar, but now there will be a loss of revenue even if the slaves are still shipped clandestinely—Barghash will not be able to collect the duty, and I do not think he would even try to, once the treaty is signed. He is an honorable man according to his lights. So they will call paying the subsidy an act of sympathy for the destruction caused by the hurricane last year. Really it is to silence the French, since they had the bad taste to describe the subsidy as the Sultan's payment to the British for a license to carry on the slave trade. So for the Lord's sake believe Frere will get his treaty. Whether it can be enforced or not is another matter. You and I know, and Col. Pelly knows, that in the monsoon a slave dhow can outrun any patrol boat that we send after it, but all the same we have to do what we can for the poor devils. I thought you would be so pleased that he wishes to entrust freed slaves to the missions, rather than set up a government agency."

"Well enough, well enough, so long as the mission does not become a cloak for a government agency..."

"Frere didn't do so well in France, where they oppose us on principle, you would think, but King Victor Emmanuel of Italy gave him a gold medal to deliver to Livingstone, and the Khedive tried to convince him that Egypt was leading Africa into civilization. Now he has got nearly all the consuls here to urge compliance on the Sultan. They were cool when Hill visited them, but Schultz, the German, went with Colonel Pelly after getting instructions from Berlin. F. R. Webb will come round for America—they dare not appear less than enthusiastic about their own emancipation policy. Bertrand is only the Vice-consul, and more Levantine than French: when de Vienne comes back from leave Kirk will persuade him to keep his navy out of it, you mark my words. They cannot face English hostility so soon after being beaten by Prussia. Paris bombarded—can you imagine that? ... He carries a lot of weight, Rebmann."

"So he does, so he does. That is not a good reason to be condescending with me... and after he has been so particular about freedom of conscience in Bombay that mission work is hindered."

"I wouldn't say hindered, my friend: kept within bounds, perhaps. You yourself are so scrupulous not to offer material advantages to your converts that you may not realize how strongly others are tempted to put on pressure."

"But when the consuls put pressure on the Sultan they are pursuing strategy rather than succumbing to temptation? This is too devious for me, old friend. If anyone gets a signature out of Barghash I am sure it will be Kirk, who keeps his place and never visits the Sultan alone, only in the presence of his counselors, the proper Arab way.

But these diplomats of yours are in a hurry. You are ready to take down some examples of Kiswahili?"

"Yes, certainly. Fire away, Rebmann."

"In Tumbatu, for instance—you are familiar with the place, off the coast of Zanzibar?—they help you to hear the Song of the Dhow. As the vessel leaves the shore, the pulley calls watoto, watoto, children, children: as the sail is hoisted, the rudder says ao, ao when it scrapes on the sand, and as the prow strikes the waves it shouts taa wa saa, taa wa saa, the lamp of the time, the lamp of the time.

And in Zanzibar they interpret the cry of birds. They are fond of keeping caged birds too. The turtle dove calls, mama akafa, baba akafa, nimesalia mimi tu, *mother died, father died and only I am left alone. Another call is* kuku mfupa tupu, mimi nyama tele, *the chicken is only bones, but me I've lots of meat. Can you not just hear the bird calling? But the* mwigo, *the big dove, can be asked to prophesy, so you don't preempt what she is going to say. The owl is unlucky, like the silent chameleon, but he has his song too, calling* shimeji, niazime mkufu, *my sister-in-law, get me an ornamental chain, and the female replies,* usiku huu, usiku huu, *tonight, tonight. But the night-jar is followed by a wizard, so it would not do to imitate him."*

Isaac hurried up with the manuscripts and began conferring with Dr. Badger about them, when young Bartle Frere appeared, obviously sent to call him away. "You see my secretary has brought what was needed," said Rebmann, recognizing the boy's voice. "We won't delay you much longer with chatter about birds and wizards."

"Have you seen a wizard, then, Mr. Rebmann? It sounds as though you are fully conversant with them."

"I think the wizard would run away if he saw me first. So tough and talkative a Christian would surely dismay him. But if I were not shielded by this faith of mine, there is a noted charm one can get — at a price — which will make wizards think you are a tree, so that they hang their clothes on you and go away. Otherwise you could fasten phosphorescent fish bones to our door to keep them away."

"What would you do with the wizards' clothes?"

"The charm book does not say. But I suppose if you found an unwary customer you might sell them to defray the cost of the charm."

"That sounds like a good idea. But my father sent me to say the carriers are ready."

"I understand, yes, indeed. Just give me your arm, will you?" (*My boy might have been a bit older than this one if he had lived.*)

"Well, sir, I am sorry you have to go so soon. I do not move far myself, so if any of you gentlemen are back in Mombas, please remember to look me up. ... I understand you have something in mind for the freed slaves. If you had a way to see it made official... You know we are much hampered by the civil law in helping these poor fellows as much as we should like. Jones sometimes lets his heart rule his head in this matter, for which I respect him the more..."

"Provision will be made, Pastor Rebmann, provision will be made. Do not over-exert yourself trying to keep up with us. I am sure Nyondo and David will see us on our way. Goodbye, goodbye..."

Isaac remained silent, aware that Rebmann was seized with the recollection of some of the controversies that were forcing him away from the home and habits of so many years. When he chose to speak, Isaac would listen, but just as with his own father, he could not find a way into that past experience which had changed him and all about him.

"We are getting close to the harbor," he repeated.

Price was at the harbor to meet them of course. He would not trust so delicate an assignment to anyone else. Although contemptuous of the Mombasa accommodation, as of everything done before his arrival, he had arranged for Rebmann to lodge overnight in the upper room of the old cliff-top house where he had spent his first night, hoping that this would please him. It would also be easy to lead him back down the uneven steps next morning and into the rowing-boat from which he would embark.

Price had, in fact, tried to win the blind man over to accept retirement with the help of sleeping-draughts and questions about his manuscripts without for a moment comprehending the weight of grief that was being forced upon him. The East African mission had begun its new lease of life. There was no need to bring to the attention of the authorities a rambling, sightless old man who had lost his sense of European values.

Rebmann was lying on top of the made bed looking pale and listless as Price poured out his plans and instructions. Good land was going to waste, he said, and it was obvious that freed slaves should cultivate it. (Yes, yes: but at what cost in envy and witchcraft?)

He was certain that Sparshott would have to go, drawing up a long indictment. Rebmann, long experienced in disappointment as new colleagues failed him one way or another, agreed with every point, but still pleaded for Sparshott's retention.

"Why?" asked Price, "why? You have quarreled with him repeatedly. Even when you disagreed with everything I proposed last year, as though Kisulutini (or any other place) could be a refuge for your precious converts from the wiles of the devil, you still shook hands with Remington and me, though you would not pray with us. You refused Sparshott's hand, telling him, 'You know why.' And yet as soon as you consented to leave he rushed up to Rabai and spent hours in private talk with you: what was it about?"

"Mr. Price, I am old in your eyes—though only five years older than you, I am blind, and, as you allege, I have never been to Kiriama. I have been to quite a few other places, but never mind. I am still a clergyman in Anglican orders, as you are, and you have no right to challenge the confidentiality of people who come to me with their troubles."

"True. I apologize. Sparshott has never come to me for spiritual counsel, and I was thinking of him just as one of my staff, at loggerheads with the rest. Like you he works hard at building. I know that has been a sore point in the past, but I must congratulate you on the excellence of the layout of Kisulutini. If it had not been for your physical infirmity, I am sure the buildings would have been better maintained. I have sent for technical books, by the way, to supplement our small skills in that field.

As for Sparshott, I know that his wife had a miscarriage and the children are ill, but that doesn't excuse him for positive ill-will, saying he will rename his boat *The Serpent* in contradiction of our *Dove*, and that the best of the Bombay Africans, by which he means Matthew Wellington, is the only one fit to be his cook. And yet look at what Wellington has achieved, a man who accompanied Livingstone and helped to bring the body back. And after all that he is to be employed as a cook! If you ask me to re-engage Sparshott, you must give me reasons…"

"Your reasons and mine do not harmonize, Mr. Price. You must increase and I must decrease. I have accepted that."

"Well, Rebmann, that is the way of the world. We have gained much by your language work and your endurance. You must not stand in the way of a new era now."

"That may be so," said Rebmann, clambering carefully down from the bed to mask the effort of controlling his feelings.

"You organize according to your lights. Let us at least say the Lord's prayer together."

Price was happy to comply: he was too old to take lightly the task of supplanting a failing colleague, however convinced that he was always right. Each prayed extempore and without constraint.

"You prayed that God would over-rule: in this you and I are one," murmured Rebmann, now exhausted. It could not be wrong, he supposed, to pray with a sincere person, however misguided. He had often been present at his Mohammedan friends' devotions. Sparshott was more cantankerous than any of them, perhaps, but he had more spark, more emotion in him. He had almost broken his heart over that baby.

The darkness hummed with insects. The town watchmen clattered outside carrying their lamps. Every door would be closed after ten o'clock. If you were ignorant enough to answer a call or knock after that time the Djinn who had got hold of your name would, people believed, kill you on the spot. A Sparshott child wailed briefly in the rooms below, and Rebmann reached out in the dark for Emma's remembered hand.

Next morning they were to board a British naval frigate bound for Zanzibar. Price had booked a British India steamer from Zanzibar to Aden and entrusted Williams with the rest of the passage money. He gave £20 to Rebmann to use on new clothes and other necessities for the journey. Price himself and Williams would spend the night at the Methodist house, since it was too late to get a hired boat back across to Freretown.

British naval patrol-boats passed Mombasa regularly, and Price had sought their assistance when he saw how frail Rebmann was getting. All the noise and smelly juxtaposition of freight and passengers—shark meat, oil, hides, copra on an Arab dhow riding barely a foot above the water seemed too much for the blind man to bear, no matter how familiar it had become over the years. Price pleaded Williams' weak condition, afraid of Rebmann's reaction to special treatment or shelter from memories.

He need not have worried. Rebmann was acquiescent, eager, in fact to get the goodbyes over and stand in his new relation to the world. He greeted the captain courteously and asked Isaac to place him somewhere in the shade where he would not impede the work going on. Williams, physically the weaker but well aware of the strain on his older colleague, sat beside him describing in low tones what the sailors were doing.

The Kadhi and the old Governor (back to take over from Seif after the Al Akida business) came to take their leave, not just ceremoniously but with urgent, quiet speech, awakened to their own grey hairs and the flux of time: both had already been senior functionaries when Rebmann was a raw recruit to the mission. The son of the old housekeeper was there, and Tulsidass who had helped to find a surgeon that terrible night. Abdallah, portly now and slow in motion, had come down from Jimboni in his own boat, Wakefield had come from Ribe to say goodbye, Mwidani with him. Amri, long retired from domestic service, dealing in ships' stores now, came to seize Rebmann's hand. Sparshott had led him down to the harbor and still stood, well away from Chancellor, while the children, who had come with their mother to see the ship, dutifully kissed Rebmann and Williams. Mrs. Price made hearty conversation. Price prayed portentously when the time came and chivvied the visitors ashore. At last, with a rattle of chains, they were away.

II

At Zanzibar they found the British India Steam Navigation Company steamer already docked, and were able to transfer straightaway. Isaac breathed a sigh of relief, for though he would have liked more time to see the town he was fearful of exposing Rebmann to yet more emotion. But the old missionary seemed now set on his course.

Miss Tozer came to bid him Godspeed on behalf of the Universities Mission: Bishop Steere, with some new recruits, was on his way back from England. Dr. and Mrs. Kirk were cheerful and affectionate, promising a visit to Germany: they had moved into the new consulate building since his last visit. Sheikh Muhuiddin was most affected, but Rebmann reminded him that Krapf would be near him in Wurtemberg and able to read aloud letters in Arabic script. The Nasik people had come rather to meet Isaac as Polly's husband than to greet the retiring missionary. Tarya Topan, who had taken over the customs from Luda Dhamji, came to pay his respects on behalf of the Sewji family, and then came a grey-haired man whose voice Rebmann did not recognize. It turned out to be Goan Anthony, who had emerged from private service to take over the hotel portion of French Charlie's business. The German consul brought a message on behalf of the palace and passengers already on board from Natal and Mauritius were affable. Rebmann and Williams were glad to retire below and rest. There was not much privacy, but Isaac secured a lower bunk for Rebmann where he could feel his way, and at this hour the other male passengers were still pacing the deck. Williams assured Isaac that there was no need to wait for them to join in the evening devotions.

The early morning was full of nautical bustle, until they were ready to sail and old hands pointed out the pilot boat commanded by 'Admiral Bucket' with his two pet monkeys. It was a time for making acquaintances.

The ladies, especially, clustered round the blind man, fussy and sympathetic. He tried, not very successfully, to respond with small-talk and compliments. He had still to discover what was left of himself after this rupture, no longer knew what he had to give, was not ready to be drained of Africa by Europe. Williams was drained already, having missed the chance to start giving to the coast, and only waited to be refilled. Isaac, who had always been given, now needed the strength for all three and in this shadowy world of steep stairs and bolted-down tables, where the floor swayed under one's feet and the white stewards were deferential, accustomed to passengers' ignorance of their mysteries, he reached out in prayer and seized upon it.

"Is it not marvelous?" Rebmann pondered. "We embark and ask no more questions. At a set hour cups of tea and plates of food appear before us. Water for bathing is provided and musical entertainments got up for those who are interested. Seven days, is it, to Aden?"

"Yes, and there we change to a P. and O. steamer that has come from India." (New stairs, new cabins—more private, people said— guiding the blind man and the sick one down a slatted gangway over deep water, stowing Rebmann's tattered portmanteaux and the precious manuscripts all over again. New stewards, new faces.)

"So we shall be lifted up and down the locks through the canal." (Locks? Is the old man wandering again, because we have sealed the boxes but we never need locks and keys in Unika…?)

"…Which I have never seen. That French fellow was making measurements last time I was at Suez. You will have to describe it to me. And no doubt we shall touch at Alexandria, Genoa, Marseilles and so on to London. Always, before traveling, I have had to bargain and threaten in order to get set down at such and such a place. Even, as I have told you often, we overshot Mombas on our wedding trip, and were shipwrecked after the other voyage to Egypt. When Krapf brought Wakefield first, with Woolner and the others, it was even worse—54 days from Aden to Zanzibar in a *bagala* infested with rats. If it had not been for the Governor of Barawa entertaining them to a British style dinner on shore and pressing milk upon them, they might well have despaired. He was one of Said Sultan's English speakers. We always had to squabble over chicken and dates and bottles of water. Even once my dear one nearly slipped from my arms into the sea because the boat coming alongside did not hold steady. If only she could have experienced comfort like this: from the day we were married she had continually to plan and contrive, and we left it too late for her to see her sister. Perhaps the voyage to Port Natal would have been like this, only I had my eyes then. I had feared it would be too much for her, gaunt and yellow with fever as you remember her.

I never met any of her family, Isaac. Perhaps I shall have to try when we get to London. She had sisters and a brother-in-law whom she used to keep in touch with, and an old uncle of her first husband she was fond of, until he died. I know you have not met Polly's family either, but you must see the Nasik people as a clan for her, since she was snatched away from home."

Isaac privately thought it was only natural for women to be involved in housekeeping and unnatural for them to be conversing with strange men on the decks of steamers. But there was much else to occupy his mind, and he kept his counsel.

"It seems that ladies are now to be found everywhere," sighed Rebmann. "I am not at all used to it. I wonder how I shall face up to life in Germany. In England there are still, I believe, clubs where gentlemen can stay for a while if they can afford it, to which ladies are not admitted. I really have no longer any idea what things cost. They tell me my allowance is to be discussed. But there is nothing cheaper, people say, than getting yourself a hefty maid-servant who will tell you what you must eat and where you may sit while she is scrubbing the floor. I am not sure I can bear it."

"I thought Christians were supposed to respect women more than we have customarily done among the Wanika," Isaac dared to observe, sensing a certain *volte-face*. "The care of the house is women's business, but you say they may teach and give medicine as well and even do some of the secretarial work. Mrs. Wakefield used to help her husband and Mrs. Kirk, people say, was always at her desk—the joke went that the British employed two agents in Zanzibar for the price of one."

"Ah, yes, Isaac, you are right to rebuke me. There are service-able women and redoubtable ladies—you follow that, now that we are speaking English. In Kinika it is hard to make the distinction. They are there in the Bible too, and no doubt they will flower in Unika. Think what it must have been like to sit down to breakfast with Deborah or Judith: I have told you about the chief's daugh-ter in Jaga up by the snow mountain—she commands men as her father does. Jaga is like our southern part of Germany and the Ba-sel in Switzerland, where I was a student. I would like to take you there, but I am afraid they will not permit it, because you do not speak German and they do not trust me to look after myself enough to direct you. There are formidable ladies there too…

You see, I have not had all that much to do with women, and it is hard to remember that my sisters and schoolmates are fat old women with grandchildren now. Yes, I show my weakness: I am frightened of all this.

But I had a home with a wife. That you well know. It was a turning-point. I never made a long journey inland after being mar-ried—there were plenty of people eager for the fame of doing that. They like to be known as explorers, trail-blazers. I never blazed any trails myself except those few horrible days we had to cut our way through the forest between Weri-Weri and Lomi, and spend the first night without fire or water. We took seven days on the way instead of three, and I nearly got drowned when I fell off an improvised bridge. The men laughed heartily when I straddled the next one. And that detour was not by way of attracting attention. It was sim-ply to avoid having to visit Masaki again and be stripped of what little subsistence goods we had left. Perhaps it was want of faith on my part to be so concerned, but on such a journey goods mean food to eat: money in those days was not much use after three days travel inland. No-one else in the party had faith in the Lord Jesus as protector or anything else, and it might have been another way of showing off to keep them against their will on the road which had already caused them such distress. Certainly I repented of my rashness in getting us lost, and the Lord showed His mercy and provided us with wild honey and birds' nests.

Apart from that time I always took a path I had good evidence about from the local people, and asked their advice about where we could get food and water and what trade goods were acceptable. It would be foolhardy to do otherwise, and I hope you will remember that when you fancy to find your way from Islinghton to the Strand and back again. I don't think you will walk into the Army and Navy stores and ask them to accept rupees and pice. No more would I go with white beads as Speke did to the place where blue beads were accepted currency, or demand cows' milk where there are only sheep.

What could I do which the Wakamba and other guides couldn't through no fault of their own, was to take compass readings and altitudes, near enough and draw a map that might be useful to others. I admit that we were very proud of ourselves, Erhardt and I, when we hit on the idea of an inland sea. But our map had to be corrected by secular explorers: the Lord reminded us that He is the maker of all things, and just to apply our own poor brains to information received was not such a great thing compared to His command to make His name known."

"You are tired, father. You need to sleep."

"I am too restless to sleep, my son. There are too many memories alive in me tonight. Perhaps *you* ought to be up there, exposing yourself to the intricacies of European social manners. But I doubt if that is very enjoyable when I am not around to get a certain modicum of civility addressed to you. And I doubt if it's very useful either. It's not the sort of talk that you'd meet if you went to join Mr. Booth's Christian mission to the poor of London, which might be very good training for you, come to think of it.

I was reminding you of the loss of my dear wife. Well, of course, more missionaries soon came to relieve my loneliness, if such it was. But the more there are, the more risk of building a separate, second society. As you have seen with Spar...—Well, let me not name names. We are not at home here.

Missionaries apart, the big commercial Banian families knew me and my wife. The Governor of Mombas was probably tired of seeing me—about caravan questions, freed slaves questions, import questions, the tiresome business of the *Candace* people. Time and again I visited Zanzibar and enjoyed the facilities of good copyists and landed mail. The consuls and business people all knew us there, the Sultans all received us, we were in constant touch with the Home Committee, Bishop Tozer of the High Church knew me and had visited the station, which is more than our own bishop in Mauritius did. Who then says I was lost? Was I hiding somewhere for Sir Bartle Frere to come and find me?

Livingstone was not lost either, and if he had been someone other than that noisy fellow Stanley could well have looked for him. But he was at least out of sight—I never was, for someone to come blathering 'I have found Rebmann and he needs help,' 'I have found Rebmann and he needs converts,' 'I have found Rebmann he needs industrial missions'."

"My father, you excite yourself too much."

"Yes, you are right, Isaac, forgive me. You saw—and with my own eyes I did not—what he wrote: 'Rebmann does not give people what they want. He expects asceticism. He refuses them carpenters.' Indeed let carpenters be trained. Indeed, let slaves be freed. Already we have allowed girls as well as boys to go to school. But we do not buy baptisms with hammers and primers and manumission papers. Jones will baptize a man to save him from chains. He has been saved from chains himself. I see his point of view. But if that man's baptism deludes him that he is saved from sin without faith, his sins become the heavier.

Who is Frere to count heads? It took Krapf and me four years at Rabai before Mringe was baptized and, ten years after Mringe, you and your father and a handful after you. If we had been impatient, how would you be here with me, speaking in a language to which neither of us was born? Jones cries, 'Unika is not resistant as it was when Krapf and Rebmann came there: it is ready for a harvest of souls.' Then let him ask himself why it is different. God gives a time for the harvest to ripen."

"My father has told me that there were many changes."

"Indeed there have been many changes. I do not say that all of them are of our making. Dr. Krapf came looking for the Galla, and where are the Galla now? Withdrawn to the north and stripped of their power. The Kiriama have moved to take part of their place and they are more easily approachable. Is this not a movement of God's grace?"

"Indeed, it is so, my father. And then perhaps even the industrial school..."

"It may be so, and special calling will be given for it. But it is not my calling, and it would not once have seemed that industry is of great interest to the Wanika. But we shall see, we shall see. —Is Mr. Williams asleep? It shall be all right, Isaac, if you wish to take a turn on deck. I must not keep you all to myself."

The third day he had to answer the passengers. They had seen enough of water and the old hands from Mauritius and Durban had made some acquaintance with the few embarked at Zanzibar. They could no longer feign indifference to the heat. While Williams lay below most of the time and Isaac sought to memorize each glimpse of the coast, they crowded round Rebmann.

"When did I first become a missionary? How is one to answer a question like that? When, as a little boy, I first received the Lord into my heart? There is an automatic calling to mission there, but not necessarily to foreign mission. When I learned more of the faith and of the adventurous men it had inspired? All boys love adventure—I less than many, solemn-faced as I was, earning the nickname 'preacher' even at school. When I registered as a student at Basel? This had become the common ambition of pious young men in our district where piety was assumed to be a good thing, we were not making revolutions like St. Francis.

You see, I was not like Dr. Krapf, who went through a period of intellectual searching even after graduating to a parish. He established a reputation as a scholar before going abroad, and straightway plunged into individual exploits.

As for me, I was prepared to go anywhere I was sent, straight from college, and to be called by the Church Missionary Society seemed to me the most natural thing in the world. My uncle on the mother's side, Jakob Maisch, had been sent to India when I was still a baby, and we had occasional news of him.

I had already made the missionary sacrifice when I left my home village of Gerlingen, my parents, brothers and sisters, to travel to London for training and ordination. I never really expected to come back—to tell you the truth, I do not expect it even now that I am on a north-bound steamer. Called is called and answered is answered. It was not for nothing that we chose to call our little boy Samuel."

"But how do you mean, 'never go back,' asked a lady among the passengers with some agitation. He judged her to be a young lady, but not a girl. Her skirts rustled. Her voice was anxious. "We hear you have stayed at the coast for 29 years, but the others went for leave, travel or consultation. How could you not have *expected*?"

"You will remember, madam, we are speaking of 30 years ago. We did not plan 'three years tour then furlough' or 'contract for four years service.' It would have been absurd. You invalided home those who needed to go and the others hung on as best they could. My wife lasted for 15 years: I have done 29. I am still only 55. It is simply because of my eyes..."

Isaac took his arm encouragingly. The lady unnecessarily, averted her face.

"But does not your society require missionaries to report back to the home station both for your own health and for eliciting and informing new recruits?"

"Some do, nowadays some do, Wakefield, for instance, had his leave when he married Rebecca. That was the Methodist society of course. They gave New leave as well. He started out for Kilimanjaro and died a few weeks ago on the way back again after returning—a promising young fellow, though I felt more at home with Wakefield. My wife was like a mother to him. Then there was Livingstone of the London Missionary Society, always bobbing up, here, there and everywhere. Even our CMS gave Deimler leave to go and get married, and the Sparshotts had leave not long ago. In those days the Indian Army gave leave only once in a lifetime. My brother Erhardt, after leaving us, worked ten years as a missionary in India before getting leave, and still in his second term there. Try to see 'not expect' as 'not give a thought to.'

I did not know for sure, when leaving for London, where I should be posted. My desires were all forward-looking. Even brother Krapf, remember, was originally intended for Smyrna, in spite of his interest in Africa ever since he had read *Bruce's Travels* as a schoolboy. And how many were promised for East Africa who did not come?

You see, your mind rests on those who survived their service. Think of those others who were taken when it had hardly begun— Mr. Pfefferle, Mr. Wagner, Mr. Butterworth of the Methodist mission, Mr. Taylor..."

A sense of agitation stirred the group. Isaac almost plucked at his sleeve, but refrained. Rebmann recovered his thread.

"Others were given a few years—Mrs. Krapf, Mrs. Wakefield, Mr. Pennell and Mr. Fraser of UMCA—or transferred to less arduous fields—Mr. Woolner, Mr. Deimler. But of these the Lord takes account. Humanly speaking, we hold to the plough and do not look back unless we are instructed to do so. Unfortunately Home Committee instructions are not always compatible with those from above.

It is not that I was afraid of being weakened by the comforts of home—no, no. I was never what you English call a jolly good fellow. I appreciate good food and good beds, family affection and the beauties of our south German mountains and pastures. But our background was what you call pietistic, not given to frivolity. Sentimental, yes, perhaps. Isaac will remember how I wept on hearing him and Polly teaching their children some of the good old hymns from home. I used to play them on my flageolet, finding Kinika words where they were appropriate. But I never promised my people I would return, and fended off my sisters' pleas in letters that I would go and visit them.

My father was a solid citizen, a good farmer and a pious man. I am not sure that he ever set foot outside Wurtermberg, and his service to the community was none the less for that. There are trains now in the south of Germany—it was in England that I saw a train, a horse-bus, a paddle-steamer. These things are not bad in their way. But I am not convinced that the modern affection for dashing here, there and everywhere—taking the waters, peddling goods, seeking romantic sights—is necessarily good. I should have been content to die at Kisulutini if they had left me in peace."

"But you are still in your middle years," one of the officials insisted. "With home comforts you may enjoy a long retirement, putting your papers through the press..."

Rebmann gestured towards his eyes.

"... With the help of an amanuensis, of course. And with resort to modern medical science."

He coughed. Rebmann sank into reverie.

"Germany, Germany—one of you spoke of going back to Germany. I came from Wurtemberg, and except for that one journey on my way to England I have seen little of what you now call Germany. I certainly never dreamed, as we changed from time to time the alliance of our customs unions and our defensive pacts that we should come to associate ourselves with the Prussian Empire. In your twenties you are impatient to be through with training and out on the job, overjoyed at the prospect of landing in tropical Africa. I felt like a pioneer—well, travel was not only rougher then than now but also stranger, in the eyes of my rural inland community, than it was to those island Englishmen.

I loved my family, but at that age it is not uncommon to leave home. I had been careful to keep myself from entanglements with girls. But, as I have explained, it would not do to brood or analyze one's chances—that much we have in common with a military academy. I wonder how many of my fellow-students are alive today. Theodore Hamburg died in Hong Kong 20 years ago. Schreiber, who followed me at Basel, went to India but retreated soon after his wife died. ...

No, the fruit of obedience is living in the present. And if I find the present so hard to accept, it may be because I am disobedient today, or was disobedient the day I agreed to leave Rabai. Only, since I have no means of going back—the ship cannot stop for me, I doubt whether I have enough to pay the passage back even if the doctors permitted—there must be some obedience required in my present position."

"You were telling us about your travel to London, my father," Isaac chided him gently. "Perhaps these ladies and gentlemen are well acquainted with London, but I am not, and I shall need your help."

"Some of us would like your picture of London 30 years ago," added the young lady. "The gentlemen are being called to a game of cards. I am sure you will excuse them. But I should like to hear more."

"And I," added a boy's voice, striving to sound like a man's, "I was born at the Cape and am going to London to learn business accounts: that is my father's wish. But there is much else I need to find out about."

"Well, of course, going to England at all was a great adventure for me," Rebmann resumed, "traveling by stages down the Rhine valley with fairy-tale castles above one's head and the basically pagan stories collected by the brothers Grimm coming to life in the romantic landscape. I did not like it at all. I had been brought up to think, with Isaiah and John the Baptist, that every valley should be exalted and the rough places made plain. There would be fewer dark secrets, I was taught, when the thickets where the old blood-thirsty gods were worshipped should be cleared and cultivated. That was why I, like John, was called into the wilderness. But of course I was wrong—not wrong to go, I mean, I have never for a moment thought that—but wrong to forget that John was speaking more to greedy civil servants and undisciplined soldiers than to devil-worshippers. He met his death—no retirement for him—because of a political indiscretion.

Then we came to Holland, flat and tidy, with people in fancy dress and my first sight of the cheerless sea. Following directions I somehow embarked on the sailing boat and crossed the Channel. An amiable young man who was to be my fellow-student had been sent to meet me at Harwich, and it was a good thing he had. I thought my English was competent enough, but it was sadly deficient for matters like tipping porters and interpreting announcements. I remember that one of the first things that caught my eye on landing was a huge notice with the words 'growing up to be a beautiful lady'. I could not make head nor tail of it, but later discovered that it was an advertisement for Pear's Soap.

My new friend, Ernest, engaged places for us on a London coach next day, and we spent the night at an inn. The countryside, with its tidy fields and substantial churches was reassuring.

I was already fascinated by the sight of steam trains puffing along which, Ernest said, would soon replace the horse coach for long distances all over England, though it had not yet reached Harwich. But he thought we had better be used to animal transport because modern conveniences might not be available in the countries where we should eventually serve. It did not cross our minds that in the interior of Africa I should come to a place where the wheel was previously unknown, or that before the railway network in Germany (which our Wurtemberger professor List was always demanding) was fully established, missionaries in India would be able to board a train. They opened their first railway in 1853, I am told, and Egypt soon followed suit. Can you imagine ever getting a railway in East Africa? Yet unimaginable things happen.

It took us the whole day to get to London, yet in the evening the omnibus was still running and conveyed us to Islinghton from the city. By this time I was very tired from the effort of speaking English and seeing so many new things, so I did not mark the way very closely. We had dined at four, during the last change of horses, as Ernest told me supper would be over when we reached the college: in fact the night porter had to open the gate for us. The English food was better than I had been led to expect, but for a long time I missed the thick soups and the substantial second breakfast of Wurtemberg.

The college in Islington is situated on Upper Street, a few hundred yards past St. Mary's Church. (In those days I would not have referred to feet and yards with such facility, but English people have a way of imposing their own habits on such things.) You go through the place called 'The Angel.' And the name puzzled me, for the district is characterized by taverns and low lodging-houses. But 'The Angel' is the name of a coaching-house famous as the terminus of a route that brings in farmers and their produce from the northern outskirts of the city, so we still use it in the hope that it will strike a chord of blessing in some hearts.

The 'institution,' as it is supposed to be called, but all the neighbors prefer to call it College, is situated in a prosperous district of tall, flat houses, mostly of four stories, which is the English fashion from the previous reign. It is an imposing three-storied building set back from the road and screened by miniature park.

The combination of study with practical skills on exercise stood me in good stead: we were expected to spend some time daily in the workshop or gardening. We learned some rudimentary medical practices—Erhardt was of our number in East Africa the most skilled in these—some basic surveying and mechanics and enough science roughly to classify the plants and rocks we should encounter.

The theology was of extreme interest to me, since the one reservation I had in my mind concerned my preparation for Anglican orders. I would not undertake this and then turn back as Diehlmann later did, Luther standing between him and Christ. For one of my background it did not take long experience to see that the Church of England was never truly reformed, only conformed to the political requirements of earlier times, but we were fortunate to be in the parish of St. Mary, which was truly evangelical and missionary-minded. Mr. Barlow was the Vicar. I saw no theological objection to being examined and ordained, though to minister in some of these hearty blinkered parishes would have been hard for me. It was not at that time required of foreign volunteers being ordained for the mission-field.

We were divided into four groups, according to the kind of work we were to undertake. Ordinands had to study Greek and Hebrew, and this was an excellent preparation for the translation work I was to do later. If I had my time again, I would undertake a thorough study of Arabic, but we had not then understood the value of this for East Africa. Indeed, the rigors of translation into unfamiliar languages had not yet been taken into account. Early in our stay Dr. Krapf completed a translation of one of the gospels in about three weeks! We were in a hurry to make converts, of course, especially Krapf, who believed the millennium was upon us, but we needed to take heed of Luther, who said, 'you must ask the mother at home, the children in the street and the common man in the market place how they speak, and translate accordingly!'

Indeed I had myself completed a word list before it dawned on me that A-B-C was not the best or only order for recording a language where words change significantly at the beginning. But we have the promise that knowledge shall increase and others may learn from our mistakes.

The rigorous training in English composition was of great benefit. I believe Krapf used to correct Erhardt's reports before they were sent on to London, but he never needed to interfere with mine. And of course even for English-speaking candidates those studies fitted in with what we learned on the exposition of scripture and the preparation of sermons. We also used to attend a National and Infant school to see how they were organized, especially noting the monitor system of mutual instruction.

It took a little time to get used to the common way of speaking, and many of the trade cries remain to me symbols rather than distinct words even to this day. 'Ri:dolubau//' was the cry of the

newspaper seller, and I was nonplussed to be told in an apothecary's shop 'u 1i/1 bo/1 uv this / make you be/u'. The humiliation of
bafflement is a good preparation for the mission-field, where, however much you study, there will still be some dialects unknown to
you, and these London cries with their emphatic glottal stop used
to come back to mind when I was endeavoring to follow the devotions in Arabic. It is also healthy not to be too certain in an unwrit-
ten language where a word begins and ends.

Sunday afternoons and Wednesday evenings we would make
our way in groups, according to rota, through the broad, tree-shad-
ed streets of respectable Islington to the seven tenements that made
up the Irish courts close to the Angel. I will admit that I dreaded
these expeditions, but they were well chosen in preparation for
what was to come. The nose would first be assaulted, the homely
scents of hot tar macadam, fresh horse dung and brewing malt giving way, as we passed into muddier, narrow streets, to the universal
smell of poverty."

*Urine, first of all, like a thin knife-cut in the nostrils. Cabbage cooking
and potato peel rotting in mounds beside the tenement door. Coal dust.
Children's messes. The flat stink that heralds the presence of rats. Occasionally a healthy whiff of fresh wood, as a park has been raided to eke out
the coal-fire or a fence, or an abandoned chair chopped up, cheap spirits,
both fresh and vomited. Damp washing becoming ever more grimy as it
hangs limp over windowsills or on strings overhead.*

*Little children making obscene gestures at us and joining hands to
sing rhymes in which 'orange' is frequently the only word I can make out.
The meeting room three flights up in one of the buildings is known to us
and to the recalcitrant congregation as 'St. Patrick's Cathedral.' In addition to turning the other cheek and handing out tracts, our objective is to
scale the narrow stairs—three abreast—against opposition and held our
service at the tops of our voices, drowning (we hope) the ribald interjec-
tions.*

*I am distracted from my proper devotion by receiving not only a wad
of spittle on the jaw but also a ball of mud or worse on the trouser-leg. My
second-best is already becoming threadbare from excessive washing and I
have no means of replacing it. I have taken up position behind a six-foot
stalwart destined for India and we are bawling at the tops of our voices
Wesley's hymn 'Soldiers of Christ arise.' Unfortunately our adversaries*

have anticipated the line 'leave no unguarded place,' and at the head of the stairs appears a termagant brandishing a red-hot poker.

"I have this ready for you, Bjasus," she shrieks.

"You lot come one step further and I'll do and I'll do and I'll do."

(In fact I hear only malevolent sounds. Evans has to translate them into speech for me afterwards.)

The rest of the Irish stand well back behind the angel with the flaming sword. Oh God, not my eyes! Please do not let her burn my eyes, with so much ahead to do. There is a momentary lull. Then 'We got Newman' hisses a voice behind me, more literate than the rest, and the chorus is repeated, 'We got Newman, we got Newman.' Oh John Henry Newman, I whispered to myself, whatever your sins, your well advertised conversion has given you plenty of opportunity to preach the word in your new state of life.

Stalemate. But no, Evans, without moving, raises his voice to begin Evensong.

I will arise and go to my father and will say...

It is my duty to lead the singing.

My soul doth magnify the Lord and my spirit hath rejoiced in God my Saviour...

In my heart I am speaking to the Galla, I do not expect them to understand me until I have learned the language. But instead they echo back at me, 'maknify, maknify', with peals of unholy laughter, 'rechoiced, rechoiced, rechoiced,' and another voice chants,

Hear the little German band,
Ta ra ra ra ra ra ra...

Oh God, keep me. One Sunday a man burst into tears, and they will never let him forget it, never.

A squeal rings out above us,

"Mam, Paddy's got the knife. Mam—oh, oh, oh, Paddy..."

*The termagant with the now graying poker turns her back along the cor-
ridor. In a flash, Evans is up the stairs, four of us doggedly behind him. A
surge of noise—I am amazed to find it is my own voice,* Ein feste Burg
ist unser Gott—*it is a breach of the rules to sing in German, but let them
mock that if they can. One or two curious children perch on the bench that
is welded against the back wall—the free-standing forms have long since
gone to the fire.*

Now, Lord, lettest thou thy servant...

*As we are finishing, a sad stooping man comes in to pull one of the boys
away.*

*"We are doing him no harm, brother," says Evans mildly. "Will you
not let him stay?"*

*"No harm, are ye?" says the father, all the fight gone out of him. "I
just got word that his mother died in Cork with the green mouth, just
when I had the money saved for her to come. And my old father too. God
rest his soul. There's many a one in this court shouts at you gentlemen
for want of anyone else to shout at, but it doesn't bring the dead back, and
maybe they rest better where they are. Michael, you were a bit of a scholar
once. You must try and write a letter to Father O'Meara for me."*

"We could help you with the letter."

*"Maybe you could, but there is some comfort in having your own flesh
and blood spared to do it."*

*We rake together from our soiled pockets three and six 'towards the
expenses' and offer our grimy hands in condolence.*

"That says more than sorry, your honor, Michael, come away now."

*The crowd is now milling round Michael's father's door. In the next
court the children form up and march behind us, singing in derision:*

*The Pope he is a gentleman,
He wears a watch and chain:
King Billy is a beggar man
And lives in dirty lane.*

"Some of the bravest of us would go to the Irish courts on a Saturday after the men got their pay, but this was too hard for me.

Some of the men in training complained that we were treated

like schoolboys, meals at fixed times, allowances to be strictly accounted for, gates shut at seven in the evening from Michaelmass to Lady Day and at nine from Lady Day to Michaelmass. But I could already see that this was a light discipline compared to what the mission-field would by its nature impose on us—a severe limitation on what you could get to eat, where you could go in the evening, and out of what village society—almost certainly strictly masculine—you would choose your closest friends and confidants.

I do not mean that I failed to enjoy the sights of London, for it was quite different from anything I had seen before, and I delighted both in the stately buildings and in the good-humored bustle of the street markets. A great deal of agitation was going on for the repeal of the Corn Laws, and though I had been brought up to take the farmers' point of view, requiring protected prices for stability, the terrible poverty of some of the London courts and alleys made me see the need to ease food costs for the poor. People in Ireland were actually starving, and there were families not much better off whom we passed when walking from the college to the magnificent new railway station near Euston Square and past University College into the West End. I could not forget this when my family wrote to me about the dreadful agricultural depression in Germany the next year.

Well, you will not be interested in a country boy's admiration of London, but I found it exciting to be in a place where so much was growing and changing. The College of Chemistry was founded while I was there and plans were already laid for a Women's College. Sir John Franklin's expedition set off for the North Pole. The Thames Tunnel had not long been open, and the police force and the penny post were already marvelously established.

Islington was an interesting place as well. Cruden, the eccentric bookseller, had compiled concordance to the Bible there in Camden passage, and William Collins, the poet, lived out his melancholy life there, though it was a merry place, you will all remember, when John Gilpin rode through it. Charles Lamb used to live in Colebrooke Row, Halley had his observatory there, and Defoe had attended a non-conformist seminary in Islington. Long before that Islington Fields had been the place for compulsory archery practice, but clergy and judges were exempt from that. So altogether ordinands and evangelists were made to feel very fine fellows, far too fine, I'm afraid, to take seriously the Chartist protests which just then were thought to be an affront to church and state. We were going to be missionaries and eschew politics. But politics, like gin, is hard to avoid unless you recognize it when you see it, and we could have been shown more actively where the bounds of discretion lay. You will often be praised for stopping a man beating his horse but you may be expelled for stopping the same man beating his wife or his servant. We are taught to render to Caesar what is his, but not always to recognize Caesar when we meet him in a foreign land.

But I am afraid as long as we had got up our proof texts and our parables we did not always set our minds to these difficulties. A pleasant Saturday outing was to take the river-boat for four pence from any of the London bridges. Waterloo Bridge—that used to be the Strand Bridge—was said to be the most magnificent in Europe. King's College and Somerset House lay on one side and the great Lying-in Hospital on the other, Westminster Bridge was already famous through Wordsworth's sonnet, and the ancient City of London was open to view from Blackfriars and London Bridge. CMS Headquarters were at Salisbury Square, off Fleet Street, and a little too near the open sewage of the River Fleet, which I understand has now been hygienically enclosed.

From Islington to Paddington or Bank you could get a Shillibeere's First Omnibus, a pretty wooden carriage with garlands of flowers painted on it, for two pence halfpenny, or the same fare would take you form Islington to the starting-place in the country.

It was drawn by three horses and picked up passengers who hailed it along the way until the full complement of 27 was reached. There was a conductor inside to take the fares and assist ladies mounting and dismounting by the back steps with their packages. Departures were regular, every hour and a half from each end. In fact by my time there were many competitors, some offering a more frequent service by having only 12 passengers and two horses, but there was something special about Shillibeere's. By the time I left London you could buy *Moggs' Omnibus Guide* to look up the timetable and fares. This was fashion that London had copied from Paris and the bigger German cities would copy it in their turn. I suppose the day may come even in Africa, where ferries already offer a regular service, that we shall have something of the sort.

The Lord blesses some of us with such pleasant experiences during our time of training so that we have some mental sustenance, stored like the camel's, for the dreary days that are bound to come, emptied by sea-sickness or dancing attendance on petty authorities, when one is cut off from the work in hand. But they must never intrude upon that work, and in the second year my mind was all on my ordination exams and the wonderful experience of ordination itself.

The service was conducted by the Bishop of London and I can hardly express to you the joy and peace which I felt at being entrusted with the Lord's ministry, and the sense of brotherhood with my fellows, especially those enlisted for missionary service.

After assigning me, to my great joy, to work beside Dr. Krapf in East Africa, the committee then considered how to convey me there, and found it most economical to book me on the sailing ship *Arrow* to the Cape from Southampton in February 1846. From the Cape I should take another vessel to Zanzibar and there meet assistance on my way to the coast. This plan surprised me, as I had expected to follow Dr. Krapf's route by the Mediterranean to Egypt and the Red Sea, so approaching the lands celebrated in the scriptures. But there is no place to which the scriptures do not point us, and so I was content. After my valedictory commissioning at the old Islington Parochial School, I was accompanied to the South Western Railway Terminus at Nine Elms, near Vauxhall, on the south bank of the river, and there entering the steam carriage was waved off by a number of officers of the Society and a group of students from the College. We joined our voices, over the hissing of the engine and the commencing clatter of the wheels, in the hymn 'All hail the power of Jesus' name' which had been written to send off the first missionaries to the South Seas, and I waved my handkerchief after them until I withdrew it from the window quite black with smuts from the engine.

Two of the gentlemen in my carriage seemed disturbed by this fervor, and took shelter behind their newspapers, although the jerking of the carriage could hardly have been conducive to comfortable reading, but another person, somehow concerned with the Transatlantic mail, questioned me closely about my commission and appeared to take a great interest in it. He was traveling with his wife, who wished to try the mineral properties of the waters in Southampton. He told me that East Africa mail could be transmitted more cheaply through Southampton than through France, despite the preponderance of French commercial vessels at that time.

The journey took us through pretty and fairly prosperous country and at the Terminus Station, near Southampton Docks, I found myself in the company of a prospective fellow-passenger who, being experienced in such matters, showed me how to get aboard the ship to sleep, though it was now late at night, and so avoid the expense of a night's lodging in the town. No food was served at that hour, but we had fortified ourselves with meat pies at Basingstoke and stowed some bread rolls in our pockets against future uncertainties.

The whole of the next day we lay at anchor as the passengers assembled and stores, fresh water, cargo and spare tackle were brought aboard—I, landlubber that I was, observing with great interest and learning the quaint vocabulary of ships and sailors. Southampton is blessed with a double tide, owing to the waters parting round the Isle of Wight at the mouth of the estuary, and this is hastening its development into a modern port for ocean-going vessels. So it was already a matter of signs and numbers, none of the old-fashioned notices you would sometimes see tied to the shrouds of vessels in the London docks, showing their destination and when they hoped to sail. On the second day, when wind and current were in our favor, we unloosed and bowled fairly along, turning eastwards into the Channel.

The seagulls scooped and shrieked overhead, targeting on the waste food and slops we poured in our wake. Their raucous cries frightened me, as though devils were contending for our souls, reluctant to let me follow my calling: porpoises somersaulted and in the grey February light I was leaving behind the shores were backed by skeletal trees, hardly showing a hint of greenery.

At Calshot Spit I got a premonition of the desert, the curving bank of barren sand against chill water, the mechanical light resting at the end of it and only a cottage or two to house the men who would tend the light and deal (in what manner I dared not conjecture) with those who missed its warning.

We spun past the neat quay-side villages of the Isle of Wight,

Portsmouth, marked by its Martello Tower on our left, and so to the open Channel. The rolling motion of the boat made me slightly queasy as we lacked steady impetus from the wind. I concealed my uneasiness, conscious that we were not yet out of sight of land and terrors lay ahead. But pride goes before a fall: we loitered a whole week in the Channel on account of contrary winds. Here was the first test of patience to be tried in the years ahead.

By day I read and studied a little. By night the illumination of the lanterns was dim, and I did not find much congenial converse among my cabin companions, younger sons of merchants and farmers going out to try their fortunes at the Cape. I found one older man who could give me a little information on the original inhabitants of that country, though he knew nothing of the progress of the gospel among them.

I comforted myself with the scripture as the weary days passed. Isaiah heard the Lord say:

I give Egypt as your ransom,
Ethiopia and Sheba in exchange for you.

And again:

Who are these that fly like a cloud
and like doves to their windows?
For the coastlands shall wait for me.

There was a continual slapping and groaning from the rigging and one's body was never for a minute still, except in dead calm, or the few days' respite we had taking on stores at the Cape Verde Islands.

At Cape Town, after a voyage of eleven weeks, I first set foot on African soil, giving thanks to God who had brought me so far safely in his service. It was winter-time there—not cold, but more moderate then I had anticipated, and some of the Dutch buildings put me more in mind of Germany than of Britain. I had an introduction to a clergyman there, but found him at first away from home, so took lodgings at the home of Mr. Janitz, a German apothecary who was the agent of the Moravian Brethren in that place.

The local people I observed, and some more yellow than black, seemed to be working in the dock or market, all busy and all clad in at least some segment of European dress. How I should have liked to visit them in their home places and observe how the gospel was being preached: but I was supposed to keep in daily touch with the docks, and none of the brothers could enlighten me much about African homes.

After about a week we set sail for the east coast, but the weather was not in our favor, and we had to sail as far as 41 degrees south in hopes of meeting a westerly wind. Perhaps you people are seasoned travelers and would not bat an eyelid at this but for a young man from the middle of Europe to be talking about the open ocean with nothing but a few planks of wood and some limp canvas between himself and the South Pole is a terrifying experience. He has embarked, let us say, for Nineveh and is being carried (this time without willing it) in the direction of Tarshish. I was indeed crying:

> The waters closed in over me,
> the deep was round about me,
> weeds were wrapped about my head
> at the roots of the mountains.

Well, naturally they laughed at me, but in the course of time we found our wind and were to sail north and east along the coast of Africa.

> Who hath gathered the wind in his fists?
> Who hath bound the waters in a garment?

Was I so puny a preacher that I needed to ask? I must confess I was very happy indeed when we rode into Zanzibar. There on the waterfront was the big square house that was pointed out to me as the British consulate—further along the Sultan's palace—the harbor crowded with shipping that, I was told, had come down with the northerly monsoon and was waiting the season to return. When I saw how frail and unseaworthy these ships looked, I was the more ashamed of my nervousness on the *Arrow*, but I have never since been able to read in *Job* 41 about Leviathan with an easy mind.

Captain Hamerton welcomed me to the consulate and explained how friendly he had been with Dr. Krapf and his late wife. He introduced me to His Highness Said Sultan, and I hope I had found my land legs sufficiently to behave civilly. The Sultan very kindly offered me a passage to Mombas in one of his own vessels on the Saturday, but in fact it sailed on the Sunday.

I occupied myself with strolling round the town. Storied white houses had, from the harbor, a feeling of Europe about them, but, close to, an ambiguous oriental look. Between lay hovels of grass and matting such as my mind's eye had led me to expect, and, through a maze of twisting smelly streets some eight or nine feet wide (not so different from some in the Barbican or Hounds-ditch, save for the heat and spices) to the low-lying open space, part paved, part squelching with misery and refuse, which was the slave-market.

It was, of course (though I did not yet know it), early in the season. The first of the cargoes to be shipped north in September had lately come in from Uniamiesi, and others were expected from the hinterland of Kilwa. From Ukambani and the Benadir coast there would be goods rather than persons. Those coming south from Ethiopia would consist of choice girls and eunuchs, liable to be snapped up quickly. All the treaties up to the last were carefully worded so as to avoid interfering with these special delicacies, and even now I suppose it is not possible to unwrap every shrinking female or pry into the anatomy of a well-dressed male passenger accompanying his employer. Everything I saw fascinated me. Of course, I did not realize that crew of ten—as on any mercantile dhow—would be slaves. It was not obvious."

"You did not object to sailing on the Sabbath?"

"I did not see myself in a position to object, on board the King's vessel, and there is work to do on any ship on a Sunday, whether she lays to or not. Indeed, a sailing ship might require more manipulation to stand than to go. Even in my land safaris I did not see a need to halt on the Sabbath, so requiring more provisions to be carried and making the men's loads heavier, provided we left time for divine worship and, if possible, kept our exertions moderate. If you have ever marched with dwindling water supplies you will know that you dare not slacken pace until the water necessary to life is found. It would be good if we were equally mindful of the living water... The Sabbath is made for man and thank God it is. If the law did not regulate human industry, some of those poor workers of London would hardly have seen daylight or met with their families. My wife has often told me how she used to accompany her first husband (though for modesty's sake he would try to prevent her) when he was gathering evidence on Sabbath observance for his committees and reports. And suppose, she used to think, these poor women had not been able to procure a mutton pie or a plate of whelks for their husbands on a Sunday, their only midday meal at home, how would they have been able to leave their kitchens and go to church—admitting that even so they might not go because it was the only time they had to wash their scanty change of garments by daylight, and also because the pulpit tended to use difficult words and the pews to be both hard and chilly. So among us in East Africa someone may object that she does not have pots enough to bring two days' water at once for the family. Our Mohammedan porters are expected to work with us on a Friday, and if we observe the days of rest applicable to each local community we might have none left for the march.

However that may be, I reached Mombas on Wednesday, and of all the excitements of landfall this was the greatest, since now I had come home. Someone from the ship was sent to tell Dr. Krapf—who had known, of course, for several months that I was on my way, but had no means of anticipating the actual week or day—and he hastened to embrace me and take me to his house on the cliff-top just above the harbor.

To my eye everything was delightful—the pleasantly distant view of the sea, the towering castle flying the red flag of Muscat, the narrow busy oriental streets of what we now call the old town, the stark contrast of dark skin and white flowing robes, the lively eyes of the curly-headed boys, the palms waving in the breeze and the clusters of men squatting round the brass coffee pot.

Well, the dhows are not in better repair now than then, the fort crumbles a little more from year to year, the bright-eyed boys have grown a middle-aged leer, the breeze stinks of fish and sewage, the coffee is stewed and sour, the red flag has flown for Zanzibar against Muscat as well as for Muscat against Mabruki, and Rebmann can see none of it as the naval-steamer, painfully skirting the reef, churns him away from home."

The silence was unbearable as some of them could see the coast white in the heat haze and low buildings beautified against the distant wilderness. Brava? Marka? Mogadishu? No-one aboard this steamer would need to distinguish them, undertake the perilous search for slavers or water, live out the gospel with a handful of dates under the shadow of a cracked earth wall.

"But," Rebmann jerked awake, "the question and the answer are still the same."

III

"How did you live, then?"

"Physically, you mean? Well, I joined Dr. Krapf in the house the Governor of Mombas had given him, two fair-sized rooms, quite adequate for us. They were the top part of the seven-roomed house the British naval officers had occupied in 1824. The steps Lieutenant Emery had built led right down to the harbor, and we had the use of the well they had dug too. We used to think of it as the top of a cliff, till British visitors laughed at us as country bumpkins and said it was just a little bank compared to a proper sea-cliff. Krapf had labored himself to build an extra room on the roof when he heard I was coming: the Arab shops, and those rented to Indians, were nearby along a narrow crooked street, within what was left of the old town walls. The Governor could not raise enough tax to keep them in good repair and since then new buildings have spread beyond them. There was even an old Catholic church built by the Portuguese, very much broken down and being used as a cowshed: it seems to have been where Lieutenant Reitz was buried. I had an idea that we might have taken over the old site, but Krapf would not hear of it, since he felt it had bad associations with the Portuguese occupation and was in any case revered by the Hindus on account of the cows. The Great Fort, the Governor's Residence, towered then as now, over Arab-style houses of the town. The older ones were storied buildings with terraces and windows in the Spanish style, but outside the walls were square wattle and daub cottages and others built more substantially of coral rag, roofed with banana leaves and secured by hinged doors made of planks. This was *mji wa kale*, the old town. The warmth of the climate made these dwellings tolerable, even heavy rain soon dried off in the compulsive heat, unless there was a ditch to collect it.

The women, mostly Mohammedan at least by profession, were generally more clothed than their inland neighbors, but seldom protected by the black cloth *buibui* or spider which envelops the women of Zanzibar. Also they pursued their traditional market role with zest, as well as cultivating the sugarcane and other crops of the humid tropics. In Zanzibar to this day no woman engages in selling, and the men of all communities are prevented by superstition from offering after dark salt, incense, needles, thread, ginger or eggs. On the mainland it would take the most severe catastrophe to inhibit trade.

Magnificent wedding processions used to parade through the streets of Mombas, and you would hear the strange, haunting tone of their trumpets and drums from curtained enclosures. The place seemed to me prosperous, but less so, Sheikh Ben told me, than in the Mazrui days ten years before, before Said Sultan subdued them by force of arms and cut them off from the rich produce of Pemba. But the town crier would still parade with his long horn, and the complex alliances of Arab, Swahili and inland peoples kept their balance with scrupulous attention to the symbolism of rank— Jumbe, Sheikh, Tamim, though they could no longer afford to give all the elaborate presents tradition required. Apart from cash on his accession and provisions on feast days, a Sheikh (as functionary not as man of learning) was expected to give a cloth to every child born, a gown piece to every bride, four fathoms of cloth for each Swahili burial and provisions for all visiting Wanika. Dr. Krapf warned me against getting mixed up in their political intrigues, as the Sheikh of Kilindini, Muallem Shafei, had tried to involve him, but my own particular friend, Sheikh Ali Ben, the Kadhi, was devoted to religion and learning, though less zealous than some of his kind in promoting popular education. There were three men of law at that time—one for the "Three Houses" and one for the "Nine" and one appointed by Said Sultan to keep the Omani Arabs happy, since, though few in numbers, they were in his special care and then still belonged to the Ibadhi or Shia denomination of Islam.

The customs master was, as everywhere, a Banian: when I became head of station he was Lakshmidass, and we went on well enough. Since these people never brought their women with them, and tried to conceal the liaisons they subsequently made, their social life was greatly restricted. During his father's time, Lakshmidass told me, they used to come to the coast only seasonally, but the volume of business now required them to keep a representative all the year round, each brother taking his turn to have a holiday in India.

We had a housekeeper who was able to maintain the apartment when we were not using it, a widow with a little boy. When he grew up and was able to support her, we brought in one of the new Christians.

Krapf was eager to start a missionary station where we should have more independence. Yet there is no place we can go which is without the freedom of the gospel. Nor is there any place we can leave our closest grief or our suspected guilt behind. I was young then, eager for martyrdom, certain that all our burdens can be cast upon the Man of Sorrows. I had yet to learn that even when you lay your burden down, the arm still aches from having carried it. Krapf needed to get away from the house that was full of memories of his Rosina and their baby. (The first, you will remember, they had to leave buried under a tree by the roadside in Ethiopia.) I failed to understand this, and so I failed to help him. You have probably all read in his book how we went to Rabai and were offered by twelve old men a plot of land which they must have identified before. It was not for sale, they insisted, but for use, since they consider land a gift from God that cannot be bought or sold. (Would that we Christians had so clear a conception of the gift of God!)

Of course they were elders, not 'chiefs,' but we had not yet learned to understand this.

Dr. Krapf was kind enough to consult me as to the choice of station, but as a newcomer I had no knowledge with which to oppose his decision. It was, in fact, a good one and Rabai Mpya, that is to say New Rabai, is a valuable station to this day. It pleased us to be starting in a place called 'New' which would, we expected, enlighten Great Rabai, the *kaya* or citadel nearby. However, Great Rabai was also sometimes called 'New,' since it had taken precedence over the older citadel called Vokera. Well, we were in the service of one who shall make all things new, and we had reason to be happy that the people had welcomed us into what they saw as the heart of their settlement area. The ridge was narrow at that point, only 70 or 80 feet across, with its scattering of some 25 homesteads, high up and ringed with trees, defensible against the attack of Galla or Maasai raiders. The population of even Great Rabai could at that time be numbered in hundreds rather than thousands out of Dr. Krapf's estimate of 4000 for all the Rabai people.

I had not, on that first visit, myself seen Great Rabai, which was a mile round, with three entrances in the triple palisade enclosing 80 homes and two men beating a great drum to announce the coming of strangers. It was at the gateway of Great Rabai that ritual operated — a black bag hung there containing powdered bones and organs of slaughtered enemies, to be carried out before battle to ensure success. Then there was the *kisuka* or little devil, some saint's image preserved from Portuguese times, and the more common coconut shell to ward off any who might be tempted to steal from people's palm trees. Was it for the same reason, I wondered, that an empty coconut shell used to be left on a grave? It seemed a good image of the Resurrection, but I soon found that it had not always been empty — the strong drink in it had been consumed by some spirit or bird or totem beast. That way it made a good image of the transience of ritual.

The *jumba la mulungu*, a little shrine some three or four feet high, stood near the entrance and was said to give protection to any items left in its care. Certainly theft within the community was unknown.

In times of peace the population would spread outward — in fact during our time three more *kayas*, stockaded fortresses, were built for the Rabai alone, Fimbana, Chang'ombe and later Kijembeni, and each of the twelve communities have their own. (Some people count them nine, but Dr. Krapf insisted that they should be twelve, and indeed this would symbolize their old affiliations with the twelve Swahili lineages of Mombas, the nine and the three.) But in the course of years you might not find many people in the *kayas*, for they scattered to cultivate the fields and thin the protecting woodlands for their use. Similarly in a British city you may see a great cathedral standing in the old symbolic centre, but the Methodists and the dissenting chapels follow the people out to where they live and work and bring in a spiritual harvest.

You have heard how we toiled up the ridge to confirm our bargain after spending the night at Abdallah's plantation nearby. Krapf was in the worse state and needed sole use of the one donkey we had with us: sometimes we were reduced to crawling, supporting one another on account of our fever and exhaustion. We might well say, 'our strength is made perfect in weakness.' Krapf had to rest on a cow-skin in Jindoa's house before we could make our bargain. Jindoa was the headman of the settlement.

This was the first Nika house I entered, and I looked about me curiously, so far as the dim light permitted, for the thatch was low and there were no windows. (Some of my colleagues later protested that the house I had put up for my three servants had no windows: they might have refused to live in it if it had!) It appeared to me to be a single, large, round room, but I later came to understand that its divisions were marked out symbolically by the furnishing. A corn-bin in one section with three stones for the fireplace mat indicated the kitchen area, and this was full of kitchen utensils, gourds, baskets, pots, forked sticks to use as spoons and a grinding slab with its pebble. A low bench of sticks bound to cross-pieces was the bed, and its leather coverlets would regularly be soaked in sea-water to remove insect pests. A stool and a few mats sufficed to identify the sitting-room with its water-pot and calabashes for drinking, the opening backed with strong parallel logs which could be jammed into place at night: a poorer home might make do with sacking.

We found the air pleasant, due to the elevation, and good cultivable land on which we proposed to demonstrate to the local people how to improve their lot. Indeed, their agriculture could and can be improved, and some of our experiments were successful, though we were over-optimistic of vines and apple-trees. But we had yet to take into account the fear of armed incursions which made the Rabai people modest in their undertakings, and the prevalence of envy and magic which might restrain them from any enterprise tainted with singularity.

So our intentions were well suited. What we did not remember—young men as we still were, despite our physical weakness, and confident that our plans would bear fruit whether we lived to see it or not—was that the long steep climb up the ridge would become a burden when we had invalids to carry and ladies or, hopefully, children among us.

In building, also, we did not consider this. I had, in fact, been offered a frame house by the Home Committee, but deferred to Dr. Krapf's greater experience, and refused it. A hut in the local style, we thought, would suffice us. After some delay, the people made it to our measurements, 24 feet by 18 and 18 feet high, rather than try remodel the two houses they had offered. Later we strengthened the foundations and laid it out in the Swahili manner, to allow more separate rooms and shade. We did not remember that, according to our program, we should not always be at home to make the frequent repairs that style of building demands. We added gradually, by our own handiwork, a kitchen, stable, store, oven and a hut for public worship.

It has never been difficult to hire a boat between Mombas, Rabai and Kisulutini. The nature of the boat is hard to predict. In the poorest dug-out canoe you may have to huddle on the floor and trust that not much water will be shipped. In an eight-oar boat with a sail you may complete the journey in three hours, and of course there are various degrees of comfort in between. We missionaries did not usually aspire to eight-oar boats, and in some places the channel is too narrow for rowing, so that you have to use poles to keep off the bank. There is a lot of poling to be done if you go up to the channel to Mwakerungi, the nearest point by water to Ribe. You cannot see much from the creek except the hills looming ahead, for the water's edge is dense with mangroves, intertwined with a kind of convolvulus creeper having pretty blue flowers.

After the first steep 100 yards from Jimboni, it is a weary climb of some five miles to Rabai Mpya or a pleasant hilly walk of similar distance to Kisulutini where I have lived so long. Later Krapf put up a thatched shelter at this 100 yard point to rest in if one had to send for carriers or wait for a boat to bring guests. There are enough people about (though you would not think it, peering ashore through the mangroves from the estuary) to provide porters or litter-bearers if necessary. Later we learned to meet visitors with donkeys saddled, but though Mombas is locally famous for the size and strength of its donkeys, fed on millet rather than grass, our early faith in them has tended to diminish. Sparshott, who had, in later years, a boat of his own, also seemed to have a way with donkeys, but it might be unbecoming to pursue comparisons …

The waterway being so easy I did not make the short day's march to the coast until some months later. As the crow flies it is not much more than 12 miles, and not without narrow paths, as the area is cultivated in times of peace, but these necessarily meander round plantations or sacred places, seeking shallow fords over the streams or gentle slopes down the hills, so progress is desultory. One descends from each ridge and its exposed red soil to the rich loam of the valleys, each a step lower and full of luxuriant growth. Then natural salt-pans and a maze of shallow inlets bring one to the ocean shore, and there is still need to find a ferry boat over to the island.

So we were established. Our fellowship together was sweet in those days, as Krapf labored to teach me the language and customs of the surrounding people, and this was, and always will be, a prime object of the pioneer missionary, to establish an example of peace and concord. Alas that the devil so easily subverts the work, but, if he can be held back from doing so for a while, new relationships at least will have been founded, so that there is a spread of opportunities for witness.

It appeared to the Wanika at first that we had come to repossess the fortress of Mombas: they must have remembered Owen's occupation 20 years before at the invitation of the Mazrui, and, considering the tension between clans and factions within the island, it was a natural enough conjecture. After the British withdrew Owen (who had acted without consultation) it took Said Sultan seven years to expel the Mazruis, and his Omanis recouped their expenses by slave-raiding, right there near the coast, where people had previously been middlemen, not victims. Might we not be thought to be bringing the Mazruis back from exile to Takaunga, or doing a bit of raiding on our own account?

Some said our big boxes brought from the ship contained armed men—as though they knew the story of the Wooden Horse of Troy. This rumor persisted for years: they might have seen our few gifts to them as harmless yet, given the complexity of move and motive up and down the coast, perhaps they were wise to 'distrust the Greeks even bringing gifts.'

At the same time they felt a right to the gifts! On safari we found that even people begging for food refused to cut grass for the donkey in return. The Wanika used to demand two dollars worth of cloth whenever they were called to audience with the Governor of Mombas. This was the value they put upon themselves. Perhaps they saw it as a payment for fulfilling a civic duty.

The women never felt it necessary to ask permission to draw water from the reservoir we had constructed for our own use, or thank us for it. Yet all people learn by imitation, and I remember my dear wife, in later years, weeping with joy when a crippled boy to whom she had given a piece of meat returned with the gift of a coconut.

Some felt us to be connected with the Seyyid's government, alleging that we received a kind of tax. What tax? The freewill offerings were modest enough and long in coming. Certainly we sought protection from the Governor of Mombas from time to time, but we were also at his beck and call for translation services or to account for our doings.

We set up our home with the help of Amri, our Kamba servant, who was also helping Dr. Krapf to learn Kikamba. I soon started teaching a group of boys: Jindoa's son, nicknamed Shehe or supervisor, was one of the quickest at learning. We made the centre at Bunii, two miles from Rabai, to give access to more interested families.

We also kept open house for visitors. They might come just in courtesy, to welcome us among them, or to request some material aid—cloth, cash, seed or medicine. They would come to observe our oddities and hear our stories. But do not think these people would come straight to ask our advice: the kindest came to offer advice—'Don't buy your grain from such a one, he is over-charging you.' 'I see you are heavy with fever: try chewing a bit of this leaf.' 'When you hear such and such a noise, close your door: it is dangerous to leave it open.'

Just so, I hope, you might welcome a foreigner settled among you but would not run to him with your own problems unless he advertised himself as a doctor, pastor, lawyer with a familiar qualification: a brass plate written in Chinese would not impress much.

We began to hold services on Sundays as soon as the worship place was ready. Dr. Krapf would fire a gun, then ring a hand bell."

It is hot. Yesterday Amri swept the beaten earth floor that, covered by a banana leaf thatch supported on poles, at present constitutes our church. At one end we have a small table made in Mombas with a piece of white cloth on it and a wooden cross made in Egypt. On each side we have placed a wooden kneeler.

Sweating in my cassock and bands, I wield a twig brush removing the leaves and stalks that have crept in during the night, a trail of ants, some dog dirts. My flageolet lies on the table with the big English Bible, pages of the Kinika gospels and some hymn texts carefully folded inside. It is our first public service, though some of the elders have sat quietly through our prayer-time in the house. We have explained to them what we mean to do and that everyone is welcome. (Was that wise? Was it even true? Do I really invite the Saha's supercilious smile, Mam Kemba's drunken belches, Me Hari's darting eyes, eager to uncover conflicts that can be dealt with acrobatically and at a profit? Am I to keep the tune going towards the provocative breasts of Abe Mlega's nubile daughters? Fortunately it is not my service and not my invitation.)

Dr. Krapf is robed and ready. Amri, Ndune, Abe Ngowa seat themselves ceremoniously facing the table. (Will the time come they ask for another day off because attending church is still work? We have not demanded it of them, but they are in an obscure sense on our side.) I set out to lead the singing, first playing through the melody.

How sweet the name of Jesus sounds...

Krapf bawls out the words, not very tunefully. No-one else can read, of course. Amri, who has often heard us sing it at home, makes a manful attempt at the first verse, filling in with Yesu wherever it seems to fit the tune. A black dog I recognize as Jindoa's peers in, crosses the floor expeditiously and strolls away.

"We will learn the song while we are waiting for the others," *I offer hopefully.*

Jina lake Yesu tamu ...
Tamu,

chorus the three men.
"Yes, but to make it fit the tune we need to use the whole line."

Jina lake Yesu tamu.
Jina lake…

Recall they have a good notion of the tune. I also can whistle some of theirs, but my grasp of the language is not yet up to writing an original song for them. Soon (I thought) they will do it themselves.

Here come the heavyweights now. Jindoa, seeing that all is well in his province. The Saha, his big belly protruding, looking for amusing subjects of gossip. Abe Gunga with a small boy between his knees, possibly my first sight of Isaac. Abe Marunga with a stalwart son—Marunga, that is—carrying a mat. Abe Konde with his grave ceremonial face. They tuck themselves neatly on the floor. Clearly there will be no women. Later a few boys slip in at the back and Mringe limps along.

Dr. Krapf explains that we shall pray to God through his son, Jesus, and at the end of each prayer we shall say 'Amen.' They are to join in if they feel it appropriate. Then we shall continue to learn the hymn and the Lord's Prayer. Then we shall read briefly from the holy book. If there are any questions we shall deal with them outside.

There are gestures of assent and we proceed, the congregation whispering the stressed phrases back at us. A few more men come in with walking-sticks, signifying that they are Kiriama, but they appear to understand all we say. (They are so much on the move nowadays, making north to their old settlements on the Mangea and Sabaki rivers, that they have to be adaptable.) We repeat one more verse of the hymn and then leave the church.

It has taken about three hours. I am exhausted and the hand-written pages are damp. Krapf is tired too, but he has had longer practice at this sort of thing. Mringe has a question about the birth of Jesus: Mringe will always have questions. Our servants hastily disperse. The Saha settles expectantly in the shade of a tree.

"Thirsty work, all that singing," prompts Abe Konde.

"That is because we are still new to it," replies Krapf artlessly. "When you are accustomed to our way of worship we shall use the prayers from the book and then it will not take so long. And since the women did not come today, they probably have your food ready. We should like to start the service on time so that they can come too."

I have not often wished to be a painter, but Abe Konde's face at that moment is something that will stay in my mind for ever. He seems to puff himself up like a turkey. His extended hands imply hunger of a ferocity which the sleek bare torso renders improbable. His voice becomes squeaky.

"But we came for maneno, for discussion, and where there are maneno, there is also food. I know you have no women, but the men who wait on you, where are they? What sort of council is this?"

"It is not a council, brother," I interpose, "it is a time for praising our God and giving thanks. When you visit us in our home you are welcome to food. But the house of God as you see, has no cooking-place and no water-pot. Our people do not work on the special day we call the Sabbath. We want you to see this as a religious time."

"But at a sacrifice people eat..."

"We do not have that kind of sacrifice. When you have learned more of the book we shall explain what the Christian sacrifice means..."

"He is saying that there is no food, Abe Konde," the Saha announces with a malicious grin. He is saying that the wisdom of the white man is better than food. You are not here to eat: you are here to say 'A— min. A— min, A— min' like a donkey. And then you pray. Were you asleep, Abe Konde? Perhaps their spirit will strike you for being asleep — 'give us this day our daily bread,' our daily corn porridge, do you hear? That is what their God gives. They do not need to cook it. But the relish they have to get for themselves." The Saha roars with laughter.

Abe Konde turns away, offended.

"Rebmann," says Abe Gunga gravely, "this is something we ought to have talked about together. Jindoa would have put us right. But now I must take the child to his step-mother. Stay well."

"Go well, Abe Gunga."

"But when the angel said to her..."

"Brother Mringe, I am sorry. Let us talk about it tomorrow. I do not yet know enough words to..." to explain the mystery of the Virgin Birth from a parched mouth in the noontide heat in a language I started learning barely six months ago, to a culture which insists on early marriage.

They drift away, puzzled, disappointed.

"Not a bad start," says Krapf cheerfully.

I tear off my cassock and my socks and dip a gourd into the water-pot the servants have left standing in a cool place. I seize a couple of boiled eggs and a mango and throw myself on the rough mattress.

"Did you listen carefully to that Kiriama man speaking?" asks Krapf reflectively. "The sibilants..."

Resolutely I shut my eyes, and so fall into temptation. I conjure up a picture of myself going home from morning service on a bracing autumn day, to my mother's hot meat soup and apple cake, and a vision of the tall, white angel announcing the Lord's command to a humble girl, amply clothed, as yet unaware of the terror before her.

How can I give this picture to Mringe, deformed, tormented, outcast, daily exposed to the bare legs and shoulders of beautiful girls who will soon be hustled by their families to the expected defloration, the welcome husband? What would happen to a Nika Mary—could she stay alive to bear the baby? Might she not be whipped to death in the forest? Or sold into exile? Would the muansa *scream out its message of fear while the holy child was disposed of at dead of night? Or would old women come with unguents and emetics as soon as the signs were seen, and then a Digo man would get a cheap slave wife? Did Joseph pay any bride price? Did Mary have to live in his mother's house, with piercing looks and everyone telling significant dreams? Oh Lord, give Mringe understanding, and help me with the language...*

I sleep, exhausted, and wake to shouts and imprecations and long shadows. Somebody's daughter has lingered too long in the plantation: if these are the words that greet the slightest deviance, what manic laughter would disrupt the visit of an angel?

"Many is the time Amri bailed me out of trouble when I was mistaken in a message given or over-charged for some item of food. It was he who taught me to disperse the fiercely biting black ants with fire and recognize the dangerous trees whose coconuts were ripe and hard and liable to fall on one's head. He showed me how to scrub off with earth the sticky resin from a cut banana stem, and how to distinguish a cheeky greeting from a civil one and answer in good measure.

He was able to communicate with the Wanika around us at this level, but the most complicated things I had to learn for myself, not from scholarly lectures but embedded in stories and bits of gossip."

"Pastor Rebmann," put in Williams, who had been assisted on deck for a breath of air, "I am afraid our friends are getting confused. I am not very clear myself, though Mr. Price plans, with a large work-force in future, to send people to specialize in particular areas. You have told them that a lot of peoples are grouped together as Wanika—the Rabai, Giriama and so on. Please try to make it simple."

"They cannot possibly be more confused than we were, Williams," boomed Rebmann. "You have to remember that we went ashore hardly knowing any names of peoples except the Galla, whom Krapf had sought out in Ethiopia. Captain Boteler, who had traveled the coast in the 20s and published his account of it in 1835, was an excellent observer, but he speaks almost entirely of Arabs and Soallese, by which he means Swahili.

We really knew very little, you see, until gradually we were able to ask people what names they used for themselves and for other communities. The Kiswahili language therefore was a good starting-point, but not enough for us. We saw that those called Arabs had generally higher status than those called Swahili, and Swahili had more expertise in modern ways of living than the Nika and other inland communities. What we learned afterwards is that a man is never (or seldom) a Swahili and nothing else. He may be a Zanzibari, an inland convert to Islam or belong to Masiwani, the Comoros, or Visiwani, the Bajun islands. The Arab called the northern Swahili *Hamara* or *Abba Suffa*, possessors of clothes, as distinct from the Arabs or Southern Swahili who were *Mulusha*. Some of the Swahili retained beliefs and superstitions of the Nika people. They underwent a form of initiation and a few even entered the age-grades of the communities they were allied to. For instance one Liwali of Takaunga was initiated elder of the Kiriama. Perhaps he got some security from that during the Mazrui troubles, for the Kiriama also have a relationship with the Mvita 'house' of Mombas. We cannot expect you to take in all these details any more than I could comprehend all the enmities and alliances of the Irish courts but I would have had to try if my life's ministry had led among them. Even in pious Gerlingen you would drop some bricks if no one warned you that the school teacher's daughter had run away with a Roman Catholic or the miller's brother (for all our pacifism) gone for a soldier.

When we first went ashore we knew three names for people—Swahili, Galla and Wanika—and the number of spellings those three names got from different travelers you would find hard to believe. Oh and the Portuguese used the name Mozungulos, who may have been the Wanika: there were also the Zimba cannibals in those days, who seem to have disappeared, they were just in transit. They are remembered with so much fear that Said Sultan changed his mind about Krapf and allowed him to preach the gospel when he heard that the word of God had changed the hearts of cannibals in the South Seas.

But most of us started with less sensational matters, like births, marriages and deaths in our neighbors' families."

A wedding is coming up in Jindoa's household. But the bride is not of his family. I must be ashamed if I cannot understand the situation. I have already been rebuked for failing to recognize his livestock. Eventually I am made to understand that the bride must be escorted by her father's mother.

"Is this not so in England?"

I am by now tired of distinguishing between Germany and England, so assert more knowledge than I have.

"Not so. Her parents escort her. The grandmother may not be alive."

"Just so. The grandmother is not alive, so her eldest daughter must give the escort. Jindoa's wife is the eldest daughter of the grandmother."

"I understand. She is an aunt to the bride."

"Well, in a way she is the aunt." (I have used the wrong word again.) "But she is not the sort of aunt you mention because her mother got only daughters by her first husband, which did not please him; not that we Rabai do not value daughters, but we need at least one son to carry on the line. So, you see, the bride's father is the son of the second husband."

"I see. And they had no daughters?"

"Oh, they had daughters all right. But Jindoa's wife is the oldest daughter of the bride's father's mother. You see?"

"I see, yes, in a manner of speaking. The house is smoky, as the evening meal is being cooked, and noisy as the small children are shooing the chickens indoors. I am perched on a low stool, trying to balance a gourd of gruel in one hand and fan myself with the other. In this decent, orderly house it is not yet time for palm wine to be served. The gospel of Luke *printed in Swahili is beside me: we are still working on the Nika version: we have a rule never to speak without the book in hand. In church I carry the big leather English bible. In preference to the German with its harder style of print, to indicate that they will have all this in their language soon, but I need to write down and translate any passage I mean to use outside* Luke, John *and* Genesis *which Krapf is completing. I do not trust myself to do it extempore."*

"And who will pay dowry for you, Rebmani, when you have chosen yourself a wife?"

"It is not our custom to pay for a wife, Sheha. *In fact some fathers give a gift along with the girl. But we are here for God's work as you know. I do not think a girl of my tribe could easily come so far to marry me."*

"Not to marry you, to be married to you: are the two things not different in your language?"

"To be married to me. Thank you, Abe Marunga, for putting me right. Perhaps God means Krapf and me to live alone." I should have liked to say *'A good wife who can find? She is more precious than jewels.'* But how to say it? *'More precious than beads'* does not sound right. I have got used to being laughed at, but the scripture must not come into derision.

"Huh, you do not speak truth, Rebmani. Does not your God say in the first book that it is not good for man to be alone? Kiraf was telling us about that as he looked for the right words to set it down. Only if you seek a wife round here, you have to find a dowry, even if you go to work for the Banians in Mombas and make money yourself, since your father is far away."

"I am not looking for a girl, Jindoa."

"No, I see you are not. Maybe the Governor will have to come from Mombas to fix you up. Or your friend Abdallah bin Pisili, though you tell me your religion is not the same as his."

"His is the religion of law. Ours is of love."

"Love, heh? And you are going to be bachelors? And you do not want children? Rebmani, I do not believe you," chuckled Abe Marunga. *"And if you do not marry, how will you take titles, tell me that? How far can you go up in your society as you are? Reading is enough?"*

"Reading books is for anybody. Don't you see Jindoa your son, Shehe, is beginning to read? And Seyyid Sultan can also read. The Kadhi reads. Jomsic reads. Abdallah reads. The King of Uniamwesi has had his sons taught to read in Arabic."

"So? He does not want to pay people to read for him? Hear, young Shehe, your teacher says you will get a title for reading."

The boy grins but knows better than to answer in front of his elders. He is sure reading would not bring him cattle, but I already know he is sure I should give him a cloth.

"You may get a title for reading, for honor, to say you are learned, but that does not give you advancement. Krapf is doctor as well as reverend. We have titles like King or Duke—Seyyid, shall we say—that pass from father to son. But the mark of advancement a person like Krapf or me

might get in Germany is to put a von *in front of his name, or in England
Sir. But only if you deserve it—not by asking or by paying money." (I believe that was true then. Perhaps it is not anymore. Perhaps it never was.)*

"So—like I say—von Kiraf. Sir Rebmani?"

"Ludwig von Krapf. Sir Johannes Rebmann. But it will not be so."

"Why not?"

*"Because we have chosen to spend our lives bringing you the gospel
in East Africa."*

"And your king does not give a title because of the gospel?"

*"No. I do not think so. I have not met the king. But it is the King of
Heaven I serve first."*

*"So you said. Yet your clothes are not finer than Abdallah's, and when
you were plastering your house your hands were torn and bleeding like
a laborer's. I do not understand it, my friend," went on Abe Marunga
painfully. "I have reached Muaya rank: you see it by these amulets. It cost
me a lot of money, but still I am not proud. My sons come to learn from
you because I am interested in anything new. If my palm trees prosper I
shall come at last to the Gofu order and wear the ivory armlet. Everyone
will know that I am one of the leading elders of Rabai. I cannot become
*headman because that belongs to my friend here. I cannot become *Jumbe*,*
*because only the Swahili do that, and it costs them—heh, you have not yet
seen how it costs them in presents and feasts when they put their name up
for a week to be approved for office."*

*"Bana Hamade, who visits us on behalf of the Governor of Mombas—
you would call him *Jumbe?"*

*"Yes, that is right. The one who grumbles that you will not give him
wine to drink."*

*"Indeed not. His faith forbids him wine. I told him that if he became a
Christian he might drink it in moderation, but I would not otherwise put
the weight on his conscience. He was most annoyed."*

"Well, the worse for the Mombas people."

"You choose among them, then? Or the Swahili do?"

*"No second man puts his name up, or he would have to give even
more. And we, the active age-group of Wanika, give them our support.
Without us they cannot administer their area, and so we have our say and
get presents instead of giving them. Is that not sense? But you, you come
here reading and writing and singing like a child, and boasting that you
are not afraid of the *muansa. I cannot make it out."*

"My friends, release me now: my head is spinning with the words I do not know. I will go to rest early."

"No, indeed you may not go now. The food is nearly ready—my wife, is it not so?" insisted the hospitable headman. "Kiraf is away and it is bad for you to stay all by yourself. Tell us one of your stories—you never miss a chance to do that—and then after eating we will let you rest."

"All right, if you will bear with me. We started talking about a wedding. I will tell you the story of the wedding of Cana in Galilee..."

"So what time of year was it? Why did the servants not tap more trees?"

"The wine did not come from palm-trees. It came from a kind of fruit that you press..."

"Like the Kamba pombe?"

"No, not a spirit... I do not mean pepo, a person's spirit, I mean pombe we call something like sipiriti. The wine came from a small soft fruit. My father grows such fruit in Germany."

"Well, but six little pots. What good would they be for a wedding?"

"Not little pots, big jars, up to my waist, like this, holding..." (What is the word for firkins? What do the English mean by firkins anyway? Oh Lord, I am tired.)

"So, if you mean storage jars you should not have used the word for little pots. And you mean that when you get married you will not have to tap the trees?"

"Our friend is tired, Abe Marunga," intervened Jindoa. "We promised to let him rest. He has told his story, now let him eat and drink."

Politely they turn away to other topics, but I am still cramped on the little stool gazing up at the smoke-blackened thatch which helps to keep down the mosquitoes.

"You were saying that the bridegroom is from the A-Yombo clan. But he is a Rabai, not a Digo?"

"Oh yes indeed, though it is said that all the lineages of that group have Digo names. Of course his father has checked it, and the female lineage as well—all very satisfactory."

"You know, we must have shared some history with those other communities since they came south from Shungwaya, or how should we have the same names and clans?"

"My brother was doing business with a Kauma man the other day, and his lineage was called Amwa gudza Mzungu, European. How could that be when these people only came a few years back?"

"There were **Wareno**, *the Portuguese, but that was long ago, before our people came to these lands.*"

My head is splitting, splitting. There are four clans, and 18 male lineages within them, I have worked out so far, and ten female lineages—I shall never get them all straight! A man belongs to his father's male clan and his mother's female clan. (What for? They hardly ever mention it, except that a slave belongs to his owner's female clan.) Other Wanika have clan club-houses so you can watch who attends, but for the Rabai you just have to keep it in your head. If I start to nod I shall fall off this stool and that will be a disgrace...

A small, fat, naked child stumbles in with a puppy, and they tumble together on the floor. It is dusk outside—that dusk the books tell you hardly occurs in the tropics, but all those years I had my sight I hardly managed to catch exactly the moment darkness falls.

Jindoa's wife, Me Shehe, is a little late with the meal, perhaps flustered by my presence. She has patterned cloth tied round the waist and thrown over one bare shoulder. Her oldest daughter, carrying gourds of water and running out to dispose of stay husks of rice, wears the pleated cotton skirt of tradition and an amulet on a string of coconut coir bobs over her scarcely budding breasts. Jindoa has a rice paddy down by the stream. There had been an older wife who died, but her daughters are married now and one young man, Endoro, remains around the place, eagerly working at his father's fields so that he may define his own holding and marry soon. But he is not here with the elder visitors. The moon is nearly full, and no doubt there will be a dance tonight for which he is making himself beautiful.

A pleasing young man, Endoro, who once asked me, 'who is Jesus Christ?' but grew impatient before I was through with the answer. I must learn the art of the nutshell. His plain waist-cloth will be well oiled tonight, and the brass wire of his collar and amulets will be shining more than ever, liberally anointed.

The girl pours out water ceremoniously over my hand before three men begin to eat, rice prepared with coconut and goat's meat. The women and children wait for us to finish. By the time we have eaten our fill it is dark. Jindoa, because of his rank, has a little Swahili earthenware lamp with a wick floating in oil. The girl brings it closer as she removes the eating tray and offers palm wine.

"Drink with us, Rebmani; you say you are a bachelor, but we cannot treat you as a boy. You are welcome."

"I know of the welcome Shehe, and I thank you, but please excuse me this time. You have seen that I am getting confused. It is a weakness but I struggle to overcome it."

"You are getting on, Rebmani. So long as you do not let a girl marry you instead of being married by you. Go and rest. Shehe will escort you."

"But Shehe is still eating."

"He must learn courtesy first. To us it is more important than learning books. So —how do you say it? —God be with you this night."

"Thank you, Jindoa. God be with you this night, and with you, Abe Marunga."

We shake hands solemnly, hooking the little fingers in sign of friendship, and Shehe skips along the path, deftly kicking a coconut husk out of my way and holding back intrusive branches. It remains my duty to thank him and give him a little picture from my store before he runs back to his supper.

"I remember evening after evening staggering home, not drunk with wine, though that would have been easy in so hospitable a place, but overcome by the day's effort to understand what was said to me and tabulate the information for future use. The house would be open, of course—no need to lock anything up among the Wanika at home, where courtesy rules and an item forgotten by the pathway will be brought back to the owner. Caravan safaris have their different rules. The only stores we ever had stolen at Rabai were taken by a visiting Swahili. However vehemently people may beg, near home they do not steal. Amri says it is the same among the Kamba.

Amri would have set up the lamp and a basin of water for me to wash. He might hover about to ask if I wanted anything further, but knowing that by this hour I must have eaten in the homes I was visiting. I would commend each one I had met to the Lord by name as I toweled myself and sank on to the bed of wood and rope. How shocked my mother would be at the rough unironed sheets and the perfunctory devotions."

The drums are beating from the dance enclosure. A skittering amid the thatch—rats, bats, monkeys? I do not have the strength to go and see. There is a hum of insects and the hooting of a kind of owl. A distant lowing of cattle—untimely. Perhaps the Saha's cow, after all, is giving birth: he was worried about her. Father, help me to be patient with the Saha, the

Master of Ceremonies, a lively old man, great fun to talk to, but I was near to anger when he chased the children back to their dancing from hearing bible stories the day of the Youth Festival. He is no fool: he knows that if they come to love the Lord there will be a change in their dances and the sacrificial victim need not be hunted at the great initiation, since Christ our Passover has already been slain for us. Jindoa says that Rabai boys do not kill (I have a notion it is the junior elders not the boys), but the warning not to visit Yumbo given to Krapf by the headman of Great Rabai, could not have been quite without foundation. There was something he was not supposed to see. And if not the Rabai, then the other Wanika for whom we have equally a burden before the Lord...

What a wonderful thing it would be if the Saha himself could come to Christ—all that quick wit, the respect he has within the community, yes, and that appreciation of change too, for it is only ten years since the Kamba brought cattle-rearing here as their major industry, and who loves cattle better than the Saha? ...

"Some of these Kamba came as a result of the great famine of 1855 to join others who, working in the caravan trade, had become accustomed to the luxuries of the coast—palm-wine not least—and chosen to stay rather than return to their comparatively harsh country—although they exaggerate the harshness to make sure predatory caravans avoid the place. They may feel at home even to the extent of allowing the Wanika to bury their dead, at the fee of a cow, since there is no empty bush in which the bodies can be thrown away. Most of the Wanika bury their own dead and mark the grave, but the Ribe—who claim seniority... when a regional council is held, the Ribe speaker must be heard first—used to have the custom of leaving people at the point of death in a stockaded village in the forest. In this way they escaped both the sorrow and the ritual contagion of the last struggles. But where will you find such a secluded sport now?

So how to approach these Kamba? They were not like other people. Their preternaturally acute hearing gave them a kind of claim to foreknowledge, and their mechanical arts were so advanced that they made false teeth out of the bone of an ox.

They did not seem to be interested in the services or the school. Krapf was getting on with the language, and perhaps Amri could interpret for me, if only he were a bit more sensitive to our meaning.

The Kamba also were changing rapidly. They were growing maize, though they still preferred a diet of milk and blood. When they came to visit the Wanika and Swahili they put on some clothes as well as their leather tails and blue and white beads—that is the grace of being considerate, for the older Nika men always wear a cloth or two, and carry a skin or raffia bag to emphasize their dignity. The Kamba say they learned dancing, exorcism and incantation from the Wanika, and that must mean learning new beliefs. If some, why not others?

You may recall Krapf's story of a young Kamba man who one day assaulted the son of one of our headmen as he was working in the field. The young men were eager for a formal declaration of war. Young men are headstrong. Remember King David and all those discipline problems. The elders did not shout them down, though they had a customary right to do so. Instead they flattered their sons.

'We need you to defend the *kaya* against raiders like those Kamba. We shall be at risk if you all go off mounting a raid. Besides, it is time to bring in the harvest. At least put off your plans till it is safely stored.'

So they waited, and their friend recovered. The Kamba were no more eager to start hostilities in defense of one young hothead than our people were, so they brought a sheep and slaughtered it and poured the blood out before the injured man. Then they brought money to restore the peace. It is written that the love of money is the root of all evil, but money that is not excessively loved can be a blessing all the same. It is much easier to pay compensation in coins—and privately too—than to drive along a herd of goats or pack sacks of grain and rice that everybody will want a share of.

Again, in such a case everybody has to visit the sick person, both his age-mates and older neighbors. So we would go along too, and with all that youthful energy around we might start singing one of the hymns I had written or translated—

Jesus Christos, fania
Moyo wangu muvia,

'Jesus Christ, make me a new heart,' and soon there would be a hearty chorus, for the people are essentially musical.

We had got past the distresses of the first days, when mothers would hide their babies at our approach and the bigger children would run away. In fact their regular pattern of life with strong family attachments, traditional tastes in food and story-telling and a lively practice of popular music, often reminded me of the small towns of southern Germany. As I got to know them better, the communal divisions of the Wanika also reminded me of our small German states, sharing so many interests yet so determined, in those days, to preserve their separateness by keeping up some independent coinage or complex sets of weights and measures, or an over-stylized form of dress.

On visits such as these to the sick I had opportunity to learn the names of more young men, and some of them would come and visit me and listen to stories, since they all enjoyed hearing new ones and retelling them. Krapf was working on the translation of a book of bible stories, but I could make shift to tell some, and I knew what the young men would like—Joshua and Gideon, Jonathan shooting the arrow, the Prodigal Son. Some of them had seen the crumbling wall of Mombas town: it is easy to picture it falling down to a great shout and the sound of trumpets.

All had seen the Omani soldiers here or there, their seven-foot pikes not much in use on land but their little round rhinoceros hide shields always carried like a badge of office. In the rainy season you must hold them high over your head to prevent the leather being rotted by dew on the shoulder-high grass. All were skilled in the use of the bow. A few had served in caravans and come home to enjoy the fatted calf.

They would tell stories in return glad, perhaps, to anticipate the elders' role, stories of the people's migrations in the past, of the other 'cities' they had broken away from, exploits of Mombarak at Pemba and Mombas, Swahili hero stories which have carried far and wide. One, who had Mohammedan friends among the Swahili, passed on the inland notion of cosmology. The distance the sun has to travel daily, he said would take a man 500 years to do on foot, and the moon gets fatter as it thinks of praying on the 15th of the month, and then wanes as it reflects on its sins.

I learned, like the rest, to repeat the last phrase after the speaker to show I understand him. When my sight failed I came to realize what a good help to memory that is. I have sometimes heard old men repeat my address almost word for word, though the substance of it must in the early days have been unfamiliar.

But there were two things the young men would never talk about—the initiation and the *muansa*. This was a kind of hollow drum, which one rubbed, making a noise said to be that of a ferocious monster. I am not well acquainted with ferocious monsters myself. It was Krapf and Livingstone who encountered lions and raiders: the one rhinoceros I met at the crossing of the Lumi river politely turned its back and fled away. I and my bible were credited by the party with achieving this. My own worst moments had more to do with ritual expectorations and the sprinkling of blood and fat. So I was not as alarmed as I was supposed to be at the raucous noise. The distant baying of hyenas always seemed to me more disturbing, but since all Wanika show respect (as towards kin) to the hyena and the kasiji bird, one could not do anything to drive them off.

We were instructed to lock ourselves in and hide from the peril announced by *muansa*, but Krapf always refused to do that. He would deliberately leave the door open to show that we were not afraid. Perhaps some people were genuinely frightened, but it always seemed to me rather like refusing to join in a party game with a blindfold: after all, the secret was not impenetrable—you could buy the instrument openly from the Digo if you could afford it. I was nervous too when he refused the elders' first present of a goat fearing it would give offence. True, we did not have the resources to start on an institutionalized exchange of gifts. As he said, you must give enough to show people that you care for them, not so much as to let them think you richer than you are. All the same, Krapf was often ill during those early years, and I would be the one to bear the burden of his decisions.

Perhaps we were wrong to use the word *muansa* for all the festivals heralded by the same noise. There was the women's festival, and that very strictly organized. A woman who absented herself could be fined a goat or a cow. Then soon afterwards came the elders' *muansa*, for which the women swept the paths in advance, and after that must hide away, together with the uninitiated. Payments changed hands—whether for participation in the festival itself or admission into something it portended I cannot say with certainty.

The same horrid sound would occur when some poor misshapen baby, or one presenting in unusual fashion, was to be strangled at night in the bush. One would lie awake at night trying to think of any way to save the child, or stop it happening again, but we had no women missionaries to nurse the infants if we had been able to rescue them, and no local woman would have dared do so. Perhaps in this case the noise was just a warning for strangers to keep away from a bad business.

The ordeals were held more silently: I never actually saw one being administered to test the guilt of the accused by red-hot metal, hatchet, needle or poison—perhaps it was carefully arranged that I should not. But one would often enough see the scars of burning and blistered lips pierced by the needle, or hear of a mysterious stomach complaint, and as the practitioner received clothing from both parties, a sudden increase in finery might make us suspect a trial had been hidden from us.

And yet, nasty as all this is, Europe also knows its midsummer rituals and its mystery societies. The Swahili, professing to be Mohammedan, though they lack much of the practice of that faith, do as much or more harm when they celebrate their New Year in July, not only taunting the Hindu Banians but at times throwing them bodily into the sea, so that some have drowned. And this without even the excuse of intoxication, for the rule of abstinence at least is kept pretty strictly in Mombas. In other ways the celebration seems positive: after sea bathing, the women cook the rice and the men (on this one day of the year!) the relish. Then all their fires are put out with water and rekindled.

The Banians in their turn make merry when the first consignment of goods for the year is exported, letting off fire crackers, beating drums, and in their superstitious ways soliciting good fortune and fine weather. Sometimes they also distribute rice and small change among the people. Like others, they become more talkative when there is a festival.

Once five Teita men came to see me with their little bags and walking-sticks. They are lighter-skinned than the Kiriama and their sticks are different, fashioned for steep hill slopes. They turned aside to see the mission, as a curiosity, when they were coming to the coast to sell perfumed oil, of which they gave us some. Their visit prompted my first journey to Kadiaro later on."

"Pastor Rebmann," put in Williams, "you have told us the different Wanika. Now you talk about others, like the Kamba and Teita, who are not Wanika at all."

"We want to know about souls being saved," put in a passenger. "It is not important what they call themselves."

"It is like remembering that you and Krapf are from Wurtemberg," added Williams, "Erhardt from Bavaria and Pastor Harms from Hanover. You all sound like Germans to us."

"I suppose we do," laughed Rebmann. (What a long time, Isaac thought, since I have heard him laugh. When Mrs. Rebmann was there they often laughed. Perhaps, after all, he is like other men, and helped by a change of air and voices.)

"But in my heart I know I am — was once — a Wurtemberger, the language I speak is not hard and cold like the clipped speech of Berlin, and I would not thank you to offer me a pickled herring or a military title... The language of our translations is put together from the way many people speak. It has to be so.

The people who inspired fear when I was new at the coast were the Galla, proud, fierce warriors who colored the imagination. Erhardt used to say they had a commanding presence but would not look you in the eye. And where are the Galla now? Self-sufficient in their homeland but otherwise, like the Sumerians and the Phoenicians, submerged by those who came after them. Their leader, Dado Boneat, was killed when they succeeded in repulsing a Maasai raid, and after that they were defeated by the Somali, who would have liked to make them Mohammedans. My brother Krapf's great concern was that this should be prevented: otherwise they might have spread Islam with the sword before we made our way with the ploughshare.

One Galla came to see me with two Kiriama, out of curiosity, after they had made their business visit to a Swahili trader. He was civil to me, speaking a few words of Kiswahili, and the others assured me that he would not hurt me but that he would be regarded by other neighbors as a sorcerer who was potentially dangerous:

therefore if I wished to make a visit to Galla country I should be sure to get acquainted with several members of the community first. In fact, after consultation, we left the Galla to the Methodists.

Another time a group of Galla came with some Kiriama, having been robbed on the way, and very cowed and miserable they were. We put them up for the night and managed to speak to them through an interpreter. They are men like other men, though what the world knows of them is that they seek above all else the trophies of emasculation. They string them on a sort of head-dress."

There was an indignant rustle of skirts as certain questions were suppressed.

"Have I...? No, I have never actually seen one. It would not make for good business to wear it on a trading trip. ... After their heavy losses in battle, the Galla were harassed by the Kwafi, a branch of the Maasai, and so for 15 years they have hardly troubled the coast.

We should have trusted the Lord to overrule. The scripture says:

Their camels shall become a booty,
their herds of cattle a spoil.
I will scatter to every wind
those who cut the corners of their hair,
and I will bring their calamity
from every side of them.

'Those who cut the corners of their hair,' you see, that was Buiya to the life."

"Who is Buiya?"

"Well, the Methodists—this was much later, of course—received Galla regularly at Ribe to help them with the language, and made some converts too. Buiya was one who was literate and was particularly gifted in the story-telling sessions they used to have for training. He was baptized together with his wife—or a wife, I should say, perhaps. The trouble came about because he was required to inherit a widow...

Inherit a widow? I would refer you to the book of Ruth, madam, and to the questioner who asked Our Lord about marriage in heaven. Devout Jews may marry a dead brother's wife even to this day. Our problem was that Buiya already had a wife. (Even if he had not, he would naturally have wanted to raise up children in his own name as well as his brother's. Most men do.) Of course that did not appear difficult to the other Galla, especially since Buiya was an important man with four-inch plaits on his head to signify as much, and would have been able to afford wives if he had not been a refugee.

Cut off the plaits? What for? A Jew in New Testament times was not forced to barber and shave himself like a Roman soldier, was he? We are concerned with men's hearts, not their hair-styles. Of course I was forgetting your English distinction between Round-heads and Cavaliers, but I believe the descendants of both went in for wigs and powder! Anyway the man kept in touch with Wake-field, but I don't remember the end of it, if, in fact, there was an end. He may be reasoning out his priorities still.

In East Africa you do not see people prostrating themselves in the streets at the time of prayer as, I am told, happens in other Is-lamic communities. To some extent people choose the role that suits them, as the Welshman may do in London or the Greek in Cairo. During my time the Omani Arabs in Mombas have abandoned the Ibadhi sect for the orthodox Sunni position, but in Zanzibar they refuse to change.

Once we had some idea of the structure of what Krapf called the 'twelve tribes' of the Wanika, perhaps eager to see a parallel with the twelve tribes of Israel, we tried to make our first map of in-land parts — the mission map, I mean, long before we got embroiled in the business of the Great Lakes — just to show where Rabai, Ribe, Digo, Kiriama and so on lived in relation to known places on the coast: it was published in the *CMS Intelligencer* in 1849. I would not like to say that Krapf was muddled — he organized things inside his head in the high intellectual manner — but for the rest of us getting about was difficult. He even speaks in his book about extending the journey to Uniamiesi and *hence to the west coast*. We had simply no idea what we were talking about. Our only excuse is that no-one else did either. Well, that is not completely true. We heard later that as early as 1852 a caravan of 40 porters led by three 'Moors' from Zanzibar reached Benguela with a cargo of ivory and slaves. This was four years before Livingstone crossed the continent in the other direction, and of course the route may have been used many times before. But since they clearly did not *want* to make the story public and spoil their monopoly, I do not see that we can be blamed for not knowing about them.

Preaching the gospel is not as simple as writing a sermon and getting people to read it but in different languages. If they have a different meaning for a word in different places, you must take this into account; 'spirit' for instance, is to the Rabai a kind of demanding child, to be propitiated by gifts and fast movement, but the Digo see 'spirit' as an enemy and give it a name accordingly — Galla, Somali, Kwavi."

I have my English New Testament and some sheets of paper sewn together and a couple of pencils in my pocket. It is too hot to think of carrying an inkhorn, though that might endear me to the elders with their snuff-horns dangling.

I have not brought my precious manuscript for it always gets soiled and greasy on such occasions. We are sitting under a shady mango-tree opposite Abe Gunga's house.

For he had commanded the unclean sprit to come out of the man. For oftentimes it had caught him and he was kept bound with chains and fetters; and he brake the bands, and was driven of the devil into the wilderness.

So far plain sailing — or nearly plain. Is 'devil' the same as 'unclean spirit'? 'Lord of the unclean spirits'.

For the first draft that will do.

And Jesus asked him, saying, what is thy name? And he said, Legion: because many devils were entered into him.

And he said, 'raiding-party' because many spirits had entered him.

"But raiding-party is not a person's name."

"Spirits enter one at a time. A person may have as many as twelve spirits, but they all want different things."

"He asked the name of the man, not the name of the spirit."

"The possessed person can be given a new name. Is that what happened?"

"Ha," says Jindoa sharply, it is a good thing we keep no pigs here. You would to fill them with the spirits, Rebmani, wouldn't you?"

Someone explains the joke to the Saha.

"By no means," he retorts solemnly. "You get one of my goats in that *condition and I will demand replacement for the whole herd. Those pig-keepers ran away? You let me see anything like that happening to my animals..."*

"Indeed, I have no power to do it, Saha. *But would it not be worth it to get the man healed?"*

"Worth it? Worth *it? A bit of red cloth and a few bangles is all it will take to heal him. And a thank you, maybe, to the helper..."*

"And when the pigs ran to the lake, what then?"

"The spirits cannot cross the water."

"They can, you know, to Zanzibar, to Pemba."

"Ooh you have traveled far my brother!"

"No need to have traveled, whether I have or not. Even our town of Mombas is across the water, and people have seen the spirits there. They bang on doors and splash water in the night."

"In Zanzibar the Sheikh ties them up in a bag for Ramadhan so that they do not disturb the mosque people in their prayers. Can you do that pastor?"

"No, I can do nothing of myself. I can only ask Jesus..."

"But you have paper. Of all the kinds of Keti *for drawing off spirits, paper is the best."*

Drums are beating a little distance away, not a single drum, but the pattern of the exorcising dance, coming from Me Hari's place.

"Our expert on these matters was Me Hari, a small woman, going a little grey at that time. She always wore the traditional cotton skirt of many layers, to which she sometimes added a red cloth of the kind often given to appease a clamorous spirit. She was one of the most influential women around New Rabai, a diviner whose dreams would indicate which one of the ancestral spirits required to be appeased by sacrifice, and what characteristics the chosen beast should have. To some extent she may have been influenced by the hope of reward and meat, even more by the attention of a community which rarely saw the need to thank women, even if they showed outstanding ability in managing their homes and families. But she was also skilled, no doubt, in observing signs of trouble in a household, incipient quarrels or disregard of the known wishes of the dead. By putting a finger on these, and bringing those affected into the public eye, she may indeed have staved off further evil."

Shrieks and groans follow the noise of the drums, and Nyondo appears on flying feet.

"Father, come, Pastor, come."

We understand at once. The woman is flinging herself about, flailing at the ground, uttering strange cries.

The other women, urged on by Me Hari, circle in the dance. Most of them have come from the fields, bare-breasted, shaggy-haired, wearing only their everyday ornaments and their pleated skirts. Some are distended with pregnancy. Their heavy feet stamp in time. Others come running to join them. Their digging-sticks lie around and some put down platters of ripe vegetables. Little girls have been pressed into service to hold naked babies, some with an amulet round the neck or a string of beads defending the loins.

"Woman, stop that," Abe Gunga is shouting, but to no effect. The dance continues.

"The black goat for sacrifice," Me Hari announces in sepulchral tones, "and blue beads for the afflicted one."

The woman writhes and grunts.

I stand aghast. I have seen this before, but never before have I felt the pain tearing at flesh as my friend suffers. I have not thought about Nyondo's step-mother very seriously. Now I am required to receive the iron into my soul.

"Pray, pastor," begs Nyondo, my child promise.

"Pray, pastor," urges Abe Gunga.

"Well, are you not going to pray?" shouts the Saha.

"For me it is to give goat after goat: they are ruining me because I care for the traditions. You, your work is only to pray and read—ba-be-bi-bo-bu. What use is that? Pray, Rebmani, if you came here for praying!"

Sweat is running off me. My arm aches. I can hardly lift it. I am not strong enough for this: my faith is not sufficient. I have no virtue to be drawn out of me in the act of healing. But somehow my arm raises itself and points and a weak voice produce the words,

"Ich gebiete dir in den namen Jesu Christi dase du von ihr ausfahrest."

The drums continue, but the woman goes limp. The men are staring at me, though their wives still labor in the dance. They are not surprised not to understand my words, but something in my aspect puzzles them. With a great effort I repeat in Kinika,

"I charge you in the name of Jesus Christ to come out of her."

The woman does not stir. The dance jerks to a close. Out drums sub-
side with a sophisticated diminuendo. Me Hari is staring at me but she
does not speak.

"No goat," says the Sana *judiciously.*

I am trembling violently. Someone helps me home. Amri prepares my
bed, Krapf brings the fever medicine and is sensible enough to keep quiet.
It is three days before I can trust my feet again and meantime Abe Gunga's
wife has brought me gruel and cooked plantain in silence. She has not been
beaten. (There is some testimony in the state of near nakedness.) Some of
the men have been inspecting their goats anxiously, but none of them has
jumped in to the creek.

"There was a time I was credited with casting out a spirit myself, and this put me in a false position, like Paul and Barnabas at
Lystra. For of course the spirit had not responded like Legion to
the Holy Name but like a pet dog to the voice of command. Krapf's
first entry to Rabai was wonderfully blessed by thunderstorm, and
helpers were often ready to claim for us the credit of timely rain.

Just so, many of our rainmakers and herbal doctors make acute
observation of the skies, vegetation and of patients' symptoms before issuing their pronouncements. On my way to Jaga I encountered a 'rain-doctor' who used a certain kind of wood dipped in
water as an elementary thermometer. I venture to think that I also
could have set up as a rain prophet, so predictable were the cloud
sequences over the high mountains. The procurement and preparation of materials here and there may conveniently occupy the interval until the rain one has 'manufactured' is ready to fall.

Who can say how much trust the practitioner puts in his par-
aphernalia? I suspect that many a fashionable doctor in Europe
would not care to certify the effectiveness of his remedies without the passing of a magic number of golden guineas from hand
to hand, how many patients might lose faith if the remedy were
produced from the greatcoat pocket instead of the expected little
black bag. Many pertinent questions about the faith come from the
practitioners of these pseudo-scientific arts, and I should not be
surprised if in the days to come many of our staunchest churchmen
issue from them.

I remember my father—a sober man, if you ever knew one—

telling me how in his youth, some ten years before I was born, he was one of those gathered in our cathedral city of Ulm to watch 'the Flying Tailor' launch himself from the Tower in an attempt to fly, and perish. This project, which seemed so persuasive at first, immediately came to be ridiculous. Yet I remember Captain Speke telling me some 20 years ago that Sir George Cayley had sent his coachman into the air for a short time with one of his gliding machines, and because no fatality occurred, there was little public comment.

Me Hari never did any harm that I know of: indeed in Dr. Krapf's opinion, she upheld public order by giving some spiritual support—perhaps at the Headman's suggestion—to decrees which our easy going neighbors did not take very seriously from the secular authorities."

I go back fearfully to the shade of the same tree, with my magic notepad that 'traps people's words.'

'Then the whole multitude of the country of the Gadarenes round about besought him to depart from them; for they were taken with great fear; and he went up into the ship and returned back again.'

"Now, that ship, was it bagala *or* dau *or* mtepe *or* mtumbwi *or* ngalawa?" *A lively debate ensues.*

IV

On the first Sunday the passengers and such of the ship's officers as could be spared took their places in the lounge for divine worship. Mr. Rebmann, the only clergyman aboard (apart from a Portuguese priest of Roman persuasion who naturally pursued his private devotions) was consulted. He consented to give the address but, being blind, requested the Captain to read the service as usual. The missionary's demeanor on board, and his rambling reminiscences conveyed to those who cared to stop and listen to them, had aroused some apprehension, and a few young passengers were excused from attending on grounds of indisposition. Nonetheless, the congregation was alert, expecting something, to say the least, out of the ordinary, when Isaac led Mr. Rebmann forward to the reading-desk, clothed in rusty black and a much-mended surplice. (How attentive the young man was, they thought, how modest and well-spoken. If socially it was a little awkward, all the same he was a credit to the mission.)

"In the name of the Father, and of the Son, and of the Holy Ghost, Amen."

The voice was heavily accented, produced with an effort, but it was confident, perhaps even a little arrogant, practiced provocative.

"For many years I have been preaching *to* East Africa. This morning I am preaching *from* East Africa. I take it that this is what you require of me. In any case, my knowledge of the rest of the world is newspaper news, casual conversation, hearsay. I was called to East Africa. East Africa has made me what I am.

It takes 40 years for a mangrove to grow to full size, and a man would be a fool if he spoiled the main growth by hacking out the young shoots before they are ready. Apart from any urgent need for his own building, he will let the poles mature and then, each year in the slack months, take rental from the dhow owners who employ casual laborers to cut and trim them and portion them into bundles for sale, so that with the next monsoon they can be sent out to the treeless northerly coasts.

So with a convert to the gospel—an attachment to the rough wood of the cross—you must allow him time to grow before you ship him elsewhere to places where the word is eagerly awaited. Mission is not the work of a single season.

The mangrove is long-lasting, useful for construction, seasoned by salt water and tides. In the dry heat of Aden it will shore up a roof for 100 years, in the debilitating moisture of Mombas, only for five. So with the Christian character. If the surroundings are not supportive, it must seek spiritual refreshment to uphold it.

We find mangrove already growing. I have not heard of a man planting seeds in a swamp where there were none before. It is not like the mango tree which, strictly, belongs to noble owners and so, though you and I may enjoy the fruit, has taboos attached to it, and brings pleasure more than nourishment. All the same, you can make a canoe, either *ngalawa* or *mtumbwi*, out of mango wood so long as you scorch it over a fire and caulk it to make it watertight. Just so, even the proud can be of service after they are burned out and scoured.

The mangrove used in a ship may acquire taboos—though I have not come across any—because all ships are more than inanimate objects. They have names, figureheads, symbols like the magic eye which is painted on the prow from here to China: they have characteristics and are to be known, gentled or commanded like a horse. It would weary you to list the kinds of boats which ply up and down this sea-board, some, since ancient times, sewn with fiber and pegged without any help of iron. Those from Pate and Lamu in this style have a camel's head on the prow with its leaf charms and white harbor pennant, and a black and white striped pole on the stern. You could well picture them in Venice or exotic Brighton. Each kind has its own ritual of naming and commissioning, and its own incantations to call a blessing on each journey, as you may have heard singing at night from the *jahazi* in Zanzibar harbor. But the wild tree of which they are made is just a tree, and so, like the Holy Tree, is available to us all.

Similarly, man in a state of nature (though we lack examples of such a state) is restricted only by his necessities, but in a social state he is hedged about with duties and prohibitions. Safety and property impinge on him. The condition of marriage limits his, and even more her, separate freedom. Wage labor, military service and all sponsorship restrict us. Worst of all does the state of slavery restrict us, and it is indeed our Christian duty to root it out. Here lies the irony of serving the Lord under a Mohammedan monarch, whose powers forbid one to harbor a runaway slave.

And yet such is human perversity that a slave may himself own a slave. This is the final irony of lost humanity: he can even become a Governor or a commander of troops, such is man's reliance on what he owns. Yaqut, the Abyssinian, was appointed Governor of Mombas by Said Sultan's father and Ambar, another slave form Ethiopia, followed him. Yaqut left Said Sultan his property when he died, as slaves must do, 500,000 dollars, the profits from his large estates in Oman: in any case he had been unmanned in the course of slavery and could have no heirs of his body. This may make one trust him in cases where both close kin and known rivals prove dangerous.

In 1834 another Abyssinian slave was actually in command of the Baluchi soldiers in Zanzibar, could he not successfully have made a palace revolution? Perhaps he could, but that would have been to identify himself with the other slaves rather than with the other commanders, and this he did not want to do. Even in Russia, where recently it has been forbidden to export female slaves to the Turks, families rebel against this law, believing that their beautiful girls can win favor and employment for their brothers better than if they remained free and pure. So we, who are freely bidden to become humble disciples, often agree to bind ourselves to some more glittering illusion of title."

There was a rustling of skirts as a couple of ladies felt themselves close to fainting and demanded the attendance of their daughters in less polluted air.

"As a slave harshly commands his lower slave, so an officer, giving an order to a private soldier, may himself go in fear of a superior officer. The factor who brutally demands rent depends for his own employment on a greedy master. Even the missionary, eager to open a distant region to the gospel, may be told, 'your faith is too great: the money is not forthcoming.'

In Jesus Christ we become free men. But freed men in East African society still have some ceremonial obligations to the household where their ancestors were bound in service. So the fact that we are free in the Lord does not make us disrespectful to those who formerly had claims upon us—kinsfolk, neighbors, the traditional authorities. Only the service we give them is out of love, not fear. Luther says, 'A Christian is bond-servant to none but has a duty to everyone.'

A slave must belong to one of three classes: he may be *mzalia*, born into slavery, or *mjinga*, a raw, untrained person captured into slavery, or *mateka*, a captive of war or pledge for debt handed over to fulfill an obligation. No slave in Mombas is *mjinga*: the city is too sophisticated for that. People sell what is unfit for their use. But in the Christian life, no-one is useless. We may be born into the faith, trained and instructed as a foregone conclusion to serve the Lord: we may be new converts, won over to Christianity but in need of guidance to make us useful: or we may be booty captured from another religion and bringing what skills and insights we have learned there into the service of a new master. I am not asserting that any person is completely without access to God, but in all faiths, not least the Christian, some are more sensitive and better instructed than others and these are they in whom the Lord delights when they come to understand that they are ransomed by blood.

The dreadful thing about slavery is the capture, the separation from loved ones and familiar objects, the terrors of the march and the market of which the late Dr. Livingstone has written so eloquently. Do not let anyone tell you that the African—for all that his cruelties may be different from our cruelties and his apparent indifference to pain and grief not quite equivalent to the famous British stiff upper lip—is not distressed by the break-up of his family and yes, let me say it, by removal from his local shrines. He is a man at heart as we are, and it is not only slave-masters who forget that. Because of the comparatively small communities in which he lives, with intense local attachments and subtle differences of language, he may bear removal even more hardly than we who come from larger confines and have been more schooled in individuality. Above all, we have the promise of one who is with us even to the ends of the earth. Without that promise, if I myself believed that my personal God and angel inhabited a certain tree in a village in Wurtemberg, I do not see how I could have survived 29 years away from that place.

The Niassa person who helped me so much with language study had been through at least four hands before he came to the coast and was freed. The terror of being available for sale, even if the immediate conditions are tolerable, has driven many to escape from their masters, and it is said that thousands live by choice in the woods to the far north and south of us, at once protected and segregated by the surrounding forest. They call the northern settlement Maas Ngombe, and have perhaps achieved what Nat Turner tried and failed to do in America, but with less loss of life. (You see, we in East Africa are not so ignorant of the outside world as they often are of us, until we get an explorer's volume to make us briefly fashionable. Every schoolboy knows now where Kilimanjaro is. Captain Colomb's book about rescuing slaves is the one that people will read for its own excitement and its lack of charity. Sullivan's is a better book and will be less popular.)

Traders, unreasonably, find this patrolled 'Liberia' a hindrance to free passage: without commerce it would not have come into existence.

But once the great break from home and family has been made, and the terrible risk of the land export route bypassed (for the British have no right to inspect ashore, and perhaps 15,000—some think many more marched northwards in a year, of whom less than a third survive), the state of slavery itself in Zanzibar and the mainland plantations is less grievous than that which prevailed until recently in America. Society would take offence at heavy punishments or deliberate sale of a slave's wife and children. Indeed, I have heard worse stories of porters on expeditions, where free men may be given ten or 20 lashes for quite trivial offences. Mr. Stanley, in particular, still punishing other innocents for the unfortunate circumstances of his own birth, is said to mete out summary execution."

A gasp floated in the air of the makeshift chapel. To stretch one's mind to other points of view might conceivably be a Sunday duty: to exclude one's own kind was quite another matter or, if the hideous innuendo pointed at one not of one's own kind, then what solecisms had already been committed?

"On Zanzibar at least two thirds of the inhabitants are, technically, in a state of slavery—so many, in fact, that they could combine to change their lot if they saw means of making a better living independently. One thinks, for instance, of Toussaint L'Ouverture. But perhaps theirs is more like a state of serfdom—the word is a bit painful to us from the middle of Europe who have not all that long completely outlawed it. The bargain made by the plantation slaves is one that the intimidating trade unions of the west might well emulate. They reckon to work from eight in the morning until five, except in the peak agricultural season, when they need to start earlier or if it is a matter of clearing new ground they get piece-rate terms. Their basic ration used to be cassava and shark-meat, with a bit of coarse cloth for clothing. The slaves keep produce from their privately cultivated plots and half of what they earn when hired out to pursue their trades. I don't know whether the allowance may have improved since replacements are harder to come by.

In the 1820s French slavers were making their purchases South of Cape Delgado at a dollar a head, confirmed by a bill of lading. The goods have gone up since then. In Egypt the Franciscan nuns used to buy sick girls and admit them to school, since they could not afford the healthy ones. My own church does not permit this, but if it did I should not like to be faced with the decision. Think how you would spend your money, if you picture yourself as a rational, muscular Christian.

Part of the agreement in Zanzibar, urged upon the Sultan by the late Colonel Hamerton, is that the slaves should be allowed to bury their dead. Previously the bodies were thrown upon the beach, where dogs ravaged them.

Promising slave boys, whether local or imported, are given an Islamic education and also taught a trade if they show attitude, so that both they and their elders should benefit. And what a place Zanzibar is for the enterprising tradesman: apart from the specialists who work the small shipyards, there are people who make the four kinds of local shoes of wood, plain baobab bark, plaited baobab bark or the three-fold ox-hide—makers of rings, bracelets and belts, plain brown *joho* cloth (such as they weave in blue on the other islands) or delicate *bushti*, the finest being of camel hair, the checked *miswaya*, face masks for fine ladies, shields for export, ropes, hooks and pulleys for string-making, pots mats, baskets and stools of every description, elaborate reading-desks for the Holy Quran carved out of a single piece of wood, drums, hoes, doors and whole ceilings ready to be fitted into place.

There are rope walks on several of the islands where as many as four one-inch strands are twisted together on an axle to great lengths, and there have been attempts at mechanical sugar milling. It can take you a year to note down all the special words related to this fine craftsmanship. In this bustle of commerce, slave and free compete in their skills, their prices, their advertisement.

What a place, also, for the eager linguist, since the slave population represents nearly every inland area. The first generation, all the same, soon learn to communicate with fair facility in Kiswahili: they have to, to survive.

So you may feel complacent that in most European societies slavery has been defeated. Even in America it no longer legally exists. I hope no-one in this congregation is involved with that semi-slavery which still exists in remote places round our oriental coasts. To illustrate, I remember a shipload of workers from Kilwa being asked *in French* whether they were enslaved or had put their marks on a voluntary contract. Such a question is surely not likely to get an enlightened answer. Also when I was staying in Zanzibar in 1858 I encountered a French vessel full of voluntary laborers (so I was assured) in the harbor, only every one of them had a wooden ticket fixed to his neck. You would not countenance this? I cannot see you but I do not sense the odor of guilt around me. You congratulate yourselves that you have done your best for emancipation and are so a cut above the slaves of Zanzibar who have come to terms with their condition. What kind of compulsion lies on the worker in Europe you know better than I, who have been so long away. I hear of moves for reform. Whether they demand as much self-sacrifice from Christian manufacturers as we impose on British Indians of other faiths who must give up their slaves, I cannot say.

You see the institutions of sin bear some resemblance (forgive me) to the British fighting man. Even when legally dead they show an unconscionable reluctance to lie down. For two years now the slave market at Zanzibar has been closed—no, hardly two years. For all the fulminations of wrath and buckets of tears hurled against it, in a town where 80 Europeans now live and hundreds visit on naval or other duties, hardly out of nose-shot of French Charlie's, where all of these need to call for their weekly groceries or their safari stores or their gentleman's board and lodging, within bell-call of a church with a robed choir and what the hurricane had left of an organ—two years ago the slave season opened on the first of May, as though it might be grouse or spring vegetables!

Sir Bartle Frere had come and gone. Everyone knew the Sultan would soon have to sign the treaty. Perhaps that was why the ownership of the main site had already passed to Jairam Sewji, a British Indian from Cutch, known to us all. Honorably, finding his plans to repave the market and erect awnings were already out of date, he presented a large part of it to the Universities' Mission. Their Mr. West bought the site of the whipping post, and there the new cathedral is already going up: the site was dedicated on Christmas Day while African children rescued from the slavers sang 'Jerusalem the Golden' and ladies wept.

I rejoiced myself, though I was not able to go over for the ceremony. But remember, most of us who were concerned had not found it impossible to spend time on Zanzibar before the site was redeemed. And even as we rejoiced, slaves were still being smuggled across to Pemba, which has been better off than ever before, since the hurricane left it a near monopoly of clove trees. 'He sendeth rain upon the just and the unjust.' When the treaty was signed, 3000 slaves were cooped up in Kilwa, awaiting shipment. What happened to them, I wonder? They must have been far from home, Kilwa could not offer employment to so many and who would compound his losses by feeding them when they were unsalable?

Sultan Barghash, reluctant as he was, signed the treaty forbidding sea transport of slaves, he closed the market, posting a proclamation.

The proclamation reached Mombas: it must have taken a bit longer to reach the northern ports, though no doubt the feeling of it was born on the breeze—a melancholy feeling, since it did not immediately liberate anyone but spelt financial distress for many. Consul Kirk arrived in Mombas to arrange certificates of liberation for slaves owned by British Indians. (They would not have laughed too soon over this, since there had over the years, been changes of policy over this definition: some had been freed before, but some owners had been allowed to change their status.) These were duly issued by the Arab men of law and they were thanked for their prompt co-operation.

Our Lord gave his approval to the son who answered and said 'I will not': but afterward he repented and went.

So let us consider our own condition. For the slavery of sin can also be tolerated under certain terms and conditions. The horror of it ceases to affront us if we do not see immediate prospects of harsh punishment or separation from our loved ones. We weigh the alternative discomforts of strict virtue—the loss of business advantages, perhaps, the strain of complete truthfulness to the marriage partner, the burden of concerning ourselves with the aged and sick. If we were in a situation of utter wretchedness, hiding from the police or unable through our own dissipation, to afford a home for wife and children, most of us would take warning and seek divine assistance to break our bonds. But the Day of Judgment seems far off: we are like the slave who knows that, even behind the smile of his master, there still remains the possibility of sale, whipping or starvation.

Dr. Krapf remarked on two dhows he came across not very far from our own station, packed with slaves. The ship master described them as sailors, and when the missionary party accosted them, the slaves agreed, 'we are sailors,' though their wretched condition made it clear that they were not. And what would be the profit of running a vessel packed to the gun-wales with crew, leaving no room for passengers or cargo? But those people could not trust in law or good intentions. They were too afraid of being thrown over-board if intervention failed. Just so, we may insist that the devil needs us—to copy the slippery document someone else has designed, to put the shoddy goods on display, to warm the dinner while the others are at church, to make up a fourth at cards—because it would look too singular to step out and claim our salvation.

There is yet another analogy I should bring before you. One reason this iniquitous trade has continued is that slave families do not often multiply. Even when they are settled in reasonable comfort, they seem to dwindle. The slave-owner therefore looks for replacements. In the Christian life we are enjoined to bear fruit in the spirit, but the dominion of the devil is barren, and so he must stalk like a lion, seeking whom he may devour. For he needs men and women and has many uses for them. But of what use to man is the devil? We cannot command him. There is nothing he is good for.

In Zanzibar any educated person will list for you 43 uses of the coconut. A good Swahili orator, once he gets into his strides, can enlarge on them long enough to stun any German metaphysician into silence. Do not be afraid, I am not going to expound on them all. I am not deaf to the passage of time, just blind enough to insist on your indulgence a little longer.

You can eat a coconut, drink it, shelter under the palm in its wild state, or use it as a roofing of an umbrella. You wear it as a hat, fan yourself with it, sit or lie on it, tie things up with it or haul in your boat from the sea with its rope. You can make doors, ladders, cages, clappers or mouthpieces for your *zomari* with it.

And if the mere man can do this with an everyday plant created for his comfort, what can he do with the Lord Almighty who has once humbled to become like us on earth? You can eat His flesh in the sacrament and drink His blood. You can shelter under His wings, clothe yourselves in His righteousness, and refresh yourself in the wind of His spirit. You can prostrate yourselves before His throne, gird yourselves with His armor, anchor yourselves to Him, enter through the door of His grace and rise up step by step to heaven with Him, limit yourselves to His laws, reverberate to His glory and trumpet forth His greatness.

And now unto Him who is able to keep us from falling and present us faultless before the throne of grace, to the only God, our Savior, through Jesus Christ our Lord, be glory, majesty, dominion and authority, before all times, now and forever.

Amen."

V

At Aden they boarded the P. & O. Steamer and Isaac felt a great influx of confidence that it had been managed. Williams paid over the passage money and then collapsed on to his bunk. They now had a cabin for four — Rebmann, Isaac, Williams and an Ethiopian Christian on his way to Alexandria. He was polite and devout, but unable to communicate with them except through a few words of Italian directed at Williams.

Rebmann had enquired at the port for Dr. Badger, but he was away on tour. Indeed, how else could he survive twenty years in this metallic heat. There had not been time for mail to catch up with them.

Most of their fellow-passengers had transshipped at the same time, and they found a number of travelers from India already on board. A small uniformed black boy sat in the lounge eternally pulling the rope of a punkah which gave a slight relief to the Red Sea heat. Isaac's heart went out to him, but even he could not distinguish where the shift took place, since the same child could surely not stay 18 hours on duty. The water burned your eyes, but it was certainly not red.

The British India passengers had been delighted to find at Aden English newspapers only a month old. Those who were P. & O. all the way remained unimpressed. First day out, Isaac was sitting on deck trying to read *The Daily Telegraph* to Mr. Rebmann. The departure of the Arctic expedition from Portsmouth aroused some interest in him, and speculation about the progress of mission work in northern Canada. Plans for the opening of Newnham College astonished them both. Description of ladies' dresses on the social pages or complicated sporting events caused Isaac to stumble:

up to now he had been introduced only to improving books. Mr. Rebmann in any case appeared to be asleep. He had already given warning that Englishmen went mad if confronted with a flat field and a ball.

So the intrusion of passengers was welcome enough, another around of introductions having been made after Aden.

"Well, sir, catching up with the news?" one enquired breezily.

"It might take me quite a time to catch up on," nodded Rebmann. "It is a foreign continent I am heading for."

"Go on, don't say that," answered the young man, distressed by strangeness and disability. "You're the fellow who discovered that mountain, they tell me, and never been home since. Ought to put the flags out for you, I reckon."

"Well, I don't know that that would do anyone much good," smiled Rebmann. "I got a medal from Paris after that. Extraordinary, isn't it? The mountain had been there long before I saw it and was still there the day after. If I had been able to convert the King of Jaga … Still, my father was pleased to hear about the medal before he died."

"Tell us about it."

"Well, I had never considered myself an explorer, but Dr. Krapf, whom you must have heard of, a great scholar and a pioneer, had the idea that everybody can do everything. I was young and acquiescent then if you can believe it—Williams here has been given the idea that I was always as cantankerous as I am now—so I made four journeys into the interior, one to Kadiaro and three to Kilimanjaro. Krapf arranged the porters and the stores—I afterwards found we were hard on our porters and rather short on stores—got permission from the Governor of Mombas and assured me that everything would be plain sailing, in fact he was tempted to envy me the trip.

Sailing had not so far been very enjoyable to me, and his own experience with Isenberg in Ethiopia did not sound very enviable, but I agreed that we needed to survey the possibilities of new mission stations.

To start with, men hired as porters to Kadiaro were threatened that their houses would be burned down if they did not withdraw, but this may have been more middleman pressure than personal prejudice. Emshanda, a Jomvu headman who fancied himself King of the Wanika, had started it off. We heard no more about it after the Governor of Mombas representing the Seyyid in Zanzibar, had given us a military guard.

It was a good thing Dr. Krapf had showed me how to set about the journey, since I had been hardly a year in the country and was still feeling my feet. I did feel my feet indeed, to the extent of discarding my boots more than once, but the experience was exhilarating in itself and good training for a young man. Whether it has any other importance I would not like to assert. As Livingstone said, 'The end of a geographical feat is but the commencement of missionary operations.'

When so many controversies broke out over our findings—to the extent that I was considered unable to tell the difference between snow and limestone—Krapf burst out, 'Let Geography perish. Why should I endanger my mission for the sake of science?' And I have come to think since then that the expense of the journey is only justified if it leads to the foundation of mission stations in the foreseeable future or, I suppose, gives good reasons for not founding them in a particular place.

Plenty of people have been eager to explore and invest in exploration—von der Decken's last, magnificently equipped expedition cost £30,000 and all of that, together with four lives, went to waste—five lives, if you count Kinzelbach, from the party Princess Adelheid sent to search for traces of her son. The meager resources of the church are not meant for this sort of thing.

I was embarrassed, indeed, to have so many men assisting me—six Wanika at three dollars apiece for the Kadiaro trip, to whom were added two Mohammedans when the governor found that Bana Kheri was going in our direction and asked him to assist us. But the Governor was right to doubt me and my inexperience. The fate of poor Roscher and his two remaining servants later on shows how necessary some sort of establishment is, especially when one is young and unknown to the people around. Between a sufficient party and a small army such as Stanley lords it over, there is a vast difference.

I was able to start each of these journeys from home, so that the first miles were familiar, to Mona Zahu's village and Abe Gome's, through comfortable, cultivable land. Going further inland, bush and grass grow sparser according to the time of year: the noise of birds, cicadas, thumping hooves or creaking branches intrudes more as one's hearing becomes more alert to the challenge of the unknown.

The first journey was in October, a time of light rain, starting through rich pasture and camping the first night at the village of En-gani. The second day brought us to stony, uncultivated land, dangerous because frequented by the Galla and Kwavi. It was undulating and even a slight eminence of 100 feet gave a splendid view. Here I found two magic staves stuck in the ground, each burned black, about two feet long, and wound about with tree bark. I insisted on throwing them away, but my people were disheartened, saying that the magic was as important to them as the bible was to me. This perception of theirs I found most encouraging, though they did not like my asserting that my book would destroy their magic. I could see they were uneasy, since there was no path through the euphorbia thicket, so that danger may lurk behind the rubbery, up-lifted branches. But instead of predators there were gazelles, giraffe and wild pig in plenty, and we passed the day safely. We suffered, necessarily, from fatigue, the men with head- and shoulder-loads having constantly to sidestep as they could not bend.

The next was a long day, and we camped after passing Kurun-du. In later years about 12 miles a day through rough country came to be accepted as the norm; starting very early in the morning, the leader might complete his stint by ten o'clock while the more heavily burdened porters would arrive, perhaps, at noon. It may not sound much, but supplies had to be obtained, observations taken and camp constructed before dark. The simpler the expedition, the better time it can make, but, unknowing, I was taking excessive risks by imposing such a long day on my people.

We paused for divine service before proceeding on the Sunday, and reached Kadimu at noon on the Monday, the rock masses towering like 100 footsteps above us (not a good place to meet an enemy). On Tuesday, the sixth day, we reached the mountain mass of Kadiaro which was our object.

The inhabitants of the rocky village of Maguasini, some 50 households, met us without fuss or apparent surprise. I suppose that their scouts must have observed us approach, and we had asked permission to come from the perfume traders who visited us on their way to the coast. Whereas the people of Great Rabai had burst into song, dance and drumming on Krapf's first arrival, these people maintained their dignity and reserve, and asked whether I had come to build a fortress. It was not a thought that would have occurred to me! The women and children, however, held back from us, fearing perhaps magic as they said, perhaps slave raiding which they must have heard of.

The Teita men wore a loose cloth and many ornaments of wire. The women had two ample aprons, back and front, well decorated, with necklaces and an additional cloth if it was cold. Their houses were circular or oval with a high thatch in contrast to the beehive shape preferred by the Wanika. Two people they referred to as Pare were with them, skin-clad and carrying pipes of clay and bamboo.

I made observations of the great table-land beyond and started back on the third day. I do not know whether it was from Teita example that the porters made themselves leather sandals, but I wished I had some myself, for my boots were torture to me and I had at last to do without them. The men walked inclined slightly forward if they had a heavy load on the head, making, as it were, a silhouette of the map of Africa."

"You make it sound sort of natural, sir. But wasn't it fascinating—thinking you were the first white man ever set foot there, and maybe getting new sorts of trees or flowers named after you? Things you were seeing for the first time?"

"I was well pleased with my adventure, yes; as to the first of this and that, there is precious little we know about it, and the things that strike a foreigner as magnificent are—as I used to note in Switzerland—common-place to people who see them every day. How many shipwrecked sailors or Portuguese merchants might have passed that way before me without it being known? Indeed, how many missionaries might the ancient Christian kingdoms of Ethiopia and Nubia have sent out before their light dimmed?"

"But—I mean—weren't you excited?"

"We came in order to be surprised, you know, the same as we came to pray. You can't always keep up the boiling-point in either. You are a military man yourself, I think?"

The young man nodded. He was also something of a romantic.

But he admitted that the heat and the flies sometimes knocked the imagination out of you.

"Then you know what it is like to march. One foot forward, then the other, sand gritting, sun in your eyes, sticky twigs seeming to reach out for you. Yes, you will note down in your journal in the evening something you saw—a bird, a flower—the same way a bank clerk will note down a column balanced, but the major effort has been to keep those feet moving. The excitement—well, I thought I had identified the first major concentrated settlement inland where it would be worth beginning work. I should not have believed anyone who told me that today, 28 years later, that work would not have yet begun. That is where the surprise lay."

What, after all these years, surprises? Not the dilatoriness of the human spirit, for sure. The brilliant yellow of a dying banana leaf? The mighty fortresses of ants? The glimmering line of caterpillars crawling head to tail? The sudden gasp of insight—Mringe picturing the annunciation—Me Nyondo putting the gourd into my hand when she realizes, sooner than Abraham, that I cannot see it—Sparshott, loud-mouthed and cutting as he can be, giving me a hand into the boat? I have got used even to the nearness of the ocean and human endurance of famine and the dawn bird-song. New surprises lie in wait for me: I was ready for bilge-water and cockroaches and find instead service and civility. The pillar of cloud and fire will lead even into the new Germany.

"Still, I enjoyed writing up my notes and getting back to the usual round of teaching, visiting and language study. Krapf had finished his draft of the English-Kinika-Kiswahili dictionary. The Kiswahili gospel of Luke had gone to Bombay to be printed, and we awaited the copies eagerly.

One day Abe Marungu brought a friend to see me. It was some years before he committed himself as an enquirer (he has since joined the evangelistic team at Ribe) but there was already a sympathy between us. I would not exactly say he winked at me, but it was with a sign of complicity that he told me his friend had something to suggest that would make our work easier. Amri brought us *madafu*, coconut for drinking, and some fruit. The friend took these in his stride but, man to man, he told me, this was not the way to create an impression. If we were to give a great feast with meat, as he was sure it was within our power to do—his hands were spread, his eyes dreamy—we could be sure that everyone would come. In that case they would certainly attend the church service and memorize the hymns—courtesy would demand no less. Thereupon our god would be pleased with us and perhaps grant a blessing also to Rabai Mpya.

I tried to explain that this attendance would give no pleasure to the Lord of Hosts, but my guest thought this most unreasonable. My offer to read from St. Luke about the temptations of Our Lord was also rejected. The friend had, as he explained, his farm to look to. He could not be expected to spend all day pray-pray-praying to so stingy a god. He begged to be excused because he had told his wife to bring seed ready to plant to the lower field. We watched him go.

'I do not pray to your god,' said Abe Marungu quietly. 'But I know what god means and what prayer means. That one does not. Heh, let him watch his wife, that is all. A man who does not know what respect is.

I am going now to call together some members of my order. You know we cannot invite you as you are not initiated into our mysteries. But one or two of us are arranging to go down to Jomvu to make our plans for the great market day in August. Perhaps you would like to come with us?'

We parted a little way from the door.

'Greet Kiraf when he comes and I will greet my household for you also.'

I stood rebuked.

About six months later I started my travels again, aiming at the country of the Jaga.

This time I had nine porters and the way was familiar to me as far as Kadiaro. Beyond that we got into woodland at Bugada and proceeded through thick jungle, where we missed our path, up to the river Madade.

The Teita welcomed us with sugar-cane, bananas and Indian corn, and we were glad to rest up for several days as one of the servants was sick. The people seemed afraid to look too closely at me, but Mbosa of Jawia was courteous, and Chief Maina allowed me to expound our faith to him and did not laugh.

You think it strange that I should note this? Yet how odd it must sound, the first time, this gospel with which we have grown up, if you have not had the experience of faith and charity. As odd, shall we say, as finding six years ago that a man in Rome lives without intellectual error, though he was not previously aware of it! I for my part was not happy with the libations which accompanied Maina's gift of half a heifer which my people smoked so that they could carry some of it with us. But I was immensely impressed with his prayer, the first example I had met of real spiritual fellowship on the march. I took it down word for word.

'This stranger has left his home to come to me and say, Maina, let us talk, let us make friends. I told him, Let us speak in joy, let us pray God together for the peace of the land. Let sickness leave my villages. Let this stranger see nothing evil in his way, let him not be kept back by thorns or long grass, let him not meet with elephants or rhinoceros or enemies. When he reaches Jaga, let the Jaga people receive him with joy. I invoke the spirits of my father and my mother to let him arrive, and to come back to see me again in joy.'

We left very late and camped by the river towards dusk. This was foolish, but the Lord kept us safely even when we did the same next night. My men reproved me, 'You are here with nothing but an umbrella in a place where the plundering Wakwavi often camp.' They were right, but again the Lord restrained human raiders though, deservedly, I did not get much sleep because hyenas were hanging around in the hope of meat.

In spite of a late camp, my guide insisted we left at daybreak and off the path, as he had had a quarrel with the King of Taveta. (He could have told me before.) This time I was wearing lighter shoes, but they did not protect my ankles from sharp leaves and prickly burrs, while my mind dwelt on the information that people often set elephant traps thereabouts. We did not fall into any: perhaps there were none in our way, or perhaps we were not heavy enough to break through the masking sticks and grass on to the sharpened stakes below.

This time we slept under thorn bushes, but the Lord gave me peace in the night and joy in the morning, for there in the sunlight loomed what appeared to be a white cloud but suddenly leapt into my vision as indeed a snow mountain. I come from the edge of Switzerland. The sight was too familiar to admit of any mistake, even in its extreme improbability. The men were shouting to one another *baridi, baridi,* 'cold, cold.' The sight was as sublime as it was shocking to all my expectations of equatorial lands, and I started shouting myself in the words of the Psalmist:

Great are the works of the Lord,
Studied by all who have pleasure in them.

The men gave me the names for the tremendous peaks—Kilimanjaro to the west of where we stood, Ugano to the south-west, Kikumbulia to the north-west and Verga in Teita to the east. Beyond we could see faintly the expanse of Kaptei, home of the Kwavi, and to the north the Jaga country we were heading for.

At last we had to calm down and move on. Early next morning we crossed the river Lumi, and at nearly five in the afternoon reached the river Gona, where it was possible to bathe under the great tree near our camp. The mountain streams were ice cold and refreshing, the vegetation abundant: if they had not been, we could not have sustained such hours on the move.

Next morning at eight we were pushing our way painfully through the jungle to the first trench surrounding the little kingdom of Kilema, and crossed it by a shaky tree-trunk bridge. We could see the plantation, not yet the house, and I had no doubt that the jungle had deliberately been left in its pristine state to discourage intruders.

Some of Masaki's soldiers met us, wearing loose fringed hides, and I was instructed to greet the King with grass as a sign of peace in my hand and in his. I would not at first have identified the King, as he was less splendidly dressed than some of his advisors, who wore skin caps and long garments. In conversation, however, I became much impressed by his intelligence and self-confidence.

The introductory ceremony was a long one, since a sheep had to be slaughtered in order to present me with the *Kishogno,* a piece of skin from the forehead of the beast to be fastened on my middle finger. It was the first time I had undergone this ceremony, with which I was to become familiar as a ticket of admission to the royal precincts. Here, in a little hut hidden in a banana grove, I made my presentation—calico, beads, a knife and fork, needle and thread and a few other small objects. In return I was given a cow and several sheep and goats, worth much more than my little presents. However, it rained heavily that night, so I may have got the credit for that as well!

Because of my bad feet, I was thankful for the chance to stay indoors for about a week, and the King's advisors visited me frequently, their most urgent questions relating to what arms I carried, since these were not visible. When I replied that I had only my umbrella and my trust in God, they could not take me seriously."

The night seems endless, hardly any air penetrates this thatched beehive, and now that the door is closed with a reed shutter I lie sweating, disturbed by insects and creaking noises in the roof. In her last letter my sister commiserated with me for living in a little hut, but how spacious and airy our house, with its plastered walls and gap under the eaves, appears compared with this. My feet are still covered with hard skin and my ankles swollen where prickles and insect bites have tempted me to scratch. So, though I am glad of the chance to rest, I have not taken enough exercise to assure myself of sleep. The men are not very comfortable either, feeling confined in their quarters.

I have lately seen the most marvelous sight of my life—the snow mountain in latitudes where none imagined snow could form. Should I not be praising my God for this instead of rubbing my sore and sweaty feet? It ought to be like a rainbow, a sign of confirmation, but it is more like a fairytale, with symbols and presents and conditions imposed upon one's movement. But we are not in the middle ages. This is the rational nineteenth century where we control our surroundings to the extent of being able to communicate the gospel to all nations.

Why am I here? To pave the way for a future mission and a teacher. Meanwhile my school boys are not keeping up their lessons, my neighbors are gaping at what the expedition must cost us, my porters feel that if I walk with Bana Kheri we must be of the same persuasion.

The cows here terrify me, kept in little dark enclosures to which the women bring their crushing burdens of packed grass. The young men disturb me, detached from family life in their regiments and labor battalions, working on their elaborate network of trenches and drainage channels. I am a young man myself, and could better endure the close quarters and the ache of the march if I had a woman beside me. Oh Lord, give me prudence and deliver me from the weaknesses of the flesh.

"The King favored me with two visits, accompanied by his minister and his brother-in-law. Bana Kheri interpreted for us, and I was delighted to hear that King Masaki was prepared to receive me or my 'brother' as a teacher. He required me to stay another three days, and during that time I was free to go wherever I liked. I took him at his word and climbed a hill of 2000 feet, from which I could see clearly almost as far as the coast (judging from the landmarks) though the summit of Kilimanjaro was under a cloud."

The original enquirer had backed quietly away to get a drink. Others took his place, coming and going.

"The people lived in isolated homesteads about an eighth of a mile apart, but the houses themselves are small and airless. They rear their cattle by stall feeding, treating them if they are sick with a compound they use instead of salt. They are very clean in their personal habits, but their agriculture is not well advanced.

In contrast with the equality adhered to by the Wanika, the Jaga tend to exalt a single individual, the *Mangi* or King. Questioned about the mountain, they confessed to having sent an expedition to bring back the 'silver', by which they meant the snow, but only one of the party survived, and he appeared to have been badly frostbitten. No wonder they pictured snow as being the abode of malevolent spirits. Later on, however, I came to know that they did have a word for snow and knew it melted into water.

On the last day the King's uncle and minister brought me a goat which, they said pointedly, should last three days till we reached Teita. They wanted me to come back and not to visit anywhere else. I had to explain that we might not have enough staff to return with a teacher immediately but, being pleased with my reception, did not cause trouble by attempting to search out other chiefdoms in the neighborhood. From Bura we decided to try another route and walked through the Shimba Hills to Mombas. Krapf had heard piping from some of our party making their way home, and hastened down to meet me. There were letters, from Gerlingen, disturbing letters, telling of illness in the home and surliness among old, trusted workers. I felt a tremor of concern for my mother: the news was already four months old. But my immediate concern was with our home at Rabai.

While I was away Krapf had been annoyed by two Frenchmen

from Guillain's expedition coming ashore to break stones near Rabai, and some local women had been horrified when sailors made advances to them. Abdallah also was annoyed when questions were asked about the definition of boundaries. The French insisted that they only wanted to buy produce, but there were rumors that they had tried to purchase land at Lamu and Barawa the year before.

This was the first inkling, for me, of a theme that was going to recur throughout my years at the coast, outside interests and rivalries interposed between the missionary and his spiritual meeting with the local people. At that same time, Said Sultan was strengthening his suzerainty over Siu and Pate by diplomacy, force having failed him. He could not afford to be indifferent to the behavior of foreigners in his dominions.

Soon after my return, Krapf set out on his first journey to Usambara, and returned rapturous about his contacts with King Kimweri's people. Never had a journey been made so easy for him, he said. The Wanika among his bearers were delighted with the good order of the region, and the King was most receptive towards his enthusiasm for teaching young boys, only stipulating that the instruction must be given on the spot. At Zanzibar he had outlined our discoveries to Said Sultan and been graciously received.

This was the time Krapf organized a regular congregation for prayer in the *kaya* itself, but we did not manage to keep people coming when he was away. Perhaps even to have the two of us praying and singing with our servants inside the stronghold implied some kind of confrontation with magic: the physical effort of scaling the height must have been part of the sacrifice of prayer."

"I thought the object of all your endeavors was to convert the Wanika," put in another passenger. "Never mind details. What is the measure of your success?"

Official, this one. Frere in miniature. A bit younger than me: shorter too, I can tell by the direction of the voice. Has had to lay on his authority in India because of that. Thank you, God: I am beginning to listen like a blind man, not like a normal man in a blindfold. This is the first time I am conscious of it. And I have, after all, the authority of the licensed predikant. *Who does he think he is?*

"In the Christian life, my dear sir, there may be victory but there is no success. The counting of heads lies deep in the secrets of the Lord. That Isaac here stands beside me, tends like a son, reads and writes for me in English, Kiswahili and Kinika, that is something you may use as a measure if you wish. But for all those with whom I contended, as Jacob wrestled with the angel—and did not realize, until the hurt upon him, that divine power had to be exercised through him, not by him—how can I answer for all those? Except that Jacob has to have a new name. I do not mean just a new name in baptism, though there is that too. I mean that you cannot wrestle without gaining an intimate knowledge of the other person.

The object is to win men for Christ—any men who happen to swim into the net, not just Wanika. The Galla were our first object, but it was the Lord's will to commit the pastoral care of the Galla to other hands: I am not sure that I ever heard the name Wanika until I came to these shores we are now leaving."

A kind of death it is, and Price did well to see the shadow of it on my face, though he did not think I overheard him say so. A simple soul Price, doing the obvious thing so proudly and overlooking the obvious cost: he will build his tower in the vineyard and others will pay for it.

"Krapf was introduced to New Rabai because Abdallah, the plantation owner, who is still a Mohammedan and still our friend, had borrowed ten dollars from him to keep himself out of jail, and acknowledged the obligation. So Abdallah made Krapf known to Jindoa, the headman of New Rabai. Jindoa never became a Christian either, but he allowed his ten-year-old son to come and learn to read and write. The boy did not persevere, since he wanted clothing and other inducements, but who knows what may come of it in the long run? Jindoa, like his friends was disappointed that our 'magic' book could not at once tell fortunes or heal the sick. But when he said later on that the young people might adopt our customs though the old could not stomach them, he was perhaps speaking a truth he would not have chosen, just like Balaam. It was his nephew who compared the evangelization of the Wanika to filling a dry river bed—the small daily drops appear to effect nothing, and yet one day a mighty torrent comes roaring from somewhere out of sight.

At first, you see, it was utterly clear to me that any person, Nika, Arab, Swahili, Kamba, was potentially a brother or sister in the Lord. This is a joy you are given to see you through the first hard days when fever racks you and you are confused by different languages and your stomach turns up at the soggy porridge. I can hardly remember the strength of desire I had in those days for my friend Digeller from Basel to come and join me. Yet now I may not think of him for a year together.

Then, when the new light clouds over and you become aware of the strain of getting along even with German-speaking brothers, you are easily discouraged. In this time—from the fifth year, say, when I was concerned with my dear wife's safety as well as my own, and our very continuance at the coast seemed to depend on the tolerance of unbelievers—I began to say (and this is only too abundantly on record) that the church could only be brought after what I called civilization. This was the theory that CMS had applied to New Zealand: possibly by now they have got more civilization than Christianity. As we say at the coast, 'It is its own good things that bring trouble to the mango tree' when the stones are sucked dry and thrown all over the place. I felt that all the towns Paul preached in were in the Roman sphere of influence—he would have had to travel a long way to find any that were not—and that their roads, buildings, systems of writing and of law, were necessary for the foundation of the faith.

Of course they helped, though neither Britain nor Germany took very kindly to them in the first place. But the Jewish community and its scriptures helped most of all. The Greek language was useful and I had not yet come to see that here the Arabic language helped us, giving us theological terms that found their way into Kiswahili and an urbane culture within which our people could travel and see something of the world.

Britain had not yet, remember, officially taken over India, even, and precious little has their doing so fostered Christianity, as Sir Bartle Frere bruises his conscience on the question. But I would have liked Europeans to have more power to protect me and my converts. I was behaving as though St. Paul's appeal to Rome had been altogether to his advantage: it did spread the word wider, but at the cost of execution."

There was a long silence. The pulse of the ship's engines could be both heard and felt. It was evening now, and there was a murmur of conversation as passengers who had dressed for dinner came on deck hoping for any breeze that might cool the air. Rebmann could smell the scent; hear the rustle of stiff, fresh shirts not yet limp with the heat. Isaac could see cigars glowing in the darkness and the extraordinary low-cut dresses of the ladies. He was oppressed by a sense of artificiality: no-one was at home, everyone conversing deliberately, without explicit irritation or passion, to keep the temporary community in good order.

"I have often referred to the Wanika as being backward and low on the scale of civilization. By my mother's standards, this is so. She could never have conceived of sitting down to table separately from her husband and sons. A rough earth floor or an unglazed window would appear to her as ungodly as a bare-headed woman suckling her child in church, though our ancestors three or four centuries back might not have thought any of these odd.

Arrogance is a major sin of Europe, and so we Christians must guard against it, but arrogance is not peculiar to us. The Jaga no doubt look down on the Wanika for their want of educational organization. The Teita would rebuke them for frivolity and the Kamba scoff at their unmilitary ways. They in their turn mock the stalled cattle, the dingy black robes, the filed teeth, just as they find me clumsy and unmanly. Yet in the Lord's eyes none of this matters. He chooses me for the Wanika, the Wanika for me. We are to make the best of it.

I was also at fault. Some of the questions I had asked at first, in the language I was so eager to think I had mastered, were, I now see, not rightly understood, and so naturally I did not get the right answers to them. Any missionary has to see his mistakes and go on continually learning more, or else blunder in heavy-footed like Sir Bartle Frere and his henchman Price. For the Lord spoke through the mouth of Jeremiah,

seek the welfare of the city where I have sent you into exile, and pray to the Lord on its behalf, for in its welfare you will find your welfare.

If I had been asked, as a young man, to report on the Irish courts in Islington, I might have said that the men and women were drunk much of the day and night, dirty in their persons, neglectful of children, defacing their surroundings and contemptuous of our attempts to preach to them. But I should not have been able to describe what necessities forced them from their native land, what painful labor, led them to seek oblivion in the bottle, or what daily hostility they had to endure. Sojourners themselves, they did not meet in us that hospitality which comes so readily to the Wanika, and there were few of them I could have put a name to.

So it is only when one has begun to understand how people live that one can challenge their beliefs by presenting an overt alternative. We had to think and pray hard, for instance, about the right time to introduce a small portion of liturgy, for a prayer recited before the terms are understood is no more than a written verse from the Koran that the illiterate buries tied to a live kitten in the hope of wreaking his vengeance.

Price accused me of having 'a morbid concern for the sensibility of the native' — such a concern, that is, as my son Isaac shows for you when he removes his hat at meals and deftly handles a knife and fork, which his own society does not require. For instance, there is the matter of the bell.

Among our people a bell is connected with demonic possession and so to be approached with caution. Krapf used to ring a hand bell after firing off a gun to mark the Sabbath, but I discontinued the practice. I should not dream of summoning a servant to table or children to school with a bell, and my wife understood this.

Now Price came recently with a big bell which he proposed to set up in the church. I protested, but he got his way and most church-goers heed the summons. This seems to him a *Victory over Superstition* which, he says, could have been achieved 28 years ago if my obstinacy had not stood in the way.

Well, that is one way of looking at it. But if, during those 28 years, people had not got a bit used to the idiosyncrasies of the white man, they might still have run away from the bell. And now that they do not, what is gained? An imitation of an English village church. I do not recollect that Holy Scripture has anything to say about bells. The drum we used to beat linked our message: with other messages given in the community. It signified our coming in, not their going out. But soon enough they will want to be going."

VI

"We had made many preparatory journeys, received one valuable helper and buried another, before we baptized our first convert. He was Mringe, a small suffering man, crippled by cancer with an effect akin to leprosy. He had the idea that God should do something special for him to compensate for his suffering in this life. Now, no doubt, he sees that the special good thing was *through* him to open the way for the Wanika. He must have thought deeply even before we came, since he proposed to Krapf an idea of the transmigration of souls which Krapf thought he had learned from one of the Khoja Mohammedans who still remembered his Hindu origins, but I think it may have been a Nyika idea expanded with Mringe's peculiar metaphysical exactness. Mringe tried hard to bring his friend Ndune to the new way but Ndune listened mostly when he was sick. Once recovered, he was sensitive to the taunts of his agemates and returned to their drinking parties. You will have read Dr. Krapf's book, of course, which explains that he had instructed Mringe and in course of time, since his death was coming close, I, Rebmann, baptized him, not daring to take more time to complete the instruction or, to put it better, to complete my own language study and so be sure I interpreted his answers rightly. Dr. Krapf was away at the time. In any case, I was the one in Anglican orders: Krapf had entered the Lutheran ministry while still at Basel.

You may have heard that I changed my views on baptism afterwards, became very hard and selective, not at all like a good, tolerant, middle-of-the-road Church of England parson. You will not want to talk about all that now. But, you see, baptism is the bringing of a believer into fellowship—what fellowship? That is what it is all about. If I say that Mringe could become a Christian because of his disease, that is not to say that he was not a true believer. It is to say that he could enter into a potentially new fellowship because he was an outcast from his own society. We had to give him half a dollar (a Maria Theresa dollar that was, if you can think so far back) to get his own house built, because at his mother's place he was not able to read or in fact make his own decisions like a normal man. If he had been healthy there would have been a host of ties to hold him back—his need to have marriage alliances within the society, trading links and work groups, an attachment also to the dead of his line achieved by magic and heathen ritual. Who can be the first to come out of such a society, and into what?

I—and Erhardt after me—was alone, a young a man, a bachelor, not regarded therefore as full-grown, not even British, which was beginning to have a fearful significance in those days. Krapf had been known longer, and at least he had had a wife and two children, though they died. I remember I used to be offended when people greeted me simply, *'Yambo, Rebmani,'* *'U hali gain, Rebmani?'* I was looking for the respect due to a pastor, a foreigner, a bringer of the good word. But of course I should have seen myself as a boy in their eyes, lacking any category into which I could fit. There was a place for a Kamba or a Jaga who would settle nearby, bring his woman and exchange merchandise or work at his trade. (At that time they did not intermarry.) There was a place for the Arab or Banian who would bring in his own people and make wealth for them. But we were nonentities and we were offering baptism into nonentity.

The next enquirer was Abe Gunga, Abraham, the dear father of Isaac here and the closest friend of all my life. He was the only comrade present with us at the baptism of our little son. He too had been an outcast from his society, being thought mad. I did not see him in the days of his supposed madness, but it set him aside, half in contempt, half in awe, for there may be something prophetic in the aspect of one who is not normal. We struggled together for many years before his baptism, along with Isaac, and perhaps if these two alone were the fruits of 29 years of toil it would be enough, for their progeny shall be many nations.

Abe Gunga tried hard to learn the book. How often have I heard him reading aloud, in later years, in his slow, deliberate way, in the little cottage of which I supplied the doors and window-frames with my own hand, or in Erhardt's house which we sometimes left for his use. I remember his gasp of delight when he seized on the meaning of a sentence for himself instead of spelling it out word for word. He was gracious, too, to accept Isaac's beginning English with the aid of my dear wife, which I thought would not have been useful or appropriate for Abraham himself. Brother Krapf has recorded his happy fellowship with this good man on their southward journey, and how Mohammedan observers were affected at seeing them reading the bible or praying together. I myself was more than once saved from a dilemma by his sensible interpretation of scripture.

Abe Gunga never asked for a present for himself, and was early persuaded not to recover a debt by force, as others would have done, by drawing on the debtor's palms for wine up to the value owed him. He was the first to bring a freewill offering to our place of prayer—a fowl, I think it was—and later, when we were building the Church, he brought along a goat. This encouraged the others to bring a little grain or offer voluntary labor.

And yet how I contended in spirit with this man, and sometimes in harsh words too—Isaac will judge better than myself how harsh. For, having come so far, he failed to prevent other relatives sacrificing on the grave of his father to appease the *koma* spirits. He told the elders openly that their trust in circumcision and the attendant ceremonies was useless, but nonetheless submitted Isaac to it. I was disappointed, but the scripture did not give me ground to rebuke him, and Isaac would indeed have been outcast if his father had held firm. However, I was desperately worried, for the ritual which used to be held at the *kaya* now occurred in the open plantations, and therefore under less strict supervision by experienced men. In fact, several of the boys died."

Isaac left the group and stationed himself for awhile by the rail, wrinkling his eyes against the dazzle of the sea. He recalled the first sense of betrayal that he should be treated like the rest, he who had been a mission boy from the age of five when his father first became the friend of Rebmann, always clothed, regular at whatever classes started and restarted, dogging Mrs. Rebmann's footsteps, carrying her chalk or her ink bottle, unoiled, drinking sweet tea, fearless of the *muansa*.

"You have to have a wife like other people," my father says fierce in the flickering light of the cooking fire. My own mother is cooking, and I am glad of her return, but I have got used to the other one, with her many charms and her red cloths, who followed my father in his wild wanderings and looked after me while my elder brother, Gunga, stayed with the sad young mother in grandmother's house. Mother now wears a cloth tucked under her armpits and washes our clothes well. She drives rats out of the house with a terrible fervor.

"You must know what other boys know, so you must enter into manhood with them, so that you may earn respect and the new faith you have will be taken seriously."

My father's double knowledge frightens me more than the knife or the grease or the contempt of the other boys. I am tempted to blame him for that contempt, but it is less his keeping me separate than their rejection which has given rise to it. Perhaps if we are brave enough not to withhold our children it may be different. If Polly could see…

So they sent me to the Kungwi *in preparation for* unyago. *I had been less schooled in impassivity than the others and it was all I could do not to laugh at the screech of the* muansa. *It would have been hysterical laughter, of course, if I had failed to control it, for the mud dressing on my head, the symbolism of leaves and white clay, the icy water that I knew was meant to reduce pain, worked on me like a nightmare. Did those others have nightmares too? Did they know more than they dared say? Would they be afraid of water and the Holy Ghost? Would we truly be age-mate brothers? Most have been friendly to me: a few have come to Christ. The instructor was careful with me and restrained some of their taunts, seeing that otherwise some Christian fathers would be more stubborn than mine. I did not flinch outwardly but I bitterly resented the reserve that grew up inside the home. Only Mrs. Rebmann could be a mother to me now.*

"Abe Gunga's wife of those days wheedled out of him clothes and medicine to satisfy the spirits who so clearly oppressed her, whether they were coastal spirits indeed or desires we might give a cruder name to. I had silenced them once but, alas, I had not cast them out, for although she had once professed a desire to pray, I suppose she was only praying for what the spirits had failed to procure for her.

She certainly showed pleasure in the cottage we built them, close to ours, and yet seemed, even when we were concerned with their safety, to be eyeing our pots and pans, measuring what we might in time of danger leave behind us. And up to the time we left for Zanzibar (leaving very little behind us: Me Shabani had not been able to size up the English housewife) there was still no believing community, apart from the missionaries, to receive a new convert.

Then there was Abe Ngowa, a very headstrong man, the kind who always makes a sensation: if we had daily paper here he would be continually in the headlines. Stanley would consider him a goldmine.

Abe Ngowa, who was once in my service, was quick at learning to read, but he kept making a step and then falling back, vowing obedience and again falling back. His main difficulty was that he had the reputation of a rainmaker, and after he renounced the charms he was always in trouble with people if the rain failed. I think he had also been in trouble when it failed during the time he was still practicing! But afterwards people said he had seized the rain and hidden it in his little spelling book and catechism. Once he escaped his persecutors by traveling with Krapf from Ribe to Mombas. Young men used to shout insults at him from the tops of their palm-trees. One time we let him bring his wife and children to take refuge with us because he was being pestered to pay for some oath that he could not afford.

Like other people, we lived in a neighborhood. Although it was Abe Gunga who knew my heart and bound me most closely to the Nika, I was dependent, like any newcomer in a strange land, on neighbors and tradesmen. Even in a pietistic place like Gerlingen, one must not assume that the butcher, the baker, the candlestick maker will all be brothers in the Lord. One gets along.

Jomsic was one who raised our hopes in those early days but turned out to be a disappointment. He had been a Kadhi and knew how to write Kiswahili in Roman script. He professed great interest in the faith and was, indeed, useful in taking copies of the Kiswahili gospel to show others. He claimed to have been deprived of his Kadhi-ship for adherence to Christ, but it later appeared that there were other and less creditable reasons.

Some people who were not close neighbors we met in the course of their work and ours. Bana Kheri, for example, had accompanied me to Jaga and also acted as a guide to Dr. Krapf. I had not at first understood what a big trader he was in his own right, perhaps not, as Krapf claimed, the only Swahili man to understand the inland peoples, but the only one willing to share his understanding with us.

Bana Kheri had a brother, Mua Muira, right down south in Magugu, so naturally Dr. Krapf was glad of the chance to stay with him during that journey he made to survey the possibilities in Usambara after his return from Europe. In such a way relationships are cemented, and though foreigners may estimate porterage there at a pound a mile, it does not mean that families do not find ways to keep in touch and further one another's interests.

One had to respect Bana Kheri's stalwart defense of his Islamic faith, even though it was sometimes an embarrassment to us because it looked to the other porters (those of them who had grasped that we were not Mohammedans ourselves) like insubordination. We were sad to hear of his death at the hands of the Maasai. I have heard since that other Jaga districts grumbled because he had led me to his own trading contacts. But what else could he do? If a German visited London when I lived there, I would find him lodgings in Islington, not to show partiality but because it was familiar to me. It would be absurd to suppose the African less circumscribed and particular than we are ourselves, or than Our Lord was in His life on earth, knowing which people had perished when a building fell down in Siloam, who was getting married in Cana or what sort of woman was drying His feet with her hair. The gospel spreads in Unika as in Galilee, where some fishermen haul up their nets and come to listen while others turn their backs and go on working.

Local contacts gave us hope, though not yet assurance, of conversions. But Rabai was only the beginning. At the centre of my thoughts were the wonderful opportunities enlightened people like the Jaga seemed to offer for spreading the gospel. It appeared that even greater kingdoms lay ahead. I knew I had disappointed Dr. Krapf by returning so soon from my first visit. It was arranged that I should go again later in the year and proceed at least as far as the kingdom of Majame.

I left in November—1848 that was, the year of revolutions, though they may have lost a bit of steam before the news filtered through to us by way of old newspapers.

Ordinarily docile piece-workers were crowding into the market towns of south Germany making protests: they had no experience of strikes or agitation. In Paris more sophisticated gestures were being made, perhaps not more effectually. In England the Chartists, whom I had failed to get acquainted with when I had the chance, were drawing up their third and last petition. It was presented to parliament in three cabs while the enormous supporting procession was stopped on the south side of Westminster Bridge. And here was I bound up with village affairs in East Africa, trying to decide which kind of footgear would cause me least discomfort. (If not, I would have been watering my father's vines and never aware of possible choices in boots!) Some great ceremony was going on among the Somali, but we only heard whispers of it.

We were more concerned with the news that Maasai were raiding in force across the route to Jaga. For the sake of witness, it was decided that I should go on as planned, but seek out Kikuyu country and then Mbelete if progress from Bura to Jaga looked impossible. In fact, of course, the Lord has His own plans for me on that journey: I never saw a Maasai, and in consequence the Kikuyu have not yet heard the name of Jesus. They meet outsiders chiefly by supplying them with tobacco, and are not keen to let them in on their source of ivory. We had changed our tactics with the times, and my 15 Swahili porters, under Bana Kheri, were armed with muskets and bows and arrows. This would not have been welcome news in Gerlingen and Kornthal, where the community had special exemption from military service.

Since we heard nothing alarming at Bura, we followed the old route as far as Kilema, taking only three days. Masaki, however, raised difficulties about my going on to Majame, and I remembered his former instruction, 'Do not go anywhere else.' Although Kilema was a kingdom in miniature, its soldiers were well organized and could have turned nasty towards us. However, as it happened, Mamkinga, the sovereign of Majame, had already expressed a desire for a European among his sorcerers. (So quickly does news travel in the interior, especially when it concerns strangers. Would not then the news of the gospel spread equally fast?) Masaki therefore could not avoid sending a message to Mamkinga of Majame about me, and he dispatched soldiers to escort me, with his brother

Kilewo to make my arrival the more sure. Masaki could not dispute it. I was in the position of Joseph, who may have regarded the arrival of the Ishmaelite slave traders as marginally advantageous. Humanly speaking you would have expected it to teach him to stop telling his dreams.

We marched up and up, through empty, undulating country as cold as Germany in November, very different from the luxurious banana groves we had left behind. Part of our way had lain amid the foul odor of rotting bananas, part through all but impenetrable jungle, where a fruit which struck my weary palate as exactly like a raspberry helped to keep us going.

At the Weri-Weri River we had to wait for the tedious ceremony of *Kishogno* to be completed before we were allowed in to rest in a house belonging to one of the King's kin. There I was visited by Muigno Wessiri, a Swahili medicine-man who had acquired great influence with the King and desired to inspect the presents I had brought. I had to explain that they were much depleted by Masaki's demands.

I was told that medicine from a distant tree had to be mixed with the *koshogno* to eliminate any harm that might come from my visit before I could have an audience with the King. Certainly my porters and I were glad enough to rest in a safe, well-watered place, but I was beginning to have suspicions about these three-day journeys to collect herbs.

Common-sense suggests that you should replant near your own home any article that might be urgently required if, for instance, your sworn enemies should offer to negotiate a truce.

On the evening of the sixth day the King appeared with a great retinue while yet another beast was strangled for the *Kishogno* and rain obligingly began to fall—perhaps that was what we had been waiting for. I was expecting the strip of skin, but was less than delighted to find some noxious mixture splashed over my face and front from a cow's tail used as a brush. However, I had to put the best face I could on it; after the rain I was allowed to join the King and we then withdrew to a little hut for me to present my gifts. These were accepted, but the offer of teachers obviously gave the King more pleasure, and the next day he presented me with a sheep. Both his words and his manner assured me that he was more interested in my person than in gifts, and accepted my assertion that the teaching of the gospel rather than profit was my object in coming to see him. He even said he would have allowed his son to attend my school if I had been able to stay there permanently. Alas, how easy it is to deceive one who has been brought up in the simple practice of telling the truth: Mamkinga played with me like a cat with a mouse.

I had to stay with Muigno Wessin for another 17 days before the King would allow me to leave. It was now the end of January and the hot season was starting, though at those high altitudes there was also plenty of rain which gave us some relief. It also caused the rivers to swell, and there were not less than 20 between us and Bura, but we made our way without mishap and took the shortest road back to New Rabai.

My third journey to Jaga—I could not know that it was to be my last—began in April 1849. It was the rainy season, a year after my first sight of the snow mountain, which I already knew had been ridiculed in Europe by armchair geographers, and I had a much bigger party, 30 men, most of them Wanika, and what we considered an ample load of presents. We would have been wiser to carry more provisions too, for running out of supplies when heavy rain detained us, I was forced to revisit Kilema, which I should have preferred to avoid, and inspect a parade of between 400 and 500 troops.

A rhinoceros fled at the sight of me and so my stock was still high with the porters. As they were dilatory in moving out of a makeshift hut of banana leaves in which about ten of us had spent the night—I under my umbrella for added protection—I cut the Gordian knot by knocking the construction down while they were still chanting choruses inside. To my relief they roared with laughter and were as grateful as I was to reach Majame, after crossing the Weri-Weri, and be offered shelter.

Our position was not, however, really funny. Mamkinga came to see to me with the expected friendly demeanor but it soon became clear that he had no intention of letting us go on to Uniamiesi. Muigni Wessini continued his practiced methods of extortion while I lay ill with fever and dysentery in a smoke-filled hut: he would be hailed as a financial wizard in Europe, I fancied, teaching people to wring even more blood out of a stone. The weather continued wet and cold: my porters were also being plundered or threatened if they did not hand over the little trade goods they had for subsistence. All we got in return was one old tusk for the purchase of food. I was reduced to tears of vexation: as you know, I did not look for gifts for trade or profit, but I could not go empty-handed to the great king of Uniamiesi, nor could I risk my people's lives if we had not enough left for barter on the way. So we had to determine to make our way home forthwith and having got leave to do so, meet the final humiliation of paying a fee for the parting blessing to be spit (literally) in our faces by the rascally court. Even one of my Swahili porters, who retained a finer garment than most of us could boast at the end of a wet and thorny march, was forced to hand it over, and I cannot blame him if he never wants to join a missionary expedition again.

We then lost our way—as I have told you—trying to avoid more depredations by Masaki, and I was thoroughly made a fool of and also reduced to bitter repentance. Well, the latter was good for me and the former may have renewed the cheerfulness of my party. We were exceedingly glad on the tenth day to enter the district of our prayerful friend Maina. We were able to use the wretched tusk to procure maize and beans at Kadiaro and so proceeded homeward. I felt so weak that I sent the main body ahead with a request to Krapf to supply me with wine and biscuits. However, struggling on to Ngoni in Duruma country, I received generous hospitality there. This made me feel able to proceed to Rabai Mpya, and I met our good Amri on the way bringing me supplies. His face lit up when he saw me able to walk, and for the rest of the way we were happy to exchange our news. The main item from Rabai was our two expected colleagues, Erhardt and Wagner, had arrived but were both very sick with fever.

The other principal event on the home front concerned an admirable act of discipline. The community had fined the elders a cow for allowing Sheikh Gabiri of Mombasa to cut more trees than they felt could be spared for ships' timbers. This led Dr. Krapf to remark that our civilized republics have still much to learn from those of uncivilized Africa!

I was happy to meet with old and new colleagues and put aside my disappointment at not attaining my goal. Erhardt looked at the point of death, but in fact he was the one who recovered. The Goan servant, Anthony, whom he had brought with him from Bombay, was also sick, and at that time rather a burden, as we had not expected his arrival. However, the ways of the Lord are strange, and it was Wagner who died at the beginning of August and was buried at New Rabai. Krapf translated the burial service into Kinika and gave an address on 1 *Thess*.4.xiii, and we sang a hymn together so that enquirers could indeed see the Christian hope triumphant."

The first of August—hot, hot, hot, and dry. We have had to adopt the Mohammedan custom of burying before sundown on the day of death. Panda and Abe Ngowa have dug the grave for us for a small fee: this is more familiar work to them than laying foundations of houses. The grass that two months ago swished against our faces is still long but coarse and yellowed, and a whitish dust lies on it: all flesh indeed is grass. The dust intrudes between our toes, into our throats, beneath our eyelids: I can hardly swallow—shall I be able to give out the tune on my flageolet? Erhardt and I have knocked together a coffin. Anthony has washed the body and swathed it in white calico, Mringe looking enviously on. Krapf has transcribed the lesson and put together some notes for the sermon. I have made copies of my Kinika version of 'The Lord's my Shepherd.'

Wagner is a cipher, lying in the coffin: he has been seven weeks among us, ill all that time: he has hardly walked from one home to another or mastered the simplest of Kinika greetings. We have no letter in his handwriting, no report to the mission of his hopes and fears. Only Erhardt, who got to know him a little on the voyage, will have to go through his little box of private possessions and write to his mother, while Dr. Krapf composes a request for another missionary. And yet here lie all the passions and hopes and ardent youthful sacrifice of a young man like myself, or like a cadet eager to serve his country and butchered before he can strike the first blow. Or like a beast strangled to produce, primarily, only the little patch of skin for Kishogno.

I gaze around trying to understand. Krapf, robed over his usual nondescript shirt and trousers, is sweating profusely, his features sharpened by another recent attack of fever, a haunted look that may be recalling other funerals. Erhardt has recovered some of the stocky strength and blond blandness of feature which I already recognize as individual character. He is reading through the verses, screwing up his eyes against the sun. An-

thony, lean, brown, handsome, his crinkly hair smoothed with some kind of pomade, wears a look of surprise which has hardly been lifted since his arrival. It is an advantage to us to have another English speaking Christian on the station, and his attempts to vary our diet and smooth our tattered clothing are welcome to us, though frustrating to him. But I wonder what wild enthusiasm for mission led him and Erhardt to rush into partnership without considering that he has no Roman Catholic priest within hundreds of miles and no sufficient outlet for the perfection of his puddings and starched tablecloths. The probability of an early death has been starkly presented to him, and he is taking it very well.

Mringe crouches besides him, his melancholy eyes fixed, I am sure, on the prospects of white robes and golden crowns. He has shrouded his misshapen body hopefully in a piece of patterned cloth, and his lips are working over the hymn-sheet. We are thankful for his strong, clear singing voice. Jindoa stands stiffly, got up in all his ornaments of wire and beads as befits a civic representative: he has had little more than an introduction to poor Wagner through an interpreter. Abe Gunga comes next to me in sympathy, waving away the book since he will not pretend he has more than begun on the letters: his face is creased with genuine feeling—his friend has lost a helper who might have relieved him of a burden and, somewhere far away, a mother has lost an unmarried son. He is aware of our hope and looks to see that we shall persevere in our declared intention not to put little pots of sustenance on the grave or align it with any place we find a comfort in. Abe Marunga and his son stand at a little distance, having laid down their hoes when they heard the news. Amri has put on a long cloth for the occasion, and glances from one to another of us to make sure we are in good health. Abdallah has graciously come over from Jimboni to support us in our grief: he wears a long white robe and an embroidered cap, looking suddenly old and worried.

Krapf speaks the sonorous words familiar to none of us in that language. I am making an effort to concentrate, Panda and Abe Ngowa stand by, streaked with sweat, to complete their office. Ashes to ashes, dust to dust. The first time in Kinika. The shadows are lengthening. Abdallah must stay the night. Of course there is room. Inevitably.

"Our servants stood by us for the funeral. At Kisulutini we reckoned to have three of them, for water and firewood had to be fetched and many visitors fed, and the relationship is inevitably a close one.

It seems to me that old India hands—I hope there are none within hearing, but I've said it now—habitually draw out volumes of information from their domestics. 'I had a Bengali once' you hear them say, or 'have you ever tried a Tamil?' as though it were a kind of liquor or cigar: (see how fast I am learning your language). I have never managed to assume quite that proprietary tone. For one thing, it is not to be taken for granted that the other person wants to work for you. He may take some persuading. And when he is coaxed into it, his office may be as much to display and explain you in the eyes of the village as to keep the lamps filled and the water-buckets cool.

Of course our staff changed from time to time, as one would go away on his own business and another young man be brought in to learn the secrets of waiting upon the white man. He might, for instance, need to distance himself before seeking a bride, since once upon a time people were jeered at for entering our service, and it was even thought more respectable to sell oneself into indentured slavery than to work for the mission. Of course it was something to do with the borderline between male and female roles, yet certain sorts of domestic work were acceptable in the Banian or wealthier Arab households.

So Amri was attached to Krapf, Anthony to Erhardt, Salamini, the ex-slave, in later years to me, and Abe Ngowa with a kind of emotional frenzy to all of us. How many water-carriers and cooks to my dear wife I would not like to count. We valued what they taught us of ideas and manners, trusted their support to bellow out a hymn or take a message, but I would not say we secured our most reliable believers among them: there is a kind reticence necessary to the relationship.

Three months later, Dr. Krapf set out on his first journey to Ukambani, leaving Erhardt and me to cement the comradeship that was already evident between us. I had given all I had to the work and I almost envied his having more to give. That was wrong, of course. The cruse of oil is replenished however little it held in the first place. Erhardt was full of life and had a delight in God's gifts which upset Dr. Krapf. He brought in white sugar and strong beer from Zanzibar, not ashamed to trouble the consul on our behalf. He got tobacco from the Digo. He could see nothing wrong with engaging Anthony along the way, especially as the Wanika were not anxious to enter domestic service. He discussed with me long and earnestly the necessity of building a better house, and I came round to his point of view after the kitchen fell down, undermined by white ants. I did not resent the rebuilding of the kitchen, but the agony on Anthony's face, desperately lonely as he must have been, with only his craft and an occasional boat trip to Mombas to console him, taught me a lesson. If Dr. Krapf had been trained in Islington, we thought, he might have been less certain that walls stand upright through prayer and metaphysics. The prophet Amos, after all, though a shepherd by trade, was familiar with the plumb-line.

But our mentor was on his way to meet Kivoi with a Nika headman, Mana Zahu, and eleven bearers. That the journey was sensational goes without saying. It was an armed party, and they started with the threat of a skirmish in Duruma country: the assailants settled for a modest half dollar's worth of cloth to allow them passage. There were threats of Maasai raids: these did not in fact occur, but in the circumstances it is not surprising that the porters demanded more money, especially as they had to cross long waterless tracts before rain fell. Soon after investigating the Athi River, they reached Chief Kivoi's village, but Kivoi was primarily a trader and his mind seemed to be set more on ivory than on recruiting teachers. He proposed to take Krapf on a long journey to see the country of the Kikuyu, some of whom had put on a dance at the village, and the Ndorobo. Krapf, however, refused, partly because of the hostility of the Wakamba to his Wanika porters and came back to Rabai after seven weeks.

In spite of the difficult march, he became ever more convinced that the first of chain of mission stations which, he proposed, was to span Africa from Rabai to the far west, should be among the Wakamba. He felt that 36 missionaries would do it, on an annual expenditure of £4000 to £5000. One assumes that at this rate, with the long, long, porterage involved, they would all have to stay single. However, Krapf was frustrated in his hopes of finding a route from Ukambani direct to Uniamiesi or to the sources of the Nile and those still surviving Christian remnants on the Equator of whom he had heard in Shoa. Perhaps he was right to be searching for them. Those Catholic priests in Zanzibar declared that thou-

sands of Christian Galla collect regularly at Goijam market. But that
was hearsay: they had not yet been to see for themselves.

Later on Krapf agreed that Kadiaro was a more reasonable
stepping-stone to the interior. This did not prevent his feeling that
'two is company, three is a crowd,' and that Erhardt should be able
to set himself up in another place. His vision was exciting, but we
were three people half a day's boat ride from one extreme edge of
the continent, without a mortar board to plaster our walls with or
a tent for safari!

Erhardt was, in my eyes, busy. He had set up a little dispen-
sary and estimated that in a year about 100 Rabai, nearly as many
Swahili, and a handful of others came for treatment. Considering
that this was extra to their traditional medical practices, we were
pleased. It gave him opportunity to talk with the patients and to
accept presents of food by which some showed their appreciation.
The Wakamba often brought fowl: the Wanika were more skeptical
of the outcome and so reluctant to offer payment in advance. Erhardt's biggest worry was that some would come for medicine but
not follow his instruction about using it. He appreciated the chance
of approaching the traditional healers who, he felt, had some special knowledge above their fellow-villagers but might be uncertain
how it was linked with the superficial ceremonies accompanying
the cure. Their red and blue beaded sticks did not appear to offer
much relief to boils, but their poultices and inhalants were often
effective. Dr. Livingstone used to say that you must treat these doctors as professional colleagues and not poach their patients without
permission, but the patients themselves might be less scrupulous.

Krapf, though, was impatient to be up and doing, so in February, having determined to revisit Europe that year and propose his
grandiose plans to the Home Committee, he took Erhardt with him
on a survey of the coast from Mombas to Cape Delgado. Perhaps
the trip was intended to instill a spirit of adventure: they met some
interesting people and at Niali Krapf insisted on going ashore lying on his back in a dugout canoe. It capsized in the heavy surf and
left him and his Swahili sailor drenched on the shore, until Erhardt
was able to persuade the unwilling skipper to send a larger boat for
them. I sometimes think Dr. Krapf's theological education—some
ten years earlier than mine and so nearer the high tide of romanti-

cism—must have omitted the book of *Proverbs*. He seemed to have no idea of prudence as a virtue.

Their return from Zanzibar to Mombas took five days instead of the normal one and a half, and they found me at Rabai with scalded feet owing to an accident when visiting these low, dark houses where cooking and all is done inside. No doubt Krapf was glad to be away from us weaklings, reaching Aden in a fortnight and Trieste 30 days after leaving Mombas, which for those days was something of a record.

Found a mission and move on, when you have taught the evangelist who will be the leaven in the lump. Found another and move on again. (Is this what you would recommend in an English parish?)

They say nowadays that missionaries are only in transit, so there should be no missionary bishops, only bishops of the local church. This sounds very impressive and conforms to St. Paul's practice. Krapf was at one time eager to take Paul's missionary journeys and his celibacy as our guiding light, but Paul's journeys were made by the most sophisticated means available in his time. He used the Greek language as being common to the civilized world.

In highly literate societies it may be possible to translate the scriptures and the liturgy and then pass on. But in a mixed society that means learning a new language every few years and investigating new sensibilities and superstitions of the people. For if we are to be all things to all men, we must not knowingly offend them—as by offering meat to a Banian—nor must we lightly excuse our own ignorance, for our work begins with learning and that takes time.

In this way influence spreads, and we get new light on people we thought we knew. Does not this happen everywhere? One day I passed a little shepherd boy dallying by the wayside with his friends. I did not recognize him, though my eyes were good then. I am sure he never attended our school or services. Yet from somewhere in his tattered garments he drew out a Christmas picture and an Easter picture which could only have come from Mrs. Rebmann's little stock, and explained in a matter-of-fact manner to the other boys. 'See, this is where Jesus was born among the cows and donkeys: and this is where they nailed him to the cross so that he died.' He had knowledge, not conviction, but that knowledge was of pride and interest to him, and was shared.

Meanwhile Dr. Krapf on our behalf associated himself with the great—Prince Albert and the ancient Baron Humboldt among others—and had dinner with the King and Queen of Prussia, followed by the presentation of a gold medal, since they were assured that our more humble wants were amply provided for.

Nothing had been said about how the new missionaries were to be accommodated. (Later on Dr. Krapf said he had made an arrangement with the Chief of Kauma, but I had not been told of it.)

Of course they were meant to disperse eventually, but they must have somewhere to roost and get acclimatized.

I had already engaged myself to marry Mrs. Tyler, whose acquaintance I had made by correspondence through Dr. Krapf himself. It is still not clear to me why the marriage was such an offence to him. Erhardt was planning to get leave to find himself a bride in Germany. Obviously we would need more adequate accommodation even though it might not be as good as the stone-built house where we rented rooms in Mombas. The young men had helped us to find a piece of open ground, 30 stony acres. We were told that it could not be sold—only the *Kambi* elders must agree to the transfer—but the customary present to show respect for a transaction would be accepted. The 30 dollars we offered was welcome, together with a present of clothes for each of those party to the agreement which was drawn up—I have told the tale so often that I remember exactly—on 18 November 1850, the third day of the fourth month by Wanika reckoning.

I had often discussed with Dr. Krapf the need to expand our quarters, so I did not expect the thunderbolts that later fell on my head. If all our settlements were to be temporary in nature, I wondered why he had been allowed to bring wheels, a mill, a stove, a plough back from Europe! And did marriage cease to be weakness of the flesh if the second wife, Charlotte, whom he married in 1855, could be kept in Germany away from the mission field?

We had hoped to interest local people in our building project and particularly to bring home to them the advantages of permanent tracks. Their paths were scarcely 18 inches wide, and though they did have donkeys to carry goods for trade, this must have restricted their use, even before the more remote conception of wheels had been introduced. Even those neighbors who had urged us to move shied away from helping with the work.

Said Sultan had already brought in from India 5000 dollars worth of copper pice, to supplement the rupees and Maria Theresa dollars and so make small exchanges more practicable, but cash exchange for labor did not seem attractive. Cash exchange for goods was a very different matter, though you can easily understand why the traders preferred to go on giving change in millet rather than in small coins.

So Erhardt and I toiled alone, making a path along the ravine that runs between Rabai Mpya and Kisulutini so that our goods could be transported. We then started on two small cottages, one for Erhardt and one for me. But in neglecting to build a church at the beginning, when so many of the neighboring homesteads challenged us with their little thatched shrines, we failed to put first things first. Nor did we take into account the need of privacy related to study, to instruction, to translation and the hope of attracting more people to devotional meetings. Our potential congregation was much bigger than it had been at Rabai Mpya.

I had given up my idea of asking for agricultural missionaries. Krapf would not have allowed them to stay in one place long enough for fruitful experiment. Besides, I was beginning to see how interwoven the agricultural pattern was with the people's way of life (just as it was in the vineyards of Wurtemberg). In fact I had such a strong preconceived notion that the inland African is a subsistence farmer, living from hand to mouth, that I failed at first to see how sophisticated the Rabai economy was. I should have been better instructed if I had listened to Professor List of Tubingen, who used to be regarded as a great son of Wurtemberg and the economic genius of the greater Germany which has since swallowed us up.

All down the coast, in the comparative security of Said's suzerainty, commercial opportunities were opening up and people started to move out into plantations and new settlements. Having cultivated more land, they needed more labor, and slave holding became common, even among those who had once dreaded slave raids. The people of Mombas bought slaves from among those captured further south and sold them to the Wanika for two, three or four cattle apiece. Cattle owners like the *Saha* were sitting pretty. With the cattle, the Mombas people bought ivory from the Kamba for export.

Most people grew some grain to be on the safe side, but coconut palms had first been planted in the district some 50 years before, and the Rabai took over from the Digo the supply of palm wine to their northern neighbors, being paid in grain. A man with eight or ten coconut trees could consider himself comfortably off, and this made some of them lazy. The constant tapping, of course, reduced the productivity of the tree in other respects. The use of donkeys conserved physical effort, and in their traditional calendar every fourth day is a day of rest when the elders take council together. Some of the rank and file spend whole days, as the saying goes 'as drunk as the *kitosi* bird.'

The grain (millet or Indian corn) with copra from the coconut trees, is paid over to the Jomvu for cloth, beads and pots. Even better, an astute Rabai person will take a percentage on trade he mediates between the Jomvu and the Kamba, since he has learned to communicate with the Kamba in neighboring markets. Swahili traders have depots among the Rabai too, and negotiate for them purchases from Mombas. Our friend Abdallah had put his family on to a good thing.

All this we began to learn through our move to Kisulutini, but we had to put a hasty roof of palm thatch on our unfinished cottages because our attention was diverted to other things. Mringe, our first convert, eaten up by the cancer, was nearing his end, and I felt it right to baptize him at Rabai Mpya.

The Nika custom is to throw away cancerous bodies, not bury them in the Mohammedan way, but we were to give Mringe a Christian burial on our own ground. Ordinarily the custom of the Rabai (but not all the Wanika) is to bury those who die 'clean' in the *kaya* inside the palisade and those who die at a distance outside it, as close as they can. A family will even exhume the skull when opportunity offers, to bring it nearer the citadel—this is expected to prevent drought. Like the rest of us, they may not have freedom of movement in time of fighting or pestilence. But Mringe was not regarded as a whole man, and his mother made no attempt to disturb the grave.

Dr. Krapf returned in April 1851 with the Rev. Christian Pfefferle and the three workmen. Pastor Diehlmann, who was to have come too, had left the party at Aden for doctrinal reasons. Pfefferle died within a month. This left no companion for Krapf in his new adventure among the Kamba (since my own commission was specifically to hold the home base) or for Erhardt to initiate the work in Usambara.

Krapf felt we should not have taken the initiative in building, especially as Swiss workmen were on their way to help us. (Why, I wonder, if building had suddenly become a sin.) But little enough help we got from them, even when they had been nursed through their sickness under the roof we had built. So for years afterwards we were chastised for using our strength on the new station (as though honest work were not a witness) while Kaiser and Metzler were praised for wanting to transform themselves from workmen into preachers.

Krapf said he had spoken to them of me with great respect, but I wonder whether they listened, or what sentimental image of the mission-field they had. Hagermann was a better worker. When fit, he put in some time at Rabai, and was able to support himself by working for Europeans in Zanzibar while waiting for the passage home. I was accused of not respecting artisans: that is untrue, but I did expect the respect to be mutual. Perhaps they were just upset by Pfefferle's dying as soon as they arrived. Kaiser went back to Germany saying that Dr. Krapf had ministered to him 'as though I were the master and he the servant.' But the pair of them had accepted my nursing on the assumption that I was the servant, and complained that Erhardt and I left them in the daytime to go about our other work.

Dr. Krapf's confidence in his plans to start a station among the Kamba was undiminished by loss of staff, and he set out in July after the rains, with 30 Wanika porters and about 100 Kamba going home. This proved to be more than he could keep in order, and I was surprised that he allowed them to take an oath, together with other Kamba caravans in the vicinity, not to run away if they were attacked by the Galla and Maasai.

Something like a pitched battle followed, in which the Wanika were not conspicuous for their bravery or the good doctor for his skill with firearms, but fortunately there were enough experienced Kamba to repel the robbers. After two weeks the party reached the Yata plateau, and although Mailu wa Kiwoi, with whom Krapf had made a prior arrangement, had left the district because of famine, another 'chief,' Mtangi wa Nsuki, gave him a place to build inside his own compound.

Krapf was uncomfortable there, because the place was chilly after the heat of the coast to which we were accustomed, and his Wanika party insisted on returning home with another caravan even before the tiny hut they had constructed for him was either rooted in or provided with a door. Not surprisingly, his one servant, though a favorite, ran away, under these difficulties. Krapf is a man like the rest of us. The complete lack of privacy became unbearable, and he decided to make another visit to Kivoi.

This also had its difficulties, because Krapf was hardly well enough to keep up with his reluctant guides. He found Kivoi engaged in dispute which might easily have led to war. Krapf's telescope and umbrella were of some service and peace was at last agreed on. After this Kivoi and some Embu visitors, as well as his own people proposed to escort Krapf to the Tana River which he had long desired to see. You must all know what happened next— an encounter with robbers in which Kivoi was killed and Krapf isolated, still holding on to his telescope, in danger from hunger, thirst and wild beasts as well as enemies. He was still in danger when he managed to trek back to Kivoi's relations, since it might be thought that he ought to have saved his friend's life, but he was still under the Lord's protection and reached home safely seven weeks after starting out, during which time many rumors had been flying about.

We were greatly relieved both to see him back and to hear him admit that the immediate setting up of a station at Yatta was beyond our resources.

But there was no rest in him: perhaps our old south German quietism was excessive, yet this reckless energy consumed him and gave no quarter to other opinion.

Erhardt felt that, with two missionaries short and two of the three workmen disabled by illness, the London directives about planting new stations must be subject to discussion on the spot. Krapf would not agree and the tension mounted. I had been made accounting officer, but at this point Krapf insisted on separate accounts and even threatened to resign if Erhardt were not removed.

He spoke of being 'only a visitor' at New Rabai, which was absurd. The original house had been planned modestly for the two of us: would it have accommodated four if Wagner had lived? Let alone Pfefferle? We had built a cottage for two families at Kisulutini, and the Yatta project had been invalidated by failure to build. He let himself go, I afterwards found, in letters. 'I am still the same old solitary wanderer.' 'It is better to do a thing myself than be held back by the weak and half-hearted.'

Well, I was a prey to emotion myself. Was I not on my way to get married? I left in October, taking Kaiser and Metzler with me. Their passages were paid for. Nobody asked me what my requirements were and indeed I could not have said, having never traveled the route before on my own, let alone with a wife. I drew a bill at Aden and another at Cairo, and was called to question about them. There had been nothing in the curriculum at Islington about the costs of getting married."

VII

"I traveled with the two sick men to Aden, where Dr. Badger so kindly put me up and found a tolerable lodging-house to suit them—if they could be suited. I admit the journey by *bagala* was exceedingly uncomfortable: it was more strange to me than to them, since they had traveled that way before with Krapf. Rats and cockroaches abounded. The strong smell of other people's provisions took away all appetite for our own, which were growing musty as the days passed, and the invalids required a helping arm to hold them steady at the heads, which were little more than a platform projecting over the open sea, screened by a piece of sacking. We put down our bedding rolls where we could on deck, seeking shade since there was no hope of privacy. By the sail were the last tattered remnants of an awning, but the best hope of shadow lay close to the side. If my two companions ever dropped off to sleep I could then contemplate the problem I had previously failed to face—how to convey Mrs. Tyler (as I still thought of her) from Cairo to Mombas. Short of shipping her right round the west coast—which clearly would cost more than I dared ask for—I could not come to a tolerable answer.

At Aden occurred the tragedy of the candle which has, in one way or another, pursued me ever since. I was carrying letters from Krapf to the Home Committee, as well as documents relating to my own expenses and the repatriation of Kaiser and Metzler. I was to hand the English letters to Badger as Her Majesty's representative in the area, to be sent by official channels while we made our way to Egypt. For that reason I had removed them from my baggage and placed them on a small table in my room, to which the servant later brought a lighted candle, as dusk was drawing on. The place appeared to be intolerably hot and airless: I had opened a shutter in the hope of catching some faint breeze and, in my absence from the room, some tiny current of air must have directed the candle flame in such a way that it consumed a large part of one of the letters. In fact, had I not been called back at once, a serious fire might have broken out.

The *Church Missionary Intelligencer* published the fragmentary material with a full account of the circumstances, and though Krapf's full text was added later by translation from a German letter, I think I have never been absolved in this world from the charge of negligence.

I managed, with Badger's help, to install my ailing charges on the boat to Suez, where I had the good fortune to meet Mr. Marchand, the Supreme Justice of Madras, who procured for us that excellent specific, Warburg's Vegetable Fever Drops. Later I requested CMS to keep us supplied with this medicine, but I thought someone might have had the foresight to recommend it to new missionaries. Survival, one suspects, is sometimes thought less honorable than martyrdom.

Then I managed to prop them on donkeys across the desert to Cairo, moaning and groaning in the P. & O. Company rest-houses on the way. It was a great relief to be met by Mr. and Mrs. Lieder at our journey's end and get their help in sending the two sick men on the next stage of their journey. Only then could I fully bring my thoughts to bear upon my approaching marriage."

"I am surprised the lady did not change her mind, then," said one of the female passengers sternly.

"Well, she could see I needed someone to organize me, no doubt. Mr. and Mrs. Lieder prompted me as to how they thought a courtship should be managed. They wanted to take us to all the famous sights, the Pyramids, especially, where you are set upon by Arab guides carrying leather water-bottles, candles and clubs — the first two for the convenience of visitors and the last to beat off competition. The expedition was interesting in an eerie sort of way, reminding us once more of the promise of life where other civilizations are obsessed by death.

I drew the line at dining in the expensive restaurant built into one of the burial chambers, though some visitors even chose to spend the night there. In fact I would have preferred to visit the Russian consul's language school but that appeared to be private. There was even a vaudeville, but performed in Italian, and the ladies were afraid there might be some indelicacy that we should not recognize. The big shops with new glass windows, the variety of camels, asses and mules in the streets, mingling with carriages belonging to the richer Turks, for which roads had been specially widened, and the variety of tongues and costumes were like a theatre. The slave market had been shifted for health reasons (the health of the free, not the bondsmen, you understand) away from the centre of the town. I did not go to see it. The soberest of us, surely, may contemplate a honeymoon once in a lifetime.

The Lieders were familiar with the Jewish section of the old walled city and the separate Greek and Coptic quarters, where they introduced me to Christians of different persuasions. Mahomet Ali's great Byzantine mosque was still being built—it took more than 30 years overall. Mr. Stephenson was preparing to start on the railway to Alexandria: Mr. de Lesseps was already surveying the site of the ancient canal. It was all very exciting, but most exciting of all was getting acquainted with the lady of one's dreams.

Well, you Englishwomen (mark it, Isaac) are allowed more initiative than others. Mrs. Tyler and I arranged to meet in Egypt to see if we could get along together. I had no doubt of it: the house was already built. She had already visited her sisters in England to accumulate what I believe you call the trousseau and bottom drawer, so perhaps she had no doubts either. She came back for me even after seeing the Great Exhibition at the Crystal Palace. She was living with the Lieders, so I stayed at Mrs. Hill's boarding-house.

We were married by the British Consul in Cairo on the third of January, a good way to start the year, everybody said. It seemed sad not to have a proper church wedding, but Mr. Lieder prayed for us, of course, and hosted a party of officials and some Coptic Christians of the ancient persuasion. After a few days of repose and visiting, we set off across the desert for four days by donkey, sleeping at the three hotel stations (more like eastern caravanserais than any European inn) belonging to the P. & O. shipping line. We had provided ourselves with admission tickets in advance. As Mrs.

Rebmann remarked, we could consider it luxurious compared with the journeys suffered by poor Mrs. Krapf in Ethiopia.

By the time we went back in 1856 the P. & O. had put on a sort of horse-drawn trolley service, but even in 1852 we did not set out unwarily alone, but in a party under the escort of an armed guard.

The hotel turned out to be a square enclosure of mud bricks, such as one has pictured the inn at Bethlehem, with a kind of stable-yard in the middle for various beasts. Rooms were squared off on the two stories, with a wooden half-door to each backed by a curtain. The only other ventilation in the room was a grating high in the outside wall. In our room we had two string bed-frames, each with a single coverlet, moderately clean. A rough toilet and washing-place occupied a separate building: the whole was sited, necessarily, near a well and a grove of date palms.

I found out that the establishment had some pails in which water could be brought to the bedroom of the traveler, and managed to procure means for my wife to wash while I stood guard outside in the upper corridor. There was hardly a breath of air and the smell of cooking from the yard below, as well as the proximity of the camels and donkeys, permeated every corner. A couple of servants were preparing a meal from the rice and goat meat brought by our guard, and helpings were ladled out to all comers at a standard fee: no implements accompanied them, and the diner had to find a place convenient to himself to lounge and eat. Nonetheless I thought it wise for us to partake of the cooked food, saving our dried provisions for the midday halt, and I had slipped into our domestic luggage a small bottle of wine as well as the water-bottle."

The old man's eyes became glazed.

I see, as though it were yesterday, Emma sitting straight-backed on the edge of the bed, dressed in a capacious white nightgown with long sleeves, tied loosely with a ribbon at the neck. Her brown hair is brushed over her shoulders and her bare feet thrust into open Arab sandals. A mantle of some dark-colored stuff lies beside her, not dissimilar to that in which the Mohammedan ladies envelop themselves, in case she should emerge into the sight of any other person, and I sense trembling, with a guilty glance at the garments folded neatly on top of the dressing case, that the substantial body was otherwise bare.

I lean against the wall, eating with the aid of a clasp-knife, choked by the hot, over-spiced food, breathless. She sits calmly eating as she had learned to eat in Egypt, a damp cloth beside her to wipe the grease from her fingers, making polite conversation about the surroundings.

"You must be tired, my love," I observe, "after all those hours on the donkey. It is not much of a honeymoon I have to offer you, with this heat and foul air."

"Oh, Johannes, we shall be fortunate if we meet nothing worse than this. It was good of the Lieders to entertain us, but now we are launched out on our own. This is the first stage towards East Africa. I am not excessively tired." Her eyes were cast down. "But since I am not dressed, if you would be so kind as to return the plates in case anyone should come blundering in... And the bucket, after you have washed your face, perhaps. I will pour the wine. I am glad you are not of the new persuasion which forbids wine entirely. And you have matches, haven't you, in case we should need the stump of candle they have given us. You will not walk barefoot though, will you? Of course, you are experienced in the dangers underfoot."

Experienced! Oh, so little experienced, despite those discreet embraces in the stifling silence of the Lieders' house. I threw open my shirt and sloshed water over, wetting the sweaty flannel underneath. I hastened to return the utensils, hardly pausing to greet with decency a Turkish naval officer and an orthodox monk who were pacing the courtyard below. It was hardly dark when I plunged back into the room and caught the glimpse by which I would always remember her, impiously or not, in season or out of season, the draperies bunched in her arms, the taste of sweet wine on her lips, the bare, pitted walls behind, the grunt of animals outside and the sour smell of hoarded fodder.

"At Suez" —he recovered himself— "we were able to get a passage on the *Abar* to Aden through six days of intense heat, with my wife's donkey traveling free of charge. I had been advised on the outward trip by Mr. West, the English Vice-consul at Suez, how to deal with donkeys or it would not have occurred to me to transport one with us. Mr. West must have seen how sadly unaccomplished I was in anticipating the requirements of ladies and come to my aid.

During that voyage I celebrated my 32nd birthday and we perhaps shocked the crew, laughing so much together and going below to toast one another in the remains of our wine without (we thought) offending the strict abstainers among the Mohammedan crew. My dear wife had brought me from London Mr. Dickens' latest novel *David Copperfield* which, though not habitually indulging in light reading, I went through so as to share her pleasure, and she had hemmed and monogrammed some handkerchiefs for me.

We spent one night in a hotel in Aden which was moderately well equipped for the comfort of European passengers, but then Mr. Badger heard of our arrival and most kindly took us into his house while I made enquiries about a ship in which a lady could reasonably travel. The ordinary *bagala*, with its complete lack of privacy and the crudest toilet arrangements would obviously have been out of the question. We found that the Nakub of Makalla possessed a slightly more comfortable vessel which plied along the coast, and we embarked on it for Makalla early in February.

From Makalla we could get nothing better than a rough *bagala*, and my wife urged me to accept the passage, which at that time of year people said, should take 'only a few days.' In fact, three weeks would have been good time, and it took us nearly four, during which we suffered the stench of accumulated bilge-water, the vermin and the complete lack of privacy natural to such a vessel. It would have been wiser to take a trading dhow which hugs the shore, so that the passage, though slower, gives more chances of relief. The *bagala* takes a bolder course, over which, in this case, the skipper seemed to lack control. My wife showed amazing fortitude, suppressing a grimace when rats scampered around our mat at night, yet managing to keep herself neat and dainty in the most unfavorable circumstances. It was a great disappointment when we overshot Mombas and carried on to Zanzibar—at least I felt it so, secretly anxious that we might lose course altogether and find ourselves adrift on the ocean—but Mrs. Rebmann enlarged on the opportunities to see other places, which she said were appropriate to a wedding voyage. (A private cabin, though it would not do to say so, would have seemed to me more appropriate.) Fortunately the customs master, Ludha Damji, opened up Hamerton's house in Zanzibar, and a German merchant welcomed us to his table, so we were able to show her a little of the town, and on the way back the dhow stayed a day at Pemba, a very pleasant and prosperous place. We were shown the arena for bull fights, a custom preserved since the Portuguese occupation. The sport appears to be much less cruel than the European version, but it is a great entertainment on the island: people take their places early and coffee and sweetmeats are hawked about, 'just like a London music-hall,' my wife remarked.

All the same, we were glad to get to Mombas and next day up to our house at Kisulutini."

"And how did she like the house?" One of the ladies demanded urgently, "the house that you and Mr. Erhardt had built with so much labor?"

"The smallness of the rooms was a bitter disappointment to her. Already wearied by the arduous walk from the landing-place, for she had refused the assistance of a litter, she was less than usual able to conceal her apprehension. I suppose I had been so proud of my workmanship as to raise her expectations unreasonably. She rarely complained. But I have to admit that when we introduced a wash-stand as well as the bed and one chair, the bedroom door had to remain ajar into her small adjoining sitting-room. She had three chairs, a table and a footstool there, so that only one guest could comfortably join us for tea, and one could not have accommodated a sewing-class there, or a nursery, if our boy had lived beyond a few days... One room, of course, had to be the store, since many of our goods were bought in bulk from a distance, and one reason for having a permanent house was to keep them in good order. The outermost or public room was the one I used for seeing people, writing, studying, arranging all the affairs of the mission. It had to double as a dining-room. Even Dr. Krapf came to admit, later on, that the house was not quite suitable for a mature lady.

I was able to make a little reservoir that year we were married, which saved a lot of labor in carrying and storing water. This was a help, though it was quite impossible to reserve it for our own use: the local people accepted it as their own without a by-your-leave, and so I was blamed later on when the Nasik ladies had to walk further afield to fetch water.

We agreed that it should be neither a German nor an English ménage, but one in which the work of the gospel came first. I never had cause to regret this and she never complained of it. We spoke only English at home, and she never reproached me for the German accent the Sparshotts make fun of, though perhaps she corrected the schoolboys if they imitated me too much. She liked an orderly routine, especially at meals. This was not always possible, with callers at all hours, but generally after dinner we would converse for a time or I would play to her on my flageolet or one of us would read aloud, before I would excuse myself to bury my head again in my manuscripts or go out among our neighbors.

Things settled down as she became able to direct helpers in the house after learning a little of the language. She did not learn Kinika as well as I had hoped—perhaps, like the rest of you English people, she thought it more helpful for other people to be taught English. She was in a delicate condition but suffered a disappointment and later took up some of the school classes, which kept her more occupied. She would copy the hymns or the ABC in big letters on to a sheet or blackboard and hang it up in the verandah for people to study. She used to hear the boys reading their ABC or syllables, and helped the women with simple sewing. They would learn the hymns by heart, and she could help them, even without knowing what every word meant in their language.

It is a heavy burden to be childless in Wanika society, but even so the women granted her a kind of respect. They could not understand us, I suspect, so seemingly old, so restrained, so happy. The women would offer her the three-legged stool to sit on even if one of their number had first to be forced away from it, and they would flock to greet her if we had been away for a time.

The *Candace* people, I remember, when they stayed with us were much concerned with her health: well, that was a bad time, but we agreed together that constant coming and going was not always an aid to the constitution, and she lived as my constant help mate and co-worker.

The house on the cliff-top at Mombas pleased her very much. All you English people love the sea. I never saw the sea myself till I traveled to England at the age of 24, and it still leaves me feeling a bit on the edge of things. There she would visit the Indian and Arab ladies, admiring their finery and trying to bring the conversation round to substantial matters of belief.

In Zanzibar there was even more to see and do, though in those days there were not many European ladies in permanent residence. Mrs. Norsworthy was there, and later Mrs. Seward, Mme de Billigny and after 1860 some French nuns.

Miss Cook arrived shortly after my wife's death to marry Dr. Kirk, our first European wedding and a great event. She is a sensible woman: I wish they could have known one another. Miss Tozer and Miss Jones of the UMCA were also too late to benefit from her experience, and so was Mrs. Wakefield—Rebecca—at Ribe, a very intelligent girl. Perhaps you would not call her a lady—you English people still puzzle me—but she quickly learned how to adapt herself, once she had got over the first fright of seeing our people inadequately dressed. She would laugh at white ants eating her husband's boots and rats drinking the water in a glass by the bedside. I did my best to protect Emma from seeing that sort of thing, but her habit was to ignore it, and then comfort me by recounting extraordinary things from St. Giles' in London: by the end of the evening we would feel almost safe in comparison. I remember Rebecca making Christmas decorations out of greenery and fashioning garlands of flowers which the black children loved as much as her own little Nellie. Only Emma had gone by then.

The days must have hung heavy on her sometimes. Perhaps she had pictured starting a school for girls such as she had in Cairo. At the Cape, they tell me, there is a girls' school for the Zulu so good that the white farmers complain of having nothing like it for their own daughters. Alas, at the coast there is still no prospect of this among grown girls living in families, whether traditional, Mohammedan or Banian, though the little ones may come to learn their ABC with us or the first *suras* in the *madrasa* if their fathers are strong believers. For girls' education it is true that the freed slave settlement is better, since no individual family can assert a right to the domestic and agricultural labor of the girls. No Mohammedan or Hindu girl living in a family here has ever listened openly to the teaching of the gospel—they are too much protected by their families. The local women ask questions sometimes, a few pray at home and quite a number come to church services, this being a social occasion, but as yet we have none ready for baptism.

Later, the Sparshotts told me that some of the Arab and Banian ladies wanted to learn English. English! I could not allow this, not by any means. I was the head of the station, after all. So once again the cry goes up, 'Old Rebmann despises women: he does not think them capable of learning!' Far from it. The question is, *what* are they capable of learning? What do they want with English? Let their husbands decide if they need to be taught English. They want company. They want visitors. Will the mission be blamed? No, I told Mrs. Sparshott, it would not do. And if, as she then decided, perhaps it is the husbands who want to learn, let the husbands come and say so. It is dangerous to take messages through the women. My wife would not have allowed it.

When we arrived at Kisulutini, Krapf was away on his second trip to Usambara. His unfortunate encounter with the French consul, de Belligny, over dinner, was made worse by the fact that he and Erhardt were staying in the British Consul's house, as we had done, while Hamerton and Said Sultan were away in Muscat. Under questioning Krapf admitted that the coast between Vanga and Pangani was not completely under Said's control. Everyone knew that already: Busaidi power worked that way. The most powerful inland ruler was then Kimweri of Usambara, Krapf's recent host, but that could change with a shift of wealth or favorable rains, new trade demands, disease decimating a rival's population or cattle, fresh alliances or the emergence of an outstanding personality.

Kimweri had his *diwans* or consuls at the coast, but their appointment had to be confirmed by Said Sultan as a king receiving foreign ambassadors accredited to him. He would give them a present to remind them of his interests and accord them the right to walk about with an umbrella, wearing special sandals and preceded by a band. As well as asserting this unwelcome fact, Krapf had brought King Kimweri's vizier, the *Mbereko*, to the island and given him introductions to foreign traders, so that he could cut out the Swahili middlemen in selling his ivory. This, of course, was what really caused offence, and Krapf was too ignorant of commerce to understand it.

In diplomatic circles there are always eavesdroppers, and this indiscretion was a trump card in the hands of those Swahili who distrusted the British, in whose camp they thought us to be. (Their love of playing cards, which Krapf attributed to the example of British sailors during Owen's brief protectorate at Mombas, was a grave offence to him. The Banians, of course, loved them even more.)"

"Your Dr. Krapf might have found himself ill at ease on this ship."

"Indeed, yes. The question does not trouble me very much. Perhaps it is on account of having an English wife. Only for her sake, not to say Her Majesty's, I find it a pity that the Jack, *Mzungu wa pili*, the second European, takes precedence over the Queen, *Mzungu wa tatu*, the third.

But, as I was saying, it was put about that Krapf had made his expedition on behalf of the French, that M. Chabot, the trader who had established himself at Lamu, really intended to found a colony, and so on. He seemed a hospitable man and, since the French interest was mostly in copra and sesame, Lamu was a good site for him. When Hamerton returned to Zanzibar he felt that the rumors could not be altogether without foundation: in fact two more French merchant houses were founded five years later, and one wonders if there might not have been more if there had not been that terrible loss of a French vessel from Bordeaux Bourbon, though mercifully the crew's lives and captain's cash were saved.

So Said and Hamerton were both angry and suspicious when they got back, and soldiers were immediately settled at Vuga on the site which Kimweri had offered for a mission.

Yet Krapf, despite Erhardt's advice, compounded his error by writing to Mr. Kuhlmann, the French consul's secretary, and refusing to go to Zanzibar to explain the misunderstanding. He has always to be right, you see. And as soon as he was back in Rabai, trouble started. I was praised as being 'humble' and 'cooperative' but Erhardt had unfortunately made a reference to the 'rules of the scribes and Pharisees' in connection with his training at Basel and Islington, and this provoked terrible wrath. I tried to say that if he was to be blamed for building, I must also share the blame, but Krapf would rattle on about his 'meager hut' and our 'pretty residence.'

Erhardt had done pretty well at languages and at geographical study: it was not from excess of humility that he doubted his chance of success in a one-man mission if Krapf, with all his vaunted experience, had failed in Yatta. Erhardt was strong-willed but not arrogant. When, early the next year, instructions came to post him to Bombay if he continued to refuse Krapf's orders, he said that he felt his calling was to East Africa and he would make the attempt on Usambara if really required to do so. Notes had been flying about—5000 miles from Rabai to London, two and a half from Rabai to Kisulutini. In the last one, saying he had accompanied Krapf up and down the Mrima coast and therefore agreeing to make a try there, all alone, Erhardt really touched our leader's conscience, for he had been harsh (I told him so) even admitting that Erhardt was not by nature tactful. Vuga now being out of the question, he settled on Tanga as a promising spot. In my opinion he suffered more there from fever and isolation than Krapf and I had ever done on our journeys.

In the meantime he visited Kimweri, taking a letter to him from the Sultan, whether of introduction or reproof we never knew. Mercifully we heard nothing more of French incursions at that time. We had daily chores and occasional disturbances of our own."

Hot hot hot hot hot. The rains are late starting this April. The heat seems to overcome all more serious considerations. By nine in the morning the sky is too brazen to look at. The banana leaves and the grass are covered with a whitish dust. The baby chicks, over whom we have rigged up a piece of old net curtain in the hope of fooling the hawks, look like bundles of waste cotton, their piping keyed down as though their little throats are dry.

Our compound is full of people—Kisulutini, should I say, is full, since only a low sisal hedge marks off the mission plot. Yesterday whole families moved up from the plantations as those furthest away brought in news of raiders approaching.

Daylight discloses that there are no raiders: the dispute is a local one. The war-horns that sounded in the evening and died away now sound again, Rabai challenging Kamba, Kamba challenging Rabai, while non-combatants of both communities are packed together here to the tune of several hundred people. A buzzing sound has continued throughout the night, sharpened here and there into the wail of a baby or the imprecations of an old man no longer able to fight.

My wife seems to be in her element. She has caused a large pot of millet porridge to be made and moves among the women in a light muslin dress that falls loosely round her, a wide-brimmed straw hat tied with a ribbon under her chin. She has collected a few half-gourds into which our servant ladles the mixture from a bucket while Isaac walks behind carrying a large basin of water into which the gourds are to be dipped for cleansing, a procedure which some fail to understand and which causes considerable delay.

Many of the refugees are women counted elderly among the Wanika, though perhaps not far beyond Emma in years, and seem shriveled above their bulging petticoats, their armlets and ankle bands click and jingle. It is really no fight of theirs. A Swahili called Jaga (no doubt because he has been in caravan service to that place) has enlisted them to help him recover a debt from a Kamba. It is the heat and uncertainly of the season rather than the small reward offered that has set them off. Jindoa, with Abe Marunga, Abe Mlega and Abe Gunga have gone down to talk sense to them. The Kamba elders are also urging the defaulter to pay his debt, and Krapf is reasoning with them.

And suddenly, as the prophet saw a cloud no bigger than a man's hand, the sky swells, the rain falls, the heat subsides, though the dust churned up in grey runnels round one's feet is still warm, like sand after the tide has gone out which, for a little while, is comforting after the white burning of the beach. The crisis is resolved. Everyone is busy. The defaulter will have to pledge part of his new crop. The warriors disperse.

Krapf staggers up the slope, half-blinded by the drops running from the hat-brim down the back of his neck and through the open front of his shirt to drench the flannel vest. Babies are crying at the shock. Women who have fashionable cloths instead of stout petticoats find them molded to their limbs and all-revealing. They cower against the house-wall or the hedge. Those living nearest prepare to walk home before dark, hoping there is sufficient dry firewood stored. My wife is singing, 'Showers of blessing, showers of blessing,' and a few of the children join in with the Nika words. The bows and arrows, I have read, symbolize rain for some communities, fertility for others. Krapf insists on walking back to his place. Erhardt is away in Tanga. Emma and I are alone after our supper of beans and cooked bananas has been served: we tell the men to let those who have provisions use the cookhouse and share a small stock of meal among those who have not. (Abe Gunga will certainly do the same.) The numbers are far too great to be able to share our hot sweet tea and hot water for washing in.

"*Showers of blessing.*"

"You have comforted many people today, my love. You must be very tired."

"Not excessively tired, Johannes. It has been quite exciting."

"In September Krapf once more set off for Europe, and as it happened we should not meet him again as an agent of CMS. So I became, by default, head of station, and was hopeful that we had lived down Krapf's indiscretion. It was a time of hope for me, in more ways than one. But unfortunately something else was to revive suspicion.

A group of missionaries from Hanover, sailing in their own ship, the Candace, under the Reverend Captain Harms, turned up in Zanzibar seeking to evangelize the Galla. (The Galla were a will-o'-the-wisp for us, you see, at every turn a bit ahead and off track.) Erhardt went over from Tanga to visit the party, but they did not get a good reception, calling to mind French ambitions along the coast and Krapf's supposed complicity. So they sailed on to Mombas and, having no permit or letter of introduction, were naturally detained by the Governor in the harbor. He sent a messenger with a letter to call me as an interpreter, but three of Harms' men, even after being warned that they had no right of passage—such fools are sent to try us—took themselves ashore and wandered up to Pokomo and the Uzi River, against my specific advice. A canoe-man on the M'toa'pa, sensible fellow, not wanting blood on his hands, so misdirected them that they were bound to find their way to Rabai. My wife and I were in mourning: we really had enough to cope with. We could not refuse to put them up for the night but sent them roundly off to Mombas next day. I could not blame my servants for refusing to escort them, but found a young man who, for a fee, agreed to see them on their way. The Governor then restricted them to their vessels and warned them that they must leave within three days and pay a hundred dollars fee to be towed out.

As it happened, I had to go down to arrange some stores to be sent to Erhardt, so the Governor asked me to mediate. Finally he allowed them to go ashore, and reduced the towing fee to the usual 50 dollars. Thereupon they lingered the whole of June in the harbor: we were thankful when they left, and more so when we heard they had reached Port Natal in August.

We had got used to being alone with our little flock, but I was still responsible for Tanga, and when I heard from consul Hamerton that year how ill Erhardt was I sent an express messenger (which must have cost the mission something like ten pounds) to recall him. The new language, the need for building, the effort of keeping a tiny group together single-handed, were altogether too much. I do not regret for a moment having done this. Our message is of life, not of death. And yet it is only in the midst of death that we are in life."

I have helped Emma to bed the evening after the funeral. It is hardly a week since she suffered the pains of child-birth here, on this very bed, the Arab midwife we had brought up from Mombas pummeling and encouraging her, calling for water and towels: there was hardly room for me to squeeze through the door, and the helper was determined that I should not do that. Indeed I am useless, at 34 hardly more acquainted with women's matters than when I was a boy, except for the evidence of my eyes in a largely unclothed society. Her earlier miscarriage was at three or four months only, and she somehow managed to dispose of the evidence all by herself. I had brought Me Shehe hopefully to sit with her, but she had not enough of the language at that time to explain her condition, and was reluctant to allow any hand to touch her.

This time her joy was so great as to overpower any false modesty: in the patchy light of the lamp I saw, myself huddled at the door, mesmerized by the loud cry of the baby, the midwife cradling the small man-creature, still attached to the cord, my wife's face radiant on the drenched pillow, her legs still arched and blood oozing.

He was perfect: tiny, it is true, but that, they said, was all to the good. A first confinement at 44 is not a joke. The human sounds he made still echo in my ear, not whimpers but emphatic cries befitting a pioneer family. Within those days he learned to turn his head towards a loud noise. He knew already how to suck. His body was firm to touch when, fearfully, I hugged him to me.

Now, her face sags with suffering. The big breasts are painful with the milk that will never nourish him. She is sore too, having stood up too soon, but we did not delay the baptism beyond the third day, knowing what we knew of other missionary families. A fever seized him on the fifth day, and it was soon over. We had no experience, either of us, in what could be applied to such little ones, and the midwife had already left. The local women were superstitious, saying my wife had left the room too early and exposed the baby. I would have liked them to trill to announce the birth, but Emma was doubtful, and the women rebuked me for having gone into the room so soon. Abe Gunga was our only comforter.

I sit on the end of the bed with my head in my hands. In spite of the brave words of the service I am overcome with sorrow, but she, she has the pain too, and I am too ignorant to relieve it. If only Erhardt were here with his little box of medicines. And suppose she were to be taken too? I remember Rosina Krapf, and the many missionary wives who have died on the west coast. I should be desolate and also guilty.

She puts a hand on my shoulder: what exertion has it taken so to move herself towards me.

"Johannes, we must learn to bear it. Did we not decide to call him Samuel because we would lend him to the Lord all the days of his life? The promise has been required of us. It is hard for you because you have had only a week to see yourself as a father. I have had nine months of being a mother, and that is a precious experience no-one can take from me. I thank you and thank the Lord that I have had it."

"Emma, you must take care. I am weak, perhaps, but I cannot bear any more. Do you think you had better go to Zanzibar for a time? Even to England? I must not risk you too."

"I shall be well, my dear, the Lord has promised I shall be well. This morning, when Samuel fell limp in my arms, and I knew—for a few minutes I dared not call you. And I thought then that if I were a younger woman you might already have been blessed, and if I were out of the way you might still have your quiver full. But we are bound to one another, Johannes, and we said that we would not withhold anything from His service..."

I cannot hold in my tears, but her face is calm, though puffed with grief, and she twists in the bed, trying to soothe the aching thighs.

"I am afraid the women will see it as a bad omen for us, my dear, but you must explain to them that I am too old. And teach me some sentences I can use to tell them. Now please you should pack all the—the clothes and things—into the box, and put it in the other house, so that we do not dwell on it. And tell them to put some water on the fire, Johannes. Perhaps a hot compress will relieve the ache here... Is that someone coming?"

I am glad to get out of the room, dabbing at my eyes, conscious that there is still earth on my trousers, that I am indeed, as the Wanika see me, not yet a man... not even Abe Samuel.

"Yes, my dear, it is Isaac to see how you are and to bring his little sister with some millet gruel for you. He is too big now to run women's errands himself."

For the first time her voice falters.

"Tell Isaac he is a comfort to me, a—a son to me—and I shall try to take the millet. I have had nothing since morning. It will do me good. He is to thank his mother and tell her we shall start on the hymns again next week."

"I did not anticipate the great solace that would come to me from Erhardt's geographical researches, especially after the dreadful time when our baby died that year. He had made many enquiries at Tanga from travelers, as I had done on my various journeys, and it was a while we were sitting quietly one evening at Kisulutini that the seeming solution to our problems, the great inland sea, burst upon us both. We were wrong to gather all the waters together in a heap, our wrongness underlined by the sentence in the map as finally published, Niassa, the name used at the coast, is a corruption of Nianja! We had not the wit to envisage both Lake Nyasa and Lake Nyanza. But Emma smiled at our excitement, and we celebrated it with a bottle of medicinal port.

I had woefully misinterpreted my ex-slave servant, Salamini, whose expositions of both language and geography were perfectly clear in themselves. All our informants, of course, were speaking from their own—or related—experience, not able to tell us how one section fitted in with the other. But our mistake gave others the clue to find out the truth: when Erhardt finally left us, late in 1855, traveling by the Cape, he took a fair copy of the Slug Map, as people nicknamed it because of the shape we had given the supposed inland sea. It was published in the *Calwar Missionsblatt* that October and in the *CMS Intelligencer*, with my comments, the following August. The interest perhaps helped to keep us both sane."

"And you have stayed in the same house up till now?"

"Oh yes, though we have had to do repairs from time to time when the rain was excessive or intruders had done damage. Not nearly as many repairs, though, as I had to do to the old house at Rabai Mpya.

Then we had to enlarge the settlement as we got younger helpers, mostly the freed slaves from Bombay, and they went on marrying and having children. Do you remember the first time you made a window frame yourself, Isaac? Sparshott came running over to tell me—we were so proud of you. Krapf thought I was indulging you with permanent houses. Bishop Tozer thought I was demeaning you, not issuing shoes and hats. Well, as your father used to say, 'he has piped and you won't dance.'

The cottages at Kisulutini always had magical properties—I would not profane the word by calling them miraculous. To Dr. Krapf—and through his eyes, it seems, to the Home Committee—

they were luxurious palaces, tempting us to a life of ease away from the rigors of missionary labor, and to overdrawing our allowances.

For readers of Krapf's book, or Dr. Speke's, the two cottages (adjacent to save building another exterior wall) appear in the picture as an impressive storied building from the roof of which I (they say it is I—I never dared enquire whether the figure behind me is meant to represent my dear wife) am holding forth behind a row of sheep hurdles to the entranced ears of some three dozen listening blacks. They appear not to be passing on their way to market—none carries produce, weapons or, as far as one can see, a digging-stick. None is even shown smoking or setting down a pot of palm-wine. One or two are gesticulating, as though calling for restraint upon the white madman who is shouting, bare-headed, into empty air 20 feet above them when he could so easily assemble their little group in comfort under the verandah and address them face to face. One could not blame them if that were it.

We did, I remember, add the verandah when repairs had to be done after our stay in Egypt, and stairs in the back, so I suppose I must have showed these to Burton and Speke as a novelty. A flat roof *does* have its uses for drying clothes or foodstuffs, or even for sitting on a cool evening. And the Book of *Deuteronomy* does specifically instruct believers to build a parapet to avoid the guilt of having any visitor fall off, so perhaps Burton drew in the fence as a sop to my conscience. The verandah certainly made the place look more spacious, but we never added an upper storey.

To Commander Trotter who visited us in 1857 to urge us to take refuge in Zanzibar, the house looked 'just right,' and he was not used to luxury, having survived the abolitionist expedition to the Niger in 1841. In fact he kept urging me to spend more on wine and provisions, in contrast to the Home Committee, who were always concerned about economy. Though he admired our (simple enough) resourcefulness in standing the legs of the beds in tins of water to keep them free from ants, Trotter and his diffident companion, Layard, could not be prevailed upon to spend a second night. They still believed the night air of the tropics to be the cause of fever in Europeans, though not able to explain how one could anywhere take refuge from the night air. Perhaps the lack of bread and familiar vegetables also alarmed them. We had sufficient, but there was famine all around and in decency one avoids excess. All the same I appreciated Trotter's support for the situation of Kisulutini as being better than Rabai Mpya, which he described as a *cul-de-sac*.

To Sparshott and his wife, used to the extended comforts of a newer generation, our cottages were native huts full of smoke and foul odors. I think Salamini and the other servants may have changed the cooking arrangements after my wife died and I moved into Taylor's two rooms next door. I kept her place for visitors and church business. To be honest, I did not notice much, but ate what they set before me when they dared disturb me. In any case, I was used to a farmhouse where life centers on the kitchen.

The Sparshotts, come to think of it, started in a two-roomed house I had designed for the Bombay people. They were right to say there was no chimney in the kitchen between the rooms. Well, he was good at building: he could improve it if he liked.

To Sir Bartle Frere, a couple of years ago, this same house merited the description of 'a miserable hut,' and Salter Price, fresh from the comforts of Bombay, considered it hardly fit for human habitation. I wonder whether Sir Bartle Frere, for all his years in the orient, has ever really set foot in 'a miserable hut.' But our cottage has been a happy home and I think our people in Rabai will not forget it."

VIII

"I had prayed for European protection from the arbitrary whims of a Mohammedan monarch. Well, prayer has its dangers. One gets more than one bargained for. All the same, I was delighted when the Seyyid's increasing regard for Hamerton started to change things. I felt it was a dispensation particularly directed towards the safety of my dear wife. We were, indeed, kept safe, though she supported many perils with true British phlegm. But we need not have doubted the protection of the Lord of Hosts: that I should have invoked Him through British diplomacy shows what a country bumpkin I still was. My wife suffered my naiveté with a wonderful patience. I had forgotten what Luther had to say about respecting non-Christian potentates. The first Mrs. Krapf had been wiser, and prayed for Said Sultan on her deathbed.

Anglicans, perhaps are meant to be gentlemen, or at least aware (as English working people are) of how gentlemen's minds work. My wife showed some shrewdness in this respect, though ladies are supposed to feign ignorance of politics. She would have dealt with Frere better than I did. The Wakefields did deal better with him. They put on dancing displays and an archery contest, even some target practice with guns, which would impress the visitors and reduce the time available for conversation.

'Good simple people, devoid of worldly wisdom,' Frere considered them. (Oh yes, reports get about. 'Leak' is the vulgar word for it.) But they put the responsibility on their Home Committee and perhaps the Home Committee respected their common sense. Nobody expects a German to have common sense."

"Your tea, Mr. Rebmann," interposed Isaac. "Do not let it grow cold."

"What did I tell you? They will make an Englishman out of you, my son, and all the coast people will go over to tea and muffins! Even my good wife could not make up a muffin such as we used to have in Islington. You see, I am not quite unaware that I am going back to London.

Perhaps I would not be, if we had managed to keep ourselves quite free from official entanglements. But to explain how it happened I have to go back a bit, for the situation was not of my making.

Captain Hamerton—he was still a captain then—had received me kindly on my first arrival at Zanzibar and told me that Dr. and Mrs. Krapf had been of great spiritual help to him. Unfortunately I was not able to retain this first good impression of him. I could not understand why his Irish blood should be considered an excuse for arrogance and excessive drinking. Of course he was unmarried— captains in India service were discouraged from marrying unless there was money in it—and in the orient could not expect a very comfortable establishment. All the same, he maintained a heavy staff at his own expense, and after he died it was found that he had accumulated enough plate and tableware to stock a small palace, let alone a rented house that actually stood in the water at high tide. It was not until Rigby took over and suggested extensions to the house that we found the Sultan had actually been paying rent for it to an owner in Muscat. This did not look very good for British prestige, so eventually it was purchased by stages.

At first His Highness would have preferred Mr. Cogan, who had been Her Majesty's Commissioner and Plenipotentiary at Muscat to be consul. But Cogan had other ideas: he established his own company in Zanzibar and took young Mr. Peters as his resident partner. Mr. Cogan had been offered the consulship in 1838, but refused it, and would have liked to get Peters appointed instead, so he tried to undermine Hamerton both with Said and with Palmerston in London. Cogan got the concession to work the guano on Latham Island, but had to give it up in 1867 after the first tidal wave had caused so much damage.

Hamerton, however, was not so easy to displace, and in due time he won Said Sultan's full confidence. He had been transferred from Oman in May 1841, though it was another year before he was appointed British consul as well as agent of the British East India Company. Around that time an English newspaper put it about that the reason Said Sultan had sent his vessel the *Sultani* to London was to recruit white wives. The calumny must have done harm to both Said and Hamerton: the real purpose of the voyage was to take Ali bin Nasser to England in state. He was to congratulate Queen Victoria on her accession and deliver letters to several important personages. (Captain Robert Cogan, the same who had refused the consulship, was in attendance, and the Governor was granted an audience and even spent a night at Windsor Castle. Said Sultan was very proud of the portrait of Her Majesty he later received: perhaps it was regard for the new young queen that had influenced him to sign the 1839 treaty further modifying the slave traffic.) But the actual scandal of the trip attracted less attention—that of the 100 original sailors only 14 survived. They were inadequately prepared for the cold and one of them was left in hospital in London, where he stayed for two years. He managed to get back to East Africa by way of Bombay, and visited Dr. Krapf at Tanga when he was surveying the coast.

In fact the *Sultani* ought not to have been so ill-prepared, since she had called at New York on an earlier voyage. There were also heavy casualties aboard the *Caroline*, which berthed in London in 1845 under the command of Captain Hassan bin Yussuf. It was the time I was preparing for ordination in October, but I ought to have had enough sense to watch the news and go down to the docks to see her. One of the crew members, an Englishman who had been converted to Islam, deserted and complained to the Anti-Slavery Society, so there was plenty of talk about it, though his charges were found to be without substance. (How would an English investigator begin to get at the truth?) I think he must have been the same man we heard about on the coast, John Orne, the only survivor of the *Essex*, who was taken by pirates off the Arabian coast in 1806. What standards of freedom or comfort would he have laid down for himself 40 years later?"

"Quite a subject for Lord Tennyson."

"Well, if you are looking for a legend.

Said had been trying to *become* one, jockeying for position as a world power, flaunting his fleet of trading shops and exchanging gifts with the great and powerful: the British were not as good at this as the Arabs because they were used to expressing themselves more forcibly. Hamerton was also a showman in his way, and this side of him delighted Said Sultan, though he could also be very tactless. For instance he gave a letter of protest about the slave trade to Said at the very moment when he was deeply offended because an innocent vessel had just been searched by the British within sight of the palace. Another time, when Said sought British approval for his intended blockade of Persian ports, Hamerton, instead of going into the rights and wrongs of his claim, alleged that he had no sailors capable of handling guns or warships: in fact there were competent sailors and plenty of guns. If they had not been in combat much, it was because Said had been restrained by his treaty obligations, though it is true there is an Arab saying deriding anyone who is 'as great a coward as a Muscatee.'

Said Sultan had presented his English-built ship, the *Liverpool*, of 1800 tons and 74 guns to King William IV, and received in return the handsome steam yacht the *Prince Regent*, a beauty of its kind but not at all suitable for Zanzibar waters, so he was permitted to pass it on to the Governor-General of India. This of course was before my time.

But when I came to the coast the story of the Queen's gift of a state carriage and harness was still being bandied about with great glee, since there were no carriage roads to accommodate it in Zanzibar. Perhaps being advised of this, the Queen ordered a silver-gilt tea service for Hamerton to present to His Highness. This was about the time of Dr. Krapf's arrival. Receiving a large packing-case from London shortly afterwards, the consul took it unopened to the palace so that the Seyyid could observe the contents without fear of their being tampered with. You can imagine his consternation when the package turned out to contain not a tea-service but a tombstone—whose and for what reason I have never discovered! I hope the gift that Dr. Krapf brought from Prince Albert in 1852 was more satisfactory. I never enquired what it was.

Fortunately Said Sultan had a sense of humor: indeed, without this faculty it would be perilous to aggrandize oneself so much. He was said often to chuckle over Captain Owen's attempts to conceal the pigs he had on board at Muscat when the Seyyid proposed to visit the ship. They might not be visible to the Mohammedan visitors but they were certainly audible and that was not all! So the affair of the tombstone was taken in good part but Hamerton was never allowed to forget it.

By the time I arrived there were already a number of Europeans living in Zanzibar—15, to be precise, in 1846, and seven of them died during that hot season. It was not exactly a reassuring situation to arrive to. We were all glad when the apothecary Lewis George was put in charge of medical care at the British Agency in 1850. Dr. Frost came two years later, and he attended the foreign merchants and sailors as well as the British. Charles Young was also setting up in business about that time—from 1854 Erhardt and I asked him to look after our letters, as we feared they might be intercepted.

To us missionaries R. P. Waters, the American consul, was by far the most congenial of the commercial set. He had left, for health reasons, before I arrived, but at that time we expected him to get well enough to return. He was an evangelical Christian and did not drink—this in itself was enough to keep him at loggerheads with Hamerton. He was the only person who had distributed Christian scriptures on the island before we came, and had arranged for the first sermon to be preached there by an American missionary on his way to Bombay. His wife was with him on the island, and they offered accommodation to Dr. and Mrs. Krapf on their first arrival.

He was, of course, a merchant. Few of the consuls other than the British were salaried and their way of doing business seemed to me aggressive and devious. Whether they could, then, be gentlemen I leave to your better judgment. Before I came, it is said, the Seyyid had written to the American President to remove Waters, but Waters opened the letter that had been entrusted to him and tore it up. I do not know whether that was the same occasion he protested against the Customs Master, Jairam Sewji, but he did so, and this showed a lack of sensibility to the situation. Waters' house was stoned and people refused to translate documents for him. He later made things up with Jairam—it was always necessary to do that. One had better not ask by what means peace was made—certainly not to the advantage of the other Europeans. Jairam, however, was too clever to put all his eggs in one basket. It was whispered that his bid to farm the customs had been accepted by the Seyyid even one year when it was not the highest: they were necessary to one another.

Mr. C. Ward was the American consul to follow Waters, and was eager to trade direct with the coast, although the treaty in force since 1833 already gave him favorable terms, 5% duty on incoming articles only, and sales of American cotton—and arms—had increased by leaps and bounds. Said Sultan was eager to keep foreign interests away from the mainland: his disputes with the French (who already had a treaty and a consul when I arrived) were mostly about their claim that they had been allowed to build depots. And there was a lot of ill-feeling, I remember, when three Zanzibaris were killed, in separate incidents, by American seamen.

Ward had severe competition from other Americans as well as foreign merchants—his employers, Shepherd and Bertram of Salem, had for a long time even tried to suppress the name of Zanzibar on their maps so as to keep out trade rivals—and of course his office gave him a certain advantage over them. So he was under pressure at both ends, and in 1850 his temper got the better of him.

He complained that the Seyyid had failed to salute the American flag on the fourth of July and closed the consulate.

Said made only a verbal apology, stating with great dignity that, apart from one occasion in honor of Queen Victoria, his guns were never fired except in response to a previous foreign salute.

(That, Hamerton told me, was in 1843, when he had belatedly managed to get carpenters from HMS *Cleopatra* to put the British flag up at the consulate. The Seyyid's *Shah Allum* gave a 21-gun salute on that occasion, and the *Cleopatra* returned it.)

This time Ward really had to be recalled and was replaced by one of the Webbs: there were so many of them that you might think W- was a tribal prefix for United States citizens. Shepherd and Bertram, though not completely happy, made a conciliatory advance to the Seyyid, and President Fillmore was gracious enough to send a friendly letter next year. He sent it by Commodore John Aulick, commanding the *Susquehannah*, so no doubt the impressive strength of the vessel was meant to be noticed as well.

The Americans, the French and the British were in competition—the Germans did not install a consul till 1860, though they were well aware of the profit to be made from cowries, exported to West Africa for use as currency. In the year Said Sultan died 20 ships from Hamburg alone called at Zanzibar. Cowries became a German specialty because the Banians would not deal in them, they had a religious objection to shell-fish, and avoided the impurity even at second hand. This one must respect, and use it as a lever for faith. Alas, Mohammedans at the coast had made a contrary use of Hindu scruples, compelling merchants to take out an affidavit in the presence of blood, though the law does not require it. Many Banians would forgo a rightful claim rather than so pollute themselves.

Said Sultan had to keep his wits about him: the British consul was not in trade, and he was also in some sort of control of British Indian commerce and British Indian nationals in Zanzibar. This was of immense importance to the Seyyid. Even now Sultan Barghash has an old Arab sea-captain interpret for him all the news in the Indian papers. This man is intemperate in his habits and so forbidden entry to the British consulate, but I am sure the other consular agents are not so strict: he must learn a lot of what goes on. It is not really surprising that Said Sultan put his trust in Hamerton.

He even put his vessel, the *Artemeise*, at Hamerton's disposal. It became known as 'the consul's yacht.' In the winter of 1852 Hamerton sailed it from Muscat to Bombay and from there to Zanzibar, arriving with the seasonal winds of 1853.

The Seyyid, whom he had left at Muscat with the flagship *Shah Allum* and his sons went down to the beach to greet him and actually embraced him. People were moved to tears. The great powers, they felt, were cementing their friendship at a personal level. This was not an absurd idea. Said himself was a man of great ability, to have raised himself (not without the aid of his dagger) from a petty prince in Muscat to acknowledged sovereign over a vast area of the coast and colonizer of the most favored island of Zanzibar. He was not the first Busaidi to have such pretentions, since the coastal people had demanded protection from Muscat in 1690, but the first to give them lasting substance. He did not see those big powers with his own eyes. His son Barghash grew nearer to that, and has become conciliatory having learned much in Bombay where his brother unwisely sent him into exile. Ever since he has had his eye on a state visit to Europe, and may yet succeed in getting it.

But it was from his father that Barghash learned to respect the technical skills that lie behind European power. Said Sultan sought out linguists and engineers to serve him and, on board his flagship, liked to conduct everything himself, giving (correctly, to the admiration of foreign officers) the word of command to get his vessel under weigh, shift her berth or bring her to anchor. His personal secretary, Khamisi bin Osman, a man of mixed blood, had served aboard the *Leven* and accompanied Captain Owen to England. He was said to be able to speak English, French, Portuguese, Hundustani and Malagasy as well as Kiswahili and, of course, Arabic. Khamisi's son Mohammed studied navigation and foreign languages in London and became captain of the fleet in the present Sultan's time. Hassan bin Ibrahim also was sent to India to study mathematics, navigation and English.

Said's eldest son, Hilal, whose Abyssinian mother had died when he was born, at one time looked like his favorite. But he took to drink, 'seduced by the Christians' as his father put it, or to far worse debauchery according to rumor, and came under the influence of the French consul, de Belligny. Perhaps the French wanted a revival of the external slave trade—certainly many of the leading citizens would have staked a good deal on getting it back—and thought Hilal was their man, but Said Sultan knew all about family rivalries. Hilal fought against being disinherited, even risking French disapproval by appealing to London. Captain Cogan met him at Southampton and the Queen received him at Windsor: her government was interested in keeping things stable.

Hilal returned to Zanzibar to be feted by the people, offered gifts by the women and welcomed with decent reserve by his family. He still refused to compromise on his status as the eldest son and was packed off into exile at Lamu, where he had strong support; Said was clearly less ruthless than in his early struggles for power.

Hilal died of consumption, it was said, on a pilgrimage in 1851. There is no point in asking what sort of death, what sort of pilgrimage. He was popular with the people but did not have the sense to bide his time. His children were brought up by His Highness as members of his own family. The year of revolutions was past, and any European power had better be a bit reticent about supporting slavery. There was no platform left for international conspiracy.

And Hamerton represented Britain. He had now become such a favorite of Said Sultan that when the consul was ill Said with his own hand attached to the door of his room, with a silver nail, a spell written by a well-known sheikh, in confidence that he would by this means exclude evil spirits and the ghost of Napier. So the story goes. But none of the Napiers represented much of a threat. I suspect that the Seyyid was remembering his own father's enthusiasms, and exorcising Napoleon, or, in fact, France.

Though not evangelically inclined, Hamerton did his duty by us missionaries.

We were all thankful when he stopped the self-styled Rev. Dr. Biallobblotsky, who had been a trial to many of us by his unsolicited visits in the name of evangelism, from setting out from Mombas to explore the sources of the Nile with only twenty pounds (out of the much larger amount subscribed in Europe) by way of funds! He rightly saw that this was bound to lead to dissatisfaction among the porters and provision agents and possible danger rebounding on the rest of us. (If only someone had foreseen the greater harm that Burton would cause in this respect.)

Naturally, the consul was primarily concerned with the political kingdom, and felt his influence was undermined by the Seyyid's suspicions about Krapf, the French and the *Candace* people. The climax of events came when, in 1854, Said could no longer postpone another visit to Muscat, where affairs were getting out of hand. On the eve of his departure he begged Hamerton to stay in Zanzibar and publicly committed his son Khalid—and so, by implication, the government—into his charge. Britain was riding high.

Of course, Said Sultan, as always, had his reasons—the month-long visit of a French flagship under the command of admiral was one of them—factions within the island, indeed within the family, might have worked ill for him, and he seemed already to have a foreboding that his end was near. We did not see him again.

So it may be that he had other forebodings too. It was in that year that he ceded the Kuria Muria islands, allowing Captain Ord to work the guano deposits. This was done freely, without demanding any *quid pro quo*, and yet the British, in his eyes, forgot it, when they peremptorily turned down his request for help against disaffection in Bunder Abbas. (By the end of 1856 they realized that

Captain Ord was making trouble with high-handedness and forced labor, and removed him from the islands long before the license was terminated. But already it was too late to pay their personal debt to Said Sultan.)

I also had my forebodings.

1855 was a difficult year for us. We had lost our little son the year before, and my wife was naturally in low spirits, since at her age she could not reasonably hope for another child. My good brother Erhardt left in April and I did not expect him to return. His health had been sorely tried by this adventure at Tanga, and when we were all at the coast in January he began to get a tumor on his arm which I felt needed the skill of an experienced surgeon. I asked Commander Etheredge of HMS *Penguin* to send his ship's surgeon up to Kisulutini, but he refused, and this seemed to be what my Mohammedan friends would call a bad omen. A Christian commodore at the Cape and a bishop in Mauritius hardly counted as protection if such practical services were not to be rendered.

Soon after Erhardt left, there were Maasai raids in our area, not of the ferocity of those that were to come, but sufficiently alarming. The Rabai people were, as so often, over-optimistic, feeling that they would be safe until all the Duruma had been killed first! The Duruma were less sanguine, and some of them alleged that Dr. Krapf had set up the Maasai to finish them off.

I took my wife to Mombas and returned to collect some of our things. Abe Gunga told me that the Maasai had been dancing and feasting and taunting our people to defend their cattle if they were men, since they considered the Nika only fit to possess grain.

We felt that we could hold out until Krapf returned from escorting a group of agricultural missionaries and mechanics to Ethiopia: he had spent Christmas in the Holy Land, and we looked forward to hearing all about it. He was to be accompanied by a new recruit, Mr. Deimler. Their journey did not start well, as they were quarantined for cholera at the Piraeus and middle eastern ports. The cholera spread as far as Vienna, and may have been connected with the epidemic which reached us a year later. In addition I wondered whether the local unrest would spread so much as to prevent their joining us at Rabai. But things turned out differently. Krapf went back to Stuttgart in July, took a course of medicinal baths and got married again. Deimler went to Bombay to study Arabic for more than a year.

Well, Dr. Krapf had suffered much, and his health might well not be up to the demands of Rabai. It appears that it was not up to the postings offered at Mauritius or Cape Town either. Or perhaps he must be a pioneer or nothing. Let us hope that the ministrations of the good Charlotte were able to bring about some improvement. Krapf's idea was that one or two Basel men might be sent out, which would enable us to take furlough if we considered it necessary. But I had already told the Home Committee that there was no question of opening up work in Kadiaro while intermittent Maasai attacks continued. I had put up argument after argument, recommendation after recommendation in writing and was not getting adequate answers. I felt that if my wife and I were going to be left alone the East African mission was as good as finished, and no-one was taking any steps to protect us. I made up my accounts and in October I booked a passage and we left for Egypt."

"Just for Egypt? Why not for Europe? Would you have got employment in Egypt? How would you subsist there? What did you expect?"

Isaac flinched, remembering that his father had been desolate, certain that the East African mission had come to an end.

"You are piercing me, as we should put it in Kiswahili. I cannot answer you. In any case I am offering you news of the coast, not submitting to an inquisition."

"My dear Mr. Rebmann…"

"Let me finish, good lady, let me finish. At the coast you do not interrupt an old man while he is speaking… If I sound sharp with you, I am being sharp with myself. I really cannot answer you. I was asked to go to Britain to meet the secretaries and Dr. Krapf, but I refused. I knew I had to refuse, without being able to explain.

In any case, Dr. Krapf declared himself not well enough to go to London. Was I supposed to be well enough to chase round the continent after him? Apparently he was sufficiently recovered to volunteer to open a new station on the Upper Nile at Khartoum, but CMS declared they could not afford that. I suppose not, if you imagine the length of communication chain that would require. Yet I was the one said to be cutting myself off and not taking converts with me on local visits. (Contact is made more when they invite *you* than when *you* invite *them.*) What right had Krapf got to report on me when he had been away from the coast for the best part of two years? And was it so important to talk face to face in those days of slow travel, long before Suez was open?

We had already had a bad enough time, with jealousies and rumors trying to divert our attention from one *bagala* to another while ours idled in the harbor, and at one point I barely kept hold of my dear wife when the small boat into which she was stepping was tossed away by the current (or by worse than carelessness, perhaps). I felt like crying with the Psalmist

> rescue me and deliver me from the many waters,
> from the hand of aliens
> whose mouths speak lies.

Costs had risen too, so that we had to draw a bill at Cairo after the one we cashed at Aden, and account for every penny.

I expected counsel from our old friends the Lieders in Cairo, but we found all the missionaries much distressed about the war in the Crimea. They could not stomach England and France being allied with infidel Turkey against Christian Russia. The Egyptians would also have preferred to see Turkey weakened so as to safeguard their own independence under the Ottoman Sultan. Their traditional ally, France, seemed to have let them down.

So our concern with changes at the coast looked parochial compared to the affairs of Europe and the Levant, which has always felt itself a wider world, so that we have marveled more at Genghis Khan's intruding into Europe than at Eastern Europe's entering the vast empire of the Golden Horde.

I also expected — and got — some reactions from London to my having left the station. I may have expected some radical realignment of forces on the East African coast. Perhaps I was wrong, but done is done. I had now completed ten years in East Africa, longer than Krapf had spent in any one place. My report on the snow mountain had been vindicated: medals and testimonials are neither here nor there, but London values them. Our 'Slug Map' had already been published and CMS had my English text to go with it into their *Intelligencer*. The Royal Geographical Society were muttering about their forthcoming expedition. I did not feel ready to be pushed about by armchair theorists who held the purse-strings. I do not feel it now.

'That obstinate old war-horse,' they will tell you, 'that German pietist, that kill-joy, blind leader of the blind!' Well, let them judge. The compliant are not always the survivors. Those who lack joy in the Lord's gifts will not be able to sing His song in a strange land."

"None of us here sits in judgment."

"So what happened in Egypt?"

"A great deal of mail flew about, that is one thing, though we were only there for a few weeks. I did not like the tone of the letters from London—why did you give up hope? Why did you spend so much money? Come, both of you, and explain to us, provided it is by the cheapest means. Or else, come, and leave your wife in comfort in Egypt. Comfort! What did they know of dust and heat and flies, these people? What did they picture when they heard of hotels in the desert to break the weary journey across to Suez? Something like Shepherds or the Hotel d' Orient? These were already set up in Cairo, but far beyond the means of missionaries. Would they be able, like my wife, to recognize the war-horn sounding as raiders approached the coast, or think it is a harmless bugle call, 'come to the cookhouse door, boys,' perhaps? Had they seen a fugitive woman impaled on a Maasai spear, or emaciated children sold into slavery to keep them alive.

So I said that when I announced 'The East African mission has been brought to an end' I meant a mission which, according to their instruction, depended on opening inland stations. Kisulutini remained in my own hand, and to get back there I must observe the sailing season, making use of the northerly monsoon in January. People were expecting us there. We had left some of our goods and undertaken to forward Erhardt's things for him."

"And was Mrs. Rebmann not disappointed to miss a visit to Europe?"

"Disappointed? I don't think so, she had been to visit her sisters less than five years before, she was more at home in Egypt than I was and we made sure she was examined by a proper doctor. She did enquire, diffidently, whether we ought not to make the acquaintance of one another's families, but I sensed a problem there. She was not much of a linguist, you see, and my sisters had no English, they might have expected her to be younger.

My mother had died before our marriage; she was the one who would have most earnestly desired a meeting. Perhaps I could not face Gerlingen without my mother. We still had the hope of visiting my wife's other sister at Port Natal.

No lady, of course, could anticipate with pleasure traveling once in a dirty *bagala*, and then we were shipwrecked into the bargain, but she did not remonstrate with me, and we were thankful to get home at last."

"You crossed the desert once more to Suez? They say we shall be there tomorrow. The mist is refreshing, is it not? I have not seen anything so much like a fog since I left England: it obscures the hillsides, as though one were driving in a carriage in the very early morning."

"The temperature is moderated, that I am aware of. I do not remember such an effect long ago: Suez then was just a jumble of wharves and commercial houses, a step on the way to Aden.

We waited for mail at Aden so long as the season allowed, and were kindly received by Colonel Thornton, much more open to the gospel than when I had met him ten years earlier, but he also was worried about what might transpire if Said Sultan died. Only my wife appeared to be quite serene, unwilted by the heat and interested in everything. I was glad she was able to enjoy society and wear a couple of her new gowns, since so much was spoiled in the shipwreck that followed. It was not really dangerous, as boys' stories would have everyone scrambling ashore on a floating spar, but annoying enough to be beached and much of one's provision waterlogged.

Mr. Alley had arranged the cheap passages for us, he was the agent of a Boston merchant, still ideal picture of the thriving American abroad. He had only been there seven months, but was sufficiently in command of things to promise to take care of our mail and parcels during the rest of his three year tour. He had already made plans for a monthly service to Zanzibar and intended to extend it to Mauritius later. As regards mail, the road to Zanzibar is paved with good intentions, but Mr. Alley's frank and boyish aspect led us to share his enthusiasm.

The passages were cheap indeed, and nasty. From Aden to Zanzibar took us nearly a month, and by that time we were ready to embark on the first filthy *bagala* that would take us to Mombas and that, against the wind, occupied another four days. Heavy rains had spoiled both our cottages and Krapf's—his was so badly damaged that we had to get his boxes carried over to Kisulutini for shelter. Once again we repaired and refurbished, but the Maasai seemed to have vanished, and we had six quiet months—not perhaps sowing much seed but removing some obstacles.

That was the beginning of 1856. In May Dr. Livingstone reached Quilimane. (Livingstone, I suppose, could go where he liked. Did anyone, I wonder, ever ask him for a tally of baptisms or object to the companies he drew his bills on?) That was our big news, but not the news closest home, for the cholera was weeping down the coast. We still find it hard to see plagues as the intervention of almighty God. What had the ordinary Egyptians done to suffer for the hardening of Pharaoh's heart? And yet the unrest of that time was not due only to Maasai raids or apprehension about the fate of Seyyid Sultan. To the Wanika the Seyyid was a faraway being represented by the Governor of Mombas and Governors might come and go without affecting them much. Each inland group was in some way related to a house or *mji* of the Waswahili, so represented on the council, and a kind of stability was maintained.

1856 was expected to be the year of *unyaro* or initiation of young lads among the Nika peoples. They were also preparing for an advance in the grades of elderhood, which occurred after a longer period. I think this is what made some of our neighbors evasive in conversation and reluctant to allow the older youths to attend our school or meetings. It gave a greater solemnity to the festivals of the *muansa* which, as Dr. Krapf had described them, were fairly light-hearted. Any reasonable person might *toboa siri*, give away the secret of the musical instrument that appeared to roar as Dutch Americans feign not to recognize the father of the family in the guise of Santa Claus. Likewise, at some of our German festivals, the domino is not seriously meant to disguise the wearer and it would be naive to pretend that licentious behavior never followed the fun. We did not hold with such goings-on in Gerlingen, but Erhardt came from Bavaria (and smoked a pipe to the disgust of our good doctor) and he could tell you a tale if he chose.

The hunt of the stranger victim, as it is hinted at in *Missionary Travels*, is something very different. I have heard the name *Mung'aro* whispered for it, and it must cause unease not only on account of the murdered man but for the hapless aspirants who are urged on hysterically to the killing. It is absurd, of course, to suppose that they smear themselves with clay so as not to be recognized: there must be some deeper symbolism in it. In Africa one is recognized not by the color of the cheeks but by the set of the ankles, the way of walking, the shoulders and the shape of the fingers. But even if the killer is actually known to the age-mates, they share the guilt and it is the guilt that binds them indissolubly together. This we challenge with individual forgiveness, and their secrecy rather than their order of seniority must ultimately give way.

But that year the cholera was raging: many people died, all were impoverished by want of labor and by the sacrifices required for the dead. The times were not propitious and the *unyaro*, if it occurred at all, did not have first place in people minds.

The first initiation became a scattered celebration by small groups. Among some of the neighboring peoples a woman's honor is ravished at this time, but not her life. If Isaac wishes to tell you more, he may, but I would not ask him to break an oath of silence any more than I would betray any confidence you brought to me as a clergyman. I doubt if he knows about the *Mung'aro*, but would not ask him. If I put such a burden on anyone it would have to be a man of my own age. I never heard again (apart from the Mohammedan sacrifices following the epidemic) if this kind of ritual is murder. These might, I suppose, have arisen from some dark consciousness of a rite omitted.

So we lived quietly at Kisulutini, consoling the bereaved as best we could and giving some counsel on the rules of hygiene."

Ndune's house is dark even in the noon of a brilliant June day. The rains are over and the heat increases, but the steams and gullies are still full and it has taken me nearly two hours to walk from Kisulutini up the ridge to Rabai Mpya, making detours where I cannot wade and pushing my way through the shoulder-high rank grass bordering the path, wary of snakes. Alas, the abundant rain of the ridge has dwindled before reaching our lower ground.

The child who was sent to call me refuses to return: he says he has messages for relations. I see now why, for by one of the smaller streams the body of a young boy lies sprawled under a cloud of flies, nauseous pools of fluid and mucus forming a trail behind him through which the cows, untended now, trample on their way to drink. I retch a little myself and shudder that Emma had offered to come with me to nurse the sick: had to tell her the climb and the swollen waters would be beyond her.

Ndune has not been attending church since his friend Mringe died, though Krapf prevailed upon him to come sometimes to the prayer meeting in the kaya. *Yet some remembered blessing has caused him to send for me in his extremity.*

"Hodi, Hodi, *it is Rebmann here."*

He totters to the door and the stench from inside the house hits me like an uncleaned stable. Ndune used to be an elegant young man, but his legs and feet are smeared with secretions now, his cheeks hollow, his eyes gummed and staring.

"Come in," he says. "Pastor, she is gone."

"You come out, rather. What about the children?"

There is a whimper from inside.

"The baby was still sucking till yesterday, but the mother was so weak, I do not know... The girl died in the night, the boy—I asked Me Shehe to take him away. A child came for him. He was well then. I do not know..."

He is holding on to the mud wall of the house, still beckoning me in. Taking a deep breath, I plunge into the darkness, guided by sound, feel for the baby who is slithering over the mother's body and dump her on the cleared ground in front of the door. The maize and millet patches have been weeded, a hoe lies at the edge of the clearing. A soiled cloth has been laid out to dry. A day or two ago, work was going on here as usual.

The baby is still plump and her eyes are bright. I suppose her to be about four months, and I pray that she has not conveyed any foul matter to her mouth. There is no need to drag out the two bodies: they tell their own tale, and Ndune himself has only an hour or two left. He collapses to the ground near me, his features drawn in a terrible spasm. I fetch water from the big pot in the house—the only medicine for his condition—but it goes straight through him, again and again.

"Ndune, the child looks well but she must feed soon. I will take her to Me Shehe and then come back to see how you are." (Even if he does not die while I am away he cannot protect her from roving beasts and snakes.) "You are very ill yourself, shall we pray to the Lord of Heaven to give you light and understanding and to have mercy on these dear departed ones?"

He inclines his head and I pour out all my petitions for his salvation and the pitiful plight of those who died in ignorance. He whispers 'Amen.' But life is precious.

"I must see to the child now. I will come back soon, Ndune."

Me Shehe has gone to nurse her own married daughter.

Ndune's little son has been sent to his maternal grandmother.

Jindoa's younger daughter cradles the baby, listens to my instruction to wash her in warm water from tip to toe and then look for a wet-nurse. She seems intelligent. Perhaps she will do it if there is not some superstitious custom to prevent it. Jindoa is out arranging burial for those who have no close kin left, I leave new names for him and the description of the boy by the stream. By the time I get back to the house, Ndune is dead. I pull a cow-hide over him and leave him lie.

Abe Mlega's wife gets me water for washing and uji to drink. I cannot stay longer for I must get home before dark: my good wife will be anxious and others will perhaps have summoned me. Along the weary way, I recall what has happened, and mumble a prayer for my own safety and Emma's along with one for Ndune, whose spiritual state I shall now never know.

Perhaps it is the good Lord's arrangement that I should be sleeping in the little parlor. Two days, three days, I examine myself carefully, turning my face away from hers at meals, avoiding the latrine I had built for us. Thank God, I seem to get all right. Among our Christians I conduct two children's funerals, but the course of the disease is so rapid that I am not called to any other death-bed.

"The disease passed us and reached Jomvu: Dr. Christie later made a detailed study of its passage.

In September 1856 Said Sultan took leave of his aged mother and sailed from Muscat in the frigate *Queen Victoria*. He ordered planks to be put aboard so that *anyone* as he put it, who died at sea should be put in a coffin and taken on to Zanzibar. The good Lord alone knows what pains he was already suffering, but he *did* die during the voyage, his body *was* brought to Zanzibar and Hamerton *did* manage affairs in such a way that his expressed wishes were more or less fulfilled.

This was not altogether simple. Said is said to have left 36 children, all of them by secondary wives, who numbered 75 at the time of his death. The only surviving principal wife remained in seclusion most of the time, putting on a gold face mask if a lady were allowed to visit her. She must have been daily conscious of failing in her office.

Thuwain, son of a Georgian mother, expected to succeed his father at least in Oman, where he had always lived: there he did so and then laid claim to the whole empire. But there is evidence that Said wanted to divide the dominion at his death, recognizing how difficult even he, with his outstanding gifts, had found it to keep the two capitals in balance. This was the easier to manage in that he had never taken the spiritual title of Imam, and had accepted nominal parity with an elected Imam in Muscat and a hereditary *Mwenye Mkuu* in Zanzibar. Nor, of course, was he Sultan in any Arabian nights sense: Sultan was his father's name, which he used as any other Arab does. The most appropriate title, if he needed one would be Seyyid or overlord. His ritual duties related to the two major codes of Islamic law and to sanctioning any capital sentence, which he hated to do. But dynasties harden and the sons, not being self-made, need the title of Sultan to define them. For purposes of suppressing the slave trade, the British may have seen an advantage in setting up Zanzibar against Muscat.

Majid, son of an Abyssinian concubine, was acting governor of Zanzibar and its dominions when his father died. Said Sultan had confided this post to an older son, Khalid, at that moving scene on the beach before he sailed away to Muscat, but Khalid died six months later, so frustrating the attempts of his Malabari mother, Shurshit, to advance his claims. It is no use tut-tutting like that to show us how shocked you are, my friend. Do not royal families everywhere marry and flatter one another as they prepare to fight to the death? But Khalid was not a popular personality: he was called 'the Banian' because of his love of money. He was deformed by elephantiasis and hydrocele, and this would not have been acceptable to most Africans, who demand physical perfection of their rulers and assurance of a healthy lineage. Perhaps it was as well that he did not have to assert his right.

Majid was 21 and his epileptic seizures could be more or less concealed; he seemed dull and biddable, but in later years showed more determination and initiative than we had expected. If he had not, he would not have got the better of his younger brother Barghash.

Barghash is, of course, the present sultan, and one must be circumspect. However, no-one will dispute that he was already an attractive figure as a young prince, good-looking, silver-tongued, quick to seize an opportunity as his Busaidi heritage had taught him. And he had one enormous advantage over Majid—he was on the ship with his father and knew what had happened. He had from the morning of 19th October to the evening of the 25th to make his plans.

The *Queen Victoria* and the escort ship *Artemeise* anchored at night five miles offshore. Not till the morning would everyone see that they had no flags flying and therefore something must be seriously amiss. Barghash had himself rowed ashore with the coffin and wanted to bury it immediately beside Khalid's grave in the old fort, but the aged Baluchi guard, Din Mahomed, stood firm and would not admit him. Mrs. Ruete maintains that there was an ominous thunder storm that night: this was not in the account I heard, but every teller highlighted his own version of the drama.

Denied the fort, Barghash could only resort to diplomacy, after hastily burying the body. He approached the El-Harthy, confident that they would like to see some changes of policy, especially about the slave trade. This had been modified under British pressure: Barghash inclined to the French. But everyone had seen Said Sultan entrust his family to Hamerton before he left. Abdalla bin Salim was chosen by the El-Harthy to approach Hamerton before light on Barghash's behalf, and got a very short shrift. The consul refused to go against Said's express wishes, and the coming of daylight showed how right he was: the whole town was weeping and wailing for its loss, and public support was strong for the new sultan, Majid. The aged Suleman bin Hamed El Busaidi was considered the repository of family wisdom, and he gave his voice for Majid.

Barghash did not give up. It would hardly have been thought honorable for him to do so, but he bided his time. Since Said came to power, there had been a change in identity. Few of the Zanzibari Arabs still spoke Arabic unless they were Koranic scholars or legal experts. In fact they were hardly physically distinguishable from the Swahili, though each, of course, knew his own lineage, and the hundred or so old island families set a great value on their traditional privileges. You could compare the situation with that of the Normans in England, who eventually identified themselves as Englishmen and forfeited their estates in Normandy to those kin who chose to remain there, or Prussia—but it would not be tactful to talk about Prussia...

It may sound like the making of nation, this drawing together of Arab and Zanzibari, but for the ruler it had one major drawback—there was no obvious pool of men from whom to levy troops, other than the slaves and the hired Baluchis. In Majid's time there were 2000 Baluchis in Zanzibar (and nearly a quarter of those belonged to Ludha Damji), a smaller garrison at Lamu and less than 200 at Mombas. They were more loyal than you might expect at three dollars a month for a private soldier, but they were five times as many as Said Sultan had needed.

Authority on the coast had been imposed, informal as it was, by at least the threat of Omani garrisons. Coastal garrisons would not constitute the same threat, even had there been an energetic response to recruitment. Said had at one time restricted to the government of Zanzibar the right to sell muskets, powder and ball at the coast. But after defeating Mombas in 1839, he lifted the ban, perhaps because it could not be effectively imposed. For instance soon after I came an English ship left the island carrying guns for Pate. How could he stop that without provoking an international incident? Mrs. Wakefield innocently told me that the ship which brought her to the coast in 1870 discharged 40 tons of gunpowder a couple of miles from Zanzibar Harbor.

Sultan Majid had plenty of cannon in Zanzibar but not enough gunners. He also had four ships carrying more than 50 guns, eight of middle size and about 20 small gunboats. But they cost a lot to maintain and repair in such humid conditions; only one had been built at Zanzibar and that by Indian craftsmen. Thuwain, of course, had his own ships at Muscat, and we were waiting for him to use them."

IX

"We happened to be in Mombas when Said Sultan died, and it was panic stations. I knew there must be urgent news when I saw the skipper of the dhow himself running up the steps to our quarters. From the window I had already seen knots of men gathering in the harbor, and something funny about the flag of the incoming vessel—my eyes were already less sharp than they had been. I ran down to meet the *nahoda*, who handed me the letter from the consul with great ceremony and then proceeded to tell the story of death and accession in high relief, while I had refreshments served to him.

I was there to check over a consignment of domestic goods and some printed materials coming from Bombay. Emma had gone to call on the Governor's ladies in the Fort, but they insisted on returning her escorted by a eunuch in great haste, as they feared unrest in the town. The skipper was anxious to be off to tell the news around: he had put on his most elaborate waistcoat and a jeweled dagger gleamed at his waist. His friends would be vying with one another to entertain him: next day he would come for my answer.

Hamerton begged us to take refuge in Zanzibar, reminding us that we should have been thrown off the coast years before had it not been for the kindness of the dear old Imam. (Said was not Imam, of course, but Hamerton did not lightly stand to be corrected.) In fact, for all that I feared leaving the gospel to the mercy of Mohammedan princes, I had affectionate and respectful memories of Said Sultan. It was his 'passport' given to Dr. Krapf enjoining on all his subjects the duty of welcoming and assisting 'this good man' and his godly message, that had enabled us to start work and travel safely. In spite of the blow-up about Krapf and the French he had continued faithful in his promise to us, and was also faithful in keeping the various treaties which set limits to the slave trade, as far as his ill-defined powers and the reluctance of his subjects permitted. His manner was dignified but he was modest in his person. We used to meet him in a plain Arab robe and colored turban, wearing no jewels. His town audience chamber was resplendent with marble and chandeliers, but his personal palace in the country was almost bare, and his *Mekrani* bodyguard of twelve coastal Arabs positively shabby. He had ordered all his slaves except the plantation slaves to be freed at his death and retain all their property. This act of clemency was not unprecedented: it represented, of course, an accumulation of merit rather than a change of heart. But the inheritors no doubt had their own households adequately supplied: to inherit a plantation without the labor to go with it would have been a dead loss. And no-one would pay wages for the acquired art of shinning up and down a clove tree.

But was the mere existence of a consul protection for us? If the coast was said to be uneasy, what about the island? A jeweled dagger can kill as effectively as a spear, and a charm accompanied by poison be a good deal more effective than one buried with your nail-clippings at the crossing of the ways. Have you ever seen a charm-book from Zanzibar? It has a measure for every contingency.

Mr. Peters, it is said, cut down a devil-tree in his own courtyard, and within six months he was dead, with five others. One can always find an antecedent to fit the event.

We did not see the need to uproot and go. But in January—1857 that was—Trotter, who is Admiral now, and Mr. Layard came to stay (perhaps I have mentioned it) and to inspect the two stations, pressing us to go away. They seemed as worried about my dear wife's health as about our safety, but by that time, gaunt and yellowed as we might be, we could judge one another's condition pretty well. She was good, as it turned out, for another ten years.

So Hamerton was a power in the land—for a time—the more so as the Busaidi seemed to think he knew where Said Sultan had hidden his personal treasures. If he did, he never disclosed the secret, and nephews and concubines hunted for them in vain. He remained bluff, high-colored, hearty, loud-voiced, but the attacks of fever came more and more often and he knew his end was near. He had come to respect Erhardt and was kind to the anti-slavery people like Colonel Trotter. I felt he only tolerated Deimler and myself. He said in so many words that a missionary would be the ruin of the Royal Geographical Society expedition which was being planned during 1856, and he must have known that I was the one invited. The Society had given me freedom of choice in the matter, but at the same time seemed to feel that the expedition would be the ruin of a missionary! I felt myself that there would be some incongruity in my joining such company, so I refused. In any case my dear wife could not remain alone in such uneasy times. Dr. Krapf also refused to go along with Burton. The Mission insisted that the Rev. Samuel Crowther had been greatly used on the Tschadda Expedition, but he, after all, was a man of the Niger country and a powerful inspiration to all who would set the slaves free.

Burton and Speke arrived in Zanzibar on the last day of mourning for the old Sultan, as people now liked to call him. Zanzibar society relies on gossip to keep it occupied, and their presence offered something else to chatter about as well as palace intrigue. They even favored us with a visit later on, and brought letters, perhaps made curious by Trotter's account of our discomforts. They made a great to-do about it, hiring a special vessel and crew all the way from Zanzibar which, I suppose, was flattering. It made me, certainly, compare our modest ideas of equipping an expedition with theirs. Burton boasted that he spent only £30 on stores for his journey inland, but I supposed him to rely mainly on an ample investment of hot air.

They were civil enough, and Mrs. Rebmann was all of a flutter to have had four European guests within a couple of weeks.

There was hunger at the time for lack of rain. We were used to it and able to bring in some rice and fish from Mombas to meet out small needs: the local people do not eat fish. We could also bring enough grain to pay those enquirers who helped us keep the buildings in good trim or gather firewood. We could not relieve the wants of the whole community.

Speke chanced to see a woman offering her little girl for a bag of millet to a trader they brought with them from Mombas. She was a skinny little thing with a big pot belly and vacant eyes, too far gone to be frightened, and the trader backed away: he must have doubted whether she could be reared to work, and the parents might not find their way to buy her back in better times.

I tried to explain that this was not slavery, but Speke's face was ashen, and I felt convicted at not being more deeply moved, but one lives with necessity. We could no more ransom all those children than we could put to school all those who in London climb up chimneys or flatten out the heads of pins in noisome cellars. The mother, herself skin and bones, heavily pregnant, did not, I am sure, doubt that she was making the best possible bargain for her family, and would get the girl back, when times improved, well fed, a virgin and a credit to her. She had no experience to suggest that, with raiders threatening the more distant fields, there might be no improvement.

I judged Speke the more reliable of the two and, as it later turned out, with reason. I would not have let Burton set foot in my house if I had known he would refuse to pay his porters and so endanger future expeditions as well as dragging the name of Britain low. The men were compensated in the end from official funds and the Sultan himself gave money to the sepoys, but much harm had been done to good relations. That Burton should later make fun of me, his host, was neither here nor there: I was not the only one to suffer from his famous wit. We know that kind of English gentleman.

Deimler had gone back to the island with Trotter, if only to prove that not every missionary spurned well-meant advice. It had already been decided that India would be a better prospect for him, so although I had been glad of his company for a few months, there was no point in his delaying further. He went to Germany for six months and got married there before the Society arranged for him to go to Nasik, where his work among the freed slaves was very valuable to us. We ourselves took our time, as Mrs. Rebmann was meticulous about the packing of our household goods, but in due course we proceeded to Mombas and from there to Zanzibar.

The warnings turned out to be timely. This time 800 Kwavi swept through Rabai to the coast and many of our friends were killed. The raiders were eventually repulsed by the Galla, though it was their last effort. It was not the last effort of the Kwavi. The great raid on Vanga was still to come.

Even the *kayas*, thought to be impregnable, were burned. New laughed in later years at the devices of the Taveta to mislead and prohibit entry—trees half cut and entrances that led nowhere. But these alone proved effective. The other *kayas* had, before his time, become too open, the forests too thin.

> You who live in the clefts of the rock,
> who hold to the height of the hill,
> though you make your nest as high as the eagle's,
> I will bring you down from there,
> says the Lord.

Colonel Hamerton had done his part. I conducted his funeral in the middle of 1857, when Majid was secure in his suzerainty. (I would not say on his throne, for the Omanis are merchant princes ruling by consensus, and each must remember that he is *primus inter pares*.) We buried the consul on one of the little islands in the harbor set aside for foreign graves. Sultan Majid attended and so did many of the overseas officials and their families: how different from the funeral of Mrs. Krapf, where the Governor of Mombas and the Kadhi, out of the kindness of their hearts, accompanied Krapf over to the mainland, since he was himself prostrated with fever almost to the point of death. Well, it pleased Hamerton to be among the notables.

Sultan Majid himself sealed up the consul's rooms and boxes till they could be officially handed over. This was the time that Speke and Burton were on their way to the interior and perhaps the whole world was changing, the innovators taking over from the diplomats. It was not my business except insofar as it affected the preaching of the gospel. Ludha Damji, who represented Jairam Sewji in Zanzibar and continued to be the right hand man of Sultan Barghash, became caretaker of the British Agency after Hamerton's death. It was a whole year before Rigby arrived to take over the consulate, and we spent that year in Zanzibar. But commerce flourished and Majid's rule did not collapse.

In Zanzibar it is customary, when you start to erect a building, to put it up on a few feet and then let it stand for some months to see what happens. If it does not fall down, you add another level. It appeared that the British agency was on a firm foundation, morally speaking, though the next consul was going to have to do something about the physical building.

Naturally anyone with a grievance was likely to side with Barghash or Thuwain against Majid. Among the young brothers, Khaleefah, Meneem, Sheneer, Nasir, Abder-Rabb and Bedran sent to Muscat a pitiful and not at all convincing account of Majid's ill-treatment of them. But Majid was not shaken.

During this uneasy time, I remember, an American ship brought me a whole pile of *Missionary Intelligencers*—years of them: I don't understand how so much mail had piled up. The promises of regular mail services never came to anything and the Home Committee never seemed to understand how long their communications took to reach us or how much our traveling was determined by the monsoon, even in the days of steam. You see how comfortable our passage is at present, but I have heard of steam liners, even, sustaining injury and damage to passengers by persisting injudiciously against the wind."

"Ah yes. One lady told me that she had been lashed on deck in order to get a little air while proceeding against the wind. I took good care to enquire about the seasons before booking this passage, let me tell you."

"You are wise, for I have seen ships' paint corroded by the spray hurled high, and white salt encrusting their funnels.

Well, the magazines were of great interest to my dear wife, as a change from visits to the decorative Arab and Banian ladies, and a relaxation for me in the intervals of my language studies. The quietness of Zanzibar was ideal for pursuing my writing—not, you will understand, a literal quietness in that close-built and often smelly mercantile town. Stinkibar, Livingstone called it, and I could never understand how one of those sailors—Devereux I think it was: they all write books nowadays if they spend three months outside home waters—could say the air was scented with clove and cinnamon. A smell of mud is the kindest thing other people call it, even from the sea. In the streets, those square pieces of shark meat they love to sell add to the more local effluvia. Then, as there are no minarets, a trumpet is sounded from each mosque to mark every one of the five daily calls to prayer: later Sultan Majid brought a brass band from Bombay, but even from those 'quiet' times shrill instruments seem to echo in my ear.

My wife was charmed to be able to get ready-baked bread and

even butter from French Charlie's: his den was dark and always crowded with ship chandlers, but it was the nearest thing to a grocer's shop we had seen since Cairo. 'French' he must have picked up as a compliment to his catering powers—it was rumored that his father was Portuguese and his mother black—but, if so, it was well deserved. Zanzibar was a pleasanter place thanks to Charlie.

Then we would walk to the eastern face of the old fort where real salt from Arabia was spread for sale at the foot of the walls, or out into the country for mangoes and oranges, passing the files of women singing as, day in, day out, they carried fresh water from the sweeter springs outside the town.

For myself, I was relieved of the constant physical demands of the mission station. Probably my father and my brother, practicing farmers, would have taken this in their stride. My training had been too compartmental—how to make a box but not how to equip a caravan, how to teach a class, not how to organize a school. Well, we live and learn.

The Wanika, it seemed, had reverted to their way of life in the fortified *kayas*. The open plantations no longer afforded them sufficient protection and (God forgive me) I was afraid of what I should find on my return to Kisulutini. So I took comfort from my selfish interests. Captain Gordon of the *Hermes* presented me with a copy of *The Languages of Mozambique* by Dr. Bleek, which contained a vocabulary partly derived from Mr. Koelle's *Polyglot Africana*. How near that made me feel to fellow-missionaries across the continent. What Dr. Bleek calls Maranu turned out to be identical with my Kiniassa. I had brought Salamini over with me to help compile the vocabulary, and Abe Gunga to help with the Nika translation work.

Sir George Grey, the Governor of the Cape, wanted me to go down there, bringing with me whatever coastal manuscripts could be found. I never went, though Admiral Trotter backed the idea and CMS eventually granted permission. They thought I might look at Mauritius, as though this example could inspire me to produce ordination candidates out of thin air—I was still looking for baptism candidates myself: with the Home Committee it was always hurry, hurry, hurry. A few years in East Africa might do them good. Surely this must be: the prophet says

And some of them also will I take for priests
and for Levites.

But the time was not ripe. However, the proposal did me a favor because in seeking the manuscripts I found a new friend. This was an
Arab to whom I was introduced by Dr. Frost, the excellent Eurasian
apothecary, just before he retired to Bombay.

Abe Gunga was insisting that he must go back to Rabai for
some months to look after his affairs: I could not force him to stay,
but was privately concerned for his safety. The close fellowship between us excited remark from some people who did not directly
take an interest in the mission. I had never been able to mention his
name, even in Hamerton's presence, such is the burden of official-
dom, but the American consul of the time, Captain Mansfield, was
always interested to hear of our progress.

So was my new friend, Sheikh Muhuiddin, who possessed an
Arabic bible given to him by Mr. Waters but had not at that time
read it, being satisfied of the truth and adequacy of his Mohammedan faith. He is a rich and influential man, the son of Sheikh Al-
Katani, and has reason enough to maintain that his scrupulous observance of the injunctions of the Holy Koran has been rewarded. It
was only when I was able to demonstrate that I, too, had studied his
scriptures and could quote them verse by verse, translating from
my own German copy into Kiswahili, that he was challenged to apply himself likewise to the study of the Holy Bible.

Many nights we sat up late together discussing religious questions and recounting our own experiences of God's favor. When he
came to know how long I had been in East Africa, and how much
language work I had done, he told me in the most moving terms
that if any person had done as much to propagate his own faith he
would hide him in the apple of his eye, give him all he possessed
and become his slave. I could only beseech him rather to pay my
toil and study by considering for himself the claims of our scriptures. I also expressed a desire to study Arabic with him, for the
scripture portions which should have helped me frame my translation into the coast languages were far from accurate. Better knowledge of Arabic would assist me in the understanding of Kiswahili.
A few months later the sheikh invited me to visit Arabia with him

to pursue this study, but I still felt I must not leave the coast without express permission of the Society, and I feared for the security of my wife.

I still needed Abe Gunga beside me, and therefore sent a messenger to request him to return to Zanzibar as soon as he could. This was our good friend Mohmess, who had served 20 years before as a sepoy in the Bengal army. He was deeply impressed when he arrived at Rabai on a Sunday and found my faithful friend keeping the Sabbath with three other men, reading and speaking to them.

Abe Gunga arrived at our rooms in Zanzibar at Christmas Day and, as my wife said, we could have looked for no better Christmas present. He brought with him one of the prospective converts, a maker of charms, who had been of service to Abe Gunga's family when he was considered mad. We showed him the book in which his friend had found a better medicine, and he readily agreed that his patient was cured and stood in no more need of charms. I hope he has stood by his resolution not to make any more. Me Shahani, they told me, also had confidence in her husband's recovery and was making another attempt to pray.

The people, he said, wanted me to go back. They were tired of being forced to carry burdens for the Governor's soldiers who had, in addition, relieved them of any cattle the Maasai had not taken. They had come to appreciate our fair dealings with them. (Indeed, over the next year or two many artisans came to me seeking work, so that they might excuse themselves from unprofitable labor for the officials.) But I told them, 'Rebmann has piped to you but you have not danced, he has mourned to you and you have not wept.' This is a verse they easily remember because of their own proverb, 'If a tune is piped at Zanzibar people dance to it at the lakes.'

Naturally Abe Gunga enjoyed the comforts of the island and the esteem in which he was held; few of his inland countrymen walked there as free citizens. I had come to feel that G-O-N-J-A would be a more accurate presentation of his name, but he found this confusing so I did not press it. He was a tower of strength in such evangelistic contacts as we had, explaining to Mohammedan gossips who wanted to know what we were about that the missionary had come a long way for the purpose of teaching them the book but they had not bothered to receive his instruction.

I was tempted to wonder whether Brother Krapf had been right in deciding to leave the island for the mainland, but of course our grand strategy of the chain of missions demanded it. In fact the island was opened to the UMCA when they fell back from the rigors of the Shire country. This also had advantages for us as our own Bishop, in Mauritius, never visited us for purposes of confirmation or ordination, as the need later arose. I was allowed to put some of my people under instruction with Bishop Tozer of the high church UMCA, though not to involve him in ordinations or consecrating buildings. This was not a matter of prejudice but of the separate jurisdiction of our two societies and our two dioceses.

I was glad enough to lend some of my vernacular material to a Roman Catholic priest—Catholic work was just beginning in the area—and to act as an interpreter for some Arabs with the American consul. But we were marking time. The months went by without our hearing of a new consular appointment or how Speke and Burton were getting on. However, a year after Hamerton's death, Captain Rigby turned up to replace him, having been delayed by a serious accident in Bombay which continued to cause him intermittent pain. He proved to be an affable person, long interested in East Africa and acquainted with the Somali and Amharic languages.

Possibly he was just in time, for Majid had in fact, under the guise of a prospective cruise, taken refuge on one of his ships in the harbor, and might (though no-one said as much) have gone into exile. There was already a knot of disaffected Swahili notables in Goa, and no doubt he could have found a place of safety in some quarter of the Indian Ocean.

In fact the British owed him some consideration, for he had been hard pressed to renounce his father's restrictions on the slave trade, and always refused. His secretary, Ahmed bin Naaman, was unpopular and bore the nickname *Wajhaya*, Two-faced, but I do not know who else could have better kept conflicting elements in play.

The consul graciously invited me and my wife to his first official dinner party, and sent me supplies of beer and port when I went down with chickenpox, an embarrassing malady for a grown and bearded man. He saw no difficulty in continuing the East African mission, and by the end of the year had given an official letter to the Governor of Mombas, with a formal seal, which made me feel (rightly or wrongly I now wonder) that East Africa had been opened to us by Christian hands. He had been waiting for a convenient time, he told me, to consult with the Sultan, who was in mourning for the death of two dear brothers from smallpox. They were Jamshid and Hamdan. I wondered myself which of the pestilential little brothers it would grieve him to lose, but my wife rebuked me for lack of charity and so I prayed for the salvation of those who remained. (Of course, the only one of the family who later professed a change was the Princess Salme, who would become Emily Ruete when in a vastly interesting condition.

She was by that time already under a cloud because of her intrigues in favor of Barghash. She had to seek the aid of a British naval vessel to snatch her away to Aden while she was supposed to be ritually bathing at the beach, and there she was married to her lover just in time to make an honest woman of her, as you might say. This bit of romanticism on the part of the navy might well have caused a diplomatic incident.

Nothing could be less conducive to respect for baptism among reputable Arabs and, being by that time cut off from the moderating influence of my late beloved wife, I began to work out new rules for baptism more in conformity with apostolic practice.)

I now felt ready, indeed eager, to face the privations of Rabai after an absence of nearly two years, leaving my wife for the time being in Zanzibar.

For all the good welcome I received after my long absence — and at Rabai Mpya, now reduced to a couple of hundred people, even the drinkers stood up from their pots to greet me — it was grievous to find many people had died as a result of Maasai raids.

Abe Gunga said it was a cleansing of the nation for letting the old order go to pieces, as people prided themselves on their herds of cattle, ceasing to pay attention to their neighbors and despising those who were poor. Wakamba and Digo women were even offering themselves to Rabai men in return for palm wine.

He persuaded me that the judgment might bring respect for the word of the Lord, which previously the people had valued less than their cattle and their toddy. There is a lot of the prophet Amos about Abe Gunga.

Certainly, as in the days of Noah, those who were not depraved were foolish, claiming that the Wakamba would be attacked before or that those who had no cattle need fear nothing. The Maasai threatened them before attacking, and some men guarding their plantations were astonished to find that the fires they had seen were kindled by Maasai, not Wakamba. Among the dead known to us were Abe Mabaya the Saha, who had been Master of ceremonies of the heathen rites, an impressive person for whom he had a sneaking regard, and one of his brothers, the large family of Zumbe (who himself died while we were in Egypt), Abe Mamkale, an old man who was speared while leaving the *kaya*, and some of his womenfolk who were trying to run away. But of course there were many other casualties, both Kamba and Nika, men, women and children.

And yet when others were killed Mam Kemba was spared—he who had the audacity, before we took refuge in Zanzibar, to demand of me a black sheep to be led ritually along the western boundaries and be slaughtered as a defensive charm! Perhaps he needed a longer time for repentance. I blame myself now that I did not visit Mam Kemba more often, but the palm-wine had such a hold on him that one gave up expecting him to be able to hear a word.

Abe Gunga himself had been marvelously preserved, hiding in the morning in his banana grove and the same evening, vulnerable to any eye that would look up, at the top of one of his own coconut palms. His own good house had burned down—not in the raid, as it happened, but ironically when the fields were being cleared by fire for next planting—and he was living in a grass hut, but he laughed and laughed to see me coming, and straight away strode off to the new *kaya* of Kijembeni, where he also had a house, to borrow a pot for the sailors to cook in. They were not the best of sailors, for, after the Governor had tried to delay me by offering a quite unnecessary escort of soldiers, the Customs Master came up with a boat, but the crew could not manage it. I was more eager to be off than to observe the niceties of protocol, so showed them myself how to navigate up the creek. Having experienced the Lord's power in laying to rest my worries over the privations I might meet at a long-abandoned station, I was now excited to be home again and receiving a hearty greeting from each Nika person I met. One even offered me palm-wine after a respectful salute: he turned out to be Abe Zuia, one of the three who had been reading with Abe Gunga when the ex-sepoy found them.

It was a happy time for me, for a while Abe Gunga's wife (Me Shahani, that is, not Isaac's mother, who is Me Gunga) seemed to be in her right mind, asserting that she had thrown off the badges of the nine evil spirits. Still, it was better when, after his baptism, he became firm enough to send her away and call back instead Me Gunga who had left him when he was raving.

More than one wife, you ask? Well, it is allowed in their custom, and a person cannot be unmarried from it, once it is done, however chastely he may live in accordance with the book. Not many, of course, can afford more than one at a time, but there are casual patterns of rejection and return. If a man had offered a length of red cloth to appease the spirits, he must still pay for it, must he not, even if while it is still being woven the Lord has shown him a better way of seeking peace.

Jindoa had quite changed his attitude: 'If the *mzungu* was a man who allowed people to fall on their knees before him, we would gladly do so.' He pointed out the people who were offering to be prepared for baptism, though he was not himself among them: 'These you have got already by the covering of their heads. Others are to enter the book.' I do not know what shred of scripture had given them the Jewish idea that men should pray with their heads covered. Perhaps our care to keep our hats on outdoors because of the strong sun had impressed them as a kind of ritual: one has to be constantly alert to the devil's eagerness to mix up the essential and the arbitrary.

One of the six 'probables' was Dena, grown in grace since I had had to rebuke him for adultery. Another was Mua Mwamba, named for 'rock' just like Peter, who died suddenly before he could be baptized. I went to his house with medicine and found him already dead with his head on his wife's lap. I did not have all that long acquaintance with him, yet he was faithful to death, even adjuring his wife to go about her agricultural duties as usual and not permit heathen ceremonies over the grave. She kept her part in this, an astonishing thing for an uninstructed woman in her deep distress, but told us she could not assert authority over her husband's kin. Of course not, but the dancers and instrumentalists dispersed without argument when they saw me coming with cloth for the burial, and after that they started to call me *Mkulufundi*, teacher.

You see the people ordinarily stay indoors for some time after the death, which one respects, but when it is time to move towards the grave for burial they perform a dance called *Wira,* and before the grave is filled in they sprinkle sacrificial blood on it and place in the hand of the deceased a piece of skin from the head of the slaughtered animal. Then they put up a carved wooden headpost, but Brother Krapf used to be adamant that this was not an idol, only a memorial to the deceased, so we never objected to this part of the ceremony. Mwamba's wife did not attempt to move the body near the *kaya.*

I did not pay much attention to mission housing or property on this visit, as I was sure of coming back soon. I felt a new confidence in our mission after that blessed welcome and signs of fruit. So I returned to Zanzibar to reassure my wife and catch up on my correspondence, though anxious over news just received from Delhi about the tail end of the mutiny and from Jiddah where there had been a massacre of Christians.

I now wrote to London that we should have more missionary support and that there was urgent need of a medical man. If only one could be sent to learn the language before myself made the visit to Europe that they had been clamoring for, that would prevent another gap in the occupancy of the station. We were perhaps ready to receive some of the Bombay Africans too. A doctor would have advised me to leave at once, but the manuscripts had still to be prepared for publication. Cholera and smallpox were menacing us and extreme fatigue may render one susceptible. I had advised my wife to stay within doors as much as possible and avoid too much exertion.

A visit from the *Candace* people had made me apprehensive that we might again fall into dispute with the authorities, but there were no repercussions. Two missionaries remained out of the original party: one had died and the two mechanics were returning to Natal. I advised them to stay in the Roman Catholic house in Zanzibar and involved myself no further. All the same, I was glad to hear their news of Mr. and Mrs. Moffat at Kuruman, whom they had told about their previous visit to us. So closely is Africa drawing together in the light of the gospel.

I was pleased, too, to receive a courteous visit from Albrecht

Roscher with regard to the planning of his expedition—no mission involvement there. He went to join Burton and Speke near Bagamoyo, from where they sent a complimentary message about my map.

The first screw steamer to visit Zanzibar, HMS *Lynx*, called near the end of 1858 and took the Sultan and a hundred other notables on a day's cruise to mark the event. Majid, not to be outdone, had the ships of his fleet, dressed overall; fire a royal salute on Christmas Day, and next day paid a state visit to the British consul. This recognition of a Christian festival impressed me greatly, though of course it had diplomatic rather than religious overtones. It was always the Queen's birthday which the Sultans celebrated—once with a bonfire of a pirate dhow but generally with a feast, servants staggering to the consulate with a whole roasted sheep, accompanied by piles of pilau and pyramids of fruit.

But the fleet looked impressive—I had gone over from the mainland to spend Christmas with Mrs. Rebmann—Thuwain was still threatening Majid's ascendancy and relying on French support. By this time Burton and Speke were on their way to Zanzibar and Roscher had set out on his own. He was only 22: we ought to have found a way to stop him. He reached Lake Nyasa but only two brothers remained in his service. One was murdered with him near Musewa in 1860. The other, wounded by an arrow in the hand, escaped and made a report. The Sultan was shocked, and promptly had the murderers arrested and executed before witnesses, Captain Grant being one: he was preparing to set off with Captain Speke for Tabora.

Although my eyes were on the mainland and my Nika friends, a lot was happening in the great world too, and echoing in Zanzibar. America was starting towards civil war, ideas on human origins were disturbing the churches, new processes on metallurgy were coming to light in England, and a new concept about history and society in the states that made up Germany.

In 1859 loyal Arabs of the coastlands and islands flocked into Zanzibar to express their support for Majid. The days were filled with processions bearing flags and loaded muskets, shouting and playing on shrill instruments. There was cholera in the town. No wonder it appeared on the coast the following year.

Strict orders were given that no Arab *bagala* must enter Mombas harbor. Rigby had requested a British ship from the Cape, but instead it was HMS *Punjaub* from Bombay, under Captain Fullerton, which turned back Thuwain's fleet. We heard the news from an American merchant sailing out of Muscat: this was a relief to foreign residents as there was plenty of veiled Arab opposition in Zanzibar, and Indian sepoys, fleeing from the consequences of the Mutiny, could be up for hire. But the Northern Arabs were ready to withdraw in any case, seeing how firmly Majid's power was consolidated further south, and many of them were already negotiating the difficult maneuvers, tacking and laying off, needed to sail north against the monsoon. Rigby reasoned with the French, and they refrained from stirring things up any further.

A cousin of Majid, Ahmed bin Salim, bribed an Albanian *Jemadar* to murder him, but without success. There were skirmishes in the streets, with bands of armed slaves coming to parade in the town at night."

I am walking home from Sheikh Muhuiddin's house where we have been celebrating Maulid, *the prophet's birthday, which falls on 12 June. Ordinarily this would be the occasion of great festivals of song and dance which may be compared to oratorio or opera in Europe, and as many as 1800 men and women have been known to take part, while thousands gather to watch the spectacle. But this year, because of the political unrest, no public entertainments have been arranged.*

The Sheikh is ordinarily abstemious: we may sup together on flat bread with some dates or cheese washed down with milk and the inevitable thick, black coffee. But today he has entertained a group of scholars among whom I have the honor to be included. The great round tray is heaped with rice cooked in coconut milk (the coconuts specially imported from the mainland) and surrounded by the glittering dishes of meat, chicken, chutney, sauces, nuts and delicate curries. (Vegetables are not commonly to be had on the island, though fruits abound.) There is sherbet water and sweetmeats follow with the coffee.

The talk is gracious, witty and circumspect. I can divine from it what may be going on in the palace but refrain from asking questions. This is, after all, a religious holiday, not a political event. I am therefore surprised when my host insists on sending me home with an armed escort. Groups of splendidly attired young men lounge about the streets, and some withdraw to the shadows as we pass. A few rattle their weapons or shout questions about who I am. This is entirely unfamiliar to me, amid the flares of torches and chanting from a hidden doorway what has for so long become homely is suddenly menacing, as foreign as Prussia or the Indies.

I recollect that my dear wife has recounted to me the scene of a play she has attended (how extra-ordinarily lax the English church is in respect of such frivolities) where bands of retainers strut and threaten one another in some Italian city. Here there is the same theatrical improbability.

Emma may be anxious for me, though she is safe enough, for three respectable families have apartments in the same house. Her visits, I fear, are less exciting than mine. She must always climb up twisting wooden stairs to the ladies' quarters off a gallery round the inner courtyard, with no sight of the busy street. Their etiquette demands that she shall accept three cups of syrupy coffee, perhaps with some sugared delicacy besides, and make conversation, limited by her knowledge of the Swahili tongue. The children have to be admired, many of them sickly through close confinement and adorned, for some reason, with red, yellow and white patches of their cheeks.

"Matters grew more extreme as the weeks passed. Barghash had been promised safety so long as he left the island, but he kept delaying departure and in October he barricaded himself in his country house (it had been Khalid's and was named Marseilles to stress his allegiance to the French) and called a rebellion.

The call did not get much response, though a number of people sailed over to the mainland to be safely out of the way, and some proposed emigrating to Muscat. One British Indian was killed and one wounded, so Rigby was wondering what he could do if the other 5000 claimed his protection. Country houses were burned and clove plantations destroyed. Business came to a halt in the town: it looked bad for the Indians but in fact the money-lenders' stranglehold over the estates was strengthened.

Majid set up headquarters in his own country house, but it took him nine days to make up his mind to ask the British navy to attack his brother: when they did so, Marseilles was empty: Barghash had escaped into the town. Artlessly, he took refuge in his own house, which was soon surrounded. The classic motions followed. Rigby in person rapped on the door and gave a time limit to surrender. Barghash emerged in tears a few minutes before the time expired, gave up his sword and was marched to the palace by British guards.

Leniently enough, he was sent into exile in Bombay on board HMS *Assaye*.

I seemed to be the only white man not surprised at the devious-ness of the political currents, and was relieved to hear a few months later that the Sultan had put the disaffected El Harthy in irons.

When I returned to Mombas, rejoicing in the first rays of the morning sun as though they welcomed me, instead of grumbling, as I had often done before, at the discomforts of the voyage, it was to find that our Mombas house had been disfigured by the Arab soldiers and it took me a month to put it to rights. I had no immedi-ate plans for baptisms, since we still felt the need of a chapel and community buildings, but it seemed to me that Christian families were beginning to move mountains in their witness.

They had to: for this is when I first heard the horrible news of human sacrifices. Hoping to combat the cholera, the Moham-medans — but the believers in name only, for their scriptures could never allow such a vile superstition — had offered living beings to some dark primeval god in their mind, drowning the victims in the sea or burying them alive. Some said that the principal men had been involved in these practices, but the Kadhi of Mombas, whose judgment I had learned to trust, said it was only one of them and he deservedly died soon afterwards.

In June of 1860 I brought my dear wife back to Kisulutini for a short visit, and we resumed our household there in October. We were delighted when people brought her a fowl. They had asked for no presents, though still distressed by their losses in the Maasai raids and the reduced labor available for planting.

The house at Kisulutini, which had come through the fighting in good shape, had again been damaged, though not destroyed, by the heavy rain of that year. Since the Lord kept the Israelites a long time making bricks in North Africa, I could not repine at hav-ing to perform similar labor a little further south. However, I was able to get workmen from Mombas to repair the broken roof of our half of the building while I spent some time in the town revising my translation of *St. Luke* with the Kadhi's help. The other cottage, which Erhardt and then Deimler had occupied, was quite broken down, and for this reason I suggested to the Home Committee that we could only, at present, accommodate an unmarried missionary.

I had also built a little room to be used as a chapel instead of having our fellowship meeting in the palm grove. Abe Gunga and Isaac had been baptized at Pentecost, and the following Easter we welcomed Joseph Dena, David Mua Zuia, Jonathan Lugo and Yohannes Zuia. This last was an earnest young man, and soon after his baptism, asked whether he would be allowed to go to a traditional wedding. I said he could go provided he did not drink too much: it would be absurd to enjoin total abstinence when nature provides wine in such abundance. I had another problem, though, with Johannes. His own children were not believers, and he failed to stop his eldest son putting charms on a mango tree. We had to burn it down, of course, but Isaac, here, and one of Johannes' other sons retrieved some of the fruit.

Abe Mlega also brought me joy, though he was not baptized until later. He was a person of some dignity, an elder like Abe Marunga, his friend and mine, Abe Mlega requested me to cut off charms which signified his membership: I never asked him to do that, but for his own peace of mind he wanted to show his change of allegiance. I felt it was a bit hard that he then had to pay a large fine to the elders for disassociating himself, but he did so cheerfully.

Then Abe Ngowa, our old servant, kept turning up, so in the end I baptized him after stringent examination, by the name of Mua Ringa, with his three children, and made him caretaker of our house in Mombas. With such a vivid personality it is hard to keep the new name in mind, but my wife always managed it.

A time came when Abe Ngowa quarreled so violently with his wife that he cut her head open. She had been a slave, and he thought she was not good enough for him, and accused her of being unfaithful. Then it was all remorse and agitation, so he sent for me and we managed to get a doctor with the help of a young Indian merchant who was a friend of mine."

After lunch in Mombas. All the shops will be closed. Only a few vendors in the shade of verandahs will be offering chunks of pineapple or sherbet water. Even the coffee sellers have retreated from the sun. We have pulled the curtains of our upstairs rooms, but the bright sunlight penetrates. Emma is lying down with her shoes off reading some back issues of Mr. Dickens' Household Words *which her sister sends her in great bundles from time to time. I am dozing heavily, having spent the morning haggling over domestic stores and the purchase of iron sheets and nails for house repair. In the evening I have a translation session with the Kadhi. Tomorrow, if the stores are ready, we should be on our way home to Kisulutini.*

A great commotion from a distance—shouts of rage, screams, blows—perturbs the room. Emma is on her feet in an instant, shoes on, scarf over her head, as a child is heard running the upstairs—'Teacher, come! Pastor, come! Father says come.' Emma is on her way before I have pulled myself together.

I follow barefoot, my shirt unbuttoned. The child is Ngowa, the first-born after whom the parents were named and we follow him the short distance to their quarters.

Me Ngowa lies in the courtyard, bleeding from the head, shoulder and leg. Abe Ngowa is weeping, not touching her, the great truncheon with which he has been laying about him lies at his feet. The younger children are wailing.

"Ngowa, what happened?"

Emma is wiping the blood with her scarf, dipping water from the water pot she has found in the little room, making soothing noises.

"Mother had been out since early morning. Father sent me to look for her. When he saw us coming, he started to beat her."

"Ah, sinful man that I am. I have killed my wife."

"Johannes, we must move her into the shade. Or—no, we will rig up a shade over her. Ngowa, bring me the chair from our house, the tall one."

A chair is brought and a sheet from our washing line rigged up on a rope. Emma runs for scissors, cotton cloth for bandages.

"Teacher, get a doctor—I will do anything, pay anything—my jealous temper—I thought myself too good—save her, save her."

Doctor? I have heard that among the Banians there is a person with some medical knowledge. He has come to stay with one of the merchants, perhaps raising money for further studies.

"Will you be all right, my dear, if I go to look for help?"

"Of course, Johannes, I will stay with her. Only get your shoes—the sandy soil will burn your feet at this hour. Ngowa get the other children to be quiet, please: they are disturbing your mother. Mua Ringa, come and tell her you are sorry. She may not look as though she hears you, but she will know. Then bring any cloths you have—good—and we will put them under her head—so."

Upstairs for shoes and, yes, money may be needed, down headlong to the shopping street—almost deserted—to Vekaria's store. I batter on the wooden door—"Hodi, hodi". A string of leaves is draped above it—they have just arranged his brother's marriage in Bombay. "Hodi, hodi."

Tulsidas appears on the balcony above, sleepy-eyed, his dhoti disarranged. "What is it? Does Mombas not sleep today? You, Rebmann? You want your stores in such a hurry, old friend. I thought it was murder or thieves."

We speak Kiswahili but he uses the high tone of Gujerat. "My friend, I disturb you, but we need a doctor. Do you know where I can get help?"

He is unbolting the door, and I am thankful to take shelter inside where it is dark if not exactly cool. My eyes are throbbing with the afternoon sun. I sneeze full of the smell of curry powder, dusty grams, husked coconut for export, pale brown sugar in sacks. The cloves and cinnamon sticks are in glass jars. There is still a faint scent of the morning jose stick. A crude printed picture of Shiva hangs unframed on the wall.

"I hope your good lady…"

"She is well, Tulsidas. It is my servant's wife who has been injured and is bleeding."

"Come, come—Raju, see to the door for me."

He slips on sandals and pushes the lank, black hair out of his eyes. Outside a clothing store at the far end of the street he raises his voice and the conversation continues in a language unknown to me. But within a few minutes a lean man in shirt and trousers, carrying a bag, joins us on the pavement.

"I pray it may be in time," says my friend, leaving us. The doctor speaks English. He learned it at the Robert Money missionary school in Bombay, but I do not ask about his medical background. He staunches the bleeding, stitches the head wound, which he declares not to touch any vital parts, and gives instructions for nursing the patient. Then he bows and withdraws.

Emma is determined to stay near Me Ngowa. Abe Ngowa is hysterical, demanding counsel and reassurance. So we stay another week. I hand a discreet thank you for the doctor through Tulisdas's shop. Since Me Ngowa has been a slave, no-one brings a complaint on her behalf. At the end of the week she is able to walk and instruct the children in their household duties.

"The wife got treatment, but did not rest long enough, being perhaps eager to vindicate herself by hard work, and so died. I thought that Mua Ringa's haste to get assistance showed that he had not intended murder, but he himself felt the need to run away to the north and hide. He took copies of the gospel translations with him and, getting some Kiriama companions to join him in the bush, instructed them in the scriptures. I hear that they have now increased in number and that Chancellor and George David are putting them up for baptism. Well, I have no more part in it except for prayer, but Abe Ngowa was a memorable man. There was a Kiriama man who also approached us because he was accused of holding up the rain: maybe he also joined the group and learned something of the water of life.

Then there was Abe Sidi—chief, he liked to call himself—I hear that he too is about to get himself baptized, with a wife. He always had a tremendous presence, I will say that for him, and would set young missionary all of a flutter. They did not see the implications of his gathering former slaves around him—who is to say they were legally freed?"

"Come, sir," interjected one of the passengers, "I may go and live where I like and follow a leader. In this year of grace, why may not they?"

"Well, sir, I expect you can," answered Rebmann good-humouredly. "I cannot see you, so I have no comment. But if you happened to be a member of Her Majesty's army or Her Majesty's navy, or an inmate of one of Her Majesty's prisons, or a bound apprentice, you would not be so under the present law. Quite a lot of laws need changing...

Sultan Majid was doing well, and trying hard to meet us on the slave issue. Like his father and brother, he staked much on foreign friendship, enforcing measures which were bound to be unpopular. Said Sultan had burned down a village near Kilwa when the people were found guilty of slave raiding. Majid took on the even bigger problems of regulating the annual visits of the northern Arabs. This may also have served to curb the expansion of private interests, but inevitably it led to further clashes with his brother Thuwain.

Their dispute dragged on over the years because of the annual subsidy payable by Zanzibar to Oman. The conflicting claims for power after Said Sultan's death had been submitted to Lord Canning as arbitrator, and he sent Brigadier Coghlan, the British political Resident at Aden, to Zanzibar to make a report. This was late in 1860 and the decision was that Majid must go on paying, not to indicate guilt or subordination but simply as a makeweight for the smaller revenue of Muscat. Well, nobody likes being made to pay, and there is no distinction between the private and the public purse. The decision was announced a few weeks after the French put up their big barrack in Zanzibar town which kept us all guessing and added credibility to any candidate they might favor. People said it might be a hospital or a convent: there were rumors of incursions on to the coast. Of necessity, Majid had to look around him cautiously.

In fact there was nothing sinister, and the first Catholic missionary had, actually, been in conflict with the French consul. Abbe Fava had the building put up and then went to seek for staff and funds to run it as a Catholic mission. They purchased more than 100 slave children from the market and made a home for them, and later, when Abbe Horner took over the new site in Bagamoyo, the British navy also provided them with rescued slaves, more than they could cope with: Dr. Kirk would have liked to subsidize them. No one who knew Abbe Horner would still fear—as we had done at first—that his charges might be used as indentured labor in Reunion. So the big building became the hospital. The Catholics also started the first Indian school in East Africa, but the Indians did not persevere. Perhaps they would have preferred English to French, but we never had the staff to go in for such frivolities. We did benefit, indirectly, because consul Rigby stepped in smartly when he found the Sultan had permitted a Roman Catholic mission in Zanzibar, and requested similar rights for the Protestants. I was just as glad that the Universities' Mission rather than the Hanoverians took up the opening. There were altogether too many Germans about for my liking, remembering Professor List's old doctrine of expansionism. The new consulate kept changing its title, as the North German League developed into a full-fledged empire and one year Rigby gave a Christmas dinner for Germans alone. Nowadays you will find a German engineer on every steamship up and down the coast, and talk of a permanent repair yard, and yet when I left Germany as far as I know we did not even have a navy!

In such a diplomatic situation, Majid knew the rules: he paid the subsidy, and by the time he died was £50,000 in debt. That may not sound much to you, but Zanzibar did not have many sources of revenue, and Majid did not have his father's genius as a trader. He also had more competition to face than Said ever had.

American, European and British Indian traders had all woken up to the possibilities of our coast, and with the expanded commerce of the mechanical age more young ladies were able to tinkle the ivories, as the Americans so quaintly put it, and display tortoise shell combs in their hair than ever before. They demanded these things and a few years later, when the American civil war brought about a shortage of cotton cloth which was their main item of exchange, my good wife informed me that you could get American soap, even American codfish along the coast, so long as they got their ivory in return.

In 1861 Rigby was invalided out, for all his strenuous exercise, walking and riding round the island to keep fit. He was able to draft the Anglo-French declaration guaranteeing the Sultan's freedom of action before he left, and Majid even felt secure enough to allow Barghash back. But Barghash had learnt a thing or two at Bombay, which he found in the clutch of a financial crisis. He was allowed his own carriage and had made many acquaintances on the strength of princely title. Now, back home he was receiving overtures of friendship from Ahmed Fumo Lato, otherwise Simba, the lion of Bajun, from the Sultanate of Witu. Simba was an astute performer, already receiving German travelers on his own account.

I was busy myself, and heard all this from a distance. Von der Decken came up to Kisulutini for three days with the late Mr. Thornton. (I should have said the late von der Decken too, since he came to grief on his third expedition.) He was then preparing for his second expedition to Kilimanjaro, and asked me to spend some time at Mombas assisting him. I was glad to do what I could, but so many contraptions were by then available for safari that I began to wonder how we could have managed to set out so simply in the early days, without ever having seen a folding chair or a canvas bath! Von der Decken had already come back from following Roscher's route, and in fact had to hang about for a number of months waiting for Kersten to accompany him.

Now you may think that all this has not much to do with the mission, but in fact the more explorers write books about their adventures, the more slavery-conscious Britain becomes, and the more actively do patrol boats buzz about the coast, generating in their turn more crops of memoirs and after-dinner stories. During all these years a British squadron of seven or eight small cruisers, carrying sail as well as steam power, was cruising up and down the coast trying to enforce the territorial limits to the trade of the Moresby Treaty. But this was a nominal force against the smaller and faster Arab vessels with their intimate knowledge of the area. The best time for search was from April to October, the *Kuku* or heavy rainy season and the *Kusi* or southerly monsoon that followed it. Sea shipping was restricted during the rough season, even for dhows that hugged the coast, and then came the time for overhaul or refitting of our local craft. But vessels plied between Zanzibar and Mombas all the year round.

Small naval pinnaces manned by 20 or 30 men might be days or weeks away from the mother-ship, searching the creeks and mangrove swamps for offenders. You can imagine how many British sailors died from fever or dysentery in the course of the search, so it could really only succeed if they regarded it as a crusade. Some did, but none would forget that in 1862 a whole boat's crew was murdered, going ashore for water near Cape Guardafui. They used to say that if explorers ran into trouble it was because of their own wish to venture inland, but a seaman's work was on the high seas, not to run the risk of trespassing on foreign territory. There was a bounty payable for capturing a dhow, but little enough to offset the sufferings of the sailors.

And the devil is always on the prowl, watching for a chink in our armor. In 1867, as you know, the superbly efficient relief expedition to free European prisoners at Magdala in Ethiopia was mounted. Krapf was there as interpreter, though he was not able to last out the whole mountain march. Patrol boats were drawn off for those few months to serve the monstrous logistics of the assault—a special railway, gun-bearing elephants, naval rockets, a photographic unit—and the clearance of the beach-head at Zeila in 24 hours, when all was done. Every slave trader in East Africa dived in when those boats were busy. And dhows loaded with slaves swarmed up the coast. If you let your own personal defenses down for a day, the same thing happens.

According to Captain Colomb's reckoning less than a tenth of the smuggled slaves were freed by the patrols, and something like 17,000 a year were successfully sold, not counting the seven to ten thousand absorbed annually in Zanzibar. So you can imagine that the patrolmen grew angry and suspicious and local people, not in any case seeing what all the fuss was about, resented their ordinary commerce being delayed while trading ships were searched.

At Kisulutini I was preparing to offer Holy Communion to our converts for the first time. No bishop was at hand to confirm them, but humanly speaking they were ready, and in our Lutheran tradition that was enough. But the celebration did not take place for several years. I suppose things were too good to last.

What happened was partly the fault of the British naval patrols, searching and insulting local boats that were not carrying slaves or even contraband. People took offence and called this piracy, so their feelings on this particular incident had to be vented somehow.

The Governor of Mombas, Ali bin Nasser, who had always been so courteous, so discreet, demanded to know if I had permission from the Sultan to put up more buildings in Rabai. If not, I had better pull them down again. My local people, not only church members, said they were prepared to die in defense of the mission station.

This was enough to console me for my discomfiture, and my wife, who seldom cried, was overcome with gratitude. Jindoa, an old man now, marched over from Rabai Mpya to assert his long-standing invitation to us. Mabaya, son of the old *Saha*, rounded up elders who remembered our agreement for the new site: a few even produced tattered strips of cloth which we said we had given them at the time.

It seemed very long ago. I was saddened, too, to hear of my father's death—not overcome, because it had seemed so unlikely we should ever meet again. I could not picture him any older than when I had last seen him in 1844: he was always eager to keep up with my doings, wrote the same firm, formal hand, and always sent cordial messages to my wife. My mother had faded away long before, the wisps of memory already seeming to recede before the

slow passage of the news. The first Mrs. Krapf died without knowing that her mother had gone six months before her.

I had proposed, several years before, to approach Said Sultan
about building a chapel, but Hamerton thought it inadvisable. In
the meantime Arab houses had been built in the plantations and
Banians had begun to put up their own shops in the town. It was all
sorted out in the end, but it jolted our complacency. And then one
day, when we had sent for a boat to take us to Mombas (they were
ordered from the Mohammedan village of Jomvu), who should arrive on the expected boat but Dr. Krapf and his Swiss helpers, Graf
and Elliker—more trouble.

I knew they were coming, in fact had sent a letter to await their
arrival at the harbor, but this sudden appearance brought all my
tangled feelings to the surface. Krapf was bringing out Wakefield
and Woolner for the Methodist mission. They had gone to Germany with him and plunged straight into the study of Kinika and
Kiswahili while the two Swiss recruits were at the Chrischona In-
stitute. They had a tough voyage on an Arab dhow and made their
way to Pangani, the intended site for the work. Wakefield got his
first safari experience there, Mr. Thornton, who had accompanied
Dr. Livingstone, very kindly offering to show him the ropes. But
the other three were sickly, and an unpleasant shooting incident at
Mombas on the way back was enough to finish off the spirits of the
two Swiss. Woolner was put under medical care at Zanzibar and
had to be invalided home at the first opportunity.

I still felt reverence and gratitude for the pioneer who had guided and trained me, and who had suffered so much even before I
arrived. On the other hand I was aware of his severe criticisms of
our settlement at Kisulutini and my approach to the work. I had
suffered more than once from his indiscretions, and I was pretty
sure that he would not agree to enter into debate over the linguistic
problems that were bothering me. While at Zanzibar I had made
some revision of his translations and word-lists, and sure enough
he later objected to this. I hear that he recommended that a missionary 'with a classical education' should be sent out—a very different
concern from the fire for the gospel with which we both started. He
wished Dr. Trump were here—so indeed, did I, but I did not traipse
about the world looking for scholars and linguists in preference to

digging in where the Lord had sent me.

Krapf's self-confidence had been confirmed by the public honors he received and the success of his book, which was important to him (though Erhardt and I had contributed our share to it, as he frankly admits).

As I have said, I had written to Krapf. I do not keep copies of my letters, not having the intention of publishing them. He afterwards wrote to London that I had accused him of dishonesty and of creeping into East Africa before the right time. If that is what I wrote, may God forgive me. What I thought I said was that we might have been wiser to work from Zanzibar or even Mombas for a time, and that we should assess the physical and moral strength of our recruits. Perhaps I also said that he should have consulted me before promising the Mombas house to the two Swiss. The devil seems able to conceal himself in an inkpot, or perhaps we pick our quill from some of these accursed coast birds that consort with sorcerers. However, we did not discuss these matters straight away, which might have cleared the air. He also wrote to London that I had not visited Greater Rabai since 1853, but just sat in my house reading and waiting for people to call. If he had seen what the stations were like at the end of the Maasai raids, he would have known that was not true.

That year, 1862, the church papers told us, some English Protestants were celebrating the 200th year since they were ejected from the Church of England, and were going to mark the occasion by a joint mission with the Anglicans in Madagascar. God grant they maintain a better relationship with their old enemies than some of us do with our old friends!

We turned our faces back from the boat. Perhaps I sent some message to Mombas about stores or the like: I don't remember. My good wife was already somewhat taxed by her long walk down to the creek: I had to arrange for litter-bearers to help her back over the steeper parts and, woman-like, she was concerned about feeding these unexpected guests and arranging beds for them.

Dr. Krapf was in good shape for his 52 years, but Elliker was so weak that he had to be carried all the five miles to Kisulutini. Fortunately I was able to put the two workmen in a room in a helper's house, and when Krapf left after a fortnight for Kauma (where a man wanted a well dug, which the Swiss were supposed to over-see) and from there to Zanzibar, I offered to get them organized. They were supposed to set up a station at Jibana or Biria, but I soon saw they were not up to it, and when Krapf returned in March he could see it for himself. They were in a state of physical and moral collapse, though my good wife had labored with me to set them up in health and spirits, and a single rat was enough to disturb Mr. Graf. Dr. Krapf went to pray at Mringe's grave. Then he dismissed them and they sailed for Europe early in April, a terrible waste of sponsors' money and frustrated prayer.

I had no reason to trust Krapf's judgment on recruits, but these were not for CMS so I had no grounds for comment. Wakefield, however, was a tower of strength. The plans for Pangani did not work out and so he came to Ribe, only 16 miles from our station, and became a great blessing to the work.

All this time there was sporadic famine and people came round begging for even a little cassava to eat. Hunger was most severe among the Duruma, and they trekked to Kwale in search of a bet-ter living. Many Wanika were on the move: they may be compared with the tradesman in a German guild who ventures out to improve his living in another part of the country, only to find that regula-tions from above compel him back to the overcrowded home if he has been over-zealous in striking his bargain. It becomes from year to year more obvious that the Wurtemberger has safer prospects in America than in Baden: only the Rabai have not discovered their America yet. Generally relations between the neighboring commu-nities were peaceful, but temptations come at a time of necessity, especially when Maasai raiders have recently been at work and all evil is likely to be attributed to them.

So when Mue Zuia and Lugo, two of our members, were be-sieged in their village, it was a lesson to us to find that Digo, not Maasai, were the culprits. They carried off a niece of Mue Zuia. The family's rejoinder was to take another girl hostage and try to effect an exchange, but I persuaded them to release her and raise money instead. Then a lot of complications arose because the girl's mother wanted to accept money for her and then steal her back, so as to make a profit out of the disaster. In the end we got it all sorted out, and they came back from exile in Kiriama and were reconciled with me, but it is a complex and difficult family. This shows you how impossible it is to keep new Christians sheltered and unspotted from the world. In fact, you see, it requires a good deal of spiritual discernment to get rid of the idea that you have a right over the persons of others. Many heads of families, as well as manufactories, have still to learn this.

The same year, the Sultan visited Mombas in a boat pulled by a steamer. We did not go down. But Brigadier Coghlan and Dr. Badger slipped away from the Governor's reception to visit us with a boatload of provisions and a gift of money.

Von der Decken, too, turned up unexpectedly on Christmas Day, a great addition to our modest celebration, my wife was charmed, and she did not object to our talking together in German for a bit. But, of course, such worldly pleasures lead to sorrow. She was very upset when he was killed, two years later, on to the Juba River, with three of the other nine Europeans in his expedition.

I tried to rally Emma about her 'young men,' but half-heartedly. Butterworth had survived at Ribe for only two months that same year. New who had come to join the Methodists in 1863, looked more like a survivor, but although our own Taylor enlivened the Christmas of 1864 for us, he also succumbed a few months later.

However, Sultan Majid was to do more in 1862 than make visits. He actually forbade the Northern Arabs commonly known as *Juros*, to buy and ship slaves from Zanzibar.

The seasonal incursions of these people from November to April every year—and they numbered up to three or four thousand—were becoming a nuisance. Being temporary residents, they did not much care who they knocked about: one group had recently locked the American consul in his house, wounding four servants and strutting around the town brandishing swords. The Sultan followed up his order against them with imprisonment in several well known cases, but the Northern Arabs began, in retaliation, to kidnap slaves who were legally owned in Zanzibar. Therefore a couple of years later Majid decreed that *no* boat owners should transport slaves during the January to March monsoon in any part of his dominions, on penalty of having their boats burned. (For after all it is not only in East Africa that a ship owner may claim false nationality to evade a law.) He even went so far as to say that every Northern dhow putting ashore in Zanzibar should be burned, but of course this was beyond his capacity to enforce. The Northerners owed allegiance to Thuwain. They traveled for trade, but the sight of lusher lands further south may have made them envious on his behalf. Perhaps, also, they despised the Arabs of Zanzibar for forgetting their mother tongue and appearing year by year darker in complexion.

Well, the Mohammedans have been more constant in their acceptance of all the faithful as equal in the sight of God than many Christians have. Even the Mohammedan Indians who commonly buy slave women for their use sometimes return home with them as wives, whereas the Hindus pass them on to friends before they leave.

We are speaking of slavery, my dear sir: do not *tcha* and *pshaw* at me like that as though you were the sightless innocent and I the man of the world! Hardly a Banian on these coasts—and there are thousands of them now, compared with mere hundreds when I first arrived—has failed to provide himself a black woman, or perhaps more than one. Earlier, I am told, he would have had slave girls shipped from India, but now the law is more vigilant. It still happens, no doubt, but at a cost. Can you be surprised, if families do not migrate together? If a man leaves his country not for love of the gospel but for love of money, is it strange that he wants what money will buy?

You ask what I would do about it. I would have slavery abolished sir, as you would, and people given a new way to live—would you wish for that? I hear that brother Nylander on the west coast, and some others, have done right by taking legal wives among the freed slave women: the grand-daughter of one of these women now serves with her missionary husband in Ceylon. This is what I would wish, a converted Hindu acknowledging his converted slave wife—one day it may come to pass."

X

Everyone was looking forward to a day in Alexandria, though it had been described as a rocky harbor surrounded by a waste of barren sand. It held unrelentingly to its history as a great mercantile city: hawkers already lay in wait at the dock gate with picture postcards, toy camels and beads allegedly dug up from the Pyramids. Little boys from boats called importantly, 'I say, sir,' holding up to view leather handbags and boxes of dates. Beyond that, there was little sign of the gracious city of the ancients, but the modern port was populous and busy. Isaac gaped at it, having, as he thought, adjusted to the metropolitan experience in Zanzibar, Aden and Suez.

Rebmann and Williams did not feel up to disembarking, but arranged to stay together so that Isaac could join the party being shown round the city. In the evening, Miss Philipps returned him to them.

"I shall want a full account of your day," said Williams, smiling. "I was very disappointed to miss it."

"And did not you fancy a taste of Egypt, Mr. Rebmann? I assume you ears and nose would give a strong impression, even without sight."

"I am happy enough remembering two experiences of Egypt with my good wife, madam. I have no need to add anything else."

"She must have been a very brave woman, Mr. Rebmann."

"To join a savage German in a difficult country, you mean?" replied the pastor clumsily. He had not much experience of women's voices and lacked the depth of discrimination bred into long-term blind.

"All of us risk savagery when we undertake to be led by the wedding ring," rejoined the lady, conscious that her face did not measure up to this implied levity, for this shrunken, yellow reed of a man frightened her with his intensity of feeling. "But to live on the East African coast and in such isolation from other company, that must have taken courage. How long a time did she remain there?"

"We were fifteen years together," answered Rebmann simply. "As I have told you, we made some little expeditions, but together."

"And you never asked to go to Europe?"

"Ask, ask: they were always pestering me. And now they have started again, since Bishop Tozer of UMCA came to have a look at me in 1864, and made a report, I suppose. You may have seen their church in Zanzibar—they have choir-boys in robes, candles and such-like. For all Tozer was called 'the fighting parson,' ever since he boxed one rowdy member of the congregation and offered to take on the rest, they could not stand the hardships of the Shire, so a sight of the bush is like a holiday to them now.

Not that I am condemning their churchmanship. It amuses me, but we get along very well all the same. Even the Catholics in Zanzibar were friendly, and since Abbe Horner came they have built up a marvelous place for freed slaves on the mainland, entirely in mission hands, you know. If it had not been flattened by the hurricane it would be a model now for all who are called to build schools and places of safety. They had to start from scratch again, and so they did, with hope and hard work. All the same, New was also saved from the hurricane like Jonah from the whale. There is a little Kiswahili song we made about that.

I am losing my thread... Yes, they call me and try to bribe me like a child with sweets. We will get you a publisher for your language books in Germany—or in Bombay if you prefer—or in England. You will be received with proper respect: we will have tea-parties, perhaps a medal. (It rankles with them that only the French gave me a medal for coming unexpectedly upon a mountain.) But now, of course, I shall see nothing through the press except with the good eyes in Isaac's head."

"Now, father," said Isaac, relieved to come to a pause, "these good eyes tell me that we should be getting ready for dinner, and releasing Miss Philipps to do the same. Do you not sense that evening falls?"

"Forgive me, madam, for rattling on," said Rebmann formally. "This my son has more common-sense than I. Yes, indeed, the air freshens a little and the voices that were round us have withdrawn to a distance. Let us prepare ourselves."

They went to wash and freshen their linen and ate, as usual, what was set before them, Isaac cutting up Rebmann's portion conveniently for the fork and guiding his hand to the glass. Then he helped the old man to their cabin, read a scripture portion to him in Kinika, and, after they had prayed with Williams, readied him for the bunk.

Next morning the lady again greeted Mr. Rebmann and had a chair brought close to his on deck. A faint perfume surrounded her, not yet dispersed by the bodily odors which the strong sun would induce in all of them.

"Good morning, Mr. Rebmann, I trust you slept well."

"Tolerably well, thank you, madam. Without exercise one does not drop into a deep sleep, I find. But the accommodation is comfortable, is it not?"

"I will pick up your own word, tolerably so. I had hoped that in Aden we should trans-ship into one of those amazing China clippers. The *Mei-Kang*, I hear, is the last word in fashion and elegance. But you must frown on such frivolity, and this ship is certainly more spacious than the first one.

I hope you will tell me if I try your patience or, more importantly, your sentiments, but I still have a great curiosity about your good lady. Most of us women are inquisitive, though I think she was not. I like to discuss with my acquaintances in church circles the needs of the mission-fields. So, if you will permit..."

"Ask away, my dear, if you will allow me to address you in a fatherly fashion. If you intrude too far into my privacy I shall say so, never fear. But it is a pleasure to me speak of Emma—no-one but myself, I think, ever addressed her by that name, unless Mrs. Lieder did so. She was reserved, you see, very English. Does that offend you? I was 31 when I went to Egypt to marry her, the longest I was ever away from the coast, and I have had little enough practice speaking with other ladies."

"I do see it. Your delightful Mr. Nyondo had to remind you that ladies take a long time to dress for dinner. And so as I went to change, and set out my little secret creams and lotions and brush my hair before the mirror—you must remember that girls do that—I asked myself, how did Mrs. Rebmann do all these things through so many years at the coast. Is that a daughterly question to ask?"

"It is indeed, though it had never occurred to me to ask it. I never thought of it as a problem. She had been to see her sisters in England before our marriage, so I suppose they provided what is thought necessary. In Cairo one can buy all western requirements—at least, I suppose so: I expect ideas of convenience and necessity have changed since my time. Have you seen Cairo? It is a big city and was very important for transit to the Red Sea before the Canal was opened. Then there was all the Nile trade and I dare not say what beyond.

Many of us have been opening up, as they call it, tracts of desert and lake that I daresay some back street trader in Cairo already had under his thumb, though he never thought about maps and medals from the Royal Geographical Society but only about bags of salt and grain and gum copal. Overtly, of course. Covertly he would have been thinking about strong black men to use as slaves, but not even the Khedive Ismail is supposed to say this openly. (Even Frere realized he had met his match when he found the Khedive's mother busy providing mortal souls to set up her grand-daughters in their marital homes.) Some of them would be house slaves, men and women, but even more secretly the merchant would be thinking about eunuchs, who fetch a high price... You know 14 or 15 boys will die under the knife before one survives the operation and becomes worth his weight in gold—his own family often know it too, and reap the profit ..."

Rebmann could not see the averted face, but he was conscious of a tremor beside him.

"Oh, my dear young lady, forgive me. What have I said? I cannot see you, and I am not used to the conversation of ladies other than my own dear wife. I have embarrassed you..."

The young woman took a deep breath.

"Dear Mr. Rebmann, do not distress yourself," she replied with an effort. "Fortunately no-one passed by to hear you. And it is a strange fiction to suppose that we, who are meant to sustain life and reproduce it, have no idea of the means the good Lord provided for doing so. I have done a little nursing, you see, and hope now to attend the institution set up by Miss Nightingale at St. Thomas's Hospital. One would be of little use in the east without some understanding of death, life and a reduced state of living... But, if you please, we were speaking of Mrs. Rebmann and her dresses."

"Ah yes, so many dresses and other garments we carried with us and shipped perilously to Kisulutini after the wedding. I had never dealt with so much baggage before. And tablecloths and china cups, if you please (quite a lot of them survived the journey, though they are all gone now, of course) but, when I protested, Mrs. Lieder said it was a very modest way for a lady to enter into housekeeping, and that we must accept the gifts of our well-wishers.

Cairo is sophisticated but not comfortable. I hear from Dr. Kirk that it is now connected by rail with Alexandria and more recently, I believe, to Suez as well. And we used to be so proud of the relays of horse carriages! It makes me feel an old fogey, in truth. Even more than 20 years ago there were little boys in Cairo shouting in English, 'Donkey for hire, sir. Mister, you want donkey?' I dread to think how many camels we needed for our packages... Nowadays, people say, the little boys have switched to French."

"They still use English at Aden. Did you not hear them? Those little boys—well, forgive me, you could not see them, but they had the most extraordinary way of bleaching their hair. And they were diving in the sea for coins or other trifles."

"No, I must be growing hard of hearing." (Looking back to pleasant days in Badger's house, Mr. Alley with his ambitious hopes, Emma with her new gowns. The dry, hot air full of guttural sounds.) "What were they saying?"

"Well, perhaps if you did not hear... At Suez there was one donkey they had named the Archbishop of Canterbury. Another was Mrs. Gladstone. But the other preferences—perhaps since you have been out of England they would not be familiar to you. I should not really like to repeat..."

"Do not let it distress you, my dear. I daresay I should not have understood—well, we digress. Mrs. Rebmann always looked very nice to me. Being a widow, she had a sensible kind of dress for the wedding, light brown, I think, with darker bands round it, and a big skirt, and a bonnet. I confess I wondered how all those skirts

and petticoats would fit into a wet and dirty *bagala*. But for traveling and for times of great heat she would wear a straighter kind
of dress, not low-cut, of course, and with long sleeves, fearing the
sun, but not too heavy. When I admired them she would laugh and
say that these had been the fashion when she was a child, and she
had reverted to it, but modestly. She was ten years older than me,
you see, and had a substantial figure when we got married, but at
the coast she was much reduced by fever and heat, so those dresses
which had been straight then hung about her loosely in later years.
For the heat that is not a bad thing."

"But fifteen years, Mr. Rebmann. She must have renewed her
wardrobe in that time."

"Well, yes, of course, we used to go to Zanzibar, which was a
great market for cloth, especially for the American cotton we still
call marikani. This, some years back, replaced the thinner Indian
cotton which one would have thought more appropriate to the climate. The Arab ladies would bring satins and fine stuffs, mostly not
very suitable to our way of life. Emma bought some things on that
trip to Egypt, but we lost some of our baggage when we met shipwreck on the way back. I was too concerned with arranging new
connections to enquire very closely into what was gone.

And then she could order on Bombay or London a length of
stuff, buttons, hooks and eyes (I think you call them) and so on.
Like all teaching ladies she knew how to sew. (My mother and sisters, you see, helped in the vineyard. I don't think they undertook
anything elaborate in the way of needlework.) And later, when
the ladies who had been to school in Nasik came, they had some
skill with the needle and with finer points of laundry than our man
could deal with.

I never heard her grumble about clothes—even in Mombas you
could get the black stuff for *buibuis* and that would serve on occasion. (You remember we lost our little son in a few days.) She used
to make a jacket, too, for each man baptized, and mend it when necessary. It was one of the problems when we were bachelors, Krapf,
Erhardt and I, making those long journeys through the bush with
thorns catching at our clothes and socks worn into holes. Perhaps
I would not have dared walk back from Kadiaro without my boots
if I had been married then! We were often in tatters, and had to get

an Indian tailor in Mombas to set us to rights, until Erhardt brought Anthony to help. My good wife tended us well, but she did not herself venture out far to risk tearing her dresses, and by that time we had a decent path for the five miles down to the creek where the boats put in."

"Mrs. Rebmann did not hark back to her family and her earlier life?"

"I have not yet met any of her family. There is a widowed sister in Tottenham: I hope Isaac has the address somewhere. I had to send messages when—when she was taken. But we were married in the mission, and for the mission. There is no question of looking back.

Of course we talked. Night after night we talked so that we should get to know one another better, and to pass the time, and to enlarge what light we had on the ways of God with men. She was a clergyman's daughter and her first husband was the vicar of a London parish, a good deal older than she was. They had no children. He was a great sabbatarian, giving evidence before commissions and all that—but evangelical, and prepared to have missionary preachers in his church. She was aroused by this, and would have urged him to offer, but he was phlegmatic in temper and felt no call to bestir himself away from his reports and committees. I can imagine that her fervor may have frightened him.

Mr. Tyler had an uncle who had been to the Cape—not as a missionary, no, nothing like that. He had been trying to make his fortune, as the saying goes. He was, in fact, a free-thinker of the most provocative kind, but all the same there were family gatherings at which Mrs. Tyler met him. (The vicarage must, in general, have been a dreary place: Kisulutini, with young girls scampering up to greet her, ask for drinks of water, finger her clothes and hair and ask questions, was far more lively.)

The uncle had gathered some knowledge of Bushmen speech and habits, so when he returned to Britain he was asked to take charge of a group of these people put on show for the entertainment of the British public. Yes, it sounds horrible, doesn't it? Like exhibiting a two-headed calf at a fair. Even more horrible was Mr. Tyler's assertion that whole communities were being exterminated at the Cape. Yet the people he toured with had come of their own free will, in families, to show off their skills in weaponry and music: they were remunerated, and who knows but what the opportunity in their turn to see strange people in extraordinary lands may have weighed with them and even earned them acclaim on their return home.

This Mr. Tyler did not have a great deal of sympathy with the Bushmen, whom he called Bosjemans, but when he encountered instances of extreme rudeness and provocation among his audiences at Vauxhall and Dublin—some of them being people of wealth and title—he wrote a pamphlet which I have to this day. In it he protests that, however low the actual attainments of the Bosjemans might be, they were fully human and should not be subjected to indignity. In fact he maintained that any race of men was capable of the same spiritual or intellectual achievements as any other, provided they were exposed to the same healthy and educative society.

I surmise that this document was more concerned to play off Robert Owen against the bishop of Worcester than to plead for better education at the Cape, since I find it hard to credit that both were present at the side of the author during a single performance. However, I am sure that the stories contributed by Uncle Tyler to the family entertainment lost nothing in the telling, and they made a great impression on my wife. So she questioned him closely about the peoples of the Cape and determined (when it became clear that her husband was sinking and would not be long for this world) to offer her services there as a teacher. Since no suitable opening could be found in Southern Africa, her attention was drawn by an acquaintance to the Cairo Female School. She consulted the Basel Mission and, being by then a widow, went to Egypt to join the staff at about the time I myself sailed for East Africa. (We delighted in sharing such coincidences.)

Our life at Kisulutini was simple—we had goat meat, fish, such chickens and eggs as we could raise ourselves, rice and rough meal for baking in a tin over the fire. But we could put on a good table when visitors came. Young Wakefield was like a son to Emma, and only 16 miles away at Ribe.

Our interests were local interests, though we received some letters and some reading matter from England and Germany. A villager asking, 'Are there fowls in Heaven?', which as a young man

I might have looked upon as a frivolous question, now demanded our serious attention. We needed to come to terms with the picture in the questioner's mind: if horses, lions, eagles, why not chickens?

> And every creature which is in heaven, and on the earth,
> and under the earth, and such as are in the seas,
> and all that are in them, heard I saying Blessing, and hon-
> our, and glory, and power, be unto Him.

There was still a lot of enthusiasm for a mission to the Galla, and when things had quietened down under Sultan Majid, Bishop Tozer suggested that either the CMS or the Methodists should start a station on Lamu Island. He was on good terms with both of us, but did not propose to involve UMCA in the venture.

Late in 1865 Wakefield had come over to Rabai Mpya to consult me about his first expedition to the Galla. He must have heard from the 'bush telegraph' that I was over there working on the old mud house because the whole front and half of the roof had fallen down. The first time he took only a day from Mombas to Malindi by boat. People were working heavy spells on the shore, he said, as part of the competition to get his fare, to such effect that the sail-boom of the vessel he selected broke, but none the less they had a safe passage. Wakefield was always good for a laugh.

The northern part of the coast had changed almost beyond recognition in the preceding few years. My first mission map showed Malindi as completely empty after recent fighting, but Said Sultan had told Krapf, angling for a missionary site there, that he meant to repopulate it. Indeed he did: people from Lamu and Zanzibar were induced to go there, and also to Mambrui, and in 1861 Thornton and von der Decken had seen 50 settlers building with the help of 1000 slaves and under the protection of 150 Baluchi soldiers: they worked to good effect, for Malindi is already a well-established and prosperous town. It had once been an important place, as the ancient monuments in the vicinity show. Boteler found a 'prince of Melinda' heading the Swahili in Mombas, serving under the red flag of Oman: negotiations could not commence without him, and he conversed in broken Portuguese.

Sesame had been widely planted along the coast since the 1850s, a good proposition, since it yields two crops of oil-seed every year. Perhaps you have tasted at Zanzibar the little round sweet cakes they make of it. The French merchant on Lamu may not even have known he was thought of as the spearhead of a French invasion, but Sultan Majid did not look like encouraging a mission station there. The fort of Lamu, with its three stories of balconies supported by interior arches, was more imposing even than Fort Jesus, and the Seyyids have always put one of their most trusted men in as Governor. One had a secretary, I have been told, who spoke German and English: I have always regretted missing the chance of conversing in German with an Arab. In the 1820s there were said to be four schools on the island and admission was free for the poor. I do not know if this is still so.

Wakefield and New came over to consult me about a possible transfer of mission property, and before the long rains of 1866 started I went over to inspect Ribe, and was greatly impressed, both by their construction and by their systematic progress in less than four years. We talked it over at length, and concluded that it might be best for CMS to take over the buildings when the Methodists moved further north. We even agreed on a value of £120.

My good wife was not perturbed. We thought of staying at Kisulutini ourselves and getting new staff for Ribe, but she could have borne the move if it had been ordered. All Africa, she used to say, is the Lord's, and I suspect she cherished a hope of seeing the snow mountain.

Perhaps the barrier to the Galla in Ethiopia is at last being broken down. We met several Catholic priests studying the language at Zanzibar, and I was told the two Germans made their way to Metemma afterwards. The Italian and the Piedmontese arrived separately. It seemed extraordinary that they could not trust us or one another sufficiently to pool our resources at least in language study. After all CMS reported to us evangelicals on the work of the Propaganda College in Rome and what we could learn from it.

On the coast, as I have explained before, the Lord had subdued the Galla. There were not as many of them as we used to think, and even working from Ribe the Methodists had had some success with individuals. Abe Shora, for instance, was endlessly grateful because they had taken in his family when they needed refuge.

Of course the other Galla we all knew was Dado, a charming little boy who lived at Ribe after being saved from slavers. He accompanied Mr. Wakefield to England on leave.

Yes, Dado is a Galla name, of course. I don't see why they should give him another unless he was baptized, when a lot of people take a bible name. But probably he was too big for infant baptism when they adopted him and not old enough to enter instruction. We do not encourage foreign names unless they are from the bible, and even then if your friend has been Abe Gunga up to his middle years, it is not easy to start calling him Abraham all of a sudden. With a young fellow like Isaac, here, of course it is more natural, but he still retains his given name of Nyondo. There was a baby called Rebmann when I was new to the coast, and another one called Mzungu, European—the blackest infant you ever saw in your life. I did not like that. It was just a novelty, not showing an interest in our teaching. The first Mohammedan to come to Christ on the coast is still Mwidani, as he was before. It is those freed slaves, I know it well, who have a problem over naming. We never addressed Mringe by any other name, though Johaneshi appears somewhere in the records.

This was not Deimler's fault. He encouraged the Nasik students to keep their own names and talk among themselves in their mother-tongues. They were given lectures on slavery and the history of Africa (in English, necessarily, since it was their common language). But I see their difficulties too. They would never be Chauhan or Jamnadass. If they could not genuinely be Smith or Brown either, they remained in India the minority of a minority. They had too little experience really to imagine a return to Africa. As for Dado, he was taken away from home so early that he will share some of the freed slaves' difficulties. To be able to remember the name he was born to is some advantage. Wakefield's experiment in adopting him put a new idea into our heads. We were beginning to get families strong enough, you see, to have their children baptized. It is no good undertaking this until you know that the parents will do their part. In February 1866—I remember it very well, in the slack season just before the people begin to get their fields ready for the April rains—we were putting three boys of nine or ten up for baptism: Bishop Tozer had visited us and been particularly pleased with their progress. There was Muamba, who was going to be baptized Petro, Mlangule who would become Mark, and Kango, a lovely bright-eyed curly-headed boy, quick at learning, with a big smile, perhaps a touch of the Swahili in his ancestry. I particularly asked that Kango should be called Samuel. We thought, you see, if the family would agree, we might take him for own. It was presumptuous, of course, like the apostles casting lots over Joseph and Matthias when the Lord had already picked Paul to be their twelfth man. Isaac was a ready-made son for me, and I never cease to be grateful for him. But you see in November Emma got some infection of the chest and died within a few days... I have arranged for Samuel to go to Zanzibar to Bishop Tozer's school, and I suppose he was singing in that stylish choir of theirs until his voice broke, but on my own I could not make a home for him."

"So when your wife died you were alone at Kisulutini?"

"Well, not completely so. Not as I had been alone in the early days, with no-one to share in Christian fellowship. Abe Gunga was close by, we should have been calling him grandfather by now and so were Isaac and Polly. William Jones and Ishmael and Grace Semler had been with us for a couple of years, and George David had come a little later, also from Nasik. In fact he and Priscilla were married the same day as Isaac and Polly, and that had been a very happy day for Emma. All the Bombay Africans were English-speaking and they sometimes went to Ribe or Mombas or further afield to help with the work. As it happened, Ishmael lost his Grace and their baby just after I lost Emma, so Deimler called him back to India for a while on some business. That was thoughtful, but of course I would not have gone away even if they had asked me. News of death was common at Salisbury Square. Wives would be remarked on in the *Intelligencer* but babies did not count for much.

It was a dark time and my eyes were getting worse. She was not there to remind me, 'Come nearer the lamp,' 'Let us have a candle lit for prayer time' and I would get irritable if the cook pressed me to stop and eat. I did not go out much: the long safaris were too much for me in middle life. I went to see Christian families within walking distance. Abraham was now happily settled with Isaac's mother—all of them except Abe Ngowa had attained a domestic stability which could only upset me more. Although they were tempted to spread their affections, the Nika seem otherwise well suited to Christian marriage, less harsh towards women and children than many other peoples of Africa.

Even Krapf was feeling his age: He had said he would come back if he were ten years younger, and the Magdala expedition, which he joined as interpreter the year after Emma died, proved too hard for him: he was invalided out. My old sparring partner, Abe Mabaya, was dead, and Jindoa near the end. I walked over to Rabai Mpya to see him. The younger people had become too respectful: they did not chide me for my grief. Only Isaac and Polly might bring their children to play around me and arouse an involuntary smile. If only Emma had been able to see them! I have since discovered that Polly would persuade the servants to let her take away my shirts to mend: otherwise they would have been washed to pieces without my ever noticing.

At the time of my wife's death an Estonian missionary called Tiesman was staying at Ribe, and George had gone over to help him, since Wakefield and New were both away sounding out opportunities on the north coast. Tiesman came over as soon as he heard of my trouble, conducted the funeral service and stayed for a week to comfort me. It was as though the Lord had sent an angel. His English was not very good, yet he helped me out when I broke down and wept during our English service, and just stayed close to see that I did not get desperate. I shall never forget his kindness.

The Methodists decided to stay at Ribe after all. They had spent a great deal on gifts to the Galla simply to countenance negotiations, and it was hard to see what sites would long remain central. That same year a Galla had actually visited Zanzibar and collected 750 dollars' worth of goods from Sultan Majid as a kind of premium on his willingness to trade. We could not have the gospel seen in the same light. We had not put up the proposed transfer to our parent committees and that was just as well as it turned out: with Taylor dead and Parnell sent back from the boat with eye trouble when I had been expecting him to assist me, and myself as near as possible to losing my grip after Emma's death, we should not have been able to man the station."

A tremor seized the listener, but Rebmann did not pause.

"Now for seven years I have been on my own, as you see me,

though it is only in the last three that my sight has quite failed. I have never thought it right—and nor did Krapf, who was cheerful and busy when we shared a house—to wear myself down with thoughts of how soon we may be released to join our loved ones in glory. I do not see anything in scripture to support such a point of view. When I had my sight I used sometimes to wish I had a photograph of her such as a German husband might find commonplace, but now I see her in my mind's eye as well as I ever did.

Then Wakefield got married when he went on leave, but this was not premeditated, and it would have made it difficult for him to move to a dangerous station in the north. The happy couple came back to Zanzibar with Dado, and the poor little chap was thoroughly bemused by all the changes of scene, and would pull his cap down over his eyes as though that would change his color when the sailors stared at him. He went to school in Zanzibar as long as Mrs. Wakefield stayed there: she did not come over to Ribe till after Nellie was born. Then they taught him at home—they were homely people, and had an instinct for making others comfortable with them. For instance on little Nellie's birthday—the second, I suppose—they invited all the schoolboys and other mission people for supper and gave them paper notebooks and a magic lantern show, and the child kissed them all good night. How shocking to Sir Bartle Frere, who would distinguish between the teacher and the taught! How disgusting to prudish old Rebmann who knows that kissing is an insanitary habit, displeasing to the African! And yet how innocent, because the affection behind it is stronger than the proprieties. I trust them with Dado too.

After Rebecca Wakefield died one of her pupils—Kamnazo, I think it was—wrote such a beautiful letter to her family that Wakefield brought me a copy, knowing how well it would apply to Emma (only, apart from Isaac here, we did not teach them English). I went over it till I learned it by heart.

> When I could not read, it was she herself who taught me,
> and to write also. It was *she* who taught me *all*. And to
> sew she also taught me. And when I had an ulcer she herself
> applied the poultices to it. And if I had a torn jacket it
> was she who mended it for me.

But all the people wept for Emma, not only those who had taken an interest in the teaching or the church.

But now, young lady, I shall be indiscreet again. I have not helped you much in the way of bonnets and flounces, but the world changes and commerce increases. In any functionary's house at the coast you will find a French mirror and an American clock. Even the small fezzes (the felt ones, not the embroidered caps) are imported from France, so why not bonnets and ribbons? I don't know whether this is for good or ill but certainly it can bring comforts for missionaries. I hear that nowadays you can even write with a gold-tipped pen that carries the ink inside itself, instead of leaving it in the pot to evaporate in the sun on hot days or thicken with the bodies of dead insects.

So, tell me, who is the young man for whom this information is required? What future waits you with home-made dresses and untrimmed caps?

"The future is not clear. But you assume it to be impossible for a single woman to seek service in the mission field?"

"Not impossible, my dear, but very difficult. You must examine your heart and be examined closely by your sponsors too. On a tide of victory, in the wave of conversions, you might tolerate the inconvenience and be tolerated—if you will forgive me for putting it so bluntly—by those who do not ordinarily share authority with women. But we are not on a tide of victory. It is not for me to interrogate you, since I am regarded these days as a poor example of mission work. But I see that your enquiries are pointed."

"Pointed indeed. I do not say that I have always kept faith as I ought, but I am not without a spark of seriousness. You will remember Mr. Taylor?"

"Who died at Zanzibar when he was on his way to take orders in Mauritius? He was right as rain when he left us to embark on the dhow from Bombay, and by the time they carried him ashore at Zanzibar he was beyond hope in this world. It was the year that the Basel mission celebrated their centenary, and we could not help remembering how many young lives had been sacrificed. We grieved for him. That was ten years ago, and soon afterwards my own life entered the valley of the shadow. His loss was outweighed by my greater loss."

"That I can understand. But you know, of course, that a girl was waiting at Mauritius with her wedding dress for Mr. Taylor to join her and bring her to the coast. I was that girl, Mr. Rebmann. I had risked everything to travel under the nominal care of a French planter's wife, and I left alone again. I did not—as perhaps I ought to have done—throw myself on your mercy and beg to be taught, chastised, given work. I wept and wept, busied myself with black dresses and fled on the next boat. My family thought I had been saved from disaster and must have my ideas made over with my winter clothes. Once the mourning period was over, I tried to enter into the social round they advised for me and became bored and rude. Now I have spent a year with cousins at the Cape, and have been calm enough to anticipate (as you surmise) but not exactly encourage an offer from one who is eager to set off and break new ground. At 32 I need to think carefully, for I see that my unpreparedness at 22 would have been a hindrance to you.

For the sake of the mission workers as well as converts, I see more medical knowledge is essential. Beyond that I do not see. Is it only a second-hand affection I can ever offer, either to the Lord or to the simple man who trusts me? He is not, perhaps, what you would call a gentleman! After all, Mrs. Moffatt married her father's nursery hand and won distinction by doing so. One can only offer what one has."

"I think, child, as well as what we have, we can offer all that the Lord of Hosts has pledged to us. Sometimes we impede the light if we fail to take and use that. And yet I am not worldly wise in these matters. How can I help you?"

"You married her—Mrs. Tyler—when she was already a widow, older than you, surely with her own views on teaching and on the place of women. Was it—there is no-one within hearing—I mean, did you marry her for love?"

"Love—love? I have told you, this is not the kind of wisdom I am gifted with. Luther sums up, 'Thus faith remains the doer and love remains the deed,' one follows from the other, you see. Yes, I loved her. We had not met, but Dr. Krapf had put us in correspondence, taking as excuse some point of missionary practice. From the letters one senses devotion and uprightness of character. She was prepared to give up a comparatively comfortable position in

Cairo, to join me. Is that not love? I was prepared to heed the counsel of my Wanika associates that marriage makes a boy into a man, however much one's fellow missionaries may see it as an indulgence—probably you would not call that love. She was my wife and she gave me a son at the age of 44, is that not costly? We lost the baby boy and knew that to keep her life safe we dared not risk another. We were faithful to one another without issue."

Her face is lined now, where the flesh has sunk underneath, and yellowed. The breasts that were full and firm and painful when the child was lost hang empty now, never to be fruitful, and the sleeves of her gown are loose on the shriveled arms. But we have been preserved for one another. One evening in Zanzibar she says quite simply, 'Johannes, I believe it is with me as it was with Sarah. Short of a miracle, I am an old woman now.' And so she comforts me and we lay hold of our promise.

"It was an arranged marriage, if you like, such as the Wanika or the Mohammedans or the Banians set up between their families and never question it. In Europe it is only the very rich or royal who bargain over their marriages. The rest of us maintain an illusion of free choice, though in a village the choice may be very limited. But in missionary life, as you have seen for yourself, there are not many opportunities for the customary courtship.

Both Dr. Krapf and I came out prepared to remain single. But when we found how odd, even shocking, this seemed to the people around us, and what an advantage it would be (apart from the natural desire to live in families) to demonstrate the blessings of a Christian home, we changed our minds. Krapf went to Egypt to get married while he was still serving in Ethiopia. He had known the lady slightly before, as she was betrothed to another missionary from the same training school, but the poor fellow died before they could marry. She was considered suitable for Krapf, and they got on very happily, but, as you know, she died soon after they reached Mombas. Would you say it was not a true marriage when that death claimed the Lord's first freehold on the East African coast?

You see, you are not alone in your sorrow.

Krapf married again in Germany, and perhaps this has influenced him to stay there. I do not think he could bear to bring the second lady to face the same risks here—but she is dead all the same.

Rebecca Wakefield also had been engaged before, but the first young man died in Ceylon before she could join him, and left a message for her, 'The Lord will provide.' Would she have been better to spend the rest of her life weeping and pressing flowers? They will tell you that Germans are sentimental, but I don't think she would. And I suppose Wakefield will have to marry again because of the little girl. Of course I am a German and not a Prussian. Is that Isaac coming? I have been trying to impress the difference upon him."

"Good morning, Mr. Nyondo, I expect you heard what your godfather said?"

"Good morning, Miss Philipps. Yes, I have learned that lesson. I am to fling myself into the nearest ditch if I see a Prussian hussar coming. To be honest, I would do the same if he were a Galla or a Maasai in full war array. And now Mr. Williams has been giving me a lecture on the Samurai of Japan. I really wonder if it was wise to allow myself to be persuaded away from Rabai, where most of us are peaceable people."

"Nothing venture, nothing win," smiled Rebmann.

"Yes, my father, of course. And now Mr. Williams would like me to help him write out his report. His hand is still very shaky. I think you will not mind, as you have company here."

"Go, of course, my son. You are a great help to us."

"I have some idea what it is like to be lonely, Mr. Rebmann."

"Yes, and that will help you to comfort others. Truly after my wife died I felt alone: it was like when my eyes dimmed a few years later—a constant sense of deprivation. The Lord is always present, but of course one takes that presence for granted, as, after the first few magic days one takes for granted the presence of the marriage partner. Yes, it exists, it upholds, it keeps one from desperation. But those who criticize our pietism must be a bit reasonable.

Archimedes jumps out of his bath in excitement—once. *Eureka. Eureka.* He has the knowledge of displacement. He lives with it. He does not—once the first few attempts have led to cold stares and whispers—shout every time he gets into a ferry boat the mystery he has uncovered.

So we—admitting that a little more excitement might confirm our apostolic succession—wake every morning to renew our prayers and our commitment. But we do not *daily* endanger our breakfasts by rushing into the kitchen to shout 'The Lord is risen indeed and has appeared unto Peter!' Me Hari would be sent for, if we did so, to perform exorcism, or a guard dispatched regretfully with chains by the Governor of Mombas. Divine love is 'new every morning' but earthly love also persists: you accept bereavement as you accept a fever, but it shows on you bodily.

I could no longer reach out to young Samuel. Of course I sometimes had to go down to Mombas for stores and workmen, but I did not feel like going to Zanzibar where we had had so much pleasure together. No officials came to see me, though they sent proper, little notes.

And then I got from the Home Committee a letter of rebuke and counsel which reduced me to tears. It spoke about spiritual stagnation and the effects of this on my flock. *I* may have been stagnating. It is true I had not followed up the plan for Holy Communion and let the daily public prayers lapse. But the congregation never failed to meet and their requests for baptism and admission to the sacrament did not give me any impression of stagnation, though some may have been slow to master the instruction offered.

I accepted the admonition in good part. It is the duty of the committee to keep us up to the mark. I had been too often left to cope with the station alone. But if I needed that counsel, I needed it sooner than I got it.

Mr. Mee wrote the letter in August 1867, some nine months after the death of my dear wife, a time when any man may have difficulty in finding his way. I might have taken it better from Mr. Venn, who had for so long been my director. But it did not reach me until seven months after it was written, by which time much might have changed in and around me. In fact the Sparshotts had arrived, and it was already too late to comply with the letter's instructions about that year's Annual Report.—Are we bankers, in any case, to be always filling in forms and columns? A printed letterhead indeed!— We never failed to send in our returns on plain paper thinned with sweat and rusty ink, so much thinned that they had to remind us not to write on both sides of the sheet.

The direct mail was generally slow, though a letter from Zanzibar might reach us in peaceful times in as little as a week.

During the troubled days after Said's death you might have to wait nine months for an answer from London, not more than that.

But from London to Bombay there was already a weekly mail taking only 24 days, and for years I had been reminding the Home Committee precisely when letters should reach Bombay for the rapid onward transmission. Regularity in observing such details is of the greatest help to us in the field.

I replied feelingly to Mr. Mee that in Africa one learns patience and that Dr. Krapf's early insistence on rapid conversions had been misplaced. I hope we both learned something from the exchange. On the mission-field, doubt of one's own calling is almost the most terrible of the devil's weapons. I have experienced it and narrowly achieved victory over it. Certainty of committee guidance is another, and on this perhaps the devil and I have to call it quits.

The letter dealt in part with my relation to the Bombay Africans. They were still not acknowledged as English speakers who, like the rest of us, needed training to reach out to their African brethren in a new place. A white or black skin is not the point. I had had 20 years to get used to the Nika and they had not. Livingstone used to say that a local man could teach us things that even the best trained Nasik worker never knew.

The Nasik people were good in their way and felt a second liberation when they were away from the caste-ridden atmosphere of Bombay, but their very Englishness irritated me. I felt that all Englishness belonged to me. Even now in Isaac's clear-cut consonants I hear an echo of the one who taught him. It was William Jones with his polished, solemn phrases who seemed bent on upsetting me. (See how I treat you already as a missionary confessor—brace yourself to it!)

'They work hard, just like white missionaries,' some people say, making the quite unwarranted assumption that every missionary knows what work is. Their attainments are formidable. Therefore I am blamed for not treating them 'just like white missionaries,' again assuming that to be the best way. I thought I was treating them like guild apprentices, who live as younger sons to their masters, but then I am not supposed to know what it means to be father."

Miss Philipps was called away to attend a lady who had fainted, but Williams had come on deck and two listeners still remained, bemused, one gazing seaward for enlightenment, the other racking his brains for a pertinent question to which a brief, factual answer could be given.

"I understand that the task of the Bombay Africans is not to be as good as us but to be, for mission purposes, better than us. They are expected to have a remote recollection of their mother-tongues that will allow them to learn languages quickly; on this their usefulness depends, since we have no English language school in which they can teach on first arrival. They are supposed to merge with the people, teaching new skills in their daily tasks, cleanliness and decency in the clothes available, harmony and cooperation in homes that are not above the power of the people to build. For this reason I designed their two-room cottages and built the first myself, close to the mission to emphasize our unity. I had started four more, but after Emma died the heart went out of me; if Parnell had come, he could have had Semler's house. The Sparshotts found the four still with their temporary roofing of palm thatch, and looked askance.

There is no allowance from the Home Committee for the Bombay Africans, and I therefore understood that they were not to be given money, but allowances of food and clothes which they could supplement by their own efforts, and encourage the Nika to do the same. Perhaps it was not clear to them that we missionaries, if we had no private income, did not have personal spending money either. We drew a bill for our requirements out of a common purse, though the idea of individual budgeting was soon to come.

So soon a storm broke over my head. Tea and coffee were not luxuries to people trained at Nasik: they should be available weekly. They were used to wearing shoes every day, not only on Sundays. (What Nika person has shoes, unless he makes himself sandals after the Arab pattern?) Their wives were not accustomed to grinding their own corn or fetching their own water.

I came afterwards to see, during those long days when I waited in the dark for Isaac to come and take dictation, that there was a contradiction in the very word 'freed.' They would lead me down to the church sometimes to hear how Jones or David handled the catechumens—not too often, or they would think I was interfering. They are eloquent, though less fluent in Kinika than in English, but they fail to touch on the fears of the people.

They have had their own fears—of whipping, starvation, sharks, humiliation. But they have never known what I may call the metaphysical fears of the community—of omens, evil spirits, forbidden acts that have become detached from their moral imperatives, just as devout Jews fear mixing milk and meat. And so they forget to offer liberation from these.

The Wanika at present do not fear hell-fire: it seems to them like another ordeal from which they will emerge unscathed if they are innocent. Separation from a God whom you have always had to coax and propitiate may not seem such a bad thing.

Even Isaac, I believe, attached to us since childhood, hardly understood the compulsion on his father to buy off the spirits which afflicted his wife, or the terrible effort of becoming different.

The Bombay Africans thought me too exacting in teaching the whole history of the Old Testament before baptism. How does one understand the New Covenant without the Old? How better could the Nika relate the promise to their own migratory and eventful history? But in Nasik, African history was something learned in a lecture, not the assurance of clan identity and divine protection.

Let me be fair. Although Jones riled me, he was the only one who, to my knowledge, sought blood brotherhood and some way into the rank order of Nika society. I do not know what success he has had: that may depend upon his not telling me. And with his piercing eyes and unruly hair he is the one who might, in an unguarded moment, be taken for a man of the coast: the others are too smooth, too tightly disciplined. Of course there is restraint, but the spirit of the Lord fell upon Saul and the prophets more indiscreetly, even, than the spirits that preyed upon Me Gunga. Outside the Church of England, enthusiasm need not be a dirty word.

About a year after my wife died, Sparshott arrived with his wife Margaret. He was in deacon's orders, and looked a bit temperamental to me from the start, so I left them to stew over language study and suggested he might like to take all the services. But that didn't go down well, oh no! he had to argue with me over essential parts of the Anglican liturgy... Well, my eyes were getting worse at that time, and just as I had been insensitive with Krapf, so they were with me, not recognizing how desperately I was missing my dear wife. They thought me an old man, I suppose, but I was still in my forties. So I kept my distance and plied my books rather than welcome them too effusively and have later to extricate myself. This was the time I fancied myself an epic poet, in English, if you please:

my dear wife would soon have disabused me of such fancies, but widowers set up their refuges against loneliness. The verses may still be somewhere in a box, but the only thing I had actually in common with Milton was the onset of blindness.

Poor Isaac, how you labored over the copying of that poem—new line, capital letter, indent half an inch… that was a ruse to pull myself together, no more. It would be better to face grief and grow, but we all have our weaknesses. I ought to have been pleased to have colleagues, especially another priest, but I had luxuriated in my grief: I could not let them interrupt it now.

Sparshott was thrown back on local speakers of the language as I had been, and that was an advantage: he is quite competent in it now. Margaret is a good girl, only she reminded me so much of Emma: she was always getting pregnant, but now they have three children to show for it. She tried hard at the school and did her best to make friends with the women. They even managed to hold public prayers daily, with George David translating.

One time they had all the Christians round to tea—well, to meal: Emma would not have called it tea. They had rice and meat and cups and saucers and spoons—help yourself to sugar and as many cups as you like. Tea was a novelty to most of our people, and one of the men had six cups. 'You won't be able to keep *that* up long, my girl,' I thought, not on mission allowances and all the wear and tear. But still it was kind of them to ask me to address the party, scarecrow though they thought I was. I spoke at some length on the invitation and the wedding garment. I wanted them to see that there was something more costly involved in their professions of faith than behaving well so that you got an invitation to tea. But I think some of them took it a bit literally. Margaret Sparshott, like Rebecca Wakefield, took some long time to get used to the prevailing state of half undress. Perhaps we older people had been less easily shocked in this respect: we had seen things in English slums which you, a generation later, might find it hard to credit. Visitors used to underline the point—'a dozen neatly clothed Christians met us at the landing place and 30 or 40 half naked pagans competed to carry our baggage.' How did they define those 'Christians,' I wonder. All people have the urge to imitate and to decorate: many used to make themselves elaborate leaf-hats but had so little use for them that they were left forgotten in the church.

I daresay I did go on a bit in those days about believers' baptism and the nature of marriage, since for a long time I had had no-one to listen to my ideas. Our Bombay Christians had already been taught all they thought they needed to know, and I would not have liked to sow doubt in the mind of new believers about the efficacy of the sacraments. In 1869 we were happy to admit Isaac and his father to Holy Communion. No bishop was at hand to confirm them, but we did not break our hearts over that.

The Sparshotts, like us, had lost their baby, and it pulled Margaret down. For health reasons they were advised to go to Mombas. George David tried hard to keep the school alive, but it was reduced to three pupils and again petered out. I tried to keep up the station going.

Sparshott at that time thought I was too hard on the Bombay Africans, but later he was to change his tune. Perhaps I was hard but I thought I was consistent and employed them according to their special gifts. For instance I encouraged them to take on our business with the Banian merchants and customs master who loved to hear their own language, hoping there might be an opening for the gospel also.

The society kept asking me to produce candidates for ordination—where from? The Nasik people will, of course, be the first, but we have no one else remotely near the necessary standard of education, except Isaac, and I thought him still too young—or perhaps I was too selfish to let him go. In Abyssinia Krapf had had two students reading Hebrew with him. Abbe Horner has 24 young African men learning Latin in his seminary at Bagamoyo. Perhaps my imagination is at fault that I could not conceive of such progress here. The *Intelligencer*, following Krapf, demands African Bishops. Abraham? Isaac? Jones? Semler? Zuia? each with his affinities of language, origin, generation set and rank. Paul was able to choose Timothy, both Greek and Jew, for bishop, Luke for doctor, Onesimus for freed slave. The writer to the *Hebrews* was less optimistic."

XI

"So I suppose it was because I could not overcome these obstacles that I seemed to drop out of sight of the Home Committee. They sent the Sparshotts off to the islands of the Indian Ocean to recommend a site for a freed slave settlement. He was to be priested in Mauritius.

In the islands, I hear, the difference between slavery and indentured labor is hard to make out, or the difference between planters and preachers either, if you judge by Sparshott, who came back throwing stones and calling people niggers. That is when I came to see that we were spiritually at risk: imperial pretensions could threaten our mission, our motives and our credibility.

You must not think that we were used to living in a settled state: there was always some local campaign or other going on at the coast. Mirambo was conducting a running war against the Arabs at Tabora all this time, and the expeditions shuttling up and down to look for Livingstone, or deliver stores which time and time again vanished before he got near them, brought us news from those inland regions. Then Lamu, which had been restless ever since Khalid's death, disposed of the attack from Witu, where Simba, the Lion of Bajun, was persistent in entertaining German travelers on his own account.

So when Mabruki attacked Takaunga in 1870 in defiance of the Sultan this did not seem strange, though we wondered how far his ambition might lead him. Our fears had always been of being thought to be linked, individually, with outsiders or with rebels, since this was not compatible with our calling.

We were not at risk in these internal squabbles as we had been with the Kwavi, who wanted only to destroy and take way, or with the French, who sought to embroil us. We could get along with consuls and trade agents in Zanzibar. Perhaps I was copying the Sultan's attitude, reluctant for other foreigners to intrude on to the mainland.

So it is not surprising that Majid began at this time to build his mainland harbor of peace, Dar es Salaam, offering free land to those prepared to cultivate it. He ignored Banian objections and flogged those Arabs who commented unfavorably on the climate. Like other monarchs, he needed a dream, and he reinforced it by ordering a powerful steam-tug from Hamburg to help ships through the narrow inlet to the harbor. The German merchant, O'Swald, after all, had an armed steam yacht called *The Electric Flash*, and sovereigns should keep ahead. It was then still the North German Federation—not royalty—that appointed the German consul.

Majid could not easily keep his dream to himself. At one time Frere proposed to the select committee in England a freed slave colony near Dar es Salaam which would be not an English colony but a colony of English people seeing fair play under the Sultan's protection. No doubt it takes an English aristocrat to make that distinction. I fear it may take more than a Busaidi merchant prince to evade the obvious conclusion.

These things did not affect the day to day running of the mission, but a shift of power in the Omani dynasty did. Early in 1866 Thuwain had been murdered in Muscat by his son Salim. Majid had been keeping up the subsidy, but one does not pay a parricide, particularly if he is one's own nephew! A remote relation took over Muscat for three years, so clearly the subsidy lapsed: those who had no claim to Said's throne could have no claim to compensation either. The coast was loud with threats, boasts and rumors.

The Suez Canal was now operating and the whole Indian Ocean open to the sea power of the west. Could Oman think of a sea war? Perhaps Azzan thought that Muscat would find itself once again invulnerable: he adopted a sectarian cause and flew a white flag against the red of Zanzibar. Some people compared it to the white flag on a pole that the Wasania use to entice a hippo out of the water and within range of their weapons.

Late in 1870, when the world was full of the news that Germany had defeated France at Sedan, Suliman bin Ali came privately to let consul Churchill and his assistant, Dr. Kirk, know that Majid was dying.

Barghash was the most likely candidate for Sultan, but offhand with the British. He had learned a thing or two in exile in Bombay, cultivating admirers with his private carriage and princely title. Churchill, unwell and hasty tempered, tended to favor Turki from Oman. Once in power, Barghash went so far as to surround the British Agency with troops, trying to arrest Suliman bin Ali who, discredited, had taken refuge there. Kirk, former assistant to Livingstone, kept his cool demeanor, minded his manners, bided his time. Barghash, however, had learned a lesson. Gravely he made the pilgrimage to Mecca to flaunt his respectability, taking Ali bin Nasser, our Governor, back to Zanzibar with him. We always felt a little uneasy when the Governor was away and left a deputy in charge. This time we had reason, as you will know if you have heard of the Al Akida business.

Next year Turki took over Oman: the double Busaidi dominion was reborn. Barghash refused to pay up to northern demands, kept his finances well under control, would not tolerate corruption. Fortunately, perhaps, Churchill's health soon forced him to leave. Kirk soldiered on, doing two jobs—political agent and medical officer—both of them made more difficult by the cholera epidemic which had started in Mecca during the summer of 1865 and made its way relentlessly year by year down the coast.

Kirk himself was something of a portent, making the quickest ever passage to Zanzibar from Europe, using the railway across Egypt, having the first European wedding on the island and rearing the six children born to him there.

Since my wife died I had felt cut off from all this. I even felt cut off from the life of the station—one would prefer by this time to be saying the life of the church—during those years. In Africa people come to their elders for counsel: perhaps it was part of the upheaval we had caused to offer counsel when we were still young men and find it stale when we matured. Yet how else would we fulfill our calling? Very few of us lived to be old.

William Jones was taken back to India for a bit after his first wife died in 1870—poor fellow, I felt for him. After that he went with some others to assist in Zanzibar and they came back in European dress with great ambitions. The UMCA had fine ideas. 'The permanent success of our ministry depends on acceptance of all the marked outward features of the native life from which it springs.' So I had always believed and preached. But when the good bishop (pluckily back in service by this time) also insists 'Everything like distance and separation is carefully avoided with our black as well as our white fellow-workers' he queers his own pitch, unless his missionaries are able to accept the local standards of dress and housing. CMS had, in East Africa, no specific policy and no specific funds for this question.

This was when, I believe, Bishop Tozer complained to London about me, or forwarded William's complaint from Zanzibar, and so I had to refrain from comment on his smart suits and pay him ten dollars a month. He could have got this or more translating letters for a Banian in Mombas and still been welcome to preach for us. The idea of the freed community was being obscured. But the actuality of local community remained."

Mabaya has come to visit me. Salamini lets him into the office in our old house. He must fear my sight further gone than it is, because he announces himself, 'This is Mabaya come to see you, pastor.' In fact his voice and bearing so much resemble his father, the old Saha, *that I have no difficulty in recognizing him—am on the point of welcoming him by his common name, 'Take your ease, Abe Sule.' So what is this formality? Mabaya has not followed his father into office but, after that precious herd of cattle was lost to the Kwavi, went into the caravan business and prospered. He is one of the new men.*

We gravely enquire after each other's health, the state of crops and livestock and the progress of a manslaughter case that has been troubling a clan a little to the north. Only after a decent interval is the purpose of the visit broached.

"I have come to make an enquiry about getting married, pastor. It seems to me that I have not been living in the right way."

The missionary heart should leap at such an admission. But, alas, hope does not spring quite eternal in the human breast. This does not sound like the approach of an earnest enquirer.

"I am delighted, Abe Sule, if you wish to reaffirm your marriage in church. Your father was a good friend of mine, though he did not come around to believing in Jesus, and I have always had a warm regard for

your family. But you realize, of course, that not only would you have to undergo instruction and baptism first, but Me Sule also. We might not actually insist on her learning to read, since you are both of mature age, but you would find a lot of advantages in doing so yourself. She used to come to my wife's classes, but I do not recollect seeing her in church for some time. You have discussed your intention with her?"

"Now, pastor, this is just what my father used to say—'Let Rebmani have his say and he will tie you like a bird in a net.' I did not say anything about Me Sule, did I? George David has been telling me that our Nika marriage is not right in the sight of God, and if that is so, I am no more than a boy. And if I am a boy, a bachelor, and it is now five years since Me Sule brought me a child, then I should start afresh and do it correctly—is that not sense? There is a daughter of the canoe-man from Jomvu who would suit me very well, and I would allow her to attend your classes if she wished, and even let her children go to school if she brings me blessing. What do you say to that?"

"You know quite well that I say no to it, Abe Sule. It is as shocking to me that a man should have two wives as it would be to you for a woman to have two husbands. All the same I know some of my friends had entered into that relationship because they did not hear the good news that women belong to the kingdom of God no less than men. Whether they come to confirm one of those marriages in church (and live separately from the second woman) or not—we have not yet made the experiment here—they cannot be relieved of the responsibility that having children by that other woman has placed upon them. Marriage is a state: marriage in church is a sacrament making that state holy—it cannot be used to cancel a condition that already exists. In fact I am forced to suppose that there are some things that cannot be made holy. People are better to follow their natural inclination than to drag the Lord into contradictions. I am sure that is not what George David meant."

"Well, Me Sule has a sharp tongue: I do not think you will make a Christian out of her."

"Maybe not, but she is the one you chose when you were young, Mabaya. You are not all that much younger than me: people will say you are as slow as the chameleon if you call yourself still a bachelor. Is this a time to be marrying?"

"You could think of marrying again yourself, pastor. That would be allowed, would it not, now that the first one is gone."

"It would be allowed, but I think I could not bear it, and I am not much of a prospect for a husband, do you think?"

"A Nika man of your age would not be so shy. If you would eat a bit better, to put some flesh on you, and do the house up as it used to be when our mother was there, you could get a wife from Zanzibar surely. I hear it is full of white people nowadays. Or even an Arab woman could sew and cook for you, and some of them know how to read."

We both break into laughter, knowing it to be impossible. I have a word with George afterwards and he agrees with me, but reluctantly, perhaps thinking a new start not such a bad idea. His own parents (I have to remind him) no doubt entered into a customary marriage, and his biblical duty is still to honor them, though he does not remember them clearly. I ask him to press Mabaya's sons to come to school—the younger ones, if Sule already considers himself too grown up. I wonder how many church marriages are truly sacramental. Would people in Europe submit to a course of bible readings if that were required before they could have a church wedding?

"Hodi, hodi!" at the door, and a loud rapping which we do not think consistent with good manners. I am still able to see my word lists, though with difficulty, and have my finger marking a place which has for a long time eluded me.

"Who is it?" I reply testily. One of the servants ought to be there. Perhaps Sulamini has gone off in a huff because I declared it was too early for lunch.

The door is pushed open and Abraham appears: he has grown heavier with the years but still treads with his old deliberation. The checked waist-cloth shows his seniority. He wears a singlet with it, Banian fashion, and a small cloth cap.

"Rebmani," he says, "it is I. Do I have to prove it before there is a word of welcome?"

"You are always welcome, Abe Gunga. I have not seen you lately, except at the services."

"Neither me nor anyone," growls my friend. "You shut yourself up here as though your only harvest were in books, not living Christians. You are missed."

"Most of the services are out of my hands now..."

"It is not only that. Dena was telling me you shut yourself up because there is war in your country. Is that true? You do not tell my son Isaac about it, only about church news. The Bombay people are the ones who read those big news pages that come through the post. Is it for your family that you are troubled?"

"Oh brother, brother, since I lost my wife you people here are my family. The war is far away from what I used to call my country and, oddly enough, the Germans look like beating the French. It is no affair of mine. When there is war in Witu or Tabora, does it trouble you here?"

"It comes near to doing so, since we hear of it sooner than we would have when I was a young man, and it touches trade too. Kiraf used to tell us that fighting was wrong, but the bible is full of fighting. Things like these Dena says he wanted to discuss with you, but someone at the door always says 'The old man is busy' or 'He is tired.' That is not like the old times, Rebmani. Do you want to leave us?"

"Certainly I do not want to leave, brother. Where would I go? But some would like me to, so that they can sprinkle water hastily and count heads. Is that what you would like to do?"

"How can you ask me such a thing? Young people are in hurry, as we all know. All the same, Me Gunga has waited a long time for baptism — does she not understand enough, even though she cannot read?

Well, Rebmani, that is not what I came to say. You know that of all of us I should miss you most — Isaac and I. But we see that your eyes trouble you and there is a heaviness in your spirit. If by going to your doctors in Europe you can save your eyes, then we should not keep you back. Of course we should wish you to return to us if it is possible, but that is our considered counsel, after prayer with the Rabai brothers."

Joy descends on me like a great weight of weariness, and tears gush out of my sore eyes. I put my head down on the table covered with the last of the cloths Emma brought from Egypt, frayed at the edges now and blotted with ink.

And let us consider one another to provoke unto
love and to good works, not forsaking the assembling of ourselves
together as the manner of some is, but exhorting one another.

Of course I am not free to leave at this point, but I have the assurance of a praying church. Abe Gunga presses my shoulder and leaves me alone with my wonderment. I do not refuse next day when Dena comes to invite me to a special meal.

"Later on they wrote to me from Home Committee, 'We have

often wished you to visit England. Now a formal invitation is extended: we shall welcome you with all the affection and respect to which your long and faithful service gives you claim.'

Oh yes, indeed, and leave Sparshott to supervise Mombas! What does that mean? Leave those people to preach craft work and literacy in place of the gospel? Come and print your books. The language will be used to promote trade and industry. People will be classed as Christians if they wear long trousers and work for a wage. Salvation is ceasing to grind corn and carry water.

Oh no: I was short-sighted physically then, but not so silly!

I was also depressed by lack of communication with my family. I could now hardly read at all, and Isaac was not able to make out their close-packed, Gothic handwriting. Margaret Sparshott had managed to spell out a few words for me, but not easily. Isaac wrote to Krapf for news, which he sent, but could not persuade them to use an English-speaking scribe. I was no longer traveling to Zanzibar, and in any case might be reluctant to submit private letters to a German consul who now represented a central authority unfamiliar, if not repugnant, to a rural family like mine.

The Lord over-rules: there was a method in what the Home Committee thought my madness, and I knew my sight was going before they did. I could recognize New and his men pretty well when they stayed with me on their way to Kilimanjaro in 1871: next year I could hardly read the report Kirk sent me of the terrible hurricane in Zanzibar which, by the Lord's grace, missed Mombas and Pemba. This was no time to leave the work in the hands of newcomers. The ground floor of the consulate, so I heard, was awash, the corrugated iron was stripped from the roofs of the mission buildings, the bell turret collapsed and the chapel and its organ were ruined. The clove plantations were devastated and ships in the harbor wrecked. The Catholic refuge on the mainland and its supporting farm were totally destroyed.

We had probably been foolish not to take warning from the terrible tidal wave of 1867, but I do not hear that any extra precautions were taken. I do not wonder that Bishop Tozer had his second breakdown and resigned next year. But for a Sultan, of course, there is no resigning. No fleet. No cloves. The entrepot trade badly hit. Of his major sources of income, only the slaves remained, and

Pemba, prospering as never before, had an insatiable demand for slaves. But he would not be able to satisfy it for long.

By 1872 Kirk was really ill himself with dysentery and malaria. The Bombay Presidency then chose to appoint a Major Way as consul but he never came to Zanzibar: in fact, after receiving the posting order he blew his brains out. Only in 1873 was Kirk confirmed as political agent, with two assistants and the promise of a full time doctor. He had to use his new power to convey British threats to the Sultan after Frere's visit, yet still managed to retain Barghash's trust. In Oman, Turki rapidly gave in and assented to the treaty when he heard that Frere was steaming in his direction, unsatisfied, back to London. They were all too busy to notice that my own years of service would be reduced to nothing by an official whisper into the ear of Salisbury square.

In this situation Barghash more than ever needed to consolidate his local power, and a tragedy came to his aid. Most Zanzibaris are Hadimu by descent, having their own royal line, and this died out in 1873, so the Sultan took over the functions of the *Mwenye Mkuu*. This also made him overlord of the Tumbatu, so in effect he annexed two traditional loyalties at the same time. If I had had my sight I would have liked to witness the ceremonies.

The *Mwenye Mkuu* used to be prayed for before the Sultan in the mosque on Fridays. People had to climb down from their clove or coconut trees at his approach (so that no-one should appear to be above him) and came before him on their knees. This is why we have the respectful greeting *Shikamuu*, 'I embrace your feet,' though nowadays we use it a bit loosely.

Now the *Mwenye Mkuu* is also supposed to make rain, and when Said Sultan imprisoned one, some years earlier, he is said to have disappeared, and so no rain fell on Zanzibar for three years. The people were very distressed—so, no doubt, was Said Sultan, who owned about a third of the clove crop,—and a way had to be found for the *Mwenye Mkuu* to resume his duties and make his presence known by the two special drums and the two great *Siwa* horns. A sacred horn was embedded in the Walls of his private palace too, and, some people whispered, even sacrificial slaves. I do not assert this, but I could believe it. Fortunately there has been excess rather than shortage of rain since Barghash took over the title and his technical innovations will probably dazzle his followers into crediting him with all the required powers.

You see, he is becoming Sultan indeed: he needs this title to confront ambitious foreigners. He may yet get the state visit to Europe he has been angling for. But he has lost the freedom of maneuver that his father had as a merchant prince, to haggle with his partners, to interpret oral agreements, to recoup his political losses by making, as Captain Mansfield tells me we should say nowadays, a fast buck. And I wonder whether he will have anything but the title left. Mr. Price will hardly request him, as Krapf asked his father, for a letter of safe conduct.

Said Sultan's ancestors had stressed their religious role to keep up Omani unity against the zealot Wahabi, and had filled the harbor of Muscat with purchased or captured prizes. His father, Sultan Ahmed, had signed a treaty with the British before the eighteenth century was out and watched with interest the rise of Napoleon. Said himself had consolidated his sphere of influence down the east coast. No-one could have anticipated how this would wane in the presence of more widely spread networks of power.

For me there was no question of gaining or renouncing titles. When new missionaries came I was hardly informed, let alone consulted. By that time my sight had totally gone and my prospects too, for I had come under the displeasure of Sir Bartle Frere, as you already know, and I will spare you all his comings and goings—full dress parades, audiences with the Sultan, in council and alone, manipulation of consuls, naval presence up and down the coast, even as far as Madagascar—what business had the British there? Sultan Barghash, I am told, threatened with the loss of his only major commodity after the hurricane or, eventually, British use of force, remarked sadly, 'You hold a spear to each of my eyes: which one shall I choose?' This moved me, who had submitted to the spear in both eyes and expected one to the heart. Another time he admired a fine Bible in the British consulate, remarking that it was 'a good book, which justifies slavery in principle.' He was wrong, of course, but no fool, a chip off the old block. The Sultan has his toys, his treasures and his physical eyes but, like me, he well knows when he is no longer head of station.

Sparshott's behavior was completely devilish. He admitted to throwing a stone at a man who was beating a drum outside his house and refused to stop—he even said he had done it many times before. He did not seem to care that to face such a charge contemptuously in a Mohammedan court of law was to put the whole mission in disrepute. The Governor declared that it would be as much as his life was worth to help a white man find a house again. Ironically, the one we had asked to find was not for any white man but for a party of 20 Bombay Africans being escorted from India by Ishmael Semler, yet Sparshott's attitude was 'I could send a thousand niggers from Mombas to Bombay.' This could not be tolerated, and it gave a very bad start to the new missionaries coming in. Seif, acting Governor in his uncle's absence, tried to get Price's landlord to evict him, but without success.

There was even a dispute about the mission house which we had used all those years, when Rashid of Takaunga claimed it was his. For once Sparshott consulted me, and the British consul said the owner's claim could only be made through the Sultan, so we still have the use of the house.

The proverb says, *Gongwa ni mwina wa kiza*, Mombas, is a hole of darkness. Well, it is I who pleaded, ten years ago, Mombas, poor and degraded though it may be at present, may still have an important and even glorious destiny; I still plead for it, now it has grown, for it is a place with a life of its own. Arabs and Swahili have come together, speaking the same dialect, all (at last) attending one or other of the Sunni mosques. In my young days every Omani belonged to the Ibadhi denomination, but now Sheikh Ali bin Abdallah has felt called to reclaim all of them in Mombas to Sunni orthodoxy. So powerful are his means of persuasion that one devout Ibadhi scholar in Zanzibar turned black in the face after picking up a spell which the Sheikh had inserted into a copy of one of his own books.

Arabs and Swahili, likewise, write the same topical poetry: anyone can join the coterie around either of the two dancing parties, *Mbura* and *Mrawi*, which perform every evening and give some form to current gossip and political pressure. The customs master has started keeping separate records of the town's trade, and Wanika move there freely, compared with the diffidence of their approach 30 years ago. Ferry boats keep busy from Kisauni, Makupa, Kilindini and Ras Mboroko to the mainland, and these are the start points from which the gospel can be brought to the neighboring homesteads if only our missionaries stop quarrelling among themselves.

By the time I had finished with Frere the Home Committee were begging me not just to visit them but to leave. Go to Bombay or Germany if you prefer it to print your books—anywhere you cease to be a stumbling-block. Sparshott got around to thinking it: to Price, who came last year to start a 'new' mission, it was obvious. I had come to the people as a brother but it was a father they had to have. Like it or not, they have now.

Livingstone had died, God rest him, just before the treaty to stop the slave trade was finally signed. Euan Smith came back to Mombas last year to present medals to his porters at Freretown. Perhaps they let him think I had already gone away, for he sent no word.

Price and his wife are veterans of the Indian field, survivors if you like. I may disagree with them, but there is no doubt that they know their trade. Only they have no time for old fogies like me, so to put me right they brought in four men from Islington. You may remember that 25 years ago Krapf was complaining to the Home Committee that modern missionaries were weak and effeminate— that meant me and Erhardt, who is still at work in India. Now of their four newcomers Remington has died—God rest him, he did his best. Mr. Williams is here with me under a strict medical regime: he is invalided after a year and half but is determined to seek another field and not give up. Pearson and Last are hanging on by the skin of their teeth, and Dr. Forster, who came separately as medical officer to Freretown, is already sickly.

One day some pietist will develop a thesis on that great word, 'I have toiled all the night and taken nothing, *nevertheless* at Thy word I will let down the net.' To do that is obstinacy indeed, because of course, one may be wrong. It is a risk one takes. Have you ever got up from your knees, I wonder, after praying with a Christian brother and been told, 'Well, that's settled then. The Lord has clearly revealed that I was right?' It could be so, and yet if there were certain people I have not liked to pray with, it is for risk of such an embarrassing situation.

At present George David has been sent to Kiriama and Ishmael Semler to Mombas. They are the two who know enough Kinika to replace us, and they may do it well. But George's Kiswahili is far from perfect, and if he exercises it on the freed slaves, many of whom know none at all, I fear the result.

Recently another 60 men, 35 women and 35 children have come from Bombay, claiming to be Christians. You can imagine that it will be a while before they can be useful in evangelism, but Price intends them to be an example to the Wanika of regular field labor. Very well, so long as there is no dispute over the ownership of the fields.

In January this year we were all ordered to Mombas. I was bundled into a boat with Pearson and Last. Mr. and Mrs. Price, we were told, were to have a meeting with Captain Luke of HMS *Rifleman*. Captain Luke said he was to receive all British subjects on board, since the Sultan feared unrest. (Nobody remembered that I was not a British subject.) Mabruki had visited Ribe with over 200 men and, though they offered no offence, the Sultan was afraid of risking British lives: he must already have been upset at the death of three Frenchmen looking for minerals on the Juba River. Their consul was bound to search for someone to blame.

As well as seven Europeans Price pointed out 60 'natives under British protection.' I suppose he means the Nasik people and the Banians from British India, since no-one truly native to the coast could be said to be under British protection. However our local helpers carried on very efficiently while we were away. That is the good thing that came out of the inconvenience. They neither looked for protection nor were offered any.

An armed group, ostensibly breaking away from Mabruki's rebels, had visited us at Kisulutini shortly before. They were not hostile—one even helped us to dig a grave—but I remarked that they might wish to take us hostage. The Governor was uneasy already, because a jumped up Arab officer calling himself 'Al Akida'—the same who attempted to burn Mombas town last year—had barricaded himself in Fort Jesus with some of his Hadhrami supporters (vulgarly known as fleas) skirmishing with the official Baluchi guards. In January the Sultan had to request the aid of two British ships to enforce surrender terms.

Price said he did not see anything to run away from, and I should have thought Rabai or Ribe much safer for us at that time than Mombas, torn between parties as it was, or a foreign, armed ship. What is certain is that outside interference is becoming too common."

They have hustled me up the steep stairs to the rooftop room: Last needs more support than I, feverish as he is and gasping for breath. The familiar aroma of the harbor touches many memories. It is quiet—vessels lying well out, I suppose, for easy movement. The town has drawn in on itself only whispers, they tell me, and furtive footsteps along the ordinarily sociable streets, littered with cinders and charred pieces of wood. If today's meeting fails we shall be hauled out to the Rifleman, *like it or not.*

Orders are barked below, with a slap of ropes being thrown. Last drags himself to the window, reports a naval party landing, trim blue and white, with pipes, escorting an officer along the harbor front towards the fort. I can picture their progress as far as the broad, inscribed gateway, but who knows what game of hide and seek goes on inside, Arab against Arab, firing from shadowy turrets into the glare of the noonday courtyard. I have had enough of this conflict but Emma, serene in this bare seaside apartment of ours, would have said with a smile, 'Johannes, this is quite exciting.'

"When I was young I eschewed politics, as the Home Committee repeatedly told us to do: that was why I looked for some official to bear my politics for me. Well, my time is up. Somebody else will follow my footsteps to Kadiaro and to Jaga. Since those days Zanzibar has come to swarm with agents, consuls and traders: the Gulf of Oman is thick with them: it is only a matter of time till they reach Mombas. Hamerton was once the only Briton on Zanzibar, though not the first: now there are nearly 80 Europeans, and where this happens there is threat of empire as in South Africa, where Dutch and British quarrel over Brother Moffat on his travels—'Let him pass,' 'He may not pass'—and guns and money seize men's minds to the exclusion of the gospel."

XII

Biscay lulled him. Hardy old sailors, people said, dreaded the nausea to their dying day. Williams collapsed on to his bunk and retched, Isaac, though doggedly attentive, spoke hearty words in a weak voice and, settling him in the saloon for meals, would slip away on some pretext. A steward cut out his meat. The dining-room service was slack, he said, during such weather. Miss Philipps greeted him faintly with a suspicion of brandy on her breath and a swish of heavier skirts. There was no sitting on deck now, though the hardy young officers paced out their measured distance. Rebmann mentioned to one of them in the lounge that the roll of the ship was really nothing compared to laying off in a heavily loaded dhow to make way against the monsoon, a foot above the dark waters and hung about with the smell of shark oil. The young man muttered something about the complexities of modern steam navigation and strode away—later, despite the muffling carpet, there was a hint that he was beginning to run.

Though summer was approaching, the tang in the air was unmistakably of Europe now. The wind dropped, the dinner-tables filled and the word 'Channel' crept into the conversation. They were to dock at Tilbury, and gradually the smell of mud crept aboard with the hoarse Cockney cries of the sea-gulls. Isaac, stronger but drawing a line at eggs and bacon, stood avidly by the rail recounting what he saw. Rebmann, alert now, questioned and corrected—not a carriage but a dray, not a palace but a tenement, not a washerwoman but a garbage collector.

The sounds were quite different from those he had remembered—not loud-hailers but steam-whistles, not wheries but motor-tugs. Officials came aboard concerned with health, customs, passes.

Isaac and Williams coped, Williams because he had been less than two years away, Isaac because, where all seemed so strange, no strangeness was outrageous.

Within an hour they were speeding by train into London proper, surrounded by the discharge of many steamers from different parts of the world. They had taken leave of their fellow-passengers before disembarking.

Mr. Hutchinson, the CMS Lay Secretary, met them at the station. Rebmann and Isaac were overcome by his exact foreknowledge of the train they would catch, but Williams took it for granted, and was borne away by a cousin in a cab. Mr. Hutchinson had arranged to receive Rebmann and Isaac into his own home for the first day or two, while consultations and medical examination were going on. His expectation was that Rebmann would then go quietly off to Germany to die, while Isaac could get some training at Islington and then appear as a lion in a few of the more enterprising parishes interested in foreign mission.

Both expectations were flouted and this, on balance, to Edward Hutchinson's pleasure. Rebmann, physically feeble as he might appear, was by no means senile and expressed himself forcibly in a strong German accent. He expected to be sent on deputation work and had a moving testimony to give. This was far from what reports from the coast had suggested. Moreover, he was in no hurry to return to Germany.

When he did go, Isaac was to go with him. Neither of them had ever entertained any other course. When Hutchinson demurred on account of Isaac's knowing no German, he was withered by a more or less correctly oriented look.

"When your predecessors sent me to East Africa nearly 30 years ago, sir, the least of their worries was that I had learned no Kiswahili and was not aware of the existence of Kinika. I had seen one of Dr. Krapf's early papers on Galla, a language which was not in practice ever useful to me. It was taken for granted that the grace of God and a modicum of English would suffice for all emergencies. Isaac is at least as intelligent as I am. His education has, like mine, been among people of different tongues, though he started English earlier than I and pronounces it better. He is the nearest to a son I have and he will not leave me until he has placed me in the hands of my own family. After that, give him what training seems appropriate to you. He can communicate the gospel to his own people with an accuracy no missionary ever will."

Mrs. Hutchison beamed upon Isaac, so polite, so respectful, so attentive. Mr. Rebmann frightened her a little, frail, acute, clumsy: he had already broken a china vase in the sitting-room with a sweep of his coat-tails.

"I must apologize, Mrs. Hutchinson, and beg you to clear a path for me. You know, since I have been blind I have never come across such obstacles. It was lucky for me, I suppose, that so much on ship-board is screwed down. If you shout a warning at me I shall freeze instantly like children playing statues. But it is better to keep your things out of harm's way till you find a simple boarding-house for me".

He had pleaded for Islington: they would take him to see the college but it was at last, praise be, full, and privately Mr. Hutchinson wondered how the students would look upon this image of themselves in 30 years' time.

Isaac was much more frightened of the sitting-room than Rebmann. He had judged European houses to be what the missionaries had shown him—tables and chairs on a flat floor, plates, cups, saucers, spoons, a curtain perhaps within the shutter, at best, marvel of marvels, a small piano. The most intricate item at Kisulutini had been Mrs. Rebmann's work-box, with compartments that opened out for silk and scissors. Mrs. Sparshott had gay china and a cradle that rocked, a stand for her parasols and a folding chair that could be put up in the boat. That was a delight to the people around. But this…

Polly used to say how big the missionary houses were in India, with wide verandahs and punkahs to defend you from the heat and low chairs to lounge in. But they were plain compared to all the items a rich Indian household could buy—shawls and brassware, scents and shrines, painted turrets and sculptured figures. But this…

The best Arab quarters were very fine, with tiles and cushions and texts lovingly copied from the Koran. One saw fewer things, perhaps because the women's quarters were separate and it was women (Isaac, nine years married, knew it well) who collected things. But this…

The velvet cloths on the seats and tables, and embroidered ones behind—antimacassars, he savored the word. The fringe along the mantelpiece and the gleaming fire-irons now that it was too warm (warm!) they said for fires. The embellished clocks, the china ornaments, the cut glasses in cabinets with the best plates, pictures framed behind glass on the walls and flowers and fruit carved into the sideboard, mirrors set into wood, china panels below and above the fancy handles on the inside doors, bright gas light that came on when you pulled a chain, rugs on the linoleum of the bedrooms or the polished wood of the public rooms and up and down the stairs—such rugs as would be too good to sleep on and which a Mohammedan might keep for prayer. And rich patterns on the walls that they told him were 'only paper'—*only* paper such as one might paste on the end leaves of a bible or think too good to cover a Christmas table with.

And yet Mr. Hutchinson described himself as an ordinary sort of person who kept no carriage of his own and had just a cook and two young housemaids to help his wife. These brought a jug of hot water to your room early in the morning, and cleared the table after Mrs. Hutchinson had served out.

Was this, he dared whisper in Kinika late at night, what Mrs. Rebmann had turned her back on, what Mrs. Sparshott sighed for when her husband complained that their household was low and makeshift?

"Perhaps," said Rebmann without much interest. "Maybe this is a bit above their experience, but it is what they are likely to want. You see, we are no worse off without it."

No worse. He supposed so. But he knew how Polly would stroke the velvet and arrange the dishes in the high cupboard, and set the maids to polishing.

Next day they took the bus to Bank and walked down Ludgate Hill to Salisbury Square. There was the smell of business—starched cloth and boards, grease, horse droppings, printers' ink. Isaac's eyes lifted reverently to St. Paul's. Rebmann showed excitement at the remembered cry of the newsvendor, and suggested that Isaac should take in the view from Blackfriars Bridge while the interviews went on—"but do not linger on the other side."

The Clerical Secretary, the Rev. Henry Wright, joined them and, after prayer, the expected questions were asked—how many baptized, confirmed, married, regularly communicant? How many enquirers? How much social impact—people sending their children to school, clothing themselves, abandoning witchcraft and polygamy? How many full-time and occasional teachers? How many literate?

They shook their heads at one another: Rebmann sensed it. Their minds were on New Zealand and Sierra Leone.

"I believe," Rebmann ventured, "that Mr. Booth has made some similar compilation about the situation in London. Has it been of assistance in planning the evangelistic work of the church?"

There was little encouragement to continue.

"My late wife's first husband was Rector of St. Giles' and she gave me a most distressing account... I wonder if the students from Islington still go to the Irish courts?"

"There are more and more such tenements," responded Mr. Wright. "Some of us feel that Mr. Booth diverges excessively from the customary practices of the chapels, let alone the English church. But he is venturing into savage territory, as you have done yourself, Mr. Rebmann. We had hoped that in a healthy rural atmosphere your congregation would have prospered more."

"I am a farmer's son, sir. I must object to equating rural with healthy..."

Cold sores on the itinerant farm laborer's face. A rheumatic shepherd in the dew of lambing time, with no chance to change his clothes and no comfort save the bottle. The peril of falling coconuts and the dangerous climb of the mgema *tapper up the palm frustrated that the galago lemur has already drunk from the shell he placed. The cassava diet of famine time, with sore eyes and cracked feet and purchasers eying the likely children.*

"Yes, yes, I generalize. But the climate which weakens the health of the white man may be benign to the native."

Jiggers. Ticks. Trachoma. Slaughtered breech babies. Circumcision gone septic. Me Ngowa bleeding with no-one to plead her rights. Mothers cowering at the sound of the muansa. *The* Saha *speared. Bones and genitals in the little black bag. At what cost are the shark teeth gathered that women love for their necklaces?*

"We know that you have been starved of helpers. With an increasing work-force and the mobilization of the Nasik Christians as an example to the congregations, Mr. Price is planning to extend on foundations you have built. For many years we have prayed for the uplifting of native clergy..."

"Mr. Secretary, I am not here to defend myself. I am here to be pensioned off. But there are some things you in London have to think about. They will expand, and the Bombay Christians will have their first clergy, that is understood. Even if they had not got rid of me they would have expanded, only I might have been able to put in a word or two... Jones will baptize, I know, many, many people, and he will feel in his heart that he gives me pleasure by doing so and thus will try to justify his impatience with me, acknowledging that people have made progress since my time and Krapf's. It would be more gracious and more accurate to say *in* my time...

Patience, yes, he and the others from Bombay, they have the kind of patience that repeats over and over again to the freed slaves. *Mungu kila pahali yupo, juu na chini.* 'God is everywhere, above and below.' George David is alleged to have repeated this word of wisdom 300 times at a single session. The Kiswahili is not very good but the sentiment, of course, is admirable. The question is, how does it lead to baptism or, as your report suggests, to 14 marriages among freed slaves? For baptism you need to stoop down close to each of these people and find by question and answer whether they understand what they repeat and can express it in their own tongue. It would not have been hard to teach them proof texts in English or German...

True, we must start somewhere, we *did* start somewhere, as Mr. Venn's record will show you. However, since I left home I hear they have already brought 302 rescued slaves, half of them children, and now that the settlement is crowded they *must*, of course, start.

Mr. Hutchinson, you have employed your pen and your conscience to good effect in the freeing of the slaves. Yet I wonder if either of you have ever seen a rescued slave as he comes from the ship. He is usually diseased from the hardships he has suffered, practically naked, in most cases *incommunicado*, not because he is foolish but because he has no language in common with you and his experience on board has not encouraged him to trust strangers. Do you know the smell of terror and the vacant eyes that dare not admit hope, and the terrible appetites of people who fear they may never have another chance to gratify them? Yes, they will be saved in a manner of speaking, but something more than drill and school-mastering will be required.

Jones has his eye on Kisulutini, and maybe will do better there than Price who insists, as I am sure he has written to you, that the rooms let in sun and keep out air, that the water is bad and the situation wretched. What does the letter you have on your file say? 'The mission is at its lowest ebb, while outwardly everything has an air of dirt and dilapidation.' Price thinks that he knows the orient and that a blind man cannot know what is in his letters!

Well, dirt you can clean up. If you have eyes, and dilapidation of course strictly can only occur in a stone house. Dr. Krapf need not send a man of *classical education* to tell us that. His old cottage at Rabai Mpya is safe enough from dilapidation. And Price will tell you he has to make Kisulutini his head-quarters for want of accommodation in Mombas, but if your staff had kept the peace, Mr. Hutchinson, he would not want for house room in Mombas, where we have been welcomed for more than 30 years. He may well be reluctant to keep Sparshott on and at the same time nervous of your challenging him. The quarrels between Sparshott and Chancellor, and especially Sparshott's conduct towards the African brothers, cause loss of respect within as well as for the church. I admit I have been on bad terms with Sparshott myself, would not shake hands with him, could not pray with him, could not let him think his go-ings-on tolerable to me. But I have not refused to see him, nor have I bandied words with him in public. He is changeable, you know, persuasive. He has, as the old sinners in the Irish courts used to say, kissed the blarney stone, and he can be generous when he sees the need: it was his boat that took Wakefield and his evangelist to work in Duruma when Wakefield was sorely in need of consolation.

Now the die is cast—the freed slaves will be settled (and they should be settled, instructed, employed, nobody doubts that) not for Christ but for the British. They will learn their proof texts in a language they may or may not understand, and be baptized. The Queen will not take responsibility but she will hold the puppet-strings through soft-spoken diplomats and gunboats and judicious presents. And old fools like Rebmann will not be allowed to hold back the course of history. Emancipation—yes, they have that in

America even: within weeks we heard of Lincoln's triumph and then of his death. We are not so far cut off as you suppose, sir. Clothes and book learning, they had these in some measure even before. But freedom — that is a harder word than emancipation.

So they will tell you, Rebmann does not want people to have shoes, jackets, a school, a trade. Even in Krapf's book see how I pleaded for them to have these things. When I labored as mason and carpenter did I not long for skilled workmen to help me? And last time I could see well enough to do my own repairs, I was glad there were enough Wanika to assist, rather than sending to Mombas for Swahilis. Not like 1850 when they stood idly by and watched me and Erhardt work.

But do not tell them, 'You have houses, clothes, books, money and therefore you are Christians.' Rebmann, who came to bring the gospel, is a man like other men, who misses his wife and is partial to hot broth. He did not labor for 29 years only to bring books and hammers and houses with windows."

"Your point is taken, Mr. Rebmann; the difference in view is only how to bring it about."

"Well, gentlemen, I have found it easier than I expected to change from Lutheran to Anglican. Now I have to start thinking like a Lutheran again. But I do see that the Methodists may be better adapted to the East African situation than we are. Mr. Wakefield has already, I understand, made up a local preachers' circuit. Here each man will preach within the language area he knows best, without administering the sacraments. In any case there is a lot of preaching to be done before we start on sacraments."

"Now, Mr. Rebmann, you have long experience. Sparshott and Chancellor say they cannot maintain themselves in tolerable comfort on less than £300 a year. Is that reasonable?"

"Well, sir I doubt whether the words 'tolerable comfort' could have occurred in correspondence between myself and Mr. Venn, 'comfort' was not in the picture at all. But let me be fair. I think these gentlemen may not be too far out in their reckoning. Why, 50 years ago the stipend in India was, I believe, £100 a year, and when Dr. Krapf put his proposal for a chain of mission stations his estimate worked out at about £120 per man per year. I am not sure he was thinking at all of families. But if you think of the amount of porterage required for the inland stations, then it was a low estimate even 25 years ago.

Prices have risen since and expectations have also risen. If you know there is a telegraph, you will naturally want to use it. If you are traveling with officials on a steam-ship you need a decent suit. It is not the same as bedding down a dhow. Price laid out some money on my behalf, since I have lost the faculty of fitting myself out before a mirror. We have always had to spend money on guides, carriers, boatmen, interpreters. As the places we serve in become more wealthy, even domestic servants expect more: so do trades-men and builders when their services become more sophisticated.

We used to be urged to keep a common purse. I was charged with keeping the accounts for Rabai, and you have them recorded in your books. It was Krapf who wanted separate accounts because he felt Erhardt was extravagant in purchasing groceries from Zan-zibar. Perhaps he had forgotten that after his wife's death he had begged Mr. Waters to procure him pre-cooked foods from America on account of his poor digestion. I do not judge between them. But remember that, except for the fever at Tanga, Erhardt kept strong and cheerful and he is still working even now.

Out of that common purse we used to have, traveling and stores have to be paid for, medicines you need for your church members or meat to feast visiting dignitaries. Two ladies keeping separate houses must surely be allowed some private expenses and a mea-sure of choice. I hear that Mr. Price turns up his nose at tinned had-dock when on safari! We never had the blessing of a tin-opener when I was young.

Burton in his book says that the East African mission had used £12,000 with a minimal result. I do not know where he got the fig-ure from. Nothing like that amount ever went through my hands, though I never failed to pay my porters. But even if the figure is cor-rect, taking into account passages and provision for all those who set out and never reached us, or did not survive into service, taken over 16 years with an average of three people to be supported, is it such an unreasonable figure?

It is not only that the men of the 1870s have become used to what we would once have called luxuries, but also that the work itself is expanding. I hear talk of pictures and globes for the school-

room. Well, your supporters must set out their priorities. They like
(I understand from the few comments I have received) to visualize
a little group of half-clothed children under a tree, writing their
ABC in the dust, as they often do.

But at the same time you are asking us to produce evangelists,
even bishops. At Islington we were taught to tinker, Mr. Hutchinson, to plant and to build in the intervals of philology and theology.
But we were not taught to make a silk purse out of a sow's ear.

I dislike Sparshott. I make no secret of it. But they lost their
baby, as we lost ours, and hushed their grief and kept on working.
I felt sorry afterwards that I did not go up from Mombas for the
funeral, and left it for the Methodists to take. They perhaps thought
it was ill will: in fact, it brought back too many memories. 'A voice
is heard in Rama, Rachel weeping for her children.'

There is a verse in *Isaiah*, Mr. Hutchinson, (chapter 65 and verse
20: I have laid it to heart many times) about the Lord's coming kingdom, 'No more shall there be in it an infant that lives but a few
days.' It cannot be to His glory if any infant dies because, out of
economy, the mother has missed the nourishment, the medicine or
the healthy change of scene that would have built up her strength.

I stand before you as you see me, a man old before my time,
and I do not begrudge what sufferings it has pleased the Lord to lay
upon in his service. But when you dismiss me and humor me and
say 'He only held the fort, he never sallied forth to compel the un-
ready servants to come into the banquet, his word-lists were more
important to him, so that he did not challenge governors or flaunt
his faith before Kadhis and fling it in the face of slave-owners' —
when you ease your embarrassment by saying all this, say also that
this sentimental old German wished a boy called Kango to become
Samuel at his baptism so that at least the name of his son might
remain in East Africa."

The Secretaries nodded to one another. The subject was more
reasonable than they had anticipated; they felt uneasy but not defeated. The mission field throws up strong characters.

"Now, Mr. Rebmann, I would like you to listen carefully to this
settlement. Expenses, as you say, have risen. We have no means of
comparing Germany with England in this respect and, alas, few of
your contemporaries have retired there on our invalid list. Either

they succumb earlier or they serve in situations which permit them to remain there to old age." (As I would have done. As I wished to do). "We believe you will be able to subsist on £100 a year, and we shall meet your accommodation and medical expenses while you are in London. The doctors will decide what meetings you are fit to undertake. Mr. Nyondo can be given some training here and accommodated for as long as is necessary after your return to Germany. We shall ask him to address some meetings for us in recognition of the return passage to East Africa. Does that sound fair to you?"

"I am ready to be guided by you gentlemen. I am not acquainted any more with the cost of things, and Isaac has very little experience of handling money. Dr. Krapf is the one who could advise."

"Dr. Krapf's connection with the society was broken long ago, since we could not accommodate his plans. He remains a valued correspondent, but perhaps his style of living would be a bit above your means."

"I daresay that is so. Only we must consult about the manuscripts. I am leaving them in your house, Mr. Hutchinson: you must keep them safe. The wooden box inside a tin one to keep out ants and so on. "

"As you wish. We value them highly. Now we must leave you and the doctor will come to examine you, after the office boy has brought you in a bite to eat. A chop and some mineral water? Will that do?"

Isaac attended the examination and helped Rebmann restore his clothing to order. The old man was tired, and glad to get home on the omnibus. They went to their room after a cup of tea and reassembled at the dinner table.

"There is a decent boarding-house we sometimes use," Mr. Hutchinson was saying, looking nervously at Rebmann, who had spilt some soup down his front and was kneading a linen napkin with his fingers. "But first there is a decision to be made. You see, the medical man who had a look at you thinks that something may be done for one of your eyes at least, Mr. Rebmann. That is, he would like you to go into hospital. We owe you that much care. If you had been under treatment here you need never have lost your sight completely."

Rebmann went very white. Isaac put a reassuring hand on his arm and found it trembling.

"You mean—I might get it back?"

"It is possible, I dare not say more than that. Of course, the operation is a bit painful: you have to be kept still, bandaged and so on. But I should advise you to take the chance. The Society, naturally, will take responsibility for the fees."

"Anything, anything," Rebmann whispered. "I did not want to come. I had no idea. Oh, thank you, thank you."

Mrs. Hutchinson put down the gravy boat. It was rattling on the matching saucer. A tear or two fell on the bright, white tablecloth.

"Do not distress yourself, Mr. Rebmann; after we have finished the talks tomorrow we will take you and Nyondo to your quarters. The proprietor is a motherly woman who will look after you. It is not that you are not welcome, you understand, but we have a bishop coming at the weekend and after that our married daughter. The doctor will let us know when a hospital place is ready. Meanwhile you probably have visits you wish to make and things you think our young friend should see. After the hospital we shall look into the matter of speaking engagements. And we will have to find someone who can write in German to your family. Perhaps they would be able to come and fetch you."

"To come…? Well, I don't think so. They are not great travelers. But if I had my sight. There is Mrs. Tozer—you have the address somewhere, Isaac? That is my sister-in-law, no relation to Bishop Tozer as far as I know. She will tell us if there are any other members of the family I should see. Robert Moffat is in London they tell me? We have not met but we know of one another: it would be an honor to speak with him. And these Americans, what are they called, Isaac?"

"Dwight Moody and Ira Sankey. People on the boat told us they were coming down from Scotland."

"What extraordinary names these people have! But I hear they move powerfully by their message and singing. Mr. Hutchinson, I would gladly have laid my bones at Kisulutini, but if the Lord insists on London, let us get the best out of London."

"Amen to that," echoed the Secretary. The Society had recovered from the low water point of vocations and giving five years before, but inspiration was still needed and this shabby, much-maligned old man at his table—Edward Hutchinson realized with a jolt that he might himself be in years the older—might well challenge the complacency of the good organizers who instructed the Lord in how his work should be done.

"Dr. Krapf will advise me about the manuscripts, but if I can see for myself..."

Gently Isaac urged him away, tucked him into the great double bed that every English spare room must have if it is big enough, and himself shrank into the small cot in the corner. These people perhaps understood what an affront a double bed would seem to him, though they took no exception to it. He lay marveling that it should still be daylight at nine o'clock, while next door the sound of a piano emerged from open windows, and men and women together strolled out upon the lawn.

The hospital appointment was soon made, and before Rebmann was admitted he was able to go to one of the last Revival meetings held by Sankey and Moody before their return to America. It was held at the Agricultural Hall at Islington and some of the missionary students provided an escort. All were caught up in the emotion of the packed auditorium, Isaac enjoyed it all thoroughly, seeing it as a large-scale reenactment of the penitents' bench instituted at Ribe. Rebmann was not altogether at home with the music, but impressed by the energy of the proceedings. Some of his neighbors, though not spiritually responsive, pronounced it "better nor a music-hall," and the students had exalted visions of repeating the experience in each continent they would serve in. They saw him on to the bus, bawling at the tops of their voices "It passes knowledge that dear love of thine," as compulsively as those otherwise intoxicated joined in "Champagne Charlie" or variant versions of "Come into the garden, Maud." Rebmann did nothing to disabuse them of their hope.

Except for Binns, who was preparing for deacon's orders and had questioned Rebmann long and hard during his first visit to Islington. Somehow he was still there, seeing them home (prepared to face the music for being late back at college). They talked far into the night, against the rules of the motherly woman but she supposed, considering it was church, that she had better not interfere.

Binns had not yet been posted, but he was past the point when one could decently leave him any illusions. Now all at once the future forced itself upon him: he could see it—the smelly dhow, the crowded waterfront, the coconut groves, the unpunctual lessons and the growth of trade. Thornbush, waterhole, wayfarers, dance drums, oiled skin and a gradual thirst for new knowledge. None of the three had any doubt that the Board would see it as a done thing. A call had been answered.

The hospital was vast and chilly, even in high summer, loud with footsteps and the clatter of pots and pans. Rebmann lay gratefully lost amid the straight rows of uniformed patients whose voices he had forgotten how to decipher. Since the college was on vacation, Isaac was free to visit him whenever regulations allowed, as well as taking the walks and reading prescribed for him in abundance. In due time the surgery was completed.

Rebmann lay in a torpor in the ward, or so the nurses thought. Only his lips moved, and Isaac knew that he was praying. He did not turn his head unnecessarily or disturb the bandages. He swallowed what was put to his lips but did not ask for anything. There was only one overwhelming request he had to make.

At last the day came for the trial of strength and Isaac was permitted to be with him when the bandages were removed. The silence was expectant.

"What do you see?" asked the surgeon when the pause became unbearable.

"I see light," Rebmann replied, "like heaven. I am supposed to say 'I see men like trees walking,' but it is not like that. I see green— a sort of coat, is it? I have to gather up my strength: to keep anything in focus."

Isaac approached the old man's chair.

"Is it you, my son? I see a brown hand, but the face is not very clear. All the same, praise the Lord, for He has done marvelous things. Thank you, sir, for operating…"

"You must take it quietly for a few days. I am happy that we have got so far, but I am afraid you must not go home yet. Your health in general is weak, but you have cooperated very well."

"Oh, I am tough, doctor, very tough, and much stronger than I was a few years back. I do not even give in to the cold."

It was an August day, oppressive by English standards.

"Do you know what they tell you in Zanzibar? That the soul is distributed through all parts of the body, so you must be careful what you cut off. The left leg is particularly dangerous. You surgeons take note of that! But in my case you have let the soul light into my eyes instead of letting it out. Thank you, thank you!"

Once allowed out, Rebmann walked compulsively, clinging to Isaac's arm. He was not allowed to read, and a human face or a storied building composed itself only slowly into shape. But a nearby flower, the branch of a tree, the movement of a horse-cab gave endless delight. They went to Islington by omnibus and paced about the familiar streets. They explored Westminster Abbey, the music recreating for Rebmann the haze where the high ceiling should have been. They negotiated the dangerous traffic of Fleet Street and strolled through the fashionable quarters of the Strand. They visited the patriarchal Moffat, Livingstone's father-in-law, in Brixton. He had spent 50 years in southern Africa, and his *Missionary Labours* was already published when Rebmann first set foot in East Africa. Looking forward to a public celebration of his 80th birthday, Moffat showed an interest in the east coast and envied Rebmann the company of a Bantu speaker.

September brought chilly breezes. Someone provided Isaac with a heavy greatcoat. A few meetings were held after the close of the holiday month and Rebmann, guttural, passionate, alarming, addressed half a dozen of them. People came to be comforted by the glow of their own half-crowns on the plate, left ill at ease, disconcerted by the implied ruthlessness of the divine imperative. Patience was offered instead of heart-warming acclaim, fever instead of battle, leaky dhows instead of mission steamers ploughing the blue waters of the inland lakes.

"We drew the first map of the lakes," said Rebmann casually. "Not quite right but we demonstrated that they were there."

They looked at him, frightened, and asked how many baptisms in a year. They asked Isaac what it would cost to support a native pastor. He did not know. The case had not arisen and salaries were not, in any case, support. They asked how long it took to train a school teacher. A great gulf opened.

But the Society had agreed to send Binns to East Africa. That should be enough: one to replace one. For, Rebmann could no longer doubt, the glory of autumn was fading. The most concentrated effort could hardly keep a face floating before him. Colors weakened. The wind seemed to slash right into his good eye and bite away at his confidence. The mist could not all be a product of the season.

Isaac was elegant with gloves and a felt hat, persuading the landlady to light fires before the year had, as she said, drawn in, but he was fading. The rose-wreathed wallpaper became a blur of pink. The one visit that remained was to Mrs. Tozer, who had indicated that she would be away with her daughter for the latter part of August but was prepared to receive her brother-in-law any day appointed after that. The note sounded chilly, though it was harder to interpret through a reader's voice than sharp-angled words on paper.

Rebmann asked one of the St. Mary's curates to accompany him to Tottenham, suspecting that Isaac would not be comfortable there. They found their way from the omnibus to a neat small house in a neat small row. It struck him that he had never known how they subsisted since the death of Mr. Tozer. Such questions do not arise among the Rabai.

The curate let the door-knocker fall, and Mrs. Tozer herself appeared, her face and her hair had a white blur. Her figure bony and black draped. (Why did he allow himself to think he would see Emma again, brown, mellow, smiling?).

"My name is Jenkins," said the curate cautiously into the silence. "I have escorted Mr. Rebmann because, as you know, his sight is imperfect. I believe I am addressing Mrs. Tozer." She inclined her head and led them into the parlor, motioning towards the chair.

"It is strange to meet only after being related for more than 20 years," said Rebmann heartily. "Mrs. Tozer, you are aware of my afflictions: it is just now that my sight has been partially restored for a time, or I should not have been such a poor correspondent. Any meeting that links me with Emma is a great joy."

"With Emma indeed, "replied Mrs. Tozer sepulchrally. "We refer, Mr. Jenkins, to my departed sister, who was Mrs. Rebmann. It seems strange that you should evoke the happy times when we were girls together."

"Of course I did not know her as a girl, Mrs. Tozer, but she was a happy and gracious woman. Not a day passes but I recollect our years together."

He was trying to find a focus for the good eye. Mr. Jenkins was observing the threadbare carpet and the frail curtains.

"You may well recollect them, Mr. Rebmann. It is painful for me to do so. So strong and well my sister looked when I last saw her, despite the heavy responsibilities she undertook in Egypt. She was comfortably lodged there for all the heat and the flies. She had come, you see, Mr. Jenkins, to make preparations for her second marriage. Mr. Tozer, who was living then, assisting the vicar of a flourishing parish with his schools and visiting, begged her to think better of it. 'After the rector of a London parish,' he told her, 'how can you contemplate a foreigner who has not even a decent home to offer you?' Mr. Tyler, it is true, was a good a deal older, and had left her widowed young and childless. But she said she had a call.

'What kind of call can that be?' I asked her, 'when none of us know the man and you have not even met him yourself, let alone had a chance to see his moods or his linen.' But go she would, and many the sad day I have had to think of her shut in that little airless house with black servants and not even a doctor to attend her and save the child. I have wept my eyes out for her, Mr. Jenkins. I do not see any joy, Mr. Rebmann, in recollecting all that she suffered. Would you have wished your own sister to undergo the same, I wonder?"

"Mrs. Tozer, Mrs. Tozer, she suffered in her health, as any missionary in that climate must do, but even the sufferings were sweet when we shared them for the Lord's sake. And Samuel—God forgive me, I weep still when I think of Samuel, but was he not mine as much as hers? I have never for a moment blamed her, Mrs. Tozer, that I at 34 was doomed to remain childless. I looked to you for kin, having not seen any of my own relations since 1844, and hoped to welcome your daughter as my niece. Is she not here? Or perhaps—the years slip by—she has already her own home..."

"My daughter is a teacher, Mr. Rebmann. She will be back shortly from the girls' school where she is employed. I hope that does not shock you. Your wife was also a teacher in her widowhood. She was disappointed not to find girls' education more advanced on the east coast..."

"That was one of the reasons..."

"Excuse me Mr. Rebmann, I will bring in the tea. In this day and age women must contrive to help themselves."

She flounced out and returned with a tray. Mr. Jenkins leapt to his feet to offer assistance, sad that Mr. Rebmann could not catch his glance of commiseration.

"I am sorry if you did not approve of your sister's entering a more challenging field than Egypt," floundered Rebmann. "She gave me no hint of your disapprobation. Since one of your other sisters is in Port Natal, I assumed the whole family to have some sympathy with missions."

"Their situation is quite different. My brother-in-law is an Archdeacon, and there is a considerable British community, as you would have seen if you had visited them. Year after year my sister would write 'we hope to go and visit Miriam if Mr. Rebmann's work permits'. But no, you were always too busy. You went as far as Egypt and she wrote, 'we may see you soon, if CMS insists,' but oh no, you had to drag her back to that filthy boat and get ship-wrecked into bargain. Is that proper for a lady? ... Sugar, Mr. Jenkins?"

"Indeed my sister-in-law, you do me wrong. Do you suppose any of us rushes eagerly into shipwreck?"

The door opened abruptly and a young lady, who must be Eliza, hurried in carrying a bag of books. (On second thoughts, not a very young lady, but a schoolmistress in her thirties.)

"Hallo, mother. This must be my uncle Rebmann. I am happy to see you. Fancy getting a new uncle at my age! You must find it very cold here. I am longing to hear all about East Africa. And Mr.—Jenkins, yes, how do you do? But the gentleman who wrote for you, did you not bring him? I have never met an East African, and I believe he was a great favorite of my aunt's. Are your eyes better, uncle Rebmann?"

"All the better for seeing you, I think is the right answer, my niece. But to be honest I do not see you very clearly, though the doctors did their best. I shall not read or write again, but I am grateful to have seen a little of England and I must hasten back to Germany before the light is quite lost to me. I have a sister and two brothers there, and their children and grandchildren."

"Do not fuss, Eliza," intervened her mother. "He is not used to being flustered by people like us. And you never even sent a photograph of my sister, Mr. Rebmann."

"I am afraid the apparatus does not abound at the coast, Mrs. Tozer, and we do not accumulate the sort of knickknacks people bring from India, I believe. We go, as you have perceived, to share with the people, and what they and we have would not be of significance to you. I am sorry you should have thought Emma unhappy. I can only assure you that she had all that was needful.

Thank you for the excellent tea, but I believe Mr. Jenkins has a service to take and we should be on our way. Eliza, if you would like to meet someone from East Africa the CMS at Salisbury Square will arrange it for you, but it would not be proper for me to bring Isaac here. Goodbye, goodbye."

The message had been driven home: the holiday was over. He must face Germany, and soon, before the frost bit deep into his bones. Germany was further hidden in his memory than London: the deaths of his parents, one brother, old teachers and neighbors had come to him at the coast with a kind of unreality, since his own death then seemed so much the more probable. Blindness then shielded him, but now the shield was mercifully pierced: he would have to face the village before the last loss of Isaac.

Eliza was better than her word. She arranged to meet Rebmann and Isaac on Saturday in Salisbury Square and take them out to tea. He saw how pitifully few were her chances to escape her mother, and how she was made to pay for the greater freedom of two of her aunts. The third did not visit them often. But she did not complain. He sensed that only a boarding school situation could release her, and that would not provide enough for the upkeep of the little house. She was a sacrifice at second hand.

Krapf, yet again, appeared to solve their difficulties, not in person but by letter. He was looking forward to welcoming them, but feared Isaac might have problems about traveling arrangements. He therefore wished to inform them that a Mr. Jonas, a cousin of the late second Mrs. Krapf, was traveling to London on business and would be returning to Stuttgart towards the end of October. He would be only too pleased to escort them if this accorded with the mission's plans.

XIII

The impossible seemed to be happening. Rebmann was going to Germany without being bereft of East Africa. Isaac was still beside him, the whispered warnings in Kinika belying the chilly sea air. The grayness before him might well be the Channel and the sky, or the bleak enormity of a dockyard: he was not sure of anything anymore (except the one thing needful). Sight had swept down and overwhelmed him for a few weeks like a huge bird. Briefly he could see a swan floating on a pond in the park, with clouds mirrored there that overhead spun out of his grasp. He had come to understand that he would not see a stork again. There were no storks in England.

Mr. Jonas was an old-fashioned figure in a tall hat and fur collar, unshakably benevolent, interested in East Africa but reluctant to discuss the difference of belief. At Karlsruhe they had to spend an extra night, since Rebmann had inadvertently kicked over one of the boxes, and the fuss of collecting back the documents and samples it contained had caused them to miss their train. Their guide remained peaceful, telegraphed to Dr. Krapf about the delay and did not claim any of his own expenses out of the traveling money put up by CMS. He was, as they later wrote to London, 'a true Israelite.'

Germany was a cold mist. Only East Africa swam before his eyes in true and permanent colors. Train, boat, train. Krapf booming and hearty at Stuttgart, a borrowed carriage and then his brother embracing him in the old house at Gerlingen.

Rebmann's surviving sister Katharina Margarethe—Marga for short—took him in. She was the one who had begged him, year after year to come and see them, until his marriage became a stumbling-block—a sister-in-law one could not write to direct but only greet coldly in translation: an older person whose fault it must be that there was no surviving child. It was no good explaining to Marga what happened to mothers and children in the tropics, even in the slums of industrial cities. She knew with an awful certainty that cleanliness is by the merest fraction second to godliness and a healthy appetite the next to best gift of the Lord. She had parted from her brother 32 years before in her glory, her small house spotless, her husband hard-working and obedient, her babies scrubbed and red-cheeked.

Marga seemed enormous now: the diffident pastor was lost in her embraces. She was a widow, but an unmarried son lived with her and kept his place. The grandchildren were both joy and torment to her: the elder daughter was inclined to spare the rod and spoil the child; the other failed to shield her new-washed floors with rags and permitted her husband to smoke.

Isaac was welcomed with a stiff handshake but there were objections to his sleeping in Rebmann's room. A pastor should have only the best. The fact that two of the three men must share was never directly faced. Walther was alleged to be delighted to wait upon his uncle, but could not know his habits as Isaac did and had no practice in dealing with disability. The family could not communicate with Isaac apart from the few polite phrases of German he had learned by heart.

Rebmann had to prevail. Isaac moved the wash-stand to a clear area of wall where anyone could feel his way. He substituted a makeshift pillow for the huge bolster his godfather had grown unaccustomed to and took down the heavy framed text he was liable to bump his head on. This was something no German would have dared to do, and even an Englishman (maintained Marga, who had once given hospitality to a Presbyterian minister attending a pietist convention) would have asked permission.

They endured, resolutely polite and cheerful, but Rebmann succumbed to a cold and the carrying of trays, the fire in the bedroom were an affront to Marga's clockwork household. Cocks crew, but there was no early morning chorus of birds to mark the daylight. Some owls hooted at night, and no-one spoke of thinking it unlucky.

Krapf bore Isaac off to see the University at Tubingen, the Cathedral at Ulm, to show him off to church groups, a little uneasy at not knowing what was being said about him. He had demonstrated to Walther what needed to be done.

Rebmann managed a sermon or two, and found the pointing of the canticles had changed since his boyhood. Then it was time for Isaac to go, torn apart by discomfort, cold and the parting from his almost father. This time there was no genial Herr Jonas to assist him, but Marga put up provision in plenty and Krapf wrote little notes in English and German for various eventualities. Classes were waiting at Islington, and beyond that a passage was booked back to Polly and the real world. They had their last prayer-time in Kinika and it was over, Isaac waving his precious hat violently out of the carriage window, Rebmann wiping away a tear which might otherwise freeze.

Christmas came and went, Rebmann's brother boisterous during a short visit, Marga sugary and tearful. The brother kept up the old home, but a financial collapse two years before had followed a wild boom in German investments and a large part of the vineyards had had to go. Long before Rebmann had told them to divide his own inheritance since he had no expectation of coming back to claim it. Nothing was said about that now. His nephews worked away from home, and the grapes were collected by a vintner's wagon. They could not any longer afford the horses.

Great-nephews and nieces pottered around, their treble voices hard to catch, their scattered toys perilous. Rebmann was used to baby talk only in Kinika. The pine needles in an airtight room made him sneeze. He liked to handle and smell the fir-cones before they were added to the blaze, but held back after immolating one that a younger Johannes had carefully decorated in red and gold paint. Even the blur of light was fading now.

It was a relief to stay overnight with Krapf after preaching in Stuttgart. Krapf had sent to the Rev. Henry Knight for the manuscripts and received them by the hand of Mr. Jonas on his next trip to London, the tin box within a wooden one as Rebmann had prescribed.

"Excellent," he told Rebmann. "Just a few amendments to bring them into line with modern linguistic practice. We must not confuse people further with differences of orthography. We will get them through the press very soon, never fear."

Rebmann knew that he would not live to see it. It would not be right to say, he supposed, that his heart sank. He seemed no longer to have a heart. He had never asked for publication or reward. (Lord Jesus, let me not grow cold. Stupid if need be, but not cold.)

"The atmosphere in my sister's house," he remarked cautiously, "it is not very conducive to academic work." Krapf took the point. "There is nothing else for it," he pronounced. "You will have to get married."

Rebmann swallowed hard. He would not have believed he had heard aright if Krapf had not resumed his old dictatorial manner.

"It is no use making faces about it, brother. You cannot be yourself in your sister's house. There is no match for you there. The young people are occupied with their children and their work. Your brother and his wife are working their fingers to the bone to keep the old place going. I am often away traveling myself. Marriage is ordained by God..."

"Do not discourse to me on the liturgy, brother Krapf, I pray you. I know it quite thoroughly myself. And I am in no condition for the procreation of children or the bestowing of mutual comfort either. And you know perfectly well that I am married already."

"You *were* married, Rebmann, but Emma is beyond the grave. The scripture says quite clearly..."

"I know what the scripture says, but there is no day or night I fail to remember Emma. There is no room in my life for another..."

"That is uncharitable, Rebmann. I myself conquered my sentiments enough to marry a second time and you should not be too proud. It is part of the harvest of death on the mission-field that many of us should be left..."

"And what would you have me do? Parade round the streets with a guide and a placard round my neck reading 'Blind man in search of a wife?' I have few acquaintances here and not sufficient means to set up house and have someone to drudge for me."

"You are forgetting, brother, you are forgetting. I told you the first time that you do not need a palace to house a new wife. Your pension is small but adequate. Here you are not going to send for provisions from Bombay or newspapers from England, have you forgotten that? Kornthal has lost its exemption from conscription, but the Prussian Empire has not yet deprived it of home-grown food. The lady I have in mind has also a small missionary pension. Two can live cheaper than one. As it happens there is a little house provided by her family. She has lived in India for many years, so you will find enough to talk about."

"So the lady is already arranged. Perhaps you have hired a carriage and dresses for the bridesmaids as well."

"Now, cool down, my brother. You have had reason to trust my judgment before. Mrs. Finck's elder brother is a friend of mine—Dauble, you may remember, the wholesale merchant. They fear that the lady suffers from her nerves. Her husband died in India, her brother and her only surviving son still serve the mission there. She has been used to hard work and frets at being alone and not much occupied."

"So you would have her nurse me as a distraction and put away her best china in case I break it? Does she know what a charming plan you have made for her declining years?"

"It is only a suggestion, Rebmann, but I thought it a sensible one. All I have done is to accept an invitation for you to have tea with Dauble in Kornthal and meet his sister. I told the good Marga that I would keep you here a few days so that she can air her blankets and carpets. I find Mrs. Finck charming. If you think you can do better yourself, go and get on with it."

Rebmann was really affronted, but he could not think of an excuse for refusing the invitation, and life at his sister's was becoming harder to bear. She kept recounting imagined slights and gossip 'since that black man was here,' and bewailing the state of her tablecloths and rugs whenever Johannes spilt anything. He seldom had to ask his nephew for help, but Walther seemed to think he was deaf as well as blind, and explained the economy of modern Wurtemberg loudly and simply. Poor Walther would have been something more than a lawyer's clerk if it had not been for the crash. All the same it was hard for Rebmann to remember that he had once yearned for these boys to follow in his footsteps. The other had a situation in Stuttgart and rarely came home. They appeared immune from the call of travel and adventure. Walther had once taken up the King of Wurtemberg's preoccupation with a national church, but it had never borne fruit, and of course there was no longer a King.

The widow Finck seemed to be an agreeable woman, and tough.

She had not lived in the India of railways and well-appointed bungalows but in a rural area where they traveled by bullock cart and had to learn a new alphabet as well as a new language. She had had servants, but they were orphan lads and young widows, not the splendid bearers and stewards boasted about in Zanzibar. Waste in Germany was her main theme—waste of food which would have saved lives, of land which would have maintained them. They exchanged reminiscences while Krapf and his friend talked business. Both hesitated now and again over a German word. Mrs. Finck had needed to use English in India for official purposes. And there had been very few baptisms.

Another tea-party was arranged, with Krapf as the host. This time the couple were pointedly left alone and they dared to touch on their domestic circumstances.

"I will tell you the truth Mrs. Finck," said Rebmann at last, desperately. "It is such a relief to meet a Christian friend to whom one may speak frankly. Krapf is plotting that you and I should get married. Do not be alarmed. Krapf is a pioneer, so he enjoys arranging things. I know it is out of the question. I am blind and a liability. I have only a small pension and no furniture—most of what I ever had I made myself. I do not have manners either, they tell me. My wife was a lady compared to me, but an English lady, you see. Any pretty phrases I learned were not in German. My own sister finds me uncouth. I am just telling you so that you do not let yourself be compromised... We lost our baby son," he added, completing the humiliation.

"Mr. Rebmann, do not distress yourself. I understand quite well what my brother is about. First it was an iron-monger he introduced me to, oh, a churchgoer of course, but a loud man with six children who stared at me, valuing the stuff of my dresses and my odd way of talking. Fortunately it did not come to a declaration.

Then there was an apothecary who wanted to know how people died of cholera and if I had ever seen a case of leprosy. I piled on the anguish and he fled at the first meeting.

It is only you, Mr. Rebmann, with whom I can talk comfortably of things close to the missionary heart. Let us be friends, at least."

"Friends—of course, naturally, I would not presume..."

"You think too little of yourself, Mr. Rebmann. Before I was married I assisted my mother in her blindness. I know what to do."

It was arranged of course. No-one but Rebmann himself had ever doubted it. He was still nervous, still bound to the memory of Emma but Louise was severe and practical.

"Johannes," she said when the agreement was signed and sealed, "I believe it is for the best. Do not for a moment think that I do not miss the father of my son. You would prefer an English wife, but that is not possible. Let us make the best of what we have, and it is only the sitting-room that need be decorated for these fat German *haus-fraus*. And I can read to you in English if you prefer it."

"I wish I had seen you."

She bent forward and laid his hand on her hair—springy still, though sun-dried and coarse—and over her withered cheeks, the proud nose, the thoughtful ridges of the brows.

Her son and brother approved in a remarkably speedy exchange of letters. Rebmann knew, though it irked him, that Isaac would not find it strange to marry again. He had a card sent to Eliza at her school, confident that she would not tell her mother. Mr. and Mrs. Hutchinson sent formal congratulations and a pewter teapot.

The wedding was accomplished decorously in March, and he moved to Louise's house, using her china and her linen. They lay apart in the great, obligatory double bed with its stuffy bolster, and Louise ordered and tidied him. Soon afterwards he was taken to preach at the *Missionfest* in Leonberg, and people said he had a new lease of life. He hoped not. Spring came with a few birds, but there were not many cocks crowing in Kornthal.

Louise was not unreasonable. He found the starched collars uncomfortable, and was always kicking things with his stiff, shiny shoes, but the food was much to his liking, twice a day. They agreed to dispense with the second breakfast which their mothers used to press on them when they were young and always hungry. They exchanged the memories that were not too painful, and so peopled the long, dark days. There were quite a few anniversaries—her husband's and dead children's—on which she wept, and he rated her quietly for lack of trust: at times he fell into Kinika or Kiswahili and she had to pull him back to the present—"I can understand English if you find it easier, Johannes."

Rebmann would sit in a chair making excursions into this strange world. The absurd tassels on the plush curtains (cast off, he supposed, from some richer relation) hanging on a tough cord might have been the overflow of a fertile banana tree. Louise was surprised when he asked their color. Purple, that was near enough. He dared protest at the castor oil she tried to dose him with on Friday nights: this was not the use of castor oil as it struck his sense of smell. The rag rug reminded him of the texture of those layered cotton skirts. The shiny leaves of the laurel hedge might have been designed to conserve moisture against the tropical sun.

"Do you remember," she asked, "how we used to write our names on them with a pin when we were children?"

To be honest he did not remember. The scent of May flowers no longer recalled to him the taste of 'bread and cheese,' hips harder than berries sandwiched between the scented leaves. He did remember the joy of frosty days, sliding or skating, long past, but there were no such days now, only searing, damp cold, against which your toes curled in protest in their stiff boots and it seemed impossible that you had ever fronted the cold with a beardless chin.

Louise got von der Decken's *Travels* from Dr. Krapf to read to him, and Brenner's *Forschungen*. Otherwise they shared devotional works. He had left behind in London Sir Bartle Frere's *Eastern Africa as a Field for Missionary Labour.*

Sometimes she herself read Krapf's book and questioned him about it, as together they lamented the hardness of the human heart to the proffered gospel.

Marga sometimes came over to Kornthal to sit stiffly and drink coffee (he preferred tea), and his brother or Dauble might make a Sunday visit. Occasionally Louise left him with the maid while she went to see some old friend, and this was like a holiday to him, when he would compose a sermon under his breath and look around for the chorus of assent:

Tumtegemee Yesu.
Yesu.
Twajitolee kwake.
Kwake.
Atupatie raha.
Raha.

One day he saw the crowds surging again to take refuge in the house as Emma moved calmly among them ladling out the porridge, with a young Isaac at her heels. The August heat was like a blessing. He would be persuaded now and again to sit in the porch amid the scent of sweet roses and bitter privet, acknowledging the salutations to which he could attach no faces. But the days drew in, and he found the chill strange, would look for porridge instead of soup, and marvel that the smoke of the fire was so soon drawn away. When Louise guided him up the stairs he thought he was going to the flat roof, and reminded her that *Deuteronomy* required the householder to put up a parapet.

"You can see that he is sinking, Mrs. Rebmann," said the doctor gently." I am sorry to alarm you so soon after you have embarked on married life, but he has been much weakened by fever and rough living. For a sheltered man there would have been no danger..."

"Of course I understand you," Louise answered abruptly. Why were these secular people so fearful of the truth? "I lived for 20 years in India and nursed my first husband in his pulmonary collapse. We were, no doubt, better attended than Mr. Rebmann, but climate, poor water and infection take their toll. I have seen many people close to expiry because they had no tolerable diet or shelter. I am here to alleviate his sufferings as far as may be, not to ask for the impossible."

The doctor took his leave and the invalid stirred in his sleep, moaning a little.

"I am here, Johannes," cried the wife. "Is there anything I can do to make you more comfortable?"

She had trusted in his blindness, but the voice was not quite under control.

"Do not weep, my dear. There is a lot of work left for me in East Africa."

"There is the work of prayer indeed, and I do not know enough to help you."

"You know enough for India, Louise, and I am happy that you have a son there..."

He broke into coughing and lay still, while the day fell into dusk and she moved only to draw the curtains. Autumn evenings were manageable. She had never got used again to the long light of summer.

"*Uji...*" he answered. "There is always *uji* if your conscience does not permit of palm wine. But Johannes is a bachelor name: now I am Abe Samuel."

He dozed again and opened his eyes.

"I thought I was going to be able to see."

"Would you like me to call for Dr. Krapf? He came earlier but you were asleep."

He had come with news of the Maasai raid on Rabai in August.

"It is like being back at the beginning again," he had told her. "I do not know whether we need to tell him."

"He is a good man," she had burst out, "but I cannot get near him. He is far away from me."

Afterwards she felt ashamed. A Hindu wife would not have complained: for a Christian it was unbecoming.

"No, do not call him. He will do all that is necessary. You have it all written down."

"Yes, just as you told me."

"Thank you—Louise," he said with an effort, and she knew it was an act of ultimate courtesy, for he was reaching out towards that other one. "I wish I could have seen you."

On the paper were written the words for his memorial in English, "Safe in the arms of Jesus."

In a little while the struggle for breath began and soon ended. Calmly she wrote a note and called the maid to deliver it to Dr. Krapf.

"Abe Samuel has left us to rejoin his loved ones. He is safe in the arms of Jesus."

Also on Johannes Rebmann:

Steven Paas, *Johannes Rebmann: A Servant of God in Africa before the Rise of Western Colonialism* (Nürnberg: Verlag für Theologie und Religionswissenschaft (VTR) and Bonn: Verlag für Kultur und Wissenschaft (VKW), 2011).

ISBN 978-3-941750-48-7 (VTR)
ISBN 978-3-86269-029-9 (VKW)
For introductions and reviews visit: www.chichewadictionary.org and click on 'Johannes Rebmann'.